JJ RICHARDS

The Tower

DCI Walker Crime Thrillers (Book 3)

First published by Simulacrum Press Publishers 2024

Copyright © 2024 by JJ Richards

All rights reserved. No part of this publication may be reproduced, stored or transmitted in any form or by any means, electronic, mechanical, photocopying, recording, scanning, or otherwise without written permission from the publisher. It is illegal to copy this book, post it to a website, or distribute it by any other means without permission.

This novel is entirely a work of fiction. The names, characters and incidents portrayed in it are the work of the author's imagination. Any resemblance to actual persons, living or dead, events or localities is entirely coincidental.

JJ Richards asserts the moral right to be identified as the author of this work.

JJ Richards has no responsibility for the persistence or accuracy of URLs for external or third-party Internet Websites referred to in this publication and does not guarantee that any content on such Websites is, or will remain, accurate or appropriate.

Designations used by companies to distinguish their products are often claimed as trademarks. All brand names and product names used in this book and on its cover are trade names, service marks, trademarks and registered trademarks of their respective owners. The publishers and the book are not associated with any product or vendor mentioned in this book. None of the companies referenced within the book have endorsed the book.

First edition

ISBN: 9798332064852

Editing by Hal Duncan
Cover art by Tom Sanderson

This book was professionally typeset on Reedsy.
Find out more at reedsy.com

Contents

PROLOGUE	1
CHAPTER ONE	8
CHAPTER TWO	17
CHAPTER THREE	30
CHAPTER FOUR	38
CHAPTER FIVE	43
CHAPTER SIX	52
CHAPTER SEVEN	55
CHAPTER EIGHT	62
CHAPTER NINE	66
CHAPTER TEN	70
CHAPTER ELEVEN	75
CHAPTER TWELVE	84
CHAPTER THIRTEEN	90
CHAPTER FOURTEEN	95
CHAPTER FIFTEEN	101
CHAPTER SIXTEEN	107
CHAPTER SEVENTEEN	123
CHAPTER EIGHTEEN	134
CHAPTER NINETEEN	139
CHAPTER TWENTY	149
CHAPTER TWENTY-ONE	155
CHAPTER TWENTY-TWO	165
CHAPTER TWENTY-THREE	170

CHAPTER TWENTY-FOUR	177
CHAPTER TWENTY-FIVE	180
CHAPTER TWENTY-SIX	192
CHAPTER TWENTY-SEVEN	198
CHAPTER TWENTY-EIGHT	202
CHAPTER TWENTY-NINE	209
CHAPTER THIRTY	213
CHAPTER THIRTY-ONE	216
CHAPTER THIRTY-TWO	225
CHAPTER THIRTY-THREE	230
CHAPTER THIRTY-FOUR	238
CHAPTER THIRTY-FIVE	244
CHAPTER THIRTY-SIX	250
CHAPTER THIRTY-SEVEN	255
CHAPTER THIRTY-EIGHT	262
CHAPTER THIRTY-NINE	267
CHAPTER FORTY	273
CHAPTER FORTY-ONE	278
CHAPTER FORTY-TWO	282
CHAPTER FORTY-THREE	286
CHAPTER FORTY-FOUR	290
CHAPTER FORTY-FIVE	294
CHAPTER FORTY-SIX	312
CHAPTER FORTY-SEVEN	322
EPILOGUE	329
A Note From the Author	335

"No act of kindness, no matter how small, is ever wasted." Aesop

PROLOGUE

She deserved to die, Tony thought. She'd completely and utterly destroyed him, torn his life up, ripped his heart out, made the world a place of unspeakable horrors. It would never be the same again. Not ever.

He realised he must have fallen asleep at some point because the sun was coming up; he was shivering, damp, still in his work clothes, no jacket on. He must have been here all night, wasted. He was sat on a flat, cool, concrete section of the roof of the Blackpool Tower Buildings—which lay at the base of the Tower itself—a red-brick three-storey block providing entertainment in the form of the Tower Ballroom, the Tower Circus, and the Tower Dungeon, among other things. Normally, standing on a building this size would feel lofty, high up, dizzying. But not here. The iconic tower, once the tallest man-made structure in the British Empire, which gained inspiration from the similarly structured Eiffel Tower in Paris built just a few years earlier, soared above, behind him, majestic. With its red lights on, it illuminated all, allowing him, and anyone else, to easily see in the dark. He'd once thought it beautiful, charming, captivating even. But now it just made everything look like a damned whorehouse. It was nothing more than a beacon of debauchery and thuggery, which was rife in the town, steamrollering over everything.

Still, it had been the only constant in his life, that structure, everlasting, and this truth usually gave him some meagre comfort, at least. But not today. Not anymore. She'd even spoiled that for him—because of what she'd done, right here, at his place of work. And it was *his*. It was sacrilege.

He'd been the one who'd brought her here, used his connections to get her a job working as a cleaner on the Fifth Floor, so they could be closer together. She said she no longer felt like a freak anymore, that she'd found a home. And they'd been happy together for a while—or at least he *thought* they had. But she mustn't have been. How could she be if she did what she did, with his frigging brother of all people! He couldn't even think about it. It made his blood boil, made him want to kill himself or hurt somebody else or destroy something; made his head explode. They were emotions he just couldn't handle anymore—too powerful—and they weren't going away, lingering with him every day, taunting him, overpowering him, like last night. It was no wonder he'd done what he did. It was more than justified. Nobody could judge him, not if they knew what happened. She deserved it.

He rooted in his pocket and found the bottle of Smirnoff vodka he'd been drinking the night before—the second one he'd bought. It was almost empty now, of course, but there was enough in there for one last shot, at least: *the hair of the dog.* He chugged it down and threw the bottle off the roof, hearing it smash on the street below like the crash of a mini cymbal at the Circus. Only there was no applause this time. There was nothing except for his own ragged breath; there was nobody around, not at this time. Just a stray dog wandered about, seemed alarmed at the noise, limped off down the seafront that tourists would no doubt flock to again during the daylight hours—gambling and eating greasy fish and chips and watching their freak shows, trying to forget about their meaningless lives, no doubt, just as they all were.

At forty-two, Anthony Singelmann was now single again—single by name, and by nature. He should have known. He couldn't even keep a little midget girl like her. She hardly had them queuing at the door. Or, at least, that's what he'd thought. But it seemed she had, actually, and his own brother had been first in the queue. *Well, good luck to him*, he thought. *I hope it was worth it.* He was better off without the both of them.

Tony stood up, got close to the low wall surrounding that section of roof, which had likely been put there for safety reasons, so nobody fell off. Not that he or anybody else should be up here. It was strictly off limits, but some of the staff sometimes came up to smoke. One of them had a copy of the roof door key, and Tony had made a copy of that copy at some point so he could bring her up here, show her the view—a private panorama of the seafront that few people ever got to see. It was a privilege, something else she hadn't fully appreciated. He rooted in his pocket for a ciggie but couldn't find any. He was desperate for one, must have finished them off last night. He couldn't remember—couldn't remember much of anything, except pushing *her* and watching her fall.

He got up onto the wall, tentatively—getting his balance, then stood tall. He thought about jumping, ending it all here and now. Nobody would care. He only had his brother, and now he'd betrayed Tony, took everything he had. There was his mother too, of course, but she was in a home now, could hardly speak, never mind anything else. Not that he cared.

She hadn't been a great mother, hadn't really taken care of him, which was why the other kids at school had called him Stinky Singelmann—because she never washed his bloody uniform. Still, at least she'd never hit him, and she'd *occasionally* made him some food… when she'd sobered enough to feel guilty. Not like his father. He *had* hit him, beaten the crap out of him on more occasions than he could remember, so it had been something of a relief when his old man got sent to prison—a life sentence for murder in the first degree. Tony was just eight at the time. He'd often wondered whether those genes would catch up to him eventually, whether he had that same killer instinct.

He took a breath and stepped closer to the edge of the wall he was on, put his toes over the ledge, just his heel keeping him upright now. He lost his balance a little suddenly and stepped back a couple of inches, relief washing over him, the near-death experience snapping him back to reality.

'Sod all of yer then!' he said, reaching for the zipper on his pants, but not finding it, not yet together enough to be aware he'd still been wearing his outfit and make-up, which he'd kept on after the last show.

Things had been going so well before this—by his standards. He'd finally got the role as Lead Clown in the Blackpool Tower Circus. It was a world-famous venue, or, at least, it was well-known up north, and somewhat known everywhere else too. It was *something*.

He reached inside the flap of the colourful onesie he was wearing instead and took a leak on whatever was below—probably nothing much except the paved footpath, but he couldn't be sure. He sprayed it as far as he could, back arched, not caring who or what the discharge hit. 'Take that!'

He thought he might feel better after that, but he didn't. He shook off any excess drips and put his willy away, before smoothing back his hair with both hands. He felt like an arsehole, like the lowest of the low. He didn't think he could sink much lower. And it was all because of her. She'd turned him into this, made him ugly, made him bad.

He suddenly realised how ridiculous he must appear—a clown urinating off a rooftop! He wiped at his face now, smudged his makeup, seeing it rub off on his hand. He stank of booze and cigarettes and chips, just like he did every day. He'd had enough of people laughing at him, of being humiliated, of this lifestyle. He'd liked it at first, felt famous, or important, or both. But now he realised they just wanted to debase and demean. They were cruel, laughing *at* him rather than with him. He was just another freak to be poked and prodded. He thought he might quit, move away, start a new life somewhere—stop clowning around, literally. He'd had enough of it here, of *this*. He'd lived here all his life, in Blackpool. And it was a *black pool*, for many like him, a dark place, a quagmire. Beyond the veil of the tourism industry, many people struggled, needed to self-medicate, anesthetise themselves from it all. It was time for a fresh start, to become someone else, *something* else.

Yes, that was it. He'd made his mind up: he was going to do it, going to leave once and for all. He couldn't stay here anyway; not after what he'd done. They'd find out if he stayed. Better to leave, be completely out of their minds. He looked back to try to get down off the wall, find his footing—the very first step in his new life—but before he could descend, he felt a presence there, an ominous shadow, moving closer.

He was startled, thinking he'd been alone. 'Who's that?' he

asked and began to turn his head to see who it was. If it was still night-time, he'd have assumed it was one of the other night staff, come up for a smoke, but none of them would be up here at this time. They'd be safely tucked up in bed by now, getting some well needed R&R ready for the next set of shows. He thought it might be a builder, seizing the day or something, getting ready to do some repairs. There was always something to be fixed here. It was an old building, one that needed constant maintenance—just like his fast-ageing body, which ached and creaked as he twisted. He turned some more, expecting to be told to get down, told that it was dangerous.

It was a man stood there; he could see that much now—but not much more from the corner of his eye, as he was still carefully balancing on the wall, multitasking his focus, trying to avoid falling.

'It doesn't cost anything to be nicer to people,' said the man, under his breath. *'The world will be better off without you.'*

That wasn't what he'd been expecting. Perhaps whoever it was didn't like him, thought he was about to commit suicide. Or maybe he'd seen him urinating off the building. Or both. Tony took a breath, getting ready to say something, but before he could respond, could get down off the wall and say anything at all, the man shoved him, hard, in the lower back. He hadn't been expecting that either—so abrupt, so immediate, so aggressive, powerful. Tony immediately lost his footing, couldn't do a sodding thing about it. There was nothing to grab to gain any purchase. So, he fell.

Impotent, arms flailing, Promenade rising, there was no panic—his emotions surprisingly flat, calm even—accepting. All too soon, he hit the footpath below and felt his own bones crunching, followed by blinding pain that wiped all thought from his mind. The next thing he knew, there was a stray dog licking at his face and he was looking up at the Blackpool Tower, not really sure what the hell was going on, just that he couldn't move.

The Tower remained illuminated, as it always was at this time of year, domineering over him, almost taunting; but he'd had no further illuminations about his life. It had been a mess, right from the very start, and it seemed it might be ending the same way. He took a breath, tried his best to keep his eyes open, and whispered *'help'*.

CHAPTER ONE

Detective Chief Inspector Jonathan Walker stepped out onto the Golden Mile at Blackpool, part of the seven-mile stretch that made up the Promenade. The smell of the sea air hit him immediately, mixed in with the aroma of fast foods, and candy. He hadn't been here for years—not since he'd come with his wife and kids when they'd been little, a wife he was now separated from—but it hadn't changed a bit.

'At least it's stopped raining,' said Walker, looking up at the sky and throwing the orange waterproof poncho he'd grabbed back into the car.

'You've said it now,' said DC Briggs, who'd also got out of the same car, putting her raincoat on regardless, smiling warmly at him. 'I think I'll keep mine on just in case, like,' she added, her usually subtle Liverpudlian accent a bit more obvious on this occasion.

They walked over to the Blackpool Tower Buildings, right outside the entrance to the Blackpool Tower Dungeon, a place that was unconvincingly decorated as if it was an old stone building of some sort, with a sign claiming to have '10 live actor shows' and '1 exciting ride'. It was a house of horrors, a live action dramatisation of historical stories contained within three-hundred and sixty degree sets. It was therefore somewhat appropriate, and perhaps not even a coincidence, Walker thought, that this was where the deceased was lying.

'DCI Walker?' asked a uniformed police officer at the scene, seeing them approaching and holding out his hand to shake.

'Yes,' said Walker. 'And this is my colleague, DC Briggs.'

They both shook hands with the man, getting acquainted. 'I'm PS Billings, and I'll be the Duty Officer for this case. My colleague, PC Schmidt, was first on the scene. I contacted CID once the area had been secured.' He looked around. There was a gathering of people watching, perhaps fifty or so. 'Wasn't easy with this lot hanging around,' he said.

Walker nodded. 'I can see that. What have we got here then?'

'Male, early forties according to his driving license—an Anthony Singelmann. Seemed like a jumper at first, stank of alcohol, and desperation, the way he was dressed.' He meant the clown outfit. It was hard to miss. 'But then there was this next to the body,' said PS Billings. He was motioning to some writing on the floor next to the corpse, obviously having been spray painted there by the look of it, in red paint. It said: *'Be Kined'*.

'A coincidence?' asked Walker. 'Plenty of graffiti around here.'

'Don't think so,' said PS Billings. 'It was done *after* the deceased landed. There's a bit on his leg, you see. There,' he pointed.

Walker crouched down next to the body, which had an arm and a leg twisted at an unnatural angle, and a pool of now drying blood surrounding the head. In addition to the clown attire—the colourful onesie with the frilly white collar, the large blue shoes—the man was also wearing face paint to complete the look. 'Kined? What the hell does that mean?'

'I believe a *kine* is the collective term for a group of cows, sir,' said DC Briggs, sounding pleased with herself for knowing.

'Well, that doesn't make a jot of sense now, does it,' said Walker. 'More likely that the author simply couldn't spell. I think they were going for K-I-N-D, *kind.* I'd hazard a guess that their message was for people to be kind to each other, or that this poor fella was not.'

'Schmidt, over here,' said PS Billings.

A pale, overworked-looking Police Constable walked over from where he'd been manning the crime scene line with several other PCs and PCSOs.

'Sir?' said PC Schmidt, a little wearily.

'This is DCI Walker and DC Briggs. Tell them exactly what you told me, when you arrived at the scene,' said PS Billings.

PC Schmidt looked at Walker and DC Briggs for the first time. 'It was unreal. There was an argument going on among some of the watching crowd—this lot,' he said, pointing at the onlookers. 'Some of them were convinced it was an act, part of the Tower Dungeon, some kind of promotion to get people inside. But a small minority thought it was real, and it was one of them that called it in.'

Walker's eyes went a little wider. 'So, the body had been here for a while before someone called it in?'

'It was already here when the first person arrived. And it gets worse…' said PC Schmidt.

'Go on,' said Walker.

'The deceased was still alive when he was found. He was making all kinds of moaning sounds, according to some of these folks, asking for help, he was. Like I said, most of 'em thought it was part of the act—one of the Dungeon lot. They thought he was one of their actors, drumming up customers for the next show,' said PC Schmidt. 'If someone had just called an ambulance, he might still be alive. But no-one did. Nobody wanted to risk looking stupid, I suppose.'

'Oh, my God,' said DC Briggs.

'You don't understand,' said PC Schmidt. 'Blackpool is an odd place. Things like this happen all the time—I mean, not things like *this*: a dead body. But freaky little acts and incidents. I had to help a man chained to a lamppost the other day. He was wearing a Michael Myers mask, you know the one from that film, Halloween. He was donned in nothing but the mask and some underpants. Bachelor party gone too far, apparently. Happens all the time. You get the idea. People see stuff like this in Blackpool and just laugh and walk on by. It's par for the course. It's what a lot of people come here to see.'

'So... they just watched him die,' said Walker.

'I'm afraid so. Some of them recorded it on their phones,' said PS Billings. 'Already uploaded it to TikTok and Facebook and the like. Thought it was hilarious, until it wasn't, when they realised it was real. Even then, some of them couldn't accept it. Still can't. There's one guy over there who thinks we're all in on it. Thinks some TV presenter is gonna jump out at any moment.'

'Well, we're gonna need names, addresses, and numbers of everyone—and I mean *everyone*—along with any footage taken and statements made,' said Walker. 'And that's just for starters.'

'Crikey, we've got a job on our hands here, Chief,' said DC Briggs, irritating Walker a little by somewhat stating the obvious, like she was just now realising how extensive the investigation was going to be. She was still a newbie, of course, but even she should have enough experience by now to know what was going to be a major case, and what was not. And this clearly was.

Walker looked up. 'Can't have fallen from the Tower itself then. He'd have landed on the buildings below if he had. Plus, you'd expect more damage from that height. More likely he fell from somewhere around there,' he said, pointing up at the red-brick building in front of them. 'One… two… three storeys up… and then the roof.'

'Looks like it,' said DC Briggs. 'Good call.'

'We need to get up there, take a look around,' said Walker. 'See if you can get some of the Entertainment staff to give us access, get us up there.'

'Will do,' said DC Briggs. 'Give me a minute.'

* * *

Walker stood on the section of roof just above the Blackpool Tower Dungeon entrance and looked down at the body that still lay there below. 'About here,' he said to DC Briggs. 'This is most likely where he fell from.'

A female member of the Blackpool Tower Buildings staff—a chubby woman with a tattoo of a bunch of red roses on her arm, and a hoarse voice—had taken them up to the roof via a locked door, a door she had a key to.

'I can't believe it,' she said. She was distraught. *'Tony?* Why?'

'You know him?' asked Walker.

CHAPTER ONE

'Of course. Everyone knows him. He was the Lead Clown at the circus. He was well known here,' she said. 'I've just told everyone now. We're going to take the day off. It's all a bit of a shock.'

'Do you know of anything that was going on with him at the moment?' asked Walker. 'Did he seem down or depressed in any way? Or was he experiencing any major life events?'

'Broke up with his girlfriend, I think,' said the woman. 'Some small lass he hung around with. That's all I know.'

'*Small lass?*' asked Walker. 'You mean she wasn't very tall?'

'Midget,' said the woman. 'Or whatever's politically correct now.'

'Person of short stature,' said DC Briggs. 'Or you could just use their name, if it isn't relevant.'

'Course,' said the woman. 'I heard they broke up, and now Tony is dead. It's tragic. I don't know what we're gonna do. Nobody could juggle like Tone. The show will be ruined.'

'Well… er, thank you…?' He made sure his voice went up at the end. He wanted to know her name.

'You're welcome,' she said, not catching on.

'Your name, madam?' asked Walker, wishing he'd been clearer in the first place.

'Oh. Sue Willis,' said the woman. 'I do a bit of everything here. General Maintenance.'

'Great. That will be all for now,' said Walker, and the woman left the same way they'd come. 'Write down her name,' he said to DC Briggs, so she did.

Walker took a good look around.

'What you thinking, Chief?' asked DC Briggs.

Walker was thinking a lot, his thoughts churning. If it hadn't been for that graffiti next to the body, he'd be inclined, at this point, to think it was a suicide, or a drunken accident. But someone had been sending a message with that. Either that or someone had graffitied the footpath believing the deceased *was* a part of the Tower Dungeon performance—and perhaps they were protesting it, for some reason, or… something.

'I'm thinking we've got a puzzle on our hands,' said Walker. The guy fell from here, still wearing his clown costume, stinking of booze. You'd think it was suicide but then someone spray paints a message next to the body. Where a death's meant to send a message, you might suspect it was a drugs ring, or some other organised crime. But that doesn't really fit with this, with the message that was painted.'

'A vigilante then?' suggested DC Briggs.

Walker thought about it. 'What? Someone who thinks he's Batman?' He was thinking of the Joker character in the Batman stories, the bad guy who dressed a bit like a clown, the one exhibiting symptoms of psychosis.

'Not exactly,' said DC Briggs. 'But perhaps this guy isn't as clean as people might think. Sure, his colleagues seemed to get on with him okay—or valued him at least as a member of staff. But people have secrets, don't they? His girlfriend *was* a midget.'

'What? *Person of short stature*, you said, wasn't it?' corrected Walker.

'Okay then, yeah. His girlfriend was a person of short stature. Doesn't that send just a few shivers up your spine?'

Walker was a bit taken aback. DC Briggs usually seemed open-minded about most things, but not, apparently, with this. 'Go on. Spit it out. What's bothering you? What are you getting at?' he asked, thinking he already knew and just wanting her to say it.

CHAPTER ONE

'Well, the deceased… he was a big guy, wasn't he? Tallish. And, if his girlfriend was, what, only as tall as a nine-year-old girl, then maybe—'

'Oh. I see what you're getting at,' said Walker, stopping her there, seeing she was uncomfortable with saying more, helping her out. 'You think he's been living out some kind of sick fantasy? Look, just because a man is having a consensual adult relationship with a person of short stature, that doesn't mean he's a paedophile, or that he has any thoughts of that nature now, does it? We have to stick to the evidence, be clinical.'

DC Briggs thought about it. 'You're right. Of course,' she said. 'But it still just feels a bit off, to me, that's all. A bit creepy. This whole place does, actually.'

Walker looked around. 'It is a bit different around here,' he said. 'I agree. But it has a long history. And these tourist places are typically a bit unusual to outsiders like us. We're gonna have to be a bit more open-minded on this one.'

DC Briggs smiled. 'Well, get you, DCI Walker, getting with it. I'm proud of you.'

Walker didn't smile. 'You can be proud when we crack the case. Until then, let's focus.'

He looked over the edge of the roof again. 'There's something a few metres away from the body—maybe a broken bottle. Perhaps he threw it off here before falling.'

'Maybe,' said DC Briggs, squinting at the object Walker was referring to. Luckily, the sun was behind them, warming their backs a little, not obscuring their vision further.

'A few cigarette-ends up here as well,' noted Walker, crouching down now, looking on the floor. He picked one up, looked at it. 'People coming up here to smoke, probably staff from downstairs.' He was talking to himself now more than DC Briggs. *'Did someone push you, Tony? Did someone do this to you?'*

He stood back up, brushed himself down.

'Right. Let's start talking to a few people, get a team together at the local station, you know the score by now,' said Walker. 'It's time to move.'

'Absolutely, Chief,' said DC Briggs. 'The sooner we get off this roof, the better.'

CHAPTER TWO

Walker and DC Briggs walked into the immaculate Blackpool Police Station Headquarters, a newly erected modern-looking building that had replaced the more dated, less aesthetically pleasing concrete block where Blackpool Police HQ had previously been housed, over on Bonny Street—an imposing structure that had few windows and looked and felt very much like a prison. Walker had been there before, back in the day. But not here. This was new. In sharp contrast, this new station on Clifton Road was a pristine, visually appealing affair that looked more like a contemporary university building or high-end office block than a police station. With its internal shell made up almost entirely of windows, surrounded by a sleek white frame made of modern materials, not a brick or slab of concrete in sight, it was obviously designed to provide as much light as possible. It looked like a pleasant place to be and work, unlike its depressing-looking predecessor. It was a big step up.

'Nice place,' said Walker, looking around.

'Yeah. We're getting screwed over in Skem,' said DC Briggs. She meant at their station in *Skelmersdale,* where they were largely based and spent much of their time, when they weren't being put on special assignment like this. That was more in tune with the old Blackpool station—drab, dour, uninspiring—but it did its job, *just*.

The glass-fronted desk service here also felt more like a private hospital waiting room than the usual front desk services of most British police stations. It was welcoming, professional-looking. It felt like they'd finally entered the new century proper.

'DCI Walker and DC Briggs,' said Walker to the female officer manning the front desk. 'We're going to be temporarily stationed here, working on a local case. The Superintendent asked us to come over from Skelmersdale, help out.'

The woman at the desk licked her lips and wiped her mouth with her hand, probably brushing off the crumbs of something she just ate.

'I've been expecting you,' she said. 'IDs please,' she said, so Walker passed them through the hatch at the bottom of the glass.

The woman tapped on her keyboard, several times, before looking satisfied and handing the ID cards back. 'Thank you, sir,' she said. 'All clear. You're good to go.'

DC Briggs got around Walker, so she could also see the member of staff manning the front desk. 'Apparently, they need his experience,' she said, obviously trying to be friendly, her tone playful. They'd forged a close professional working relationship over the past few months, and she knew when she could relax, and when to be on it. This was one of those times to take a breather, get to know a few people, make some connections. So, Walker let it slide.

'We've had quite a high turnover of staff over here in recent months,' said the woman. 'Out with the old, and all that.

CHAPTER TWO

Our DCI just retired and we're waiting for his permanent replacement. Is it a murder case? I'm guessing it is, since you've been asked to come.'

'Not sure yet,' said Walker. 'That's why we're here—to find out.'

'Well, Room 7B is free if you want to set up there,' said the woman. 'It's on the second floor. You'll need an Incident Room, I take it. It's all clean, I checked it myself this morning.'

Walker nodded. 'Thank you,' he said. 'I'll need a couple of rookie DCs as well, help do some of the donkey work. I have my own tech guy who can either work remotely or come over, if necessary. But I need some extra legs on the ground here.'

'I'll call the Supe and let her know,' said the woman. 'I'm sure she'll drop by later and see how you're getting on anyway. She's at a conference for most the day. I'll find out which two DCs have the lightest workload at the moment and send them to Room 7B. I'll try to get them with you within the hour, if that suits?'

'It does. That would be very helpful,' said Walker. He looked more closely at the woman's name badge. 'Reception Officer Maloney.'

'You can just call me Kate,' she said, smiling. 'Everyone else does.'

'Okay then, *Kate*,' said Walker, trying to smile back at her, though he wasn't sure if it came off as a grimace. His face wasn't that used to it. She had a nice way about her, though—warm, friendly, attractive, a little overweight but fit-looking under it, muscular. He could see how she'd make a good receptionist, and especially at a police station.

Walker and DC Briggs left the reception area just as a PC was bringing in some drunk who was shouting, reminding them this was not some posh office for a private company or something similar after all.

'To 7B it is then,' said DC Briggs, over the noise as they rounded a corner into a quieter corridor approaching a stairwell that led to the second floor.

'Yeah. Let's get settled in. We can start by going through that list of people present at the crime scene the Duty Officer has. We'll need interviews done with each and every one of them.'

'Roger that. What's the priority then, Chief? What should we focus on first?' asked DC Briggs. 'Apart from the interviews I mean. What are we looking for?'

Walker rubbed his chin as they started climbing some stairs.

'Finding out who sprayed that graffiti, I suppose,' said Walker. 'We find that out, and we may even find a shortcut to solving this thing.'

* * *

DCs Daniel Ainscough and Christopher Hardman joined Walker and DC Briggs in Room 7B at Blackpool Police Station HQ, and sat down at the U-shaped seating arrangement, one likely set up to facilitate a continual flow of communication among staff members. Walker organised himself at the head of the 'U' and the room, in front of a white board, while the others found a spot with plenty of space for their belongings. Much like the rest of the building, this had the feel of an office or university seminar rather than a criminal investigation being conducted by the CID.

CHAPTER TWO

'DC Ainscough, DC Hardman, thank you for joining us on this case. I know you must already have a pile of things to be getting on with, so it's much appreciated,' said Walker.

'No problem, sir,' said DC Ainscough, a short chap with round glasses who seemed like the sort to take his job and every aspect of it very seriously. He pushed his glasses further up the bridge of his nose, pencil in hand and notepad on the desk next to a laptop computer, ready to take any notes if necessary. He was hanging off Walker's every words.

DC Hardman, on the other hand, much like his name, seemed to be more of a *hard man*. He had a shaved head, muscular like a pit bull, like he hit the free weights regularly at the gym—maybe even the boxing punching bag too—with a demeanour that was respectful yet confident. 'We're happy to help,' said DC Hardman, speaking for the both of them.

'Right then. Let's get to it. As you already know, we have a dead body at the bottom of Blackpool Tower—an Anthony Singelmann, male, forty-two years old,' said Walker. 'Was the lead clown at the Tower Circus, apparently; still in his clown outfit when he died. Found this morning by some tourists and locals. Apparently, the deceased was still alive upon discovery, but onlookers thought it was a part of the Tower Dungeon act, thought it was all makeup and acting, and by the time someone made the call he'd already died. Looked at first glance to be a jumper, but not from the Tower itself, as the trajectory wasn't right; from the Tower Buildings nearby, a three-storey affair. However, some graffiti sprayed *after* the man landed suggests there's foul play at work. Someone wrote "Be Kined" in red spray paint, spelled K-I-N-E-D, and some of it was sprayed on the deceased trousers.' Walker took a photo of the deceased, a clean mugshot of him, and pinned it on the whiteboard with a magnet, a variation of something he always did at the start of any new murder investigation. He then pinned another photo of Anthony Singelmann underneath the clean mugshot—this time in the clown suit, his limbs all twisted, covered in blood.

DC Ainscough was getting it all down in his notepad, while DCs Hardman and Briggs just listened.

'What else?' asked DC Hardman. 'We got any statements from the onlookers yet?'

Walker picked up the first of four organised piles of A4 papers, about the size of a brick each, held together with two thick elastic bands top and side, and came over and dropped it on the desk space in front of DC Hardman. He wanted to give him a little test, see if he might be as hard as he looked—as it could be useful, later. The paper brick slammed as it hit the desk, rocking it, but the DC didn't flinch, not one iota; test passed.

'Transcripts?' he asked, casually.

'Transcripts,' said Walker. 'You can thank the Duty Officer and their team for that. They've been busy all morning—just got it to me in record time.'

'I can go through this,' said DS Ainscough, already taking out three different colours of highlighter pen from his leather briefcase, a ruler, and a silver clickable ballpoint pen. 'I'll put any actionable items in the logbook.'

Walker smiled. He was glad to have someone on his team who was on it from the get-go. 'Very good, Constable,' he said.

'I'm better out in the field anyway,' said DC Hardman. 'I prefer to stir things up, get people talking, get right up in their faces, snoop around, that kind of thing. We're not gonna find what we're looking for sat here, are we?'

CHAPTER TWO

'Maybe, maybe not,' said Walker. 'But you can come with us for now. We're gonna need to talk to a few folks down at the Tower Buildings, or at their homes, wherever they might be. And first on that list is the ex-girlfriend of the deceased. One of their colleagues said they recently broke up.'

'Perhaps it *was* a jumper then,' said DC Hardman. 'Anyone could have sprayed that graffiti near the body. Maybe whoever wrote it meant it as a warning to others, like "be kind, or you might drive someone to suicide, like this". Could be someone with mental health issues who've got their own history of suicide attempts? An artist or an art student with issues, perhaps? Everyone thinks they're Banksy these days.'

'That's an interesting theory, DC Hardman. Anything is possible,' said Walker. 'And we'll keep that in mind. I always appreciate any ideas being put on the table like that. But to me, it just feels more like a message from whoever killed this man: *be kind... or you might end up like this too*. Come on. Let's get a move on and try to figure this thing out. We haven't got all day.'

* * *

'Sarah Jenkins?' asked Walker. 'I got your address from one of the staff at the Tower Buildings. I'm Detective Chief Inspector Jonathan Walker, here with my colleague DC Briggs. May we come in and have a chat?'

They were on Abingdon Street in Blackpool, just a short drive away from the Tower Buildings on the Promenade. Sarah lived in a second floor flat above a shop that simply said, 'Charity Shop'. The building was in disrepair—a broken drainpipe hung off it limply, and there were several large cracks in some exterior cladding—while the flat itself looked down on a bus stop and shelter out front, obviously most likely chosen for its low price rather than its outlook and condition, whether it was rented or bought. Walker and DC Briggs had already found their way inside the building and were stood in front of the flat door itself, with DC Hardman being left to conduct more interviews back at the Tower Buildings.

'Yes, of course,' said Sarah, looking up at them. She was unusually short, as described, perhaps only around four feet tall, Walker thought, or less even—despite her face appearing to be early to mid-thirties. Sarah looked like she'd been crying, had evidently already been told about what happened. She didn't seem surprised in the slightest to see them.

'Thank you,' said Walker.

Sarah led them into the flat and offered a seat on a dusty old floral-patterned sofa, so faded in colour that it now looked almost completely yellowy, although Walker guessed it had once been much more vibrant. The place smelled of cigarettes and chip fat, mixed in with some cheap incense and Indian curry. They sat down and dust plumed up from the sofa, making DC Briggs cough a little, despite her obvious efforts at stifling the tickle.

'I already know what happened,' said Sarah, as she waddled over to a matching sofa chair and then climbed up onto it, with some effort. 'You're here about Tony, aren't you? Some coppers came and told me he's dead.' That was unfortunate. He should have already known that, but there were so many interviews to conduct with Blackpool Tower Buildings staff and witnesses, that he'd not had a chance to go through it all yet.

'Yes. That's correct. I'm afraid Anthony Singelmann was found deceased near the base of the Blackpool Tower Buildings early this morning, having apparently fallen from the roof above—best guess. Do you know anything about how and why this tragedy might have occurred?'

'Only what my colleagues told me,' said Sarah, wiping her eyes on the sleeve of her oversized brown cardigan. 'I can't believe it. He's really *gone*?'

'I'm told that you two were recently an item,' said Walker. 'That you broke up for some reason. Is that correct?'

Sarah shook her head, seemingly not so much in denial but disbelief, and began to cry some more. DC Briggs stood up and went over to her, but Sarah held out a hand, motioning for her to stop, so the detective returned to her seat.

'You don't understand. I did something terrible,' said Sarah.

Walker looked at DC Briggs, communicating for her to get her notepad out as usual. She always took notes for Walker in this kind of situation, and no longer needed asking. A simple look was enough. She complied, taking out her pen and notepad, ready.

'What did you do, Sarah?' asked Walker. 'What was the "terrible thing"?'

'I… I… I can't even say it,' she said.

'I'm afraid whatever it is, Sarah, you're going to have to tell us. This is a criminal investigation now. And we haven't yet ruled out the possibility of foul play.'

'*Foul play?*' said Sarah, seemingly realising for the first time—or pretending she was realising—that this may not have been a suicide. 'I thought he…'

'We do not know what happened yet,' said Walker. 'That's

why we're here: to investigate, to find out exactly what did happen. Now, what was this terrible thing that you did?'

'Well, I... I suppose I kind of had an affair with his brother, Nathan. Tony caught us together,' said Sarah, spitting the words out in the end, then glancing up to gauge their reactions. 'I'm with him now—Nathan. We're a couple. I love him.'

'I see,' said Walker.

'It's awful, isn't it?' said Sarah. 'I don't know what I was thinking. I should have ended it properly first, but I didn't know how. And now Tony is dead. Did he kill himself because of me?' Her eyes were pleading now, pleading for them to tell her it wasn't her fault.

Walker took a moment. 'Well... there was no suicide note found, but that's often the case when a person kills themself. There's no reason to suspect it's a suicide at the moment though other than the fact that it appears he fell off a building that he shouldn't have been on. His injuries are consistent with such a fall.' Walker had seen the aftermath of jumpers before. He knew what it looked like—massive skeletal damage, internal bleeding, even some damage to the footpath itself. He also knew that if Anthony had jumped from the top of the Blackpool Tower itself, even if the trajectory could have allowed him to land where he had—which it could not—there would have been far more damage from that height: the body would have been completely torn apart, head and limbs would have been ripped away from the torso, and there would have been extensive neurological damage that would have killed him on impact. From three storeys up, though, he could well have survived for a short time, as onlookers had reported.

'But everyone liked Tony,' said Sarah, eyes wide. 'I mean, perhaps not *liked* him so much, but they didn't hate him. I think they felt sorry for him. Who would do such a thing?'

'That's what we're here to find out,' said Walker. 'We're going to need to talk to his brother, Nathan, as well, of course. Do you know where we might find him?'

'Well, normally he'd be at the gym, or at work,' said Sarah. 'But I'm not sure the way things are. It's not a normal day, is it? He's a fitness fanatic, you see. A muscle man. He works as the strongman at the Pleasure Beach, hammers steel nails into wood with his bare hands, or bends the nails without any tools, that kind of thing. He's naturally big though, his hands are massive, his fingers like jumbo sausages. He can pick me up and put me over his head with one hand without breaking a sweat. It's…' She smiled, and then snapped out of it, reality yanking her back.

'Could you give his full name, address, and phone number to my colleague before we leave?' asked Walker.

'Yes, of course,' said Sarah.

'Now, is there anything else you want to tell us? We'll find out one way or another anyway. Has anything else gone on recently, any further flashpoints because of this new relationship with Nathan Singelmann?' asked Walker. 'How did Tony take it?'

Sarah leaned back in her chair, seeming resigned to the fact that she'd have to tell them everything. 'Look, there was an incident in the Red Lion last night, the pub inside the Tower Buildings near the Tower Dungeon. Me and Nathan were having a beer with the Grim Reaper, and—'

'The *Grim Reaper*?' asked Walker.

'Sorry. I mean Tom, from the show. We usually call him whatever he is that day, for fun. He was still in full costume. Some of the actors come in there afterwards still dressed up, just for a laugh, or because they can't be bothered changing, and have some drinks. There are even themed beers—we were all having a Grim Reaper Blonde Ale. Anyway, Tony came in and saw us, and he went mad.'

'Go on,' said Walker.

'He came over and started calling me all kinds of words—bad ones, the worst you can think of. Nathan got up at some point, told his brother to leave, in no uncertain terms. Then Tony grabbed hold of Tom's scythe, started hitting Nathan with it—but it's only made of plastic, so it just snapped. It was a bit pathetic really. Then Nathan dragged Tony out of there, forced him to leave, said he was acting like a clown as usual, said he should take his costume off for once. It was no contest. Nathan really is *very* strong. But I went after him—Tony. I don't know why, I just felt sorry for him, how things turned out. I wouldn't say we were even an item, really. Not *really*, really. We just went on a few dates, but then Tony started calling me his girlfriend to everyone, so I just went with it while I figured out how to let him down gently. He was a sensitive soul, you see. Anyway, at the pub, I told Nathan I just wanted a quick word with his brother before he left, and I talked to Tony outside, but he couldn't control himself. He was twisted with rage, called me a…' Sarah couldn't go on. She was starting to get upset again.

'Go on,' said Walker.

'It's okay,' added DC Briggs. 'We're almost there.'

'He called me a *slut,* and then pushed me, and I fell over, hurt my back. I think it's bruised.'

'I see,' said Walker. 'And did anybody see this?' He was thinking if someone had seen the incident, they might have gone after Tony, wanted to hurt him, to punish him. He wondered whether this might have been the cruelty someone was warning against.

'I don't know. I don't think so,' said Sarah.

'And what about Nathan? Did you tell him about it?' asked Walker, thinking this might be the result of a brotherly conflict.

'No. I told him we just talked. I didn't want any more trouble,' said Sarah. 'Nathan's a big teddy bear though. He's not violent at all. He doesn't need to be. You'll see what I mean when you meet him. I was pretty shaken up though. I was crying.'

'Does Nathan know about his brother?' asked Walker. 'That he's dead.'

'Yes,' said Sarah. 'I told him on the phone this morning when I heard. I haven't seen him yet. Said he needs some time.'

Walker took a breath, a big one. He'd got what he came for. He'd talk to her again, down at the station, if necessary. But for now, he had something to work with, at least.

'Thank you, Sarah. That will be all for now. My colleague will stay to collect the information we require,' said Walker. 'For now, I'll see myself out.'

CHAPTER THREE

Walker and DC Briggs found Nathan Singelmann at his place of work at Blackpool Pleasure Beach, banging five-inch nails into a wooden beam with his bare hands, just as Sarah had described. It didn't seem like he *wasn't an aggressive type of person* whilst he was doing it, like she said. He was pumped, veins bulging, muscles flexed, with a mad faraway look in his eyes.

'Nine!' he shouted, when he was done. 'World record! Shame we didn't record that one.'

The assembled crowd of twenty to twenty-five people or so clapped and cheered, seeming impressed with the feat, while Nathan bowed and smiled, teeth bared, the top of his nose scrunched up. It was a show of bravado, a no doubt well-practised part of the act.

When the crowd dispersed, with the show at an end, Walker and DC Briggs approached Nathan.

'Can I help you?' he said. 'Do you want an autograph?'

Walker held up his ID badge. 'Detective Chief Inspector Jonathan Walker, and my colleague DC Briggs. You're aware of what happened to your brother, Tony, this morning, I believe. Is that correct?'

Nathan nodded. 'The only surprise is he didn't do it sooner.'

CHAPTER THREE

Nathan started to pull out the nails from the wooden beam with some pliers.

'I'm sorry for your loss,' said Walker. 'Could you elaborate?'

Nathan glanced up, just for a second, looking Walker in the eyes. 'He suffered from depression. Been taking medication since he was young,' he said. 'Tried to kill himself once before, when we were teenagers. Overdosed on some pills.'

'I see,' said Walker. 'We'll look into that, check his medical records, confirm what you're saying.' He looked at DC Briggs, who nodded, confirming this would get done. 'We also believe there's been some conflict between yourself and your brother over a woman called Sarah. Is that correct? From what we understand, she started a relationship with you when she was still with Tony. That must have been difficult for all of you.'

'Look. Sarah's a lovely girl—a really sweet soul. She just didn't know how to tell him,' said Nathan. 'That's all.'

'Tell him what?' asked Walker. 'That she wanted to be with you?'

'Look, he thought they were an item, didn't he, but they weren't,' said Nathan. 'They'd just been for a coffee a couple of times. That's all. He pulled a few strings, got her a job in the Tower Buildings you see, and she just wanted to say thanks. But he thought it was more. Much more. She said she'd kissed him on the cheek, just being friendly, you know. But he took it the wrong way. That was her big mistake. He started telling everyone she was his girlfriend, and it just kind of snowballed from there. He's delusional. I mean… he *was* delusional. He was always a nice enough guy, but he could be completely detached from reality at times. She didn't have the heart to tell him.'

'I see,' said Walker. 'And I believe you're having an actual relationship with Sarah now. When did this start, exactly?'

'It actually started around the time Tony began telling everyone they were an item, so we had to do it in secret, until we'd figured out a way of tidying everything up,' said Nathan. 'This is just typical Tony. If anyone gives him any attention, or talks to him, he thinks they're his best friend. He just made everything complicated for me, as usual. He was… difficult like that. He didn't mean to be. He just didn't know how to be with people.'

'You don't seem very upset about the death of your brother, Nathan, if you don't mind me saying so,' said Walker. 'Should you be working, right now? Don't you need time to grieve?'

Nathan took a deep breath, threw some of the nails into an old tin box. 'Look, to be perfectly honest, it's all a bit of a relief. I know that doesn't sound very nice, but it is what it is. He's been a ball and chain around my ankle all my life. I took care of him at school, and then I took care of him when we grew up too. To be finally away from that… it's a bit freeing to be honest, that's all. I'm sad my brother is dead. Of course, I am. But it's probably for the best. He's never been happy. I was always wondering and stressing about what he might do to himself, or to someone else, even, looking out for him, protecting him. It was hope that was the killer—hope that he'd get better and be happier, hope that he'd find someone else to take care of him. I can deal with the pain, the grief, even the guilt that he was jealous of me and Sarah. But *the hope* I couldn't tolerate. At least it's all over now. He's in a better place, no longer being tortured by life. I don't think he ever really enjoyed any of it. I truly hope he rests in peace.'

'I see. Thanks for that. And I believe there was some kind of altercation at the pub last night, at the Red Lion inside the

CHAPTER THREE

Tower Buildings. Can you tell us about that too?' said Walker. 'So we can get your take on it. I'm sorry. But we must fully investigate all elements of any unusual deaths like this.'

'Oh, that? Nowt much to tell,' said Nathan. 'Tony came in, a bit drunk by the look of it, par for the course after a show, ranting and raving, calling Sarah all sorts—poor girl. He got it out his system, and then he left. Sarah went after him, had a quick word, and that was that. That's all I know. He had outbursts like that all the time about all sorts of things. He could be a pretty explosive character, kept things bottled up too much, probably—he was a pretty mild introverted kind of guy most of the time, but now and again he had to let it out, like a pressure cooker popping its lid. Like I said, I've had to put up with it all my life, so it's nothing new to me. It was only when he put on that damned costume and stepped into the ring, in front of all those people, that he really seemed anything close to content. At least he was distracted for a while. I'm glad he had that, glad he found something he liked to do, even for a short time.'

Nathan was now getting a little misty-eyed, not exactly holding back the tears like Sarah had been, but there was something there.

'And I believe there was somebody else with you at the pub as well, a Tom…?' said Walker.

'Yeah. Tom Neville. He's a mate of mine. We were having a beer,' said Nathan. 'He was still in costume.'

'So, I hear,' said Walker. 'The Grim Reaper?'

'That's right,' said Nathan. 'He's doing a show involving that character at the moment. Isn't life weirdly ironic.'

'Ironic?' asked Walker, but he knew what he was getting at and just wanted him to keep talking.

'The *Grim Reaper*. He comes when someone is about to die, doesn't he,' said Nathan. 'Comes to collect their soul or something. Strange that he should be dressed in that the night Tony killed himself.'

Walker saw Nathan's hands properly for the first time. They were huge—big enough to crush someone if he was so inclined.

'It's okay,' said Nathan, probably noticing Walker's reaction to seeing his hands. 'Most people look at them at some point. The doctors say I had too much growth hormone when I was a teenager, caused my hands and feet to grow more quickly than normal. It's called *acromegaly*. I never would have got this job without it though, so it's more of a blessing than a curse—at least, that's the way I see it.'

'I see. And you like your job?' asked Walker.

'I do. These seaside towns—and especially here in Blackpool—they're special. We have a long history, a real heritage. People come here from all over and we entertain them, give them something to remember, hopefully for the rest of their lives,' said Nathan, with a degree of pride.

'Okay. There's just one more thing,' said Walker. 'Do you know of anybody else who may have had any sort of conflict with your brother, anyone who had any reason to want to hurt him, that kind of thing.'

'Wait,' said Nathan, holding out one of his meaty hands. 'He did kill himself, right? Why are you asking that?'

'We're just investigating all avenues, that's all, just in case,' said Walker. 'We need to be sure. So?'

'No. Not that I know of. I think most people just felt sorry for him. Nobody I know of wanted to hurt him.'

'Because people felt sorry for him?' asked Walker. 'Sarah

said the same thing.'

'Yeah. He was a bit pathetic, you know. A bit... It's hard to explain. You had to meet him,' said Nathan. 'He just didn't connect with people very well, was always on the outside looking in. Often, he thought he was in on the joke, when actually he *was* the joke.'

'I see. I think I know the type. Well, thanks for your time, Nathan. I think that's all for now. We'll be in touch if we need anything further,' said Walker.

Walker and DC Briggs left him to it and headed towards the exit of the amusement park, hearing children screaming as the little ones passed over on rides, fairground music blazing, the smell of candy floss and sweet beverages in the air. The place was both disorientating and alluring, intoxicating.

Near the exit, there was a small booth containing a Tarot Card Reader, a mature lady dressed in black, wearing a green silk scarf around her head and strong makeup.

'Want your cards read?' she asked. 'Sometimes it's useful to know the future.'

'We're police officers, conducting an investigation,' said Walker, as he passed on by, but DC Briggs tugged him back.

'Let's take a quick look,' she said. 'Who knows, we might learn something about this place.'

'Police officers,' said the woman. 'I'll do yours for free then.' She spread a pack of cards on the booth's shelf. 'Take three.'

Walker rolled his eyes, not believing in things like this, but thinking it might be quicker just to get it over with. He selected three cards, put them to one side. 'There,' he said.

The woman turned them over, one by one, not without a little theatre. But as each card was turned, her eyes went a little wider.

'Oh, dear,' said the woman. 'Oh, deary dear. The Hanged Man, the Devil, and the Tower. I've never seen anything like it.'

Walker smiled a wry smile, thinking it was all set up.

'What does it mean?' asked DC Briggs.

'Well, it means there's been, or there's going to be some kind of sacrifice or martyrdom—that's the Hanged Man. Then we have the Devil next. This refers to addiction, rampant materialism, greed. And finally, we have the Tower.'

'The Tower,' said Walker, his interest stoked. 'What's that all about?' This card depicted some kind of tower that was on fire, looked like it had been struck by lightning.

The woman gulped, seeming genuinely perturbed. 'It means upheaval, disaster, danger, crisis, or a sudden change. It means something bad is about to happen.'

He hadn't been aware that Tarot cards contained a card that was a Tower. It made him think of the obvious—that the body was found at the bottom of Blackpool Tower, something that was a disaster, at least for his family and colleagues. Plus, he wondered whether it might be some kind of sacrifice. It sent shivers up his spine, which he dismissed as being from the cool breeze. 'Well, thanks for the reading,' said Walker. 'We'll be on our way. We have work to do.' He was glad they'd stopped for a minute or two though, discovered this potentially symbolic card. With such fortune tellers embedded in the fabric of the culture of Blackpool, most locals were probably aware of its meaning. So, it was good to know.

'Please take care,' said the woman. 'Something big is in the air.'

They left her to it, exited the amusement park proper.

'Did you see the size of Nathan's hands?' asked DC Briggs.

CHAPTER THREE

'I did,' said Walker. 'How could I not? Big fella.'

'Big enough to throw someone off a roof with ease, I'd say,' she said, glancing at Walker as they moved.

'Easy, detective. We can't go making any assumptions like that. We just follow the evidence trail, remember?' said Walker, reminding his colleague, and himself, to remain objective.

'I know. I'm just saying: he looked *strong*,' said DC Briggs.

'Point taken. I think it would be useful if we talked to this Tom character next—the Grim Reaper. See what he's got to say,' said Walker. 'Get his take on things.'

'Roger that, Chief,' said DC Briggs. 'But let's just hope death doesn't follow this guy, like Nathan suggested, or we're all in trouble.'

CHAPTER FOUR

'Tom Neville. Thanks for coming down to the station,' said Walker. 'It really wasn't necessary though. Myself or one of the DCs could have dropped by your home, took your statement from there. But it's much appreciated anyway.'

Tom Neville was a middle-aged man with boyish looks who was now starting to look a bit odd, like a boy in a man's body. He appeared to have had a relatively easy life, looking at him, and Walker wouldn't have been surprised if he spent most of his time playing computer games in his bedroom before watching back-to-back footy matches. He reeked of being single. Stank of it. He clearly hadn't been taking care of his cosmetic appearance very well, was not skilled in personal grooming—had missed clumps of beard hairs on his neck from when he'd shaved, and hairs similarly sprouted out of his nostrils like mangled cat whiskers. His hair was also greasy, like he hadn't washed it in days, and he had some kind of angry rash on his neck—most likely from a lack of cleanliness, looking at him.

'It's no problem,' said Tom with a smile that revealed badly conditioned teeth and gums, which served to underline this lack of self-care further. He didn't seem like the Grim Reaper type, whatever that was. Out of costume, he just seemed so ordinary—extraordinarily ordinary, in fact—which was perhaps why, Walker mused, he might have been drawn to such a job. 'My place is such a mess, so…'

Walker nodded. He felt the same about guests in his own home. Domestic tasks weren't his forte either. They were in an interview room on the second floor of Blackpool Police Station HQ, but Walker saw no need to record this particular conversation—he was simply taking the man's statement, and he could always record if he wanted to conduct a formal interview later. DC Briggs was busy writing some reports of what they'd found so far, so Walker was doing this one alone. He also saw no need to get her involved on this occasion. For now, this man was simply a witness, a person of interest, not a suspect.

'So, you were at the pub last night, I believe—the Red Lion—with Nathan Singelmann and his girlfriend, Sarah,' said Walker.

'That's right,' said Tom. 'It all kicked off a bit, didn't it, before… you know. It's all rather regretful now, isn't it? Did you hear?'

'Yes. Could you tell me in your own words, what happened, please?' asked Walker. 'We need to triangulate our data. It might be important for the case.'

'Course. Well… you see, Nathan's brother Tony—the man who died, who you're investigating—came in. He was upset about something. Started ranting a bit, said his brother was always stealing things from him ever since he was little, so it was no surprise he'd stolen his girlfriend too. Then he grabbed my scythe; it's a tool the Grim Reaper wields. Sorry, I was in costume. Forgot to tell you that. I work at the

Tower Dungeon as an actor. I'm just working there to get some experience. I want to be on television one day, maybe something regular, like a soap opera—Coronation Street or Hollyoaks, that kind of thing. Anyway, he tried to hit Nathan with it, the scythe, but it whacked the table and snapped. I had to glue it back together when I got home, ready for the next show. Sarah tried to calm things down, said she was never Tony's girlfriend, that he'd misunderstood, that she was sorry. Then Nathan lost it a bit and banged his fist on the table, and all the drinks jumped up like in some kind of cartoon and spilled everywhere. That startled us all because Nathan is usually pretty chilled out. Tony started laughing hysterically at that, then flipped again, called Sarah… various bad words, shall we say, and then stormed off out of there.'

'I see. And is there anything else?' asked Walker.

'Yeah. Sarah went after him, said she wanted to go alone, talk to him. Said she felt sorry for him,' said Tom. 'She came back a couple of minutes later, but she looked even more upset after that and she was rubbing her lower back. She said it was nothing, and we ordered some more drinks, but Nathan didn't stay long. Said he'd had enough, wanted an early night, so I stayed with Sarah a bit longer, finished our drinks, and then we went home too. We live on the same street, you see, so I walked her back to her place first before turning in for the night myself.'

'And was there anyone else there, watching, while all of this was happening?' asked Walker. 'At the pub, I mean. Did anyone else see what happened?'

'Not really. I mean, I don't think so. Just the barman. Oh, and I think there was some guy in the booth opposite who left when things started to get a bit too loud,' said Tom. 'But other than that, it was pretty empty, and the whole thing only lasted a couple of minutes anyway.'

'And this *other guy*, have you ever seen him before? Do you know who he is?' asked Walker.

'No. Don't think so,' said Tom. 'I wasn't paying much notice, to be honest. Probably just a tourist having a drink after the show or something. I think I *may* have seen him in there, in the Dungeon, during one of my acts. Maybe. Not a hundred per cent on that. But I don't know him as such, no.'

'Can you describe him for me?' asked Walker.

'I don't know…' said Tom, taking a breath, thinking about it. 'Like I said, I wasn't paying a whole lot of attention to him, what with everything that was going on. Big chap, I think. Tall. Middle aged perhaps. I'm not sure.'

'How about his face? It would be useful if we could arrange for you to work with a forensic artist to draw up a facial composite,' said Walker.

Tom looked into space, his eyes clouding over.

'I really can't picture anything about his face,' he said. 'Nothing at all. I only remember he was big, and I'm not even a hundred per cent on that.'

'Okay. We'll leave that then. I'll find out who was working the bar that night and talk to them instead,' said Walker. 'Maybe they know more.'

'Oh, I can save you the trouble. That would be Danny Bagley. Works at the bar Monday, Wednesday, and Friday evenings, I believe,' said Tom.

'Thank you. That's also very helpful,' said Walker, writing it all down—a little cumbersomely, not being used to taking his own notes these days. 'And just one final thing: did you have any further contact from Nathan or Tony that evening?

Anything at all? A text, a missed phone call, anything.'

'No. I did not,' said Tom, getting his phone out and double-checking, pausing while he looked. 'Nope. Nothing at all,' he confirmed, putting his phone away again. 'I'm really sorry about Tony. It's a real shame what happened. He might have been a bit odd, but nobody would wish that on anybody.'

'Of course,' said Walker. 'Thanks again for your time, Mr Neville. We'll be in touch if we need anything else.'

CHAPTER FIVE

'DI Hogarth,' said Walker. 'It's good to see you.'

Walker was sat at his desk in front of a MacBook computer, talking to DI Hogarth via a FaceTime live video stream. It was not something Walker was familiar or comfortable with. He was very much old school when it came to things like this. But needs must.

'I wish I could say the same,' said DI Hogarth. Walker was just about to say something, a bit taken aback, when his old friend and colleague said, 'You need to turn your camera on.'

Walker wasn't the most tech savvy detective, for sure. He knew that. In fact, he probably wasn't even in the bottom twentieth percentile. 'Er… How do I—'

'The icon of the video camera, oddly enough. Click it,' said DI Hogarth, sounding a little exasperated.

Walker did as asked and waited.

'There you go,' said DI Hogarth. 'That's it. I can see you now.'

'I don't know why we can't just do this over the phone,' said Walker, now getting somewhat irritated himself, 'but, anyway, what do we have?'

'Well, what we have is someone called *The Defender*. Some kind of vigilante character who's doing the rounds on various forums and chat rooms right now. There's one on Facebook called "The Tower Forum" that's particularly active at the moment,' said DI Hogarth. 'They're all talking about it—how he killed that clown. It's really got people stoked up.'

Something pinged and popped up on Walker's screen. It was a text message from DI Hogarth. Walker couldn't keep up with this new way of communicating. It was all a bit too much for him at times, but he knew he needed to use it if he was to remain in the job. He figured, if the criminals were using it, then he at least needed to be familiar with it too, before handing over any specialist technical work to more tech-minded detectives like DI Hogarth. He had to be on the ball. He needed to keep changing, evolving, to be supremely comfortable with being uncomfortable, if that was possible. He wasn't even that old, really, and other people his age seemed to be fine with it all. He guessed he'd just been too busy with work to keep up with all that crap, and now he was so far behind it was all a bit overwhelming, frustrating. But he'd stick with it for now, keep trying.

'I just sent you a link to the page. You can have a look through it later,' said DI Hogarth. 'But basically, someone's been... for want of a better word... *punishing* people who've been seen doing unpleasant things. For example, some woman had her handbag snatched on the Promenade, and some guy ran after the thief, took him down, and then bashed his face in good and proper. Another one, an old man was shouted at by a passer-by, and this passer-by got in a car only to have a brick thrown through his window. There are more of these, many more, all with the same description of a big man wearing a face mask—the ones that everyone wore during the pandemic, only his was black. And there's

CHAPTER FIVE

more still… Some of the cases involved a message being left: *Be Kind*—spelled correctly this time, by all accounts. One was an A4 printout left on a cracked car windshield, another some paint on a garage door. There was even one written on someone's forehead in a permanent black marker pen, after he'd been knocked about a bit. There's a picture of it on file—the guy got his teeth knocked out. But some folks have been supporting this violence, started calling the mystery assailant The Defender at some point, and the name stuck I guess.'

'I see. That's a lot to be getting on with,' said Walker, thinking about the big man in the pub who'd seen Tony get angry, wondering if there might be a connection, if it was the same man. But he did have some reservations given the spelling error in the latest message. The killer might just be a copycat who'd been hanging around on the Facebook Group, he thought, someone jumping on the bandwagon, but taking things too far. 'So, this Defender chap *could* have been involved in Tony Singelmann's death. But the spelling error casts some considerable doubt on whether this might have been the same person—unless he got some help with the graffiti, of course.'

'Absolutely,' said DI Hogarth. 'That's what they're all saying, anyway. I've also looked at the rate of recorded crime in the Blackpool area over the past few months. There's been a slight uptick of people reporting being beaten up in alleyways and the like, people having their cars torched, one guy even said he was dragged out into the sea and held under—thought he was going to die according to his statement. Claimed he didn't do anything wrong but someone on the forum said they saw the whole thing; said he kicked a pigeon. These kinds of reports of assault are not exactly the norm, though they do occasionally happen, as you know. However, it's the volume of such reports that's unusual. This is not the norm. Something seems to have been going down in this area recently. Whether it's an individual, or a coordinated group effort, is unclear. We'll need to look into it some more—see if all the descriptions of the offenders match, or not. There's a lot to get through. But people have definitely started talking about it, and they don't exactly dislike what's been happening either, on the whole. One person said, *it's about time the town was cleaned up*, another noted that, *people might start to behave better now*. That kind of thing.'

'Right. Well, this is all very interesting, and disturbing. Good work as always, Detective. Keep looking, if you would, see if there's anything else, look more deeply into it. I'll keep this at the forefront of my mind while working the case. In the meantime, let me know if there's anything else, and compile a list of all those who've reported a crime of this nature, so we can talk to some of them as well, try to get more detailed descriptions of the offender—maybe identify some kind of unique mark or characteristic if we're lucky; a tattoo, piercing, or scar, that kind of thing.'

'Will do,' said DI Hogarth. 'Talk soon then.'

The video feed went off, leaving Walker only with the pop-up text message that DI Hogarth had sent, and the weblink to the Facebook page he mentioned. Walker clicked on it.

'Can we focus on the case, Chief, leave our social media posts for when we get home?' It was DC Briggs. She was just walking past with some freshly photocopied papers. He could smell it, and it wasn't an aroma he disliked: to him it smelled of the building of a case. 'What do you have?' she asked.

Walker clapped his hands, getting the attention of DCs

CHAPTER FIVE

Ainscough and Hardman, who were also in the room with him, going about their business. He'd asked everyone to assemble so they could have a meeting, exchange some information, see what they'd found so far. He popped some more mugshots on the whiteboard, to update the evidence board he was creating—give them something to focus on. There was one of Nathan Singelmann, one of Tom Neville, and one of Sarah Jenkins to add to that of the deceased, Tony Singelmann. He also wrote on the whiteboard with a marker pen, and started compiling a list of 'IDEAS' to one side: (1) Facebook Discussion Group, (2) Stranger in Pub, (3) Vigilante Group? (4) Love Triangle / Tony's Brother, (5) Depression, (6) Victim Intoxicated.

'The case is growing,' said Walker. 'As you can see, and it has some complex elements. But as yet, we're still just throwing spaghetti at the wall and seeing what sticks. This is what we have so far. I've just come off a call with DI Hogarth, who's been scouring the Internet, looking for any clues or leads. It seems there's some kind of vigilante doing the rounds in Blackpool at the moment, policing people's behaviour for us. They're calling him "The Defender". Could be a possible suspect. Other possible suspects and persons of interest at the moment include Tony's brother, Nathan, and a stranger who was sat in the Red Lion pub and witnessed an argument between the victim and his brother. We need to follow up on all this. DC Ainscough, you see what more you can find out about this Defender guy, nail down his M.O. and how he operates. Even if he's not involved in this, he still needs to be investigated and arrested. DC Hardman, I want you to find out who this stranger in the pub was, bring him in for questioning. It might be the same guy. DC Briggs and I will look a little more closely at the life of the victim, go to his home, see what we can find out there.' Walker clapped his hands. 'Any questions?' There were none. 'Okay. Let's get to it then, people. Let's find out who did this. The victim, as always, is our client, and we need to do our very best for them so they can rest in peace.'

Before Walker and his team could disassemble, there was a knock on the door, and it opened.

'DCI Walker?' It was a woman, middle-aged, slim, pale, serious looking, immaculately dressed in a tight suit and blouse. 'I'm Superintendent Lucy Stone. I'm the one who requested your assistance on this case. Could I have a word, in my office?'

'Of course,' said Walker. He turned to DC Briggs. 'I'll be with you soon. Update the action book while you're waiting and file those reports.'

'Will do, Chief,' said DC Briggs, eyeing Superintendent Stone, seeming a little concerned. 'See you soon then.'

* * *

'Right then. DCI Walker, it's good to meet you again. We met at a conference one time, over in Preston, when I was younger. You gave a little talk about psychological profiling. Your work is quite well known at the Lancashire Constabulary, and beyond,' said Supt Stone. 'It's good to have someone of your extensive experience and expertise on board. We're very lucky.'

Walker took a look around her room, which like her

appearance, was similarly immaculate. Everything was neat and tidy, spotless. Even the bin had been recently emptied and looked cleaner than his kitchen worktops.

'It's my pleasure,' said Walker. 'Nice place you've got here. I can see you run a tight ship.'

Supt Stone nodded her appreciation. 'I have some concerns about your health status, Detective. Your report says you have a recurrent health condition that's being closely monitored. However, our Criminal Investigation Department is currently lacking in experience a little, so we thought it prudent to get someone of your stature in for this particular case, to take a good look at it, as I got word from the Duty Officer that it might not be a simple suicide case after all, that something more nefarious might be at play. In a word, it wasn't exactly clear, apparently, and I didn't want to miss anything. Is your initial investigation supporting this idea?'

'It is,' said Walker. 'We definitely need to look at this one a bit more closely before coming to any conclusions. There are some complex elements.'

'That's what I thought,' said Supt Stone. 'And how is your health holding up these days? Are we okay?'

'All good,' said Walker, as nonchalantly as he could. 'I'm tip-top.'

She eyed him, with some obvious suspicion. 'Well, let me know immediately if there's any change with that,' said Supt Stone. 'And I mean *immediately*.'

'Will do. I heard you have some unusual law and order issues at the moment, with some Defender character,' said Walker, wondering whether she knew about it.

Supt Stone breathed a heavy sigh. 'That's all just gossip at the moment. We have no evidence that such a coordinated attack is occurring.'

'But you have seen a spike in local crime rates for offences such as GBH and property damage, is that correct?' asked Walker.

'It is. But we do have such spikes from time to time. All kinds of socio-economic events can cause such mini-spikes, and political news too, as you know. It's not unusual, and simply coincides with these online rumours. But yes, to answer your question, of course I've heard,' said Supt Stone. 'I know everything that goes on around here.'

'Then you'll know that some graffiti left near and on our murder victim roughly matches that left near some of these less serious crimes,' said Walker, letting it hang.

'Well, I haven't read the full report yet, but that wouldn't surprise me if that's what the kids are writing these days. It might not be connected—perhaps just some trend going around on social media at the moment,' said Supt Stone. 'But it is something to consider. Anyway, I just wanted to briefly touch base with you for now, and then I'll leave you to your investigation for the time being. If there's anything I can do to further support your team, just let me know, and I'll see what I can do.'

Supt Stone was relatively young for a Superintendent, perhaps early-forties, Walker thought, sandy blonde hair, attractive if she actually smiled once in a while—but she didn't, at least not in the little time he'd spent with her. Not that he was judging her for that. He wasn't the most affable himself, far from it. Walker knew that the heavy weight of responsibility could do that to some of the more senior officers, could make them wry and cynical, forget about the human side of the job, him included. So, seeing her demeanour was a good reminder of that.

'Thank you. I'll see myself out,' said Walker. Supt Stone looked at him as if to say of course he would, and, not wanting to get on her wrong side, he didn't look back.

CHAPTER SIX

Sarah Jenkins felt Nathan wrap his meaty arm around her, enveloping her tiny frame, almost suffocating her. She panicked for a second, gasping for breath.

'I'm so sorry,' she said, as Nathan relinquished his grip on her. 'Are you okay?'

She'd come to his home. He'd texted her earlier after she'd told him on the phone what happened to Tony, told her he needed some time. But she needed to see him. She couldn't wait any more. She wanted to see how he was.

'I'm dealing with it,' said Nathan. 'I've just got home from work.'

'You've been to *work*? *Today?*' said Sarah, surprised Nathan had been able to perform today of all days. She'd told those detectives that he'd either be at home or at work, but she'd really not expected him to be at work, not really, despite this being a distinct possibility.

'Yeah. I didn't know what else to do, so I just did what I normally do. Plus, I thought bending a few nails and doing some fist hammering might help relieve some tension,' he said. 'You know how I get.' He meant his job helped to level him out, keep him chilled. If he missed a session, he was always a bit more agitated, a bit more on edge.

CHAPTER SIX

'Well done then, I suppose,' said Sarah. 'I couldn't. I just couldn't...' She started to cry so Nathan held her again, a bit looser this time, probably realising he'd overdone it the first time. He didn't know his strength, how easily he could hurt someone.

Today though, despite Nathan having gone to work and done his usual routine, he still seemed a bit jittery, which was to be expected, given the circumstances, but even more so than Sarah expected.

'Are you sure you're okay?' asked Sarah again. Nathan was sweating, covered in it, despite the house being cool and a window being open. Winter was creeping in.

'It's just... I saw Tony again, last night, before...'

'You *saw* him? What do you mean you saw him, Nathan? What happened?' asked Sarah. 'Were you on that roof with him?'

'No, no... I...' Nathan rubbed his considerable head, a head the size of a watermelon, and then scratched at his temple. 'I went after him, I mean. I wanted to talk to him, just like you did. I chased him through the Ballroom, and he went up to the second level. I grabbed him, by his collar, pinned him up against a wall. I know. Don't say anything. It was stupid. But I was angry about what he said about you. He stepped over a line: way over. I had a few words, that's all, and then I let him go. He jumped over a couch blocking the third tier to tourists, and went up higher, so I just left him to it.'

'Jesus, Nathan. Have you told the police?' she asked.

'Of course not!' said Nathan. 'And neither will you. Please don't say anything. They might think I pushed him or something.'

'Did anybody see you?' asked Sarah, fearing for him.

Nathan looked scared too. 'The place was deserted. It was late. I don't think anyone saw.'

'You don't *think*,' said Sarah. Nathan wasn't the brightest, Sarah knew, but she loved him all the same. He had a good heart, and she knew he cared about his brother, even if he drove him mad sometimes. 'And what if the police find out. Then what? It'll look even more suspicious. You have to tell them. Why *didn't* you tell them?'

'Because… I…'

'You *what*, Nathan? Tell me everything, right now,' said Sarah.

'I slapped him, in the face, and broke his tooth. He spat it out, laughing hysterically. I got his blood on my T-shirt,' said Nathan. 'It looks bad, doesn't it. I was just so angry. I don't think I've ever been that angry. I just… I love you, Sarah. And what he said was so unkind. I just wanted him to pay, that's all. I know it was wrong. I'm sorry.'

Sarah held Nathan now or did her best to. 'It's okay, my little boy,' she said, before whispering, 'but that's all, right? There's nothing else?'

Nathan started to cry now. 'No. There's nothing else, my great lady,' he said. 'That's it.'

She stroked his hair, held him close, comfortingly. 'Then there's nothing to worry about, is there?' she said. 'Nothing at all. Now where's that T-shirt you were wearing? I'll get rid of it for you.'

CHAPTER SEVEN

Danny Bagley scrolled through The Tower Forum on Facebook, reading some of the recent comments made about the vigilante Defender. He smiled, seeing how many people were on-board with cleaning up the town, scaring people into behaving better. Things had gone downhill in Blackpool over the years, the place becoming rife with drug use, theft, and violence. There was just no discipline anymore—parents couldn't teach their kids right from wrong. They were terrified of them, afraid of their own children, and these kids were growing up to rule the roost. The inmates were taking over the asylum, the monkeys taking over the zoo. Danny himself had been the victim of such an attack, bottled in a pub one night when he'd just been having a quiet drink with a mate. He hadn't even seen who'd done it, had his back to them. They'd just hit him, the coward. Knocked him out cold. He'd had to have the cut stapled back together at the hospital with a bloomin' skin stapler of all things! But that wasn't what really twisted him up, made him beyond furious. He could deal with that. What had really got him was when his own mother had been robbed, beaten, and left scarred and half-blinded in one eye. He loved his mother—she was such a gentle, loving soul—and he wanted whoever had done that to her to really suffer. He wanted anyone who did such things to suffer. They deserved no less. People should be kinder to each other, he thought, or at the very least they should stop doing these horrible things. It just wasn't right.

He read through some more of the comments on the forum on the desktop computer in front of him:

> My sister was burgled last month. She doesn't feel safe in her own home. Go Defender! [smiley face]
> At least someone is doing something now. Better late than never. I support you, *our* Defender.
> I was there this morning, outside the Tower. The Defender has stepped things up, done someone in this time. Good for him. Behave, or you'll be next!

People were loving it, Danny thought, were empowered by it. There were those who weren't quite on-board as well, of course, and even a few that vehemently opposed it and all forms of violence; but on the whole, people were supporting it, and were glad of these radical interventions.

Someone posted a photo of Tony Singelmann next, his bloodied body lying outside the Tower Buildings, next to a mugshot of him, and one of him dressed as a clown at the circus—three photos in a row.

> This clown stepped over the line. Be kinder to each other in future – D.

Wow. It seemed someone was actually claiming to be the Defender—the judge, jury, and executioner—stepping out of the shadows into the light, putting themselves at risk of being caught. But then someone else wrote on the forum too.

> No, I'm The Defender!

And then someone else.

> No. It's me. I'm The Defender!

They were all at it. All claiming to be The Defender. It was like a skit on that old film, Spartacus, where everyone claimed they were the chief protagonist as a show of solidarity. And if all these people started to punish anyone who was unkind—if they actually became a version of The Defender—then Blackpool would be cleaned up in no time, and a whole new, more positive culture might start to emerge. Danny approved. He knew it was all a bit right wing, a bit militant and extremist, actually, but things had gone way too far, and it was time for the people to do something about it. It's not like the police were doing much, so they had no choice. He prepared to post his own message. It would be okay. He was using the Tor browser, which allowed anonymity and prevented user tracking, while he'd also set up a dummy Facebook account called simply 'The Big D'.

> I'm afraid I'm the original Defender, but you all can be! Let's clean up Blackpool together!!

He pressed the 'return' key and watched the responses come flooding in.

> No way! It's really you? 'The Big D'?

> You can't be The Defender cos I am!

> Let's all work together, clean this place up once and for all. I'm sick to the back teeth of these louts.

Danny shut his computer down and took a sip of a cup of black coffee he'd made earlier, which had now cooled enough to be able to drink. He was just about to take a second sip when there was an abrupt knock on the door: three raps—*knock, knock... knock.*

'Hello? Danny? Danny Bagley? Are you home?'

A wave of paranoia washed over him. *They've found me, somehow. They found out what I did.* No. It couldn't be. He'd only just posted it. It was impossible. But then again, there were AI bots trawling the web these days, looking out for things exactly like this. He wasn't sure what to do—pretend he wasn't home? Yes. That's what he'd do. He'd just be quiet. They'd go away.

'Danny. It's the police. I can see you through the keyhole. Please, open the door. We just need to talk to you about what happened last night.'

Danny's shoulders slumped forward in defeat, and he went over to his flat door, got the key off a hook, and opened it up. There was no other way out.

'Sorry, I was... I get a little uncomfortable when a stranger knocks on the door, that's all. You know how it is around here these days,' said Danny, looking down, unable to make eye contact with the male and female detectives he found stood at his front door. 'He glanced at them. Hey, I thought you said you were—'

'We're plain clothes personnel, Danny. I'm DCI Walker, and this is my partner, DC Briggs,' said Walker.

CHAPTER SEVEN

DC Briggs looked at Walker. 'Partner? Have I been promoted?'

'Most people would consider it a demotion,' said Walker, wryly. 'Now, Danny. May we come in for a minute?' He showed Danny his ID, pulled it forward from the lanyard around his neck, letting him see it up close.

'Yes, of course,' said Danny. 'Just let me tidy up a bit.'

'That will not be necessary, Danny,' said Walker, forcing his way inside.

'Would you like to sit down?' asked Danny.

'No. That will not be necessary either. This won't take long,' said Walker. 'I believe you work in the Red Lion in the Tower Buildings? The pub?'

'That's right,' said Danny. 'I'm one of the barmen there.'

'Mondays, Wednesdays, and Fridays, I believe,' said Walker.

He knew, thought Danny. They knew everything about him. They'd come for him.

'Yes,' said Danny, frozen, like a squirrel caught with the last nut, eyes wide, staring into some headlights.

'Can you tell us what you saw there last night?' said Walker, raising an eyebrow slightly, looking at his partner. 'Specifically, the argument between Tony Singelmann and his brother, Nathan, and a girl called Sarah Jenkins. We need to know—to triangulate our information.'

'To triangle… *what?*' asked Danny. He was losing it, not quite following the conversation, his thoughts getting frantic and ragged.

'Never mind that,' said Walker. 'What do you know about the argument between the Singelmann brothers?'

'Oh, *that*,' said Danny. 'Of course. Because of what happened to Tony.'

'Yes, that,' said Walker. 'Of course, *that*. Why? What did you think we were here for?'

'Oh, nothing,' said Danny, glancing nervously at his computer, then being angry at his eyes for betraying him.

'It's okay, Danny,' said DC Briggs. 'We're not interested in what you look at on your computer. As long as it's legal, you can look at whatever you like.'

Danny breathed a sigh of relief, before wondering what they thought he was looking at. 'But I wasn't looking at anything like that,' he said, thinking they thought he was looking at something pornographic, something a bit fetish-like. 'I was just…'

'Can we just focus on last night, for now,' said Walker. 'In your own words.'

'Well, I was working at the bar, as usual. It was pretty quiet. Nathan was in there with Tom and Sarah. Then Tony came in, seemed irate, I couldn't hear much of what he was saying, some kind of argument broke out, and then he left. Sarah went after him I think, and then came back soon after. That's all I saw,' said Danny. 'It didn't last long. It was nothing.'

'And was there anybody else in the pub during all this?' asked Walker.

'No. I don't think there was. As I said, it was a quiet evening,' said Danny. 'I just remember Tony coming in. It's hard not to really. An enraged clown is not something you easily forget.'

'Indeed,' said Walker, looking at his colleague again. 'Are you sure there was nobody else there?'

'I don't think so,' said Danny, lying.

Detective Walker paused, his eyes narrowing. 'Well, if you do remember anything else, or anyone else being in the pub that night, please do let us know.'

CHAPTER SEVEN

'Okay then,' said Danny, managing to keep a straight face, but inside he was beaming. He'd managed to get away with it. They didn't have a sodding clue.

CHAPTER EIGHT

He'd followed the bastard all the way along the Promenade. It was late—nobody was around. He looked at his watch: 3:37am. The tide was at its lowest point now, the sea out right to the end of the North Pier. He held a half snooker cue up his sleeve, the heavy butt end, cupping his hand at the base holding it, concealing it. He wasn't able to bend his arm like this, but nobody could see, and he could just release the weapon at any time by dropping it, letting gravity do its thing, then catching it in his palm ready to use. It was perfect. It was like a baseball bat only better—even easier to hide; shorter. It wasn't the first time he'd done this. Sometimes, people just needed to tool up, protect themselves. And other times, they needed to clean things up, protect others; like now.

The man he was following was the worst kind of person as far as he was concerned: real scum. He was weathered like old leather and aged beyond his years, probably through a vile concoction of alcohol, cigarettes, and drug use; and probably excessive masturbation as well, he thought. He might have all kinds of horrible diseases too, paid prostitutes even to get his kicks. But worse than that, he was coarse, unlikable, and beyond rude. In a word, he was just not *nice*.

CHAPTER EIGHT

He'd seen the man get kicked out of a pub just before closing time—had been causing all kinds of trouble he was, making everyone feel bad at the end of the night, ruining their day. He had no right. He'd even tried to hit someone but had been too drunk and missed his punch. Drinking wasn't an excuse for that kind of behaviour though. Some people drank and became even nicer. It was what was on the inside that mattered, and what was in him was black and vile. You can't squeeze apple juice out of an orange, as they say, and people with a malignant personality tend to only get worse after a drink—like *him*. He'd followed the man, seen him have a go at some poor woman on his way too, manhandling her, trying to have his way with her, asking her if she wanted to go back to his place. He'd even offered her some money to do so. Vile. He was just going to step in and help when the woman had kneed the bastard right in the balls. Served him right. But that wasn't enough. He'd just do it again, night after night, making more people unhappy and traumatised. The world would just be a better place without him, period.

'You shouldn't have done that. Not tonight of all nights,' he said, under his breath, watching the repulsive excuse of a man at a distance, getting ready to approach him.

The man was stood at the railings that went all along the Promenade, with the drop down beyond them at the other side where the massive reinforced concrete Sea Wall protected the seaside town. At the bottom of this wall were some steps, which took people down to the sandy beach beyond, but there was a good twelve foot or so drop beyond the railings to these steps. If he pushed him over the side, he'd fall, hurt himself badly, but it probably wouldn't kill him, so he'd have to finish the job. But that wouldn't be a problem. He knew how it felt now—*killing*. It was a lot easier than most people thought. At least, it was proving that way for him.

He got closer now, the repugnant thug unaware of his presence, looking out into the dark night. The wind masked the noise of his footsteps, and when he got close enough, close enough to reach out and touch him, the man turned.

'Hey. What the hell do you—?'

He pushed him, hard, in the chest, and followed through, making the man slam into the railings, but he didn't go over. Not yet. He needed some help with that. He grabbed the lout by the crotch, used his pants to lift him up a tad, seeing him wince in pain, and then he released the snooker cue butt end with his other hand, caught it, whacked him hard on the head. The man staggered, almost unconscious, surprised by the attack, so he dropped the snooker cue while he was on the front foot and used both hands to hoist him over the railings. It wasn't even that difficult, almost like he wanted to be thrown, no resistance at all. He fell with a sickening *thud*, hitting the concrete steps below, yelping like a wounded animal. Of course—the guy *was* an animal, one that needed to be put down because it was hurting people. He picked the snooker cue up once more, felt the weight of it in his hand, and went down some steps where the railings ended just off to one side, getting down to where the man was below. He was moaning now, in pain, clearly hurt, but still very much alive.

He got right up close to the man's face now, holding his blood-stained T-shirt with his left hand. 'You know, you really should be nicer to people,' he said.

The man spat in his face, and he wiped it from his eyes, disgusted. And then he hit the man with the snooker cue that he held in his other hand, really hard, on the head again, and then in the face, over and over until he stopped moving, stopped breathing, his face and head now looking more like tenderised meat than anything resembling a human. But he felt nothing, nothing but disgust.

He looked up and down the beach. There was no one there—no witnesses. He was all alone.

'Why can't people just be nicer to each other?' he said, breathing heavily, looking out into the black sea, sparkling with moonlight, before preparing to finish the job.

CHAPTER NINE

'Another one?' said Walker, shaking his head. He already suspected they had a killer on their hands, that the death of Anthony Singelmann hadn't been a suicide after all, but now he *knew*.

'Same writing,' said DC Briggs. '*Be Kind*. Spelled correctly this time.'

'The writing is most definitely on the wall with this one,' said Walker. He meant it both figuratively and literally, of course. It had been spray-painted on the Sea Wall, the multi-million-pound barrier that protected the people of Blackpool from the power of the tidal elements. And next to this writing hung one deceased male, a rope around his neck, hanging impotently from the railings above. He was bloodied, severely injured.

'You think it's the same person—that did it, I mean,' asked DC Briggs, getting up close to the body, stood on the steps below, scrutinising it. Over the past few months—her very first in the role of police detective—she'd become more desensitised to such things, more objective and analytical, which was a good thing. Walker was proud of her; of the progress she'd made in such a short space of time. He was sure she'd make an excellent detective one day. But for now, she was still very much an apprentice.

CHAPTER NINE

'I'd say the different spelling strongly suggests a different writer, if not a different culprit. Maybe we're dealing with multiple copycats here, people who've heard about this Defender character independently engaging in vigilantism and escalating it to murder. It's too early to say, so I think we must keep our minds open at this point, not rule anything out,' said Walker, getting close to the wall, looking at some other writing. 'Someone has etched *The Cure* into the wall as well, next to the body. Perhaps they think Blackpool has some kind of metaphorical virus or poison, and they are the antidote, cleaning it up, making people be nicer to each other.'

'Or... perhaps someone just likes Robert Smith and his gang,' said DC Briggs.

Walker looked at her. 'Excuse me?'

'*The Cure's* lead singer—he's from Blackpool originally, isn't he? People etch their favourite bands into things all the time. I don't think this is connected to the case, sir,' said DC Briggs. 'I think it's just a bit of low-level vandalism, some good old fashioned hero worship.'

'Oh,' said Walker, a bit embarrassed. 'Yes. I've heard of them, of course. Bit jangly, aren't they? But I never knew where they were from.'

DC Briggs smiled and nodded, seeming happy she knew something he didn't. 'What is it with this guy and being obsessed with people being kind to each other?' she asked. It was morning again now, just a few days after the first killing, and the sun was warming things up again—what little there was of it anyway, as it struggled through the clouds. The sea was moving in too but had not yet reached the coast properly yet.

'Be kind, for everyone you meet is fighting a hard battle,' said

Walker.

'Sound profound, poetic,' said DC Briggs. 'Didn't Plato say that?'

'Ian Maclaren,' said Walker. 'Nineteenth century author. I did a little research on kindness for the case. Did you see how the rope was tied, at the top. This man didn't hang himself. He was hoisted up there.'

'Well, I can see that,' said DC Briggs. 'I mean, look at his face.' What she meant was there wasn't much left of it. Whoever he was, he would have been unrecognisable to anyone who knew him now. He'd clearly been battered to death well before any rope was put around his neck.

Walker looked around. 'Well, we're not going to get much down here. Anything in the sand will be washed away soon too, so we'll need forensics down here pretty sharpish. If we're lucky, we might get something on CCTV from the top side, when he was tying that rope. I say "he". I'm presuming at least one male is involved in this. They'd have to be strong enough to hoist a grown man of this size up like this. In fact, if an individual did this, they'd have to be considerable in size and strength, I'd say.'

'Like Nathan Singelmann,' said DC Briggs.

'Like anyone strong enough to lift this man up,' said Walker. 'Unless it was a group attack. That's possible too, what with all the discussions online about this.'

'A group of copycats then?' asked DC Briggs.

Walker looked around some more. 'Let's hope mob rule isn't coming to town,' he said. 'If that happens, we'll really be in trouble.' He knew he shouldn't have said it as soon as the words left his mouth. It felt like tempting fate. He'd seen that film, *The Crow*, when he'd been younger, how people went mad on what they called Devil's Night, burning everything, looting and destroying property. It hadn't been much different during the riots of 2011, when London and other cities in Britain had similarly been looted and burned. And with Bonfire Night coming up soon, just around the corner, he had a bad feeling about it.

'There's something in the sea air, sir,' said DC Briggs. 'And it doesn't smell good.'

'Wait,' said Walker. He'd spotted something lying halfway down the steps. He went down, put a nitrile glove on, picked it up. 'I think I know what this is.'

DC Briggs joined him. 'Oh. What is it, Chief?'

He popped the rubber in an evidence bag. It was black, mushroom shaped. 'I'm pretty sure that's what goes on the end of a snooker cue to protect the butt end.' He looked at his partner, glad he now also knew something that she evidently didn't. 'I used to play a bit when I was younger,' he explained. 'I think we may have just identified what our murder weapon might be.'

CHAPTER TEN

The Blackpool and Fylde Coroner's Office was located just a short walk from the Blackpool Tower Buildings, just about level with the North Pier and inland a touch on Corporation Street. The building the coroner's office was housed in was constructed at the turn of the twentieth century, a Jacobean-style affair with a symmetrical frontage and impressive-looking clock tower. It was the Blackpool Town Hall—had been since it was built—and now also headquarters of Blackpool Council. It was a grand place, for sure, and Walker much preferred it to some of the more uninspiring council offices he'd seen dotted around Lancashire, some in new builds, others in characterless buildings put up in the mid-twentieth century that had only functionality in mind and little else.

'Mr Park, I didn't realise—'

'DCI Walker,' said Mr Park. 'It's good to see you again.'

Walker and Mr Park hadn't met since the Smith case over in Burscough, and Walker was pleased to have someone on-board who he both knew and trusted.

'You get around, don't you?' said Walker.

'Aye. It seems when you do good work, you're always in demand,' said Mr Park, a man of East Asian origin who had a

CHAPTER TEN

thick Lancashire accent that always caught Walker off-guard. 'And...' He looked at DC Briggs and frowned, appearing a little confused. 'Weren't you the PC on that other case?'

DC Briggs smiled and nodded. 'Yes. Good memory. Promotion. I'm a DC now. We've been paired together. Apparently, when you do good work together, they want to keep putting out the same team.'

Now it was Mr Park's turn to smile. He might have also remembered that the then PC Briggs had been a bit squeamish during her first autopsy inspection, and he seemed pleased she'd come back for more. Not that they'd be seeing any bodies now. They'd just come to discuss the findings with the coroner. 'Please, sit down,' he said, so they did in the private office room they'd been led to, Mr Park behind one large antique oak desk, and Walker and DC Briggs at the other side. The office had varnished wood-panelled walls and a large, ceiling-high window that let in plenty of light.

'So, I've already examined the two bodies and conducted a full autopsy on each. There are some notable similarities,' said Mr Park. 'I'm sorry. Would you like anything to drink?'

'No, that's quite alright,' Walker said, answering for the both of them, leaving DC Briggs with her mouth open, ready to speak, before closing it again, probably thinking better of it. She knew they were in a hurry as the initial hours of an investigation were crucial. There was no time for tea or coffee drinking right now. He'd only come at all because the office was so close to the two crime scenes. 'The *similarities*?'

'Ah, yes. Both victims were intoxicated at the time of death with high levels of alcohol found in their blood. Each victim was killed by blunt force trauma, one to the head—our John Doe, the victim who we don't yet have an ID on—and one via multiple injuries, in Anthony Singelmann. And the injuries sustained on the John Doe are consistent with the butt end of a snooker cue, like you suggested, while Singelmann's injuries are what we would expect from a fall from a three-storey building. Amongst these many injuries were several broken and missing teeth, but it should be noted that one of these could not be found at the Singelmann crime scene. His dental records from several months ago do not document this missing tooth, so either he lost it in the interim, or something else happened that night.'

'Noted,' said Walker. 'But you must have more than that. You wouldn't ask us down here unless you had something absolutely concrete for the investigation.'

Mr Park smiled. It was a smile Walker had seen before, a look he gave him when he'd discovered something, when he was pleased with himself. 'Well, actually, there is something...' he said, milking it.

Walker let him have his moment. He knew how hard coroners worked and how crucial that work was for criminal investigations all over the country. They were some of the unsung heroes, as far as he was concerned.

Mr Park took something out from his desk—a brown envelope—and opened it up. Inside were a collection of A4 photos. He handed one to Walker.

'Thurston and Co,' he said. 'It's a snooker cue branding, and this would have been engraved in the cue. What you're looking at is a close up of a section of our John Doe's face. He'd been hit so hard with it that it's left a mark: the *Thur* part of the Thurston and Co branding. It has a very distinct font.' He handed him another photo of a snooker cue containing that branding. 'It's a match: 97.8%.'

CHAPTER TEN

'Told you,' said Walker to DC Briggs. She smiled.

'How did you know it might be a snooker cue, if you don't mind me asking?' said Mr Park.

'We found something at the crime scene, a bit of rubber that I thought goes on the end of such cues,' said Walker. 'I wasn't sure until now. But this confirms it.'

'I see,' said Mr Park. 'Nice work.'

'Okay. So, we're looking for someone who might frequent snooker clubs,' said Walker. 'That narrows it down to, like... a few hundred thousand or so. Is there anything else?'

'Oh, there's more,' said Mr Park. 'We also did an examination of the skin and found some microscopic flecks of chalk embedded in there, the type that's used by snooker players. But this is not any kind of chalk. Do you actually play snooker, Detective Walker?'

'Some. But I'm no expert. Go on,' he said.

'Well, I don't play snooker myself, but I have played a lot of billiards,' said Mr Park.

'Billiards? Isn't that, like, what people used to play before snooker and pool were invented?' asked Walker.

'Actually, I'm originally from Seoul in South Korea, an area called Gangnam—you might have heard of it?—and billiards is massive there. There's a billiard hall on every street corner. And what I learned about billiards during my youth, is that the type of chalk used is crucial. A good chalk can be the difference between winning and losing, as it reduces the number of bad contacts between balls,' said Mr Park.

'So, what has all this got to do with the case then?' asked Walker, starting to get impatient, wanting to get to the headline.

'Well, the type of chalk we found is something called Taom

chalk. It's about ten times more expensive than your average club chalk, and it's what the really good or pro players use these days. So, I'd say your killer is a pretty good player, or is at least serious about his sport and doesn't just use his cue for battering people. I'd also guess this is an old cue, one he doesn't use anymore, as every good cue-smith also takes good care of their equipment,' said Mr Park. 'As far as I know.'

'Okay. Well, that's definitely something,' said Walker, taking a closer look at the photo he'd been given. 'This is very useful information, Mr Park. Good work again.'

'Just one more thing,' said Mr Park. He took something else out of his desk drawer, this time an item of clothing, a T-shirt, neatly folded inside a sealed plastic bag. 'It's what the John Doe was wearing under his jumper. It says Kingscote Boxing Gym on it. Seems he may have been a member or affiliated with the club somehow. We've done all the forensic checks we can with it for now, and are waiting on the results, so you can take it if you like—as long as you keep it sealed.'

'I see. Looks like we've got some sports clubs to visit then. Thank you, Mr Park. It's been great to see you again,' said Walker. 'Fantastic work, as always. We'll see ourselves out.'

CHAPTER ELEVEN

Walker and DC Briggs were heading back to the Tower Buildings, back on the Promenade, when a gathering of journalists accosted them, wanting to know more about the two murders that had recently taken place.

'Excuse me, DCI Walker,' said one of them.

'The people of Blackpool need to know what's going on,' said another. 'Please.'

'Can you confirm that the first victim was the Lead Clown in the Tower Circus?'

Walker knew they'd be there again when they came back out if he didn't give them something. They'd hound him until they had some kind of a story. Plus, he had to agree that the people of Blackpool did need to know what was going on, and he was wary that with Bonfire Night around the corner, in just a few days, there could be more trouble to come if he didn't stem the tide—a tide that was increasing in intensity.

He held DC Briggs back, letting her know he was going to say something, and they both turned around in front of the journalists.

'We were going to hold a press conference soon anyway, so if you can't wait, this will do. No time like the present,' said

Walker. 'If I could have a little quiet.'

He waited while the journalists got into place, quietened down.

'Thank you,' said Walker. 'We have recently been called in to investigate the deaths of two people found here on the Promenade in mysterious circumstances. The first, an Anthony Singelmann, who was indeed the Lead Clown at the Tower Circus, was thought to have fallen from the building above, the second, beaten to death near the Sea Barrier. We have reason to believe the two incidents are connected, but our investigations are on-going. I'm afraid we don't know much more than that for the time being. But we urge the people of Blackpool, and tourists coming to the area, to be vigilant and stay safe, especially with the November fifth celebrations coming up soon. I thank you for your time.'

There was the usual clicking of cameras and flashing of lights. He knew there might be a backlash if tourists stayed away, but it was what it was. He needed to warn people and keep them as safe as possible while this thing passed.

'Do you have any suspects for these crimes?' asked one of the male journalists, a middle-aged fella with greying hair. 'The first case apparently had a message spray painted next to the body: "Be Kind". Was this signature also present at the second crime scene?'

Damn. They already knew. Walker hadn't mentioned because he didn't want any idiots copying, spray painting it everywhere, all over the town. Plus, he thought it could be the kind of information that might trip someone up if they revealed they knew about the writing at the second crime scene when they shouldn't. The journalist had obviously been talking to one or more of the many witnesses at the first crime

CHAPTER ELEVEN

scene, put two and two together.

'That's all for now. We'll let you know if we have any further updates,' said Walker, moving inside the Tower Buildings, DC Briggs quickly following.

* * *

It was much quieter in the lobby. There was a staff member there—a young man—stood behind a kiosk, giving people tickets, but there weren't many people in the queue, and once he'd served the last of them, Walker approached.

'Quiet day,' the man said. 'Usually, the queue is going out the door.'

'I guess people are staying away because of what's going on,' said Walker. 'Do you know who I am?'

The man looked at the ID card Walker had hanging around his neck. 'I do,' he said. 'You're the Detective.'

'That's correct. We'd like to do the tour. Do we need tickets?'

'You'd like to do *the tour*?' said the man.

'Yes. We'd like to do the tour,' repeated Walker. 'Go up the Tower. Take a look around, for our investigation. How do we do that?'

'Ah. I see. Well, I can give you some tickets for free, I think, and then you just go around with the other tourists,' he said. 'Is that okay? You don't need to shut the whole operation down, do you? I'd have to talk to Roger if you wanna do anything like that. He's the manager.'

'No. That's not necessary for now. We'll just take the tour,' said Walker.

The young man got some tickets together and handed one each to Walker and DC Briggs. 'The lift is around the corner. Enjoy your tour. I'm Daniel, by the way. Daniel Jones.'

'Thank you, Daniel,' said Walker. 'That will be all.'

Daniel took a seat and started looking at his mobile phone, as he had no more customers to deal with for the time being.

'Oh, one more thing, Daniel,' said Walker. 'Did you know Anthony Singelmann, and his brother, Nathan?'

'Tony and Nath? Sure,' said Daniel. 'We all do. Everyone who works here knows each other. We're like one big family—although not always happy.'

'Do you know Sarah Jenkins too? What do you think of them all?' asked Walker.

'Tony is... *was* a bit of an oddball, to be honest. But then again, you're not gonna get your everyday guy being a clown in the circus now, are you? He was quiet, a bit socially awkward, but otherwise a nice guy, I suppose. His brother is the local strongman, at the fair. He's a bit easier to talk to. Looks scary as hell when you first meet him, but he's alright when you get to know him, get past his appearance.'

'And Sarah?' asked Walker.

'She's one of the cleaners. Hard worker. I could never figure out if she was with Tony or Nath. I've seen her with both of them. Seen her kissing both of them, actually. I don't like to get involved,' he said, getting notably *involved*. 'People do all kinds of things here.'

DC Briggs stepped in. She usually let Walker do most of the talking, since he was the senior detective, but on this occasion, she intervened. 'Daniel. Are you saying that Sarah kissed both of these men, in a romantic way, you mean. Not just on the cheek?'

CHAPTER ELEVEN

'No. I saw her properly kissing the both of them on numerous occasions, right on the lips. Might have been a bit of tongue too,' said Daniel. 'Some brothers like to share everything, don't they? I don't think I could do anything like that though, but like I say, each to their own.'

DC Briggs let out a whistle, something he'd never heard her do before. She was surprised. It wasn't the picture Sarah had painted. She knew they had something now that could potentially provide motive.

'Okay. Thank you, Daniel. We'll get on with the tour now,' said Walker, leaving him alone, DC Briggs following.

They approached the lift and Walker pressed the button to go up.

'Well, that's a turn up for the books, isn't it?' he said.

'Certainly is, sir,' said DC Briggs. 'Seems we have more of a complication between those three than we first thought.'

* * *

'I don't like this at all,' said DC Briggs. They were going up Blackpool Tower in its custom-built lift from Level 6 of the building, which would take them all the way to the Tower Eye—the highest observation deck in the whole of the North-West of England. It wasn't your run-of-the-mill lift experience by any means, which are most typically, of course, shiny metal with a mirror, perhaps, and some buttons and the like. In this, though, one could see all the girders of the tower, painted red, criss-crossing and flashing before their very eyes through the glass, the landscape below getting smaller and smaller as they moved up to dizzying heights—hundreds of feet in the air now. For those uncomfortable with such heights, it was the lift from hell, the stuff of vestibular nightmares. And for those who were not, it was still likely a tad disorienting.

They'd had to wait for fifteen minutes or so before the actual tour of the tower itself had begun—before even getting to the lift—being shown some of the history of Blackpool and the Tower Buildings by a male middle-aged tour guide who seemed way too enthusiastic about it all. As part of this heritage tour, they also had to wait for several minutes in the 4D Cinema, having wind blown at them and bubbles pop in their faces and such, with Walker not enjoying this 'Multi-Sensory' experience one bit. It had all made him rather agitated. He didn't like to waste time, especially when working a time-sensitive case like this. But the staff had told them that vital safety checks had to be performed before anyone could use the tower lift, them included, so there was nothing else to do but follow the tour and wait like everyone else. Not that the tour was heaving today. There were just a small handful of folks joining them, probably just some tourists who were unaware of what had been going on, some of them perhaps not even speaking English, by the sound of it, Walker thought. There were definitely some foreigners in there.

'Almost there, Constable,' said Walker to DC Briggs, understanding that not everyone was comfortable with heights like this. Although he was not scared of heights, by any means, he wasn't exactly in his element on anything higher than a ladder either, so he could well understand Briggs' fear of it. His colleague took a deep breath as the lift came to a stop

CHAPTER ELEVEN

near the top of the tower at the Tower Eye platform, seeming relieved that they were at least stationary once again.

'What are we looking for up here anyway?' asked DC Briggs, sounding almost annoyed as they exited the lift. 'Shouldn't we be down there, where all the action is?'

'Sometimes it's important to step back, take a bird's eye view, see the bigger picture,' said Walker. 'If you know what I mean.'

'Couldn't we just use a drone for that?' asked DC Briggs.

Walker looked at her, trying to gauge whether she was being serious or not. She wasn't always easy to read. 'I was being metaphorical,' he said.

'What exactly are we looking for, Chief?' she asked again, some annoyance creeping into her voice.

'Well... as usual, we won't really know that until we find it, will we?' said Walker, giving her a little back, making it clear she was in danger of stepping over a line. 'I just want to get a feel for this whole place, see what's what, that's all. There's a good chance the killer has been up here, after all, at some point. Let's see if there's any sign. Look out for any graffiti or writing scratched into anything, that kind of thing.'

'Jeez. It's windy up here!' said DC Briggs, as a gust blew in. 'Can we just make this bloody quick?'

'We'll catch the next lift down,' said Walker. 'I promise. But let's take a good look around until then. We won't get a better view of this place than this.'

DC Briggs nodded and seemed to refocus, get herself together. At least they were on a stable platform now. It was better than the lift.

They started to scrutinise the place. The Tower Eye platform was largely enclosed, with all windows understandably locked. Walker inspected the windows a little closer; a special tool would be needed to get them open, so they were fairly secure to the public, and couldn't easily be tampered with. He gazed around some more and found the place was decorated here and there with fake plants, which seemed unnecessary and slightly tacky. Next, he looked at the glass floor section that provided a fantastic view of the Promenade and the beach below, which members of the public could stand on, *if* they were brave enough. Walker stepped onto the glass floor without hesitation and looked down at his feet, getting used to it, seeing the tower snake downwards below, fully appreciating for the first time this magnificent engineering feat achieved well over a century ago. He whistled, feeling uneasy, but going with it anyway, before something below caught his eye.

'Constable, come and join me,' said Walker.

'Oh… sir… I'd rather not. I don't like it,' said DC Briggs. 'Not unless it involves something with the case.'

Walker looked at her in a way intended to tell her that she needed to see what he was seeing, *for the case*.

'Oh, you're kidding me,' she said, before steeling herself and tentatively approaching the glass floor. Fortunately for her, she only needed to get her toes on the glass floor itself before she could see exactly what he was talking about: down below them, on the Promenade itself, was some writing so big it was easily able to be read, even from several hundred feet in the air. The writing said: 'Be Kind.'

'Somebody really does want people to be nicer to each other,' said Walker.

DC Briggs stepped back, having had enough, and grabbed onto a railing at the side of the room, evidently needing to be anchored to something for a second.

'They certainly do,' said DC Briggs. 'Now, how about you be kind to me right now, and let's get down off this thing? We found what we came for, didn't we?'

'We certainly did,' said Walker. 'Well done, Constable.'

CHAPTER TWELVE

'Thank you for coming to the station at such short notice, Sarah,' said Walker. In light of what more they'd heard about her and the Singelmann brothers, he'd requested Sarah Jenkins come down to Blackpool Police Station HQ for a further chat and a more formal interview. He wanted to ask her more about her relationship with the brothers, find out what had really gone on, try to determine if she had any role to play in the death of Anthony Singelmann.

Having gone back down to the Promenade after going up the Blackpool Tower, Walker and DC Briggs had taken a closer look at the writing they'd seen from hundreds of feet in the air, realised it was so big it couldn't be read from ground level, which was probably why they'd missed it earlier. There were already hundreds of quotes from just as many of Britain's most well-known comedians on the 'Comedy Carpet', which sat at the base of the Blackpool Tower, and as the large-scale graffiti sat close by this, it was easy to think it was part of the artwork. It was drawn with red paint, and there were other bits of unrelated graffiti here and there too, further camouflaging it. Walker had forensics take a sample of the red paint to try to determine its origin and had PCs scouring the area in an attempt to get any witnesses or CCTV footage

CHAPTER TWELVE

of the act. But he wasn't holding his breath. If the offender was smart, they'd have done it at night-time, perhaps wore a mask too. They'd be difficult to ID. But he'd got the message loud and clear, and the people of Blackpool would too. The press would love this; it would be on all the front pages in the morning—at least in any local newspapers. People would start to talk, even more than before. The rumours would escalate, snowball out of control, so they had to move fast.

They were already sat in an interview room, face-to-face with Sarah Jenkins, with DC Briggs next to Walker. Sarah wiped a tear from her eye, although Walker wasn't sure he could actually see any liquid. 'It's alright,' she said. 'I don't mind coming here. You're investigating Tony's…' She trailed off, not quite being able to complete her sentence. 'You need to know everything what happened. I get it.'

Walker turned on the recording device and got things rolling, verbally logging the time and day and who was involved in the interview, as per protocol, before moving on.

'So… you're with Nathan Singelmann, now, Tony's brother. You're having a romantic relationship with him,' said Walker. 'Is that correct?'

'That's correct,' said Sarah.

'And how long has this been going on for?' asked Walker. 'For the record.'

'Er, about two months-ish, I think,' said Sarah. She was so short that Walker appeared more like a headmaster talking to a primary school pupil, her head only just visible above the desk, her eyeline looking up at him at almost a forty-five-degree angle.

'Sorry, would you like a cushion?' asked Walker. He felt DC

Briggs sigh and cringe a little at his question, which instantly made him regret asking.

'No, I'm fine,' said Sarah, with some attitude, probably sick of a lifetime of such questions, making Walker regret his offer even more. He decided to quickly move on.

'And, for the record again, you never had any romantic involvement with Tony Singelmann, as we previously discussed, and he just, as you stated, "got the wrong idea",' said Walker. 'To be blunt, there was never any involvement with him, sexually. Is that correct?'

'Oh, God, no,' said Sarah. 'It wasn't like that. He was just a friend.'

'A friend who got you a job, took you out for coffee, and who generally hung out with you,' said Walker.

Sarah appeared a little uncomfortable with that, straightened herself, pulled the skirt down she was wearing. 'Yes. That's what friends do, isn't it?'

DC Briggs leaned forward at this point, put her hand on the table, the way you might when someone needs their hand holding but the situation isn't quite appropriate. 'We just want to know the truth,' she said. 'So, we can find out what happened to Tony.'

Sarah nodded her understanding, and seemed to ease a little, visibly relaxed a touch.

'Sarah,' said Walker. 'The problem we have is that we now have a witness who states he saw you kissing Tony… in a way that friends don't kiss, if you know what I mean.' He picked up DC Briggs's notepad, which was already on the table, and flipped through to a particular page. 'And I quote: *Right on the lips. Might have been a bit of tongue too.* Could you explain this, please?'

CHAPTER TWELVE

Sarah's face went red. 'What? Let me guess, it was Daniel who told you that, right?' she said, with fire in her eyes. 'Daniel Jones? The wanker who mans the kiosk at the Tower? Sorry, but he is.'

'So, you knew he saw you kissing Tony?' asked Walker. 'You saw him, watching you?'

Sarah breathed a heavy sigh. 'You're probably not going to believe this, but... he had a crush on me too. They all want to get in my pants. There are so many perverts out there. You've no idea.'

'Are you saying that Tony and Nathan are also, in your words, "perverts"?' asked Walker.

'No. Of course not. Nathan really loves me... I think. And Tony was just the sweetest boy,' she said.

'Man,' corrected Walker. 'He was in his forties, after all.'

'Yes, but he was really innocent, fragile really,' she said. 'I never wanted to hurt him. That was the last thing I wanted.'

'We just want to get to the bottom of this,' said Walker. 'Are you suggesting that Daniel Jones was lying about you kissing Tony? Because he liked you too?'

'Not exactly,' said Sarah. 'Tony did try to kiss me on a couple of occasions, at least one time on the lips as I remember, so Daniel might have seen that, I suppose. I tried to push him away, but I'm not that strong. I tried to tell him we weren't a couple, but he just brushed it off, said I was scared of commitment, that he understood, and would be patient. I didn't know what else to say. I was speechless. I figured he'd get it eventually, but he never did. Obviously.'

'Right. So, Daniel Jones got the wrong idea, put two and two together and got five. Tony tried to kiss you, you pushed him away the best you could, but he got the wrong idea and thought you were an item, right up until he found out about you and his brother,' said Walker. 'Am I getting this right?'

Sarah nodded. 'Yes. That's what I said.'

'And how did Tony find out about you and Nathan? That you were in a relationship?' asked Walker. 'What circumstances led to this revelation?'

Sarah gulped, looked down, appeared reluctant to speak. She shook her head.

'Go on,' said Walker.

She shook her head some more. 'It's just so awful,' she said. 'I was at Nathan's flat. We were…'

'It's okay,' said DC Briggs. 'You can tell us. You *have* to tell us. We're all adults here.'

Sarah took a deep breath. 'We were having sex, in his bed, and Tony walked in, saw us. He had a spare key, apparently, from years ago, when he'd been house sitting, or something. Nathan had forgot about it. Tony went mad. I felt like I'd been unfaithful, even though I'd done nothing wrong. He really believed we were an item. He was heartbroken.'

'That must have been very difficult,' said DC Briggs. 'For all of you.'

'And did Tony make any threats, at the time, or say he was going to commit suicide, anything of that nature?' asked Walker. 'Did he become violent.'

'No. Not really. He just called us both every bad thing you can possibility imagine, like some kind of Tourette's syndrome meltdown, and then he smashed the place up a bit and left. That was it. He never spoke to us after that, not until that night in the pub I told you about,' said Sarah. 'When he lost it again.'

Walker took a deep breath of his own. It seemed he'd hit

CHAPTER TWELVE

a dead end with this particular path, so he needed to pivot, refocus his energies elsewhere. It was something he'd learned to do over many decades in the job. He needed to get on the viable leads that he had, and quick: namely the boxing club T-shirt that the John Doe had been wearing, and talking to some folks in the local snooker clubs. It was all about having a constantly changing list of priorities and knowing what was next on the list, and then moving with it. There was no motive here, not unless the brothers got into a fight and Nathan accidentally pushed him. But that didn't really add up, not with there being a second murder and the spray-painted messages left.

'That will be all,' said Walker, perhaps a bit too abruptly, but not much concerned, more focussed on doing his job. 'You're free to go, for now. We'll be in touch if there's anything further.'

CHAPTER THIRTEEN

Walker and DC Briggs entered 'Kingscote Boxing Gym' to a cacophony of punching, shouting, and various free weights being dropped on the floor, as fighters went about their various training routines. The place smelled of sweat, rage, and testosterone. In the only boxing ring in the gym—one not in the best condition, stained and damaged here and there—a couple of men were sparring, watched carefully by a middle-aged trainer who glanced at them, but nevertheless continued shouting directions to the fighters, despite his voice being hoarse, until he was satisfied, when he rang the bell in the corner.

'Take five,' he said, in an Irish accent, throwing one of them a towel.

The trainer got down, carefully, seeming like he had trouble with his knees, and approached Walker and DC Briggs. 'What can I do for you two then?' he said. 'Hey, you're not with Health and Safety, are you? That was nothing. Did Harry complain—'

'Lancashire Constabulary,' said Walker, before the man could go on. 'We're investigating a crime in the area.'

'Ah. Well, all my boys are on the straight and narrow now, as far as I know,' said the man, shuffling, uncomfortably. 'I'm

CHAPTER THIRTEEN

Jimmy. Jimmy Butland. I'm the owner. Used to be a semi-pro myself, until I got injured. Welterweight. Just tryin' to pass on some knowledge and skills.'

'And make a few quid,' said one of the fighters, sarcastically, who was passing by, smirking, carrying some weights.

'Thanks for that, Phil-Top,' said Jimmy, his eyes going wide, telling him to back off, before returning his attention to Walker and DC Briggs. 'What can I do for you then?' he asked.

Walker took out the item of clothing that had been found on the second victim, the John Doe, the T-shirt that said 'Kingscote Boxing Gym' on the front. It was still neatly folded in a sealed and labelled plastic bag, ready to file as evidence, but the bag was transparent, so the logo was clearly visible.

'We found a man, dead, wearing this under his jumper,' said Walker.

Jimmy got closer, took a good look. 'Wait,' he said, before scurrying off, leaving them in the middle of the gym, men training all around, some continuing to glance at them, but pretending not to. A few seconds later, Jimmy returned carrying an old box with the top lip flaps folded inwards, put it on the floor in front of them. He crouched down and started to take out some identical T-shirts. 'One, two, three...' He was counting the T-shirts, one by one, as he was taking them out, putting them on the floor next to the box. 'Nine,' he said. 'That's the last one. We only had ten of these made up, for the staff to wear around town, to spread the word.' He looked up. 'We don't use them anymore as we had to change the telephone number, the one on the back.' He turned one around, showed them, pointed at the number. 'That's wrong now. I gave one to Mike the other day. Hey, Phil, you seen

Mike about recently?'

Phil-Top looked over while he was working his biceps with some dumbbells. 'Not since Steve clocked him,' he said.

'Mike was a bit of an arsehole. Bit of a troublemaker, you know? He got into a bit of a scuffle with Steve, one of our staff members—it was all legit, in the ring and that,' he added, quickly backing up, probably realising Steve might be in a lot of trouble for GBH if it was anything else. 'But Mike got some blood on his clothes, so we gave him a T-shirt to wear, to smooth things over.'

'Even though it was *all legit, in the ring*,' said Walker.

Jimmy looked a bit sheepish. 'Yeah. Even though,' he said. 'The T-shirt you have, the one you found, that must be the one we gave Mike. There aren't any others.'

'And did Mike have a last name?' asked Walker.

'Hey, is Mike *dead?*' asked Jimmy.

'We're not sure,' said Walker. 'We haven't been able to identify the victim just yet. Hence our inquiries.'

'But he was wearing this?' asked Jimmy.

'We're going to need a last name for Mike,' insisted Walker. 'And an address. Do you know it?'

Jimmy seemed to visibly snap out of it. 'His last name? I don't know. We run a very casual operation here, cash on the door, no official memberships. I don't know most of these fellas' full names, never mind their addresses.' He looked around at the men in the gym. 'Hey! Does anyone know Mike's last name? He might be in trouble.'

'Mike's always in trouble,' said one of the boxers, laughing a little, and some others followed suit. 'It's Tracy. Michael Tracy. My little brother was in his class at school. They were always ribbing him about it. They all called him Tracy, really taking the piss, treating him like a girl, until he started punching anyone who called him that. Everyone has called him Mike since then.'

'Well, it doesn't look like they'll be ribbin' him any more,' said Jimmy. 'Someone's bloody done him in.'

'Er, we don't know that just yet,' said Walker, holding his hands up, palms out. 'All we know is that the victim was apparently wearing a T-shirt that you recently gave to one Michael Tracy.'

'Got it,' said Jimmy. 'Mike might be alright,' he shouted, 'if anyone's interested.' The men all seemed to shrug, not much caring.

'We're going to need to talk to Steve too, the staff member who you said hit Mike,' said Walker.

'Oh. It really was nothing. Just some boxers doing what they do best. Steve's not in today. But I can give you his number,' said Jimmy.

'Very good,' said Walker. 'DC Briggs. Get Steve's full name and number and get some PCs over here to interview each and every man, get their take on what happened with Mike a few days ago. And see if the body can be identified now and matched to Michael Tracy. Find out where he lives if nobody knows here—driver's licence, voting records, vehicle registration, all the usual stuff—and then get DNA samples from his home once you've located it so we can get a match. We need to know who that victim is, and we need it confirmed ASAP.'

'Will do, Chief,' said DC Briggs, getting to it. She looked back. 'You waiting in the car?'

'Yeah. Gotta do a Google search, find out where we're going next,' he said. 'Hey, Jimmy, I don't suppose you or any of this lot know of any other places where Mike hung out, do you? It could be important, for the case. This doesn't just involve Mike. There are other victims too. We need to find out who's doing this,' asked Walker. 'And fast, before anybody else gets hurt.'

Jimmy tentatively climbed back up onto the boxing ring, appearing like he was thirty years older than he actually was, and clapped his hands together, getting everyone's full attention. 'Okay. Stop what you're doing. I said *stop!*' Everyone did as asked and looked at him. 'Do any of you reprobates have any idea where else Mike might have hung out? Any bars or other places you know of? Have any of you seen him, out and about?'

'He's always pissed at The Velvet Coaster,' said one of them. 'The Dutton Arms too.'

'And the Shenanigans,' said another. 'Trouble follows that bloke. He's always rubbing people up the wrong way, getting into fights—bit of a tosser, actually.'

'I've seen him at Q's too,' said another.

'Q's?' asked Walker.

'It's a sports place. Q's Sports, or something. They have pool tables and stuff,' the man said.

'Pool tables? What about snooker?' asked Walker.

'Yeah. That too. Darts. Sports on the telly, everything,' said the man. 'It's good.'

Walker looked at DC Briggs. Now they had something real to work with. 'We're done here. I'll get the address of Q's Sports. See you in the car in ten.'

CHAPTER FOURTEEN

Jonny sat in front of his desktop computer, scrolling through some of the latest comments on 'The Tower Forum' on Facebook. Hundreds of people must be looking at this now, he thought, judging by the number of comments. After several weeks of this, it seemed the movement was now finally getting some serious traction. He'd have to be careful though. Danny from the bar said the police had been snooping around, almost caught him at it—was shitting himself. But they had to take some calculated risks if the movement was to be successful. They couldn't give up now, couldn't falter just when things were starting to heat up. Jonny was adamant, completely committed to the cause, and he had damned good reason to be.

He started to write...

> Keep it up people. It's time for us to unite, take action. November 5th. Let's clean up this town!

That should do it. Sometimes, Jonny mused, the only way to foster peace is through violence. There were good battles and bad ones, and this cause was noble; he knew it in his bones. It was why he'd got involved in this thing in the first place. The police would be watching now, reading everything that was being written. But that was okay. He was using a VPN—a *virtual private network*—which currently made it look like he was posting from Luxemburg, of all places. And tomorrow he'd choose another country, maybe France. If anyone tried to track him, all they'd find would be a dummy IP address, as the VPN hid his real IP address and encrypted his online activity, allowing 'Private and Secure Viewing!'—something the VPN company had put in bold letters on their home page. Danny was using the Tor Browser, which was free and did a similar thing, but Jonny preferred the VPN, even though it cost a few quid per month, as it provided more control and offered superior functionality. It was an ongoing debate they'd been having for a while now.

Some other people started to chip in on the forum.

> I'm in!
> Me too. Let's get the bastards.
> Just one night, and this place can be nice again, like it used to be.

People were getting on board, and fast. It was happening. But the movement needed a name, something for everyone to really get their hands on, give it a feeling, an emotion, a *brand*. There were so many doing the rounds at the moment: the Black Lives Matter movement, the #MeToo movement, the LGBT Rights movement—all of which had garnered some degree of success. It needed to be something similar, comparable; something catchy. He had it: *Kindness Matters*. That was it! It would be the Kindness Matters Movement, or the KMM, for short. Easy to understand, to the point, memorable. Jonny smiled. It was probably the first time he'd smiled since his sister died last year, but it was still one bathed in sadness and regret.

> The 'Kindness Matters Movement' is born, my friends. Henceforth go forwards, and make sure people are being kind to each other. Zero tolerance. Peace out.

It was a bit extreme, a bit militant, he knew—like Danny had said. But they had to take a hard line. The government couldn't be trusted. The police: forget about it. They had to take the problem into their own hands, deal with it themselves, or things would never be right. They had to act. Nobody else would. Nobody really cared about them; not to the extent they needed it, anyhow. History would be forged by the people, at least in this small, little-known northern town. This would be their emancipation.

> Hell yeah. Kindness Matters!
> Why has nobody thought of this before? It should be law!
> Sod the law. The law does nothing for me. Let's sort this out ourselves. See you on the 5th, everyone. I'm getting revenge for my son.

That was it. That was all the people needed. Someone to lead them, to point them in the right direction, to give them permission to do what they'd wanted for years—to get rid of the scumbags who were making their lives a misery. Mob rule was making a comeback, and he'd be out at the front, doing his part, leading the way, pitchfork in hand—metaphorically speaking. He was buzzing. He felt he finally had a purpose, a reason to go on. He typed some more...

> The first rule of the KMM is to be kind, and the second rule of the KMM is to be *kind*.

The forum went a little quiet for a few seconds, and Jonny got that sinking feeling, like he'd taken it too far, hadn't really thought enough about that one. He hoped he hadn't messed up. He started to wonder if he should try to delete it, but then someone replied.

> And the third rule of the Kindness Matters Movement, is to BE KIND! Ha ha.

It was okay. They got it. That old Fight Club parody—the film with Edward Norton. It seemed apt; that also involved a revolution of sorts, a backlash from the disaffected. He'd better quit while he was ahead. It was *on*. Danny would be buzzing too. He'd have to talk to him soon. They needed to organise, plan, find some targets. They already had a decent list of local troublemakers—he'd been keeping a file on people, doing his background research—so they could start with that, maybe give some assignments out to their most trusted followers via Messenger. But there was one more thing he needed to tell everyone. He wiped his mouth, brushing away the crumbs from some cheesy Wotsits he'd been munching on, and put his hands back on the keyboard.

> One final thing. Don't forget to use the signature: 'Be Kind'.

That would do it. The police wouldn't know who'd done what.

CHAPTER FOURTEEN

They'd be chasing their own tails. There'd be too many people involved. And when the dust settled, the town would be a better place.

Jonny picked up a glass from his desk, one filled with some Special Reserve Scotch Whiskey—one of the cheaper ones; he couldn't afford more. He didn't drink much, really, compared to some people, but sometimes even he needed to take the edge off. He raised the glass. 'To you, Samantha,' he said, before taking a sip.

He was hell-bent on her death not being in vain, to make it mean *something*. She'd been depressed, as she should have been, ever since she'd miscarried her little boy, Alfie: Jonny's nephew had been stillborn at five months. It was tragic. But there was more. As if that wasn't enough, then there'd been that incident with Freddie, just a couple of years later—*his* bloody boyfriend at the time, regrettably. The bastard had hidden stolen drugs at her place, and someone came looking for it, knocked him and Sammy around, raped her. It was too much for anyone to take, all that. It was awful.

So, when some rude bitch finally tipped Sam over the edge, someone who'd been really unkind to her at the Shopping Centre, for no reason, called her this and that, she'd committed suicide shortly afterwards, slit her wrists in the bath. And that was that. Her life abruptly ended. He couldn't think about it anymore. He'd seen her before they took her body away and everything, said his goodbyes there and then. It was just so… he didn't have the words.

If only the KMM had been created before that, before his sister had been made to suffer such abuse—she might still be alive now, he thought. She may have got through it, somehow—got therapy, got medicated. It was too late for her, of course; nothing could change that. But he hoped perhaps the movement could save someone else's life. Maybe God, if he existed, had some master plan, to save many more people as a result of this tragedy. He hoped so. He hoped such utilitarianism existed. But if not, at least he might feel a bit better by getting rid of some of these arseholes, by giving some of that pain back. Maybe then, Sam could rest in peace. And maybe, just maybe, he might finally be able to get some sleep at night.

CHAPTER FIFTEEN

'Q's Sports Lounge' sat above a Tesco Express on Lytham Road, just a short walk from Blackpool South Train station. With five snooker tables, it was one of the few establishments in Blackpool that catered to the local snooker player. Walker had a feeling that both the deceased Michael Tracy and his killer might have frequented Q's at some point or another—maybe had an altercation there that other punters had witnessed, or perhaps Tracy caused some trouble that his would-be murderer had observed.

DC Briggs had gone to use the toilet before entering the bar area itself, leaving Walker to go in alone for the time being. It was still early, having only just opened, so there were no punters in just yet. He approached the barmaid and leaned against the bar. The place had a particular smell: a mixture of wood, dust, cold slate, and beer. It wasn't unpleasant—not to him, anyway.

'Hi there. Could I ask you a question?' he said.

The woman, maybe late thirties, attractive and well-groomed, blonde, rolled her eyes a touch. 'What is it, luv?' she asked.

Walker realised she probably got punters chatting her up all the time, using their lines on her. She was probably expecting one now.

'Have you ever heard anyone in here talking about people being more kind to each other?' he asked.

The woman got a bit closer. 'What?' she asked, seeming confused, and rightly so. He'd forgotten to introduce himself properly. He was probably just tired. He rubbed his forehead and started again. 'Sorry. I'm…'

DC Briggs appeared beside him, having now finished doing her business. 'He's a bit overworked is what he is,' she said.

'DCI Walker, of the Lancashire Constabulary. We're investigating, looking for someone who most likely played some snooker locally. So?' he asked.

The woman stood up, a little taller, now realising Walker wasn't just another punter trying it on. '*So?* Sorry. What was the question again?'

'He wants to know if anyone has been talking about kindness,' said DC Briggs. 'If anyone has been complaining about people not being kind enough to each other, that sort of thing.'

'Oh. No. People just come here to play or watch sports, really,' said the woman. 'They're just lads, doing lad things: swearing, drinking, messing around, having a laugh mostly. The majority of 'em are harmless.'

'And do you know a man called Michael Tracy? Or Mike?' asked Walker.

'Mike?' said the woman. 'I don't know all their names. There are too many. I just serve 'em. Is he in trouble?'

'I'd say so,' said Walker. 'I mean, it looks that way. We believe he came here sometimes, was a bit of a troublemaker by all accounts. You sure you don't remember him? May have put himself about a bit. Rubbed people up the wrong way.'

CHAPTER FIFTEEN

'Er, you got a photo?' asked the woman.

Walker looked at DC Briggs. 'Call Hogarth back. See if he's got it yet.'

'Will do, Chief,' she said, and stepped a few metres away, opening up her phone.

'We're trying to get a photo of him as we speak,' said Walker. 'It's very early in the investigation. Please, wait a minute.'

The woman nodded. 'There is this one guy who comes in here occasionally—a bit of a loner. He's trouble. Rubs people up the wrong way, as you say, seemingly on purpose. Looks like he's after a fight half the time. Most people, myself included, tend to try to ignore him, not interact with him if at all possible. I'm not sure what his name is though. Maybe that's who you're talking about?'

Briggs got off her phone and showed it to Walker. 'This is him: Michael Tracy.'

Walker took the phone and showed it to the barmaid. 'Okay. Is this the guy you're on about?'

She got closer, looked at it. 'Yeah. That's him. Definitely. One hundred per cent.'

So, Michael Tracy had come to this sports bar, a place with five snooker tables, and got murdered by someone who evidently played snooker—or who at least had access to a snooker cue. The barmaid backed off, now she'd seen the photo, but it was DC Brigg's turn to step in. She whispered in his ear.

'Chances are the offender also frequented this place,' she said. *'Perhaps got into a fight or an argument with the deceased, or saw someone else clashing with him, didn't like it?'* It was exactly what he'd been thinking, and if they were both thinking the same thing…

'I don't suppose you have to be a member to come here, do you? You don't have a list of club members with contact details or addresses by any chance?' asked Walker to the barmaid, more in hope than anticipation.

'Afraid not,' said the woman. 'Anyone can come in here off the street. We're not a proper club like that—more of a sports bar, really.'

Of course. That would have been too easy. And cases like this rarely are—Walker knew that from experience. But he had to check, give it a go.

'Any big guys come here?' asked Walker. He knew he was grasping at straws now. Not one of his best questions ever. He was thinking of the guy he saw drinking at the Red Lion pub at the Tower Buildings, the night Anthony Singelmann pushed Sarah Jenkins, the day before he was found dead.

'Plenty,' said the woman. She wasn't much taller than five feet, and Walker wondered for a second if the woman got of a lot of attention from the men because of this—whether what DC Briggs had been suggesting earlier, about some men being attracted to smaller, almost child-like women, could have some sick truth. 'Most guys seem big compared to me.'

'Of course,' said Walker. At present, they didn't know an awful lot about their killer, other than that he might be a powerfully-built guy with a thing for kindness to others—quite a contradiction since it was he who was apparently going around killing people. They needed more to get anywhere meaningful with the case. Much more. 'Do you remember anyone sticking up for anyone else, defending them, or even simply observing from the side-lines, that kind of thing?' asked Walker. 'Anything that seemed out of place. Anything that comes to mind?'

CHAPTER FIFTEEN

'*Defending* them?' asked the woman. 'I heard the rumours about that Defender guy, if that's what you're talking about, going around saving people or something, apparently. Is that who you're looking for? What is he, some kind of wannabe superhero? Here in sodding Blackpool? This isn't Gotham City. It's a bit less glamourous round here—it's all chippie papers floating around and council estates, that sort of thing.'

'We're just trying to solve a crime,' said Walker. 'You got any CCTV here?'

'No. None. The owners are strapped. We have to run things on a shoestring at the moment,' said the woman. 'It's the economy.'

'I see. Well, thank you for your time,' said Walker, realising he was banging his head against a brick wall once again, getting nowhere. 'We'll see ourselves out when we're ready.'

Walker took a little gentle stroll around the pub, taking a look here and there. There was a box full of old cues in one of the corners, which customers could evidently use. He rooted through it, found one at the bottom that didn't contain its butt end—a three-quarter length of a cue that had it's one quarter counterpart butt unscrewed and removed. He couldn't find it in the box, despite having a good look for a couple of minutes or so. He was confident it wasn't there.

'Excuse me,' said Walker to the barmaid, who was now busying herself, polishing some glasses behind the bar. 'I didn't catch your name.'

'It's Kelly. Kelly Bowen,' said the woman.

'Kelly, there's an incomplete cue here. The butt end is missing. Do you know anything about this?'

'Oh. Those are just some old cues, bits and bobs. Most serious players bring their own cue these days. Those are just for the casual player,' said Kelly. 'They aren't much good.'

'I see. Well, I'm going to need to take this, as evidence,' said Walker, holding up the three-quarter length cue. Kelly shrugged and carried on polishing.

Walker nodded, thanking her, and she went out back, doing something else.

'Bag this when we get to the car,' said Walker. 'I think we may, if we're lucky, have just found the opposite end of our murder weapon.'

CHAPTER SIXTEEN

Walker and DC Briggs arrived at the incident room at Blackpool Police HQ and took a seat, got settled, Walker shifting his bottom in his chair from side to side until it felt right—but it never did, so he had to settle and accept the discomfort. It was first thing in the morning, and Walker hadn't slept too well, hadn't been able to turn off from the case much at all. It was typical, such insomnia, while working a case, a problem he'd never really been able to solve throughout his long career, and one that had probably negatively impacted his health in the end. He became obsessed with his cases, especially ones like this— ones involving serial murderers who were still on the loose, who could kill again at any moment. He always felt like he could, and should, be doing more. He had a duty to protect the public, a fatherly duty, bound by responsibility, and it weighed heavy.

'We need to talk,' said DI Hogarth, who'd already been there before them, up bright and early, crunching data—or whatever the hell it was he did. With the case developing the way it was, Walker decided it was better to have his tech-savvy colleague stationed with them, on hand, rather than them constantly communicating via technology Walker wasn't comfortable with. This was not the time for training old dogs like him to use new tech. They had an active case in motion—a big one. So, here he was. 'There's been a development.'

Before Walker could respond, DC Hardman, who'd just walked in while DI Hogarth had been talking, dropped a newspaper in front of him. It was the Blackpool Gazette, and on the cover, it read: 'Serial Killer Warns People of Blackpool to be Kinder, or Else'. Accompanying the headline was a shot of Blackpool Promenade, taken up high, most likely from the Blackpool Tower itself, with the message 'Be Kind' spray painted on the ground—the very same image Walker and DC Briggs had viewed first-hand during their trip up to the Tower Eye. It seemed the journalists hadn't been too far behind, or perhaps they'd been already by the time they got there.

'Shit's properly hitting the fan now,' said DC Hardman.

'Damn. That it is,' said Walker. 'Not what we wanted, of course, but always inevitable, really. It's not like it wasn't on public display, for all to see. What do you have, DI Hogarth?'

'Well, the Internet is rife with discussions about this, that's for sure. It seems certain people are banding together, getting ready to cause a ruckus, or something similar, on November fifth—Bonfire Night. They want to clean up the town, fight back against people who are being unkind, or causing trouble,' he said. 'A lot of them, surprisingly, support this violence, these murders. They've even given the killer a name: *The Defender*. Some are even claiming to be him. But the general consensus is that things have gone too far, that it's time to take radical action. They're framing it as a protest of sorts.'

'I see. We'll need to notify Supt Stone then so she can coordinate things. And are you able to identify any of these

CHAPTER SIXTEEN

people?' asked Walker. 'The people who are saying these things.'

'Negative,' said DI Hogarth. 'Not the ones we've highlighted as the chief shit-stirrers, anyway, not with our limited resources. They all seem to be using third party hosting, VPNs and the like.'

Walker drew a blank on that one—as he usually did when something technical, involving computers, was said. He looked at DI Hogarth, demanding more.

'Sorry. A *Virtual Private Network*,' said DI Hogarth. 'They're hiding their IP addresses, so we can't track where they're posting from—people are getting more careful with their online activities these days. All I'm getting is a wide range of countries: Switzerland, Belgium, South Korea, Australia, the United States, Croatia. We can probably get more information from Facebook, in time, but there's also a trail of deleted posts, which are actually the ones I'm most interested in. Fake Facebook accounts aren't that easy to set up these days, you see—requires a working phone number, and more— are liable to get nixed by moderators fairly quickly if there's anything suspect. I can see there are accounts being removed here, as evidenced by the deleted posts. These are probably burner accounts, several of them, in fact, set up by one or more individuals. Best guess, I reckon they're siphoning folk off they see as serious, funnelling them into private groups elsewhere, using WhatsApp, Telegram, or something similar, recruiting them.'

'Jesus,' said Walker. 'And... can we not access these other groups somehow? I take it by Telegram, you don't mean the old-fashioned type?'

'*Telegram Messenger* is a cloud-based, encrypted instant

messaging service, similar to WhatsApp. Anything like that could have been used. Think of it like there being a pub full of loudmouths, saying they're going to do this and that—that's the Facebook forum—and then you have one or more individuals moving around them, finding the ones they think mean business, pointing them to the proper meeting in the backroom somewhere, where the actual planning might be going on.'

'I see. It's a good theory. So, the question is, can we gain access to this "backroom"?' asked Walker.

'Well, it's hard to track, that's for sure. It might be possible, given enough time, but probably not before November fifth. That's gonna be a step too far. Two days is not enough—not unless we have a team of computer-forensic technicians working on this, 24-7, which we don't, and most likely won't,' said DI Hogarth.

Walker was bloody sick of Facebook. Flaming Zuckerberk, or whatever he was called. Every single case seemed to involve it at the moment, in some way. He'd even got his own account after the last case, to try and understand it better, figure out how people used it. Still, it was the new way, and he'd just have to get used to it. At least it was another resource to use, some easy-access intel.

'Right. So, we've got two days to stop this thing, or, it seems, things are going to get even uglier,' said Walker. 'More people could die.'

'A *lot* of people could die,' added DC Briggs, who'd been listening in from the start from her seat, her eyes now wide, probably only just taking in how bad things could get.

'It's possible,' said Walker. 'I'll inform Superintendent Stone immediately so an appropriate policing response can be organised. This is clearly not within our remit. And it's her call whether it needs escalating even further up the chain of command. But an event like this, I reckon we're looking at a complex operation, riot police and more—the fire service needs to be informed also, the local hospitals too, just in case. They need to expect the unexpected on this one, be prepared. Better to be ready than not with this kind of thing. You all remember the riots of 2011, right?'

They all nodded. It had been a time of anarchy, violence, and looting that had lasted several days. It was hard to forget.

'So, are we looking at a serial killer here who's stoked a bigger fire, or has this been a coordinated attack all along?' asked DC Briggs.

'Could be both,' said DC Hardman. 'Or neither. Some things just happen organically.'

'Did we manage to find that Steve character, from the Boxing club? The one who hit the second victim?' asked Walker.

'We did,' said DC Hardman. 'Dead end, I'm afraid. He's been banged up for the past few days, over in Preston. Arrested for GBH, apparently. Repeat offender. He'll be sentenced shortly. He couldn't have killed Michael Tracy. He was in custody at the time.'

'Darn it,' said Walker, now having one less suspect to consider. 'But I still want him interviewed, find out what their fight was all about.'

'Course. I'm on it,' said DC Hardman.

We have to get through the next couple of days first without any more people dying,' said Walker. 'Maybe we can get a message out in the local press, and we can also post on this Facebook forum as well, make sure everyone stays safe and knows we're watching. It's another resource we can utilise, direct at source.'

'Oh, and there's one more thing,' said DI Hogarth.

'What?' asked Walker, getting a feeling of foreboding.

'They've given it a name. It's a movement now,' he said.

'A *movement*?' said Walker. 'You're kidding me.'

'Nope,' said DI Hogarth.

'Go on. What's it called then?' asked Walker.

'They're calling it the "Kindness Matters Movement",' said DI Hogarth.

'Oh, cute,' said Walker, but he didn't really mean it, of course. It was anything but.

* * *

By the evening of the fourth, Walker and his small team had done everything they could to prepare for another possible attack, or attacks, by their murderer, on November fifth, while Superintendent Stone had done her duty and put a much larger scale operation in place to try to police any rioting. Thankfully, there'd been no actual incidents of violence by the Kindness Matters Movement and no further action by the killer they were lionising in the interim to distract them. Stone had drawn on all possible resources they had to hand, got a small army of PCs and riot police on standby, and alerted all emergency services in the area of a possible event. All that was to do now was to hold a final press conference, so people could be better informed about the possible troubles in their morning newspapers, and make appropriate arrangements. Of course, they were still persevering to find Anthony Singelmann and Michael Tracy's killer—by continuing to canvass the area and having bobbies make inquiries while the detectives worked their way through the action book—but they now conceded that there was a possibility, at least, that this wasn't the same offender, despite them having the same apparent signature. Another possibility was that the first killing was an opportunistic murder, while the second killing was an escalation of this, with a developing modus operandi, with the killer now finding their feet, so to speak, finding a method and way of doing things. Unfortunately, they wouldn't know for sure unless there was another murder.

Walker, DCs Briggs and Ainscough, and Superintendent Lucy Stone all sat at the head of a table inside Blackpool Police HQ, in a medium sized conference room that was able to house the twenty or so journalists that had turned up.

Superintendent Stone had asked Walker to begin proceedings, so he tapped on the microphone in front of him, checking it was working properly. He wanted to make sure everyone could hear, every word.

'Okay, everybody,' he said. 'Thank you for coming down here at such short notice. We want to inform you that there's a possible event about to occur in Blackpool town centre tomorrow, during the November fifth celebrations, that we think you should know about.' There was the flashing of a camera, which sent a pain shooting to the front side of Walker's head, just above the left eye. He winced. 'Could we keep the photography until the end, please?' He waited a few seconds, making sure he had everyone's attention. He was an old hand at this now, well drilled, but some of the actions of the press still sometimes irked him. 'Now, a few of you might be aware of some of the discussions that are being had online at the moment—this concerns the two murders that have occurred here recently, which myself, DCs Briggs and Ainscough here, and my team are currently investigating. I can now tell you, the names of these two victims are Anthony Singelmann, who worked as a clown at the Blackpool Tower Circus, and one Michael Tracy, unemployed. While the circumstances of these murders were very different, some stark similarities found at both crime scenes may indicate the same murderer.' He didn't want to draw attention to the "Be Kind" signature specifically, as he didn't want all the local vandals latching on to it, confusing matters. 'This is yet unproven, but we are taking this aspect of these crimes very seriously. We want to reassure the public that we're fully committed to bringing the killer or killers to justice before anyone else is harmed, but... online groups have glorified this apparent vigilantism and people are now encouraging each other to emulate it. I'll hand you over to Superintendent Lucy Stone at this juncture, who'll be coordinating any anti-terrorism measures and mobilising riot police to deal with any possible troubles on November fifth,' said Walker, gesturing to Superintendent Stone with his hand. 'Superintendent Stone?'

Superintendent Lucy Stone stood up, back straight, head high, stone faced, and addressed the room without a microphone.

'Yes. Thank you, DCI Walker. What I would add to this, is that to the people who are engaging in such discussions online, please be warned: such nonsense is ill advised and could lead to more people getting hurt or killed. Therefore, anyone seen to be getting involved in this, or encouraging others to do so,

CHAPTER SIXTEEN

will be punished to the full extent of the law. We have reason to believe that more acts of violence might be about to occur, and not necessarily from the same assailant—so please, we urge you *not* to get involved. This will only make things worse. We take this very seriously, as we do any radicalisation to violence. A possible movement has begun to develop, which they're calling the "Kindness Matters Movement", and the mission statement of this movement, as far as we can tell, is to make people be more kind to each other, and it seems they're possibly planning to enforce this by punishing those who are not. The extent of this punishment is, as yet, unknown. But given there have already been two murders that may be linked to this movement, we have to consider that such violence could be extreme in nature if it does occur. Also, there could be more low-level violence as well, depending on the nature of punishment that members of this movement deem necessary, if indeed it is a movement and not just some people mouthing off online. It might also be the case that nothing happens too, of course—which we're hoping is the outcome—but given the ferocity of these online discussions, we are expecting some kind of event, which rest assured we will be fully prepared to deal with if any such troubles do occur. Note, these are largely discontented individuals lacking in organisation and experience, caught up in a fantasy of vigilantism that will not be tolerated. A killer is not someone to idolise, and any of this murderer's over-excited fans who're foolish enough to be carried along in mob action like this need to know they may be facing charges as severe as any sort of extremist terrorism. We have a zero-tolerance policy on terrorist acts and any involvement in them. The hypocrisy of killing and hurting in the name of kindness is there for all to see. Please, do not get involved in this. Thank you.'

Another camera clicked, this time without a flash, sending other cameras into action, and Walker cleared his throat, telling them to pack it in. 'Questions?' he asked.

A few hands went up, and Superintendent Stone picked one.

'Jenny Gould of the Lancashire Telegraph. Is the name of the discussion group referred to "The Tower Forum", and if so, are you looking into getting this discussion group closed down, to help secure the safety of the general public?'

'Yes. That's correct,' said Superintendent Stone. 'And we're waiting for a Facebook representative to get back to us, to discuss this further.'

Walker didn't want the Facebook page to be taken down just yet, though, as he thought it might be a valuable resource. It helped for them to see these discussions, in real time, while it was also useful to be able to interact in the discussion itself, either by revealing their role and position, and being transparent, or going in with a fake account and masquerading as a member of the public. He was hoping the killer might engage with his fans, his ego getting the better of him, give something away. Plus, he didn't think there was much chance these keyboard warriors would actually do anything, with perhaps only a small number of them posing anything approaching a significant threat. It wasn't an international fascist group, after all, but just a small local clique kicking off in reaction to recent news. It was, he thought, an acceptable risk, and Superintendent Stone agreed with him. They didn't want to reveal all of this to the press, though, hence her response. Some more hands shot up, and Superintendent Stone chose one.

CHAPTER SIXTEEN

'Phillip Taylor, Blackpool Gazette,' said a gentleman sat at the front.

'Mr Taylor. I saw your article the other day. "Serial Killer Warns People of Blackpool to be Kinder, or Else".' Superintendent Stone's voice was curt. Walker hadn't been too happy about it either, because he'd linked the "Be Kind" signature to the killings, something they were attempting not to specifically discuss with the public yet; but he tried not to take it too personally—the guy was just trying to do his job, he supposed, just like he was. Superintendent Stone maintained the same composure. 'What's your question?'

'My question is: given the current escalation of discussions on this topic, and the creation of the Kindness Matters Movement, how do you intend to police this proliferating problem, and could the emergence of this group be seen as a failure of the police to adequately protect the people of Blackpool?'

It was a question that seemed to have been well rehearsed, and one that may have been designed to stoke an emotional reaction. It was a tactic the press often used, but Superintendent Stone wasn't going to fall for that. She was too experienced.

'This is a fair point, Mr Taylor, and, in time, wider discussions will have to be had about whether we're doing enough to protect people from harm like this, and more specifically about whether current funding and staffing levels are adequate to achieve this. For now, as DCI Walker has already alluded to, a wide-scale operation has been put together to address the threat posed by the KMM, and rest assured measures have been put into place to guard against any possible rioting on November fifth. We have a short-term and a long-term strategy in place to combat this movement, and to bolster our protection of the people of Blackpool. In the short-term, we have organised additional resources—from the fire services, hospitals, riot police, and officers from various police stations—to adequately deal with any outbreaks of violence on November the fifth, and, as noted, we will prosecute, to the full extent of the law, anyone involved in violence or property damage or the sort of acts that might be offences under the Terrorism Act 2006. We will not bow down to such pressure. In the long-term, if our findings warrant further investigation—if this turns out in fact not to be just a lot of online talk, but something more organised—then we plan to implement a large-scale criminal investigation into this group, its founding, and all those involved, and to build a case against them ready for prosecution. For this, there would be collaboration with counter-terrorism forces, and a task force might also be set up. But for now, the seriousness of this group has yet to be determined. Again, as far as protecting the people of Blackpool, we're doing everything we can on the resources we're provided with. If the people want more, then this needs to be taken up peacefully in a political forum. Does that answer your question?'

Phillip Taylor opened his mouth to speak, but seemed to think better of it, before nodding and scribbling something in a notepad.

'Anybody else?' asked Superintendent Stone.

'Jon Dough, Lancashire Evening Post.'

'John *Doe*? Is this a joke?' asked Superintendent Stone, glancing across to Walker, motioning with her eyes for them to leave. 'We don't have time for—'

'D-O-U-G-H,' said the man, also standing up, spelling out his name. He was tall, strong-looking, but falling into middle-age with greys at his temples and a receding hairline. 'No joke. It's my name', he said, pointing at the card on a lanyard around his neck. 'May I?

Superintendent Stone looked at her watch, nodded.

'Although you are now planning for and combatting against an organised group attack, you will still need to solve the two murders that have taken place and catch the killer or killers. Are you any closer to apprehending any suspects?'

'DCI Walker and his team will be heading the investigation into these murders,' said Superintendent Stone, 'So, I'll hand you back to him for this one.' She sat down again. Walker remained seated, in front of his microphone.

'We are following a process, going through various scenarios, canvassing the area, collecting vital information to build a case', he said. 'However, this is a process that takes time. Rest assured, we're doing everything we can to catch this killer or killers in a timely manner.' He looked at his superior, raising his eyebrows to tell her he was done. She got the message.

'That will be all,' said Superintendent Stone, who promptly left first, ahead of them.

Walker stood up, also getting ready to leave and cameras started to click, rapid fire, this time with the flashes turned back on. Walker felt like it might bring on a migraine, could feel a pulsating of that left eye again, so he got out of there as quickly as he could, with DCs Briggs and Ainscough close behind. They started to climb the stairs that would take them back up to the Incident Room, but Walker stopped on one of the half landings of the stairwell, taking a breather, rubbing his head, his eyes closing as he winced with the pain. DC Briggs and DC Ainscough caught up to him and also stopped.

'You okay, sir?' asked DC Briggs.

'Bit of a headache, that's all,' said Walker, opening his eyes again.

'Maybe you should go home and rest, get ready for tomorrow?' said DC Briggs.

'Actually, I need you to look at something,' said DC Ainscough. 'I think I might have found something.'

DC Briggs threw DC Ainscough some daggers with her eyes. She obviously worried about Walker, and he appreciated that, but there were more important things to consider right now. It was just a headache, a few stabbing pains and a little throbbing, that was all. As long as it wasn't continuous, for several days, he'd be fine. That's what the doctors had told him.

'Well, let's stop hanging around here jabbering, and go see what you have then,' said Walker. 'There's at least one killer still out there, and it's our job to stop them.'

* * *

'Okay, DC Ainscough. What do you have?' asked Walker. They were sat back in the Incident Room now, the three of them joining the already present DI Hogarth.

'Well, I was looking more deeply into the history of the barman at the Red Lion pub, Danny Bagley, and I found this,' said DC Ainscough. He opened up a folder to show them a printed newspaper article, obviously taken from an online source. 'It reports on an assault of a local girl, a *Shannon Bagley*, dated just over two years ago.'

Walker's eyes went a touch wider. 'Relative?' he asked.

CHAPTER SIXTEEN

'Sister,' said DC Ainscough. 'Younger sister by three years. She was beaten and needed five stitches around her eye, had a fractured rib, and a detached retina with some possibility of permanent vision loss. Apparently, all this happened at the Houndshill Shopping Centre, during a routine trip. A gang of local girls did it to her in the toilets. They were never caught.'

'Where's that?' asked Walker.

'Just around the back side of the Blackpool Tower Buildings, in close proximity,' said DC Ainscough.

'I see. And is that everything?' asked Walker.

'In the interview with the press, Shannon stated, and I quote: *Why are people so horrible to each other? Why can't everyone just be kinder? I was just minding my own business.*' It had happened before the Defender became active, started hurting and killing people, leaving his 'Be Kind' signature. Walker was aware this could be significant.

'Well, there's that word again,' said DC Briggs. '*Kind*. A coincidence?'

'Possibly,' said Walker. 'But you know me and coincidences. We don't sit comfortably next to each other. Have you contacted the girl?'

'I have,' said DC Ainscough, pushing his glasses further up his nose. 'She did have some permanent vision loss in one of her eyes, which has affected her work as a freelance copywriter. She also revealed she's suffered from anxiety as a result of this and has been taking a course of antidepressants.'

'We'll need to interview her properly, see what she has to say about her brother, how he reacted to all this,' said Walker. 'It provides possible motive for carrying out such violence.'

'Of course,' said DC Ainscough. 'I already asked her a little about Danny, and she said he was obviously very upset and angry about what happened, as they all are, but that there's nothing they can do about it, so they have to move on. I wasn't convinced they had, though—moved on. It still seemed very raw.'

'Right. I want eyes on this guy,' said Walker. 'Get him in to be interviewed again. I'll conduct it myself. And let's see if we can get a warrant to search his home, have a look in his computer. File the application with the Magistrates court.'

'Will do,' said DC Ainscough.

'He did look a bit sheepish about something, sir. Kept glancing at his computer when we visited,' said DC Briggs. 'Assumed he'd just been looking at porn or something, like many young men do—there's no crime in that. But perhaps it was something more.'

'I think given the developments with this online forum, that's a solid assumption. We need to talk to him, and fast,' said Walker. 'Take a look at that computer. He was there the night Anthony Singelmann died, and he was likely working nearby the night Michael Tracy was killed too. He's definitely a person of interest now, but we need a little more to make him our prime suspect. Get on it, Detective Ainscough. Bring him in. And get that warrant application expedited.'

'I've been trying, sir—to get him in, I mean—but he's proving a little difficult to get a hold of,' said DC Ainscough.

'Then visit his home or see if he's working at the bar. Failing that, ask his sister where he might be,' said Walker. 'We need to get him ASAP, keep him here for twenty-four hours, all through the November fifth celebrations. At least if something happens then, we'll know he isn't involved directly.'

'Got it,' said DC Ainscough. 'I'll do my best, sir.'

CHAPTER SEVENTEEN

DC Ainscough had found Danny Bagley coming out of his home on the morning of the fifth, apparently heading out to the local shop to pick up a few things. Now down at the station, Walker had Bagley across from him in an interview room, with DC Briggs by the detective's side. At least they could now hold him for twenty-four hours, as he'd hoped, take him out of the equation concerning any possible riots or violence, if it were to happen. They were all starting to get a bit apprehensive about how bad it could get, as comments on The Tower Forum were starting to reach boiling point, with more and more people chipping in, joining the debate—despite their warnings not to. It had become feverish. Superintendent Stone had responded by getting the Counter Terrorism Internet Referral Unit (CTIRU) involved, consulting with a team of specialist officers who dealt with taking down such content and investigating those behind it. She was also holding strategy meetings, stepping up patrols in the area, and she'd put an armed response unit on standby. Walker wasn't directly involved in any of that, though, and was just responsible for investigating the killings—but he was aware of this wider operation, having been informed by Superintendent Stone.

Having done the formalities with the audio recording, Walker got straight down to business. There was no time to lose. It was going to be a big day, one way or another.

'Mr Bagley. Have you been a part of, looked at, or made comments on The Tower Forum on Facebook?' asked Walker.

'I don't know what you're talking about,' said Danny, unable to maintain eye contact with Walker, looking down at the table in front of him.

Walker sighed. 'Danny. This is important. We heard about what happened with your sister. We spoke to her.'

'Yeah. She told me,' he spat. 'Just before you picked me up. Why can't you just leave her alone. She needs to forget about it, not keep being reminded. She needs to move on with her life.'

Walker sat forward. 'Danny. What do you know about the death of Anthony Singelmann?' He let it settle for a few seconds. 'What do you know about the death of Michael Tracy.' He put photographs of the deceased on the table in front of Danny as he spoke, trying to get a reaction. 'What do you know about the Kindness Matters Movement?'

Danny looked at the wall. 'I don't know nothing,' he said. 'I work at the pub nearby, that's all. It doesn't mean I did anything.'

'Danny, what do you know about what is going to happen tonight?' asked Walker. 'If you know anything, anything at all, you need to tell us. More people might die. Innocent people.'

'No comment,' said Danny, stubbornly.

Walker looked across at DC Briggs. Normally, she might take over at this point, try to use the soft approach, but time was ticking, and Danny didn't seem like he was going to talk. He was digging his heels in. At least by having him in custody they could rule him out of anything further that might happen today—so that was something. Walker shook his head.

'Interview complete at 10:37am,' he said, calling it, turning the audio device off. They were out of time. They had to get organised, get ready. They had to move.

* * *

It was the evening of the fifth now, and things were already beginning to heat up in the way that Bonfire Night generally does—with emergency calls on the increase. But that wasn't their concern right now. Walker and DC Briggs were sat in their pool car, on standby, waiting to be alerted to any possible major events of a criminal nature—any direct and violent attacks on people, that kind of thing. It wasn't within their remit to be out on the streets, of course. It wasn't a stake-out. It was up to PCs out patrolling in marked cars to attend to any violence or trouble, to arrest any lawbreakers, and notify them if there was any link to their case. Walker and DC Briggs didn't *have* to be there, could have been analysing things back at the station, where Superintendent Stone had set up a War Room of sorts, a Command Centre to liaise with the CTIRU and police support units, including riot police and more, to coordinate responses to any scattered incidents and handle any significant activity like a full-on mob running rampage through the streets of Blackpool. She hadn't wanted Walker and DC Briggs there though, said there was nothing they could really add in the way of intel. That's why they were out on the streets, hanging around like bloody goddamned

PIs.

He could have been taking a break at home, sat with his feet up with a sandwich on his lap. Walker *wanted* to be here though. He had a feeling—that their killer would be out there tonight, looking for another victim, thirsty for blood, or whatever it was they were after. And when he told DC Briggs what he was doing, she wasn't having him sitting out here alone—wasn't having it at all—so there she was; and he didn't hate it too. They waited, with some trepidation, for the Kindness Matters Movement to set in motion, for the talk to possibly become action. What had started as what looked like two vicious attacks by one individual was now threatening to go viral. And for once, Walker would be more than happy to sit in his car with DC Briggs all night and have absolutely nothing happen. But this was Bonfire Night, of course, and things always happened on Bonfire Night. He just hoped that it'd be par for the course, that nothing out of the ordinary would happen. His expectations were the polar opposite of his hopes though.

A fire engine went blazing past, sirens on.

'Not unusual on Bonfire Night, sadly, is it?' said DC Briggs, echoing his thoughts once more, dismissing it as nothing worthy of their attention. 'Most people think this is a fun night. They don't realise how many people get hurt—children too. It must be one of the worse nights of the year for emergency services. If not *the* worst. It's just awful, some of the injuries...'

'Well, if you play with fire,' said Walker, instantly regretting it, sounding too cold. He looked at his watch. It was 7:37pm. 'Not much happening yet as far as the Movement goes. Maybe people *were* just mouthing off, trying to scare everyone into

CHAPTER SEVENTEEN

being nicer. It wouldn't be the first time.'

Right on cue, though, a call suddenly came through on the police radio, sparking it into life.

'This is PC White. We have a man unconscious on the north side of the Promenade,' said a gravelly voice. 'GBH. Looks to have been struck on the head. Waiting for paramedics to attend. Be advised, the "Be Kind" motif is spray painted next to him. Over.'

'It's starting,' said Walker, reaching for the radio. 'DCI Walker. Any witnesses?'

There was a pause. 'Negative,' said PC White. 'As far as we know. Some passers-by found him, called it in. He was alone. Over.'

'Roger that. We're on our way, over,' said Walker, putting the radio down with one hand and getting the car into gear with the other. He was just about to apply pressure to the accelerator, when another call came in.

'This is PC Adebayo. We've got attacks on two individuals outside the Rose & Crown. One of them is critical. We've got paramedics on the way. Witnesses say there were two assailants, both wearing face masks. They spray painted next to the bodies: "Be Kind". Over.'

'Shit,' said Walker. He grabbed the two-way radio again. 'Message received. We have another incident to attend to first. Be there as soon as we can. Over.'

He got on his mobile, called Superintendent Stone, let it ring. She wasn't answering. He was just about to give up when her now familiar voice spoke.

'What is it, Detective?' she asked. 'A little busy here.'

'You getting this?' asked Walker. 'Two incidents with the "Be Kind" signature already.'

'Yes, of course I'm getting it,' she said, sounding annoyed. It's my job to get it. Do you have anything to add?'

'No… Just wanted to make sure you got the message, that's all. And to request someone lets us know immediately if you get something that sounds like our killer. We're heading over to the first incident now, taking a look at the crime scene,' said Walker.

'You do that, Detective. I'll do my job, and you do yours.' The line went dead.

A riot police van drove past, patrolling the area, getting mobilised, ready for trouble.

He looked at DC Briggs, her face now gone a shade paler.

'Dig in, Detective Briggs. This could be a long night,' he said.

She nodded and looked straight ahead, down the Promenade, jaw clenched. They were going into uncharted territory, and Walker only hoped the damage wouldn't be too devastating, for the town and its people.

* * *

Three hours after the first incident had been called in—the male that was knocked unconscious on the north side of the Promenade—and there had already been too many incidents to count: two people had died so far, eleven seriously injured, and there had been numerous reports of extensive property damage too, with some arson, vandalism, and graffiti accompanied with the "Be Kind" signature. It was anarchy, and as the incidents were so scattered, it was difficult to police,

CHAPTER SEVENTEEN

even with the resources they had to hand. Walker and DC Briggs were focussing on the two incidents resulting in death, though, as there was an outside possibility that these were carried out by the same culprit—if they weren't just copycat killings, that was. Walker was concerned. They needed to figure out which it was, and fast, so the entire investigation didn't get derailed by a bunch of damned idiots clouding the water. Both had the same M.O., in the "Be Kind" motif being spray painted next to the bodies, and both had similarly been violently murdered. But it could still be a copycat because that sodding journalist from the Blackpool Gazette had linked the massive "Be Kind" graffiti to the killings, letting every man with a can of spray paint and his dog in on it—exactly what they didn't want. It was now becoming increasingly unlikely, though, that this was the same offender involved in all four murders, given the extent of the current violence, and the fact that any one of those other injured victims could also have died. It was likely that his man would strike again tonight, of all nights, but less likely that he'd strike more than once. It seemed that by the end of the night, they'd most likely have one Defender murder, and several other copycat killings and attacks—and they had zero way of knowing which was which. This did seem like a pre-planned group attack, organised violence, some occurring simultaneously and other events overlapping as far as a timeline was concerned. But they also had to consider the possibility that their killer could have done both new murders, however unlikely that might be.

The street they were on had been temporarily cordoned off with the standard blue and white police tape that said, "Police Line Do Not Cross". It had been placed about ten metres each side of the body they were inspecting, right across the street, by the First Officer Attending. Normally, they'd have an officer stood at each end, making sure no members of the public crossed that line, but this was not a normal evening. Not even close.

Despite Superintendent Stone putting a large force of various teams out on the streets of Blackpool, it was still a vast area to cover, and there were new reports coming in every few minutes. She'd be orchestrating things from the Control Room, most likely prioritising resources and allocating them where most pressing. In this case, the other officer attending had just been reallocated to another nearby incident, knowing that Walker and DC Briggs would be arriving to assist imminently, leaving just the FOA behind, one PC Johnson. The Duty Officer had apparently been held up at yet another incident, meaning that the processing of this one had been delayed. There was only so much they could do, even with the significant resources they'd been given. It wasn't that they'd underestimated the speed and intensity of the attacks so much, or the scale, it was just that Superintendent Stone seemed to be prioritising the suppressing of any mob activity and the dispersal of unruly crowds, rather than going after individual assailants. She wanted to minimise any mass damage first—show the police to be in control—save her own arse, probably, then delegate any individual investigations to CID. It was annoying the hell out of Walker. He was all about catching the killers, and as soon as possible. But he didn't want to interrupt Superintendent Stone again, so they'd just have to handle this one by themselves until reinforcements came.

DC Briggs, wearing nitrile gloves as usual so as to not compromise the crime scene, pulled a brown leather wallet out from the back jeans pocket of the deceased; a male, who was lying on the footpath on Hull Road, which lay just towards the north end of the main strip. PC Johnson was stood nearby, shining a torch, providing some light, as it was already dark and the streetlights didn't offer much.

'Name?' asked Walker.

She pulled out some ID from the man's wallet—a driver's license.

'Joshua Unsworth, born May 1992,' said DC Briggs.

The "Be Kind" motif was again spray-painted in red nearby the body. Walker thought it could be the work of the Movement, or it might just be someone jumping on the chance to settle some score or other and throw the police off their tracks. He was beginning to curse the press, and not for the first time. They all too often gave the game away, made things more difficult than it needed to be. They'd sodding given every would-be killer in the area a golden opportunity to misdirect the entire investigation, and potentially get away with murder themselves. And for what? To sell a few extra newspapers. It made Walker's blood boil. He took a careful look around, not wanting to miss anything. They needed a solid lead. All they had at the moment was some chatter on a Facebook group, some deleted posts, and an idea there might also be a private group somewhere. They had no emergent organisation with folk meeting in the flesh to coordinate everything. The supposed "Movement": it was all conjecture at the moment, an unsubstantiated theory. It wasn't like nabbing someone involved might provide the opportunity to crack them, to get the names and addresses of other members. All they'd know is aliases, like BlackpoolFCFan1234 or some shite—which was no good at all. They'd probably have a better stab at getting Facebook to reveal the identities of those who posted. At the very least, though, they needed a loose end from which they could begin untangling the knot.

'Wait. Look. They stood in it.' Walker was using his own torch now, looking at a partial footprint coming from the paint. There were several steps, before the paint went dry, and the first couple were pretty well-formed, might even be able to be used to ascertain what type of footwear was being worn, he thought.

DC Briggs was already on it, taking some photos of the footprints, up close, on her phone. 'We'll get forensics to get better shots when they're done with the last crime scene, but we can work with these for now.'

'Good,' said Walker. 'At least that's something.' He took a good look at the body now, which lay near some overfull public waste bins. 'Clear and obvious blow to the head. Some broken glass nearby. Looks like he may have been bottled. Then maybe fell over, hit his head on the edge of this metal bin. Look, there's a wound on the top right side of his head, a gash that bled,' he said, pointing with his finger. 'And there's also an injury on the front right side of his head, a line and bruising that's consistent with the edge of that bin there. Hang on a minute.'

He got over to the broken glass, picked up a paper label stuck to some of it, still well enough intact for Walker to recognise it. 'H.E.I.N., and a red star; green glass. That's "Heineken",' he said.

'Good work, sir,' said DC Briggs.

'Hold your horses, Detective. There's a chance he was just bottled in an altercation—wouldn't be out of the ordinary around here—the fatal blow happening by accident as he fell,

CHAPTER SEVENTEEN

the person responsible panicking, spray-painting the message in the hope that we'll pin it on our killer. This is becoming a shitshow. This could just be a random manslaughter, but it's now inextricable from our serial murder case because of the writing.'

DC Briggs looked around at the environment around them. The street was lined with holiday flats and hotels. 'Could be some security cams here. Will get some PCs to canvas when they can. Maybe tomorrow?'

Walker nodded. He looked in the direction the footprints were going and slowly headed that way.

'Sir?' asked DC Briggs.

'Keep your eyes out for any more paint,' he said.

DC Briggs took the torch from her belt too and they walked up the street, slowly, step by step, scanning the footpath as best they could. 'Here,' said Walker. He crouched down and pointed at one more spot of red paint. 'Maybe they stopped, had some on their heel.'

'Or turned,' said DC Briggs, looking at the building beside them. It said, "The Happy Return". It was a hotel.

'Wasn't a very happy return for Joshua Unsworth,' said Walker. He got closer to the hotel, found another spot of paint on the matt outside the door. He looked at DC Briggs, turned his torch off, and placed it back on his belt. 'Tell PC Johnson to watch that body until the forensic team turns up. And tell him not to leave it, under any circumstances, no matter what. We can't leave an unattended body. It'll make any evidence inadmissible. Got it? We're going in,' he said.

CHAPTER EIGHTEEN

Walker knocked on the door of Room 9 at The Happy Return hotel and waited. It was on the second floor, so it wasn't like the guy could just jump out of the window—not without risking serious injury, anyhow.

'Mr Williams. We know you're in there. The staff at the front desk reported that you're in your room,' said Walker. 'You're the only guest that currently is, due to all the celebrations. This is DCI Walker of the Lancashire Constabulary. We need to talk to you. There's been an incident.'

There was some activity in the room, some noise.

Walker had a spare key card that he'd got from reception but wanted to see if Mr Williams would open the door himself first.

'We're coming in, Mr Williams. Please step away from the door and put your hands where we can see them,' said Walker, as he inserted the key card into its slot and saw the red light turn to green. He tried the handle and the door clicked and opened; he pushed it inwards, cautiously. 'Mr Williams?'

A man was sat on the bed, forty-something, dishevelled,

CHAPTER EIGHTEEN

poorly groomed. 'What's this all about?' he asked, grumpily.

There were some Hoka running shoes by the door, waterproof Gore-Tex, black. Walker had seen the sort before when he'd been looking for something more comfortable for everyday use, when he'd had a bad back. He picked one up, looked at the sole. It had some red paint on it.

'You know anything about this?' asked Walker, gesturing to the paint.

'Oh, that? Someone graffitied the footpath. It's all gone nuts tonight. I'm sorry I came. Thought it might be fun here on Bonfire Night, with the illuminations and everything,' said the man. 'But there's a weird vibe. Things are kicking off.'

'And I don't suppose there was a dead body next to the paint when you stood in it, was there?' asked Walker. 'I'm sure you would have noticed.'

'A *body?*' said the man. 'Someone died? What? No. Of course… What's this about?'

There was a black face mask lying on the bedside table. Walker looked at it. 'I think we got through the pandemic, Mr Williams. What's with the mask?'

'It's for the smoke,' he said. 'It's Bonfire night, isn't it. I have asthma.'

Walker looked around some more. He looked in the minibar fridge, removed the stock list. 'Heineken beer, 650ml, stock 4, £6.50,' he said. 'There's one missing.'

'So?' said the man. 'It's not a crime to drink beer, is it??'

'Mr Williams. Stand up, please,' said Walker. The man did as asked. 'We'd like you to come down to the station, ask you a few questions.'

'What? Am I being detained?' he asked.

Walker would have preferred for him to come there voluntarily, interview him first without arresting him, buy them some more time.

'We'd just like to ask you some questions,' said Walker. 'That's all.'

'No thanks,' said the man. 'I'm going nowhere.'

'Well… in that case, you give us no choice but to arrest you for the suspected murder of Joshua Unsworth,' said Walker, getting some handcuffs from his belt and placing them on the suspect from behind. 'You do not have to say anything. But it may harm your defence if you do not mention when questioned something which you later rely on in court. Anything you do say may be—'

There was an explosion, not far away by the sounds of it. It rocked the building; a bit of plaster cracked and fell off the ceiling, hitting DC Briggs on the head.

She brushed it off. 'Jesus Chr—'

Another blast, not as ferocious as the first, but enough to scare them. Walker went over to the window, saw a car down the street on fire, a couple of youths with masks running away. Even from this distance, he could see the "Be Kind" motif had been sprayed next to the flaming vehicle. PC Johnson was doing as he was told, standing next to their body, hands in the air, exasperated, looking up at them.

'God damn it,' said Walker. 'It's like a war zone out there. Get him back to the car, take him to the station, get him locked up, and meet me back here as soon as you can.'

DC Briggs hesitated. 'But, sir, shouldn't we stick—'

'It's all hands-on deck time, Detective. Do as I say, now,' said Walker. 'Call me when you get back. And be careful.'

'Will do,' said DC Briggs. 'You too, sir.'

Walker needed to find the killer, and fast, take the momen-

CHAPTER EIGHTEEN

tum out of what was happening here, dampen these idiots' spirits, take the goddamned wind out of their sails. If they were lucky, once they got their murderer, it might just all sputter out, come to an end. He felt his anger rising, from the pit of his stomach, past his frantically pumping heart, then into his brain. It got a hold of him, the stupidity of it all, the lack of order. He lost it. He grabbed the man by the collar, dragged him over to the window. 'You see that?' he asked. 'You've turned this place into a sodding battle ground. People are dying out there. Who've you been talking to? Whose idea was this? I know you have some private online group somewhere. Telegram or some shite. We'll find it, in time, find all of you. It'll be easier if you just tell me now.'

The man smiled and shook his head. 'This place is going to be so much better after this, you'll see,' he said.

'Sir?' said DC Briggs, knowing he was stepping over a line being rough with the guy, trying to pull him back before he did anything stupid. It wouldn't be the first time, even with all his years of experience. 'Should I take him to the station now?'

Walker loosened his grip on the man, brushed his already crumpled shirt down. 'You and me are gonna have a proper talk about this soon, in a little private room, just you and me. So have a think about how you want this to go.'

'If you'd done your jobs a bit better, then none of this would be happening,' said the man, goading Walker, almost spitting on him as he spoke. Walker grabbed the guy again, but this time, DC Briggs physically pulled him back.

'Sir, I really think we should get going,' she said, pleading with her eyes, probably not wanting any more trouble than they already had; and she was right. It was enough to help him bring it down a notch—that look she gave—get himself back under some semblance of control.

Walker took another look around, sucking in a few breaths, trying to calm himself further. He grabbed the man's wallet from the other bedside unit, opened it up, took a look. He removed the cards, one by one, throwing them on the bed, until he found one of interest. It was a business card for Kingscote Boxing Gym containing their contact information. He showed it to DC Briggs, then held it in front of the man's face. He was beginning to wonder whether these louts had actually been meeting in person too, were recruiting other discontented young men, radicalising them into some budding fascist movement like the bloody English Defence League or the Patriotic Alternative.

'Like to fight, eh? You're going down for this,' said Walker. 'And so are your friends.' He was fuming, but he had to put that away now, focus on the task at hand. 'Get him out of here. And call me as soon as you can.'

CHAPTER NINETEEN

When the dust settled, and the sun finally started to come up once more, the town of Blackpool had become a warzone. Five dead, twenty-one people with serious injuries, and sixty-five instances of vandalism or property damage at the last count. It was astonishing, unheard of. This would make all the national newspapers; many of the international ones too. The press would be all over it, would have an absolute field day—it would be on TV too—and the police force in Blackpool would be at its very epicentre, including Detective Chief Inspector Walker for his role in the murder cases leading up to the wider-scale violence. It gave him heart palpitations just thinking about it, so he popped a Propranolol tablet in his mouth from his pocket, swallowed it dry as it was only tiny. The Kindness Matters Movement had made its mark: on his body, his mind, and everyone else's too. People would be grieving this morning, in shock at what had unfolded, not being able to comprehend. It was seismic.

It was now 10:36am and the weather in Blackpool was unusually calm given its proximity to the sea. It had been three hours since the last incident had been reported, and the police and emergency services were now quietly going about their work, treating the injured, processing crime scenes, getting suspects back to the station. It was a large-scale operation; even bigger than they'd feared. Walker and the now returned DC Briggs were still helping out the best they could, but it was utter chaos. They wouldn't have been able to sleep even if they had gone home anytime sooner, though—they'd have been too wired. This would take some cleaning up.

'Hey, shouldn't you be heading back now, Chief, now things are calming down a bit. Get some sleep?' asked DC Briggs, probably noticing he wasn't looking quite with it. 'I'll stay here a bit longer if you like, help get things under control. We're gonna need you fighting fit on this one, sharp. There's gonna be a lot to analyse.'

'Just a bit longer,' said Walker. There was a time when he could go for two days without sleep, even three or four with the odd power nap. But he was getting older now, wasn't in the best health, had been very much struggling with it the past few years. He was beginning to learn that he did have limitations, after all. He needed some sleep to keep himself functioning properly, he knew that much. But there was just so much to do. There weren't enough resources for something like this.

'Come on, sir. You're not going to make much progress in this state,' she said, pushing him in her most persuasive tone. 'Come back refreshed. What do you say? They need time to process the crime scenes, anyway, as you well know. It's gonna take longer than usual too, what with there being so many. You may as well take a break until they're ready. Then we can come back, try to determine if any of the incidents were carried out by our killer. We'll just pressure the CSIs if we hang around, make them feel rushed. And then mistakes could be made. And we don't—'

CHAPTER NINETEEN

'We don't want that,' said Walker, finishing her sentence for her. They were developing a good rapport together. Sometimes, it was like they'd been working together for years. Her words made Walker physically react, though, like his body took this as a signal, a sign to suddenly stop holding on and crash. He could suddenly feel the lure of his bed calling him, could feel the soft duvet embracing him and the smell of his pillows. He was exhausted. Everything biological was suddenly plummeting, his adrenaline vanishing, leaving him with nothing, devoid of energy.

He sighed in resignation. 'Well, okay then. I think I probably could—'

'*Detective Walker!* There's something you've gotta see.' It was DC Hardman, running toward them. He'd been up all night too, trying to police the chaos just like every other copper there. He was younger than Walker, fitter, looked like he'd just woken up, refreshed—but Walker knew he hadn't.

'DC Hardman. It's good to see you. What is it?' asked Walker, his mind slow, his words dragging more than usual, almost like he'd been drinking.

'It's the Blackpool Tower,' said DC Hardman. 'There's something coming off it. You're not going to believe this.'

'What?' asked Walker, afraid DC Hardman was going to say something horrific—like a fire, or people jumping. 'What, man?' he urged. 'Spit it out.'

DC Hardman smiled. 'It's money,' he said. 'And a hell of a lot of it.'

***

In the Digital Age, word travels like wildfire, something Walker had already learned in recent times during his investigations. But this was something else. There was already a crowd of people gathered at the base of the Blackpool Tower, some of them holding bags, scrambling around, picking up as much money as they could—others just stuffing it wherever was possible on their person: in their socks, under their hats, even in their underpants and knickers. It was raining with the stuff, all ten-pound notes, going everywhere, fluttering around like little butterflies. If they hadn't just witnessed a night of carnage like they had, it would be kind of beautiful. It was a stark contrast to what had been going on, for sure.

'Jesus Christ, what next?' said Walker.

It was like watching a bunch of zombies, people fumbling around everywhere, bumping into each other, eyes only for the money. A couple of fights started to briefly break out, with people trying to grab the same bunch of cash, but the scuffles didn't last long, everyone just too delighted with the situation to hold on to such quarrels, not wanting to waste any time.

'What is this?' asked DC Briggs.

'Whatever it is, someone just let this lot go, this money, from up there,' said Walker, pointing to the top of the Tower. 'Is that place open now?'

'It is,' said DC Hardman. 'I've got a couple of PCs waiting for the next lot to come down in the lift. Whoever did this is likely in that lift.'

'Well, that's something. Nice work, Detective,' said Walker. 'I'm glad somebody is still on it. We need to find out who the hell dropped this, and why. It can't be completely unrelated to what happened last night. It just can't. It's too much

CHAPTER NINETEEN

of a coincidence. Too weird. At the very least, this could be someone who's read that sodding forum, jumped on the bandwagon, decided this is how they want to "Be Kind". It might not be of any practical relevance to our murder investigation, but if they had access to that Telegram thing that DI Hogarth mentioned, and they tell us about it... it *could* be a valuable lead.'

DC Hardman nodded. 'Agreed,' he said. 'Something's fishy, that's for sure, and it isn't this sea air.'

'Right. Let's go see who did this then,' said Walker. 'And more importantly, let's find out why.'

***

When the doors to the Blackpool Tower lift opened, there were five people stood in there, including the tour guide.

'Have a good day everyone,' said the guide, seeming jaded, gesturing for people to leave, but Walker stood there, blocking everyone's path, with DCs Briggs and Hardman stood close behind, flanked by two PCs in uniform.

'Nobody will be going anywhere, not just yet, anyway,' said Walker lifting his Lancashire Constabulary ID card which hung around his neck. 'Detective Chief Inspector Jonathan Walker. We need to talk to you—*all* of you,' he clarified. 'Right now. This is a matter of urgency.'

'But the tour,' said the guide. 'There's people waiting.'

Walker looked. There were only two people waiting at the queue barrier just a few meters in front of the lift, situated behind Walker and his colleagues, in what would be a stretch to call a "queue".

'It's going to have to wait,' said Walker. 'This is very important, I'm afraid.'

The guide swallowed, hard. 'Well, I suppose we could go to the staffroom?' he suggested.

'That would suffice. The staffroom it is then,' said Walker. 'After you.'

* * *

Each of the members of the tour, plus the guide, were each questioned in turn, but there was one man in particular who immediately caught Walker's attention, a clean-cut young gentleman from Poland who was acting rather strangely.

'Mr Janowski,' said Walker. 'If you saw something or know something about the money that just came from the top of the Tower, we need to know.'

'You can call me Alex,' he said. 'It's Aleksander, but people here just call me Alex.' That was good. He was a talker. That made things easier.

'Okay, Alex. Tell me something,' said Walker. They were in a small staffroom, just large enough to contain several staff members. They'd managed to put some of the chairs out in the hallway, so the others could wait there, supervised by the watching DC Hardman and one of the PCs. The other PC had gone up the Tower to take a look, make sure nobody else was still up there. DC Briggs was sat inside the room with them.

The problem was that Walker was still running on empty,

CHAPTER NINETEEN

his body and brain not quite functioning properly, but he was managing to suck it up: a *little*. He wanted to get this done first before taking a break, as it felt like a vital step in the investigation. If people's lives were still in danger, then his health had to take the back seat for now, as usual.

'Tell me something. Anything,' repeated Walker, with some urgency in his voice.

Alex shook his head, clammed up now. He looked scared. He was already pale, but he seemed to be going even whiter before their very eyes.

'Alex. I don't know if you're aware of what happened last night, but there's been a lot of trouble. Several people have died,' said Walker. 'I'm sure you don't want to be a murder suspect. So, you need to tell us what you know. You need to tell us everything.'

The PC who'd been sent up the tower walked in holding a large leather duffle bag. He dropped it on a coffee table in front of Walker. 'Found this,' he said. He took out some bolt cutters from the bag. 'And these. The safety netting had been cut and the bag was left next to it. Presumably, they carried the money in this and then threw it out of the hole they made.'

'Thank you,' said Walker. 'But carry some nitrile gloves next time. This is evidence. Let's hope you've not compromised it. You may wait outside with the others now.'

The PC nodded, seeming a little embarrassed, and left the room.

'Alex, are we going to find your fingerprints on this bag?' asked Walker.

'It's not a crime to give people money, is it?' asked Alex, his eyes pleading for everything to be okay.

'So, it *was* you?' said Walker.

'Am I in trouble?' he asked.

Walker looked at DC Briggs. 'At the moment, it's just littering and public property damage. Unless you were coerced. What is your involvement with the Kindness Matters Movement?'

'The... *what?*' asked Alex.

Walker wasn't getting the feeling Alex was directly involved in this at all, never mind some kind of ringleader. He didn't strike him as the kind of guy who'd have a whole bunch of money to throw away either—none of his well-worn clothes or his calloused hands suggested this—more likely an impoverished immigrant struggling to find his way in a new country. So, that meant someone had given him the money for this purpose, but for what end Walker didn't know? Perhaps it was meant as a distraction while something more sinister was going on. But all they had now was a killer who'd done two murders and left the same message at each, a bunch of idiots who'd riled themselves up into running riot, and no sign of any great criminal mastermind lurking behind the scenes yet, running the show, pulling the strings. It was all a bit too random.

'Did somebody put you up to this, Alex?' asked Walker.

'Put me up?' asked Alex. 'The Tower?"

He wasn't a native English speaker. Walker had seen these types of misunderstandings before and tried again.

'Did somebody make you throw that money off the Tower, Alex?' he asked again.

Alex shook his head. 'I can't...' he said.

'Alex, this is very important. If someone put you up to this, we need to talk to them, find out why. Have you been threatened? Did somebody tell you that they'll hurt you or your family if you say anything? Do you have a family here?'

'Yes,' said Alex. 'I have a wife and young son.' His eyes pleading again, begging for them to be okay.

'And are they in any danger?'

Alex nodded his head, panic-stricken.

Walker leaned forward. 'Alex. Listen to me very carefully. We can have your wife and son, and yourself, taken somewhere safe for a while, or we can make sure they're watched until this is all over. We can keep you and your family safe. You just need to tell us what you know. If you don't, then whoever is threatening you will be free to do this again, and who knows where it'll end. To protect your family, you need to tell us everything. Do you understand?'

Alex looked down, seeming resigned to the fact, and nodded.

'Okay. I'll tell you,' he said, suddenly looking up at Walker. 'But you have to *promise* me that you'll protect my wife and son. Promise me.'

'I promise that I'll do everything I can to keep them safe,' said Walker. 'You just have to tell me who made you do this.'

Alex took a wad of cash out from his pocket and put it on the table. 'He gave me this,' he said.

Walker looked at the money, picked it up, inspected it. All ten-pound denominations, just like the cash falling from the Tower. 'And who is *he*?'

'I don't know,' said Alex. 'I was just on my way to work, walking on the street, when a big guy pulled a knife on me, pulled me into an alleyway. He was wearing a black face mask, a cap, and a… what do you call it? A head covering.'

'A hood?' suggested Walker.

'Yes. A hood. He said I have to go up the Blackpool Tower,

use the tool inside the bag to cut the net, and drop the cash down. He said to take the paper straps off the cash before dropping it. He was very clear about that. He said he'd be watching, and that I had to drop all of it, only keeping one bundle for myself. He said he knew where my family lived—had followed me home the day before, told me the street name—and that there'd be trouble if I didn't follow his instructions exactly,' said Alex.

Walker looked at DC Briggs, telling her with his eyes that they had something very important, and that they wouldn't be sleeping anytime soon. She seemed to understand—or, at least, he *thought* she did. He looked back at Alex. 'Is there anything else?' he asked. 'Anything that the man said, about the way he looked, his voice? We need every detail so we can find him.'

'Yes. There was something else. There was actually something else in the bag he gave me, but I threw it away in the bin after I used it. He told me to do that too,' he said.

'And what was it, this *thing*?' asked Walker.

'It was a can of spray paint. Red,' said Alex. 'He asked me to spray something on the ground in front of the Tower. I had to wait until there was nobody around and do it quick, while no one was looking. I had to wait a while for it to clear because there are a lot of police around today.'

'And what did he ask you to write, Alex?' Walker asked.

'No more violence,' said Alex. 'He asked me to write, *No More Violence*.'

CHAPTER TWENTY

There are logistical nightmares, and then there was November the fifth in Blackpool when the Kindness Matters Movement had been on the rampage. Walker had never personally seen anything like it in all his decades of policing. It would take weeks to process properly, if not months. But they didn't have months. If they wanted to catch whoever was behind this, and bring the movement down too, they'd have to find a quicker way before someone else got hurt. It was all over the news by now—they were having a field day with it, excoriating Superintendent Stone for her supposed mismanagement of the situation; not that she could have done much more. She was conducting interview after interview, the usual damage limitation, explaining it wasn't like a protest march or football hooliganism, that they couldn't cut off routes or kettle the troublemakers like they usually would. It had been fragmented violence, random, and she argued they'd saved many more lives because of their diligence. The press weren't having any of it, though. Walker had just managed a two-hour nap at one of the rooms in the station, DC Briggs doing the same only at home, freshening herself up a bit. Now somewhat refreshed, or at least functioning half properly again, they prepared to take on the world's media, with very little time for preparation.

'What are they saying on the Tower Forum this morning, DI Hogarth?' asked Walker, as he sipped on a decaffeinated coffee with *Oat-ly!* oat milk. It wasn't what he really wanted or needed, of course—especially in his sleep-deprived condition—but simply something that tasted good which he'd got used to. His stomach couldn't take caffeine or lactose anymore, something he'd found out the hard way after years of digestion problems and awful stomach-aches. Still, at least it was hot, and it massaged him from the inside out.

They were back in the Incident Room—Walker, DI Hogarth, and DCs Briggs, Hardman, and Ainscough—going through things, getting ready for the latest press conference.

'Seems like they're backing off. A photo of the graffiti at the base of the Blackpool Tower is on there. It now says: "Be Kind. No More Violence." They seem to have had a change of heart. Perhaps they never expected it to get so bad, went too far, regret it.'

'Too far? It was madness,' said DC Hardman. 'Utter madness. I should have been a postman or something—a nice quiet job. It's like some kind of religious cult, this.'

'Er, something else has just been posted, as we speak,' said DI Hogarth. 'It's been signed "The Defender". It says he'll let off another £100,000 from the Blackpool Tower if everyone stops the violence. He's trying to control his fanboys, bribe them. He goes on... Er... But basically, no more violence and vandalism, and he'll let off another hundred grand at some point. That's about the size of it. He's going to reward people for being kind to each other. And anyone who's not will be dealt with by him and him only, he says. So, not exactly ending the violence, but rather putting a monopoly on it.'

CHAPTER TWENTY

'Can you trace it?' asked Walker. 'Where's the message been sent from?'

'Already on it as we speak,' said DI Hogarth, tapping away on his laptop computer. 'Seems to be yet another VPN. It says it's coming from South Korea, but I very much doubt that. A place called Gwangju.'

Walker got his thoughts together. 'Well hopefully that buys us some time, at least. We'll tell the press, issue a warning that anyone involved in the Kindness Matters Movement will be arrested, and that it will be treated as an incident of terrorism, which we have a zero-tolerance policy on.'

'We need to find who this Defender character is, before this goes any further, sir,' said DC Briggs, stating the bloody obvious again. She did have her annoying little quirks, like this, as most people do if you spend enough time with them. But he'd rather be with her than without her. Plus, he was sure he had his annoyances too. 'People's lives depend on it. He seems to be the key to all this. He started it all by trying to punish hooligans and louts by intimidating them into kindness. He seems to have some influence, even if he's not in control of what they're doing'.

'Yes, it seems so. Ironic, isn't it?' said Walker. 'Quite the paradox: punishing violence through violence. He's really started something here. Seems like he might regret it though, throwing that money off the Tower, bribing them to stop. It's been a runaway train this, an echo chamber leading to mass hysteria—the mob gone completely mad. I bet a lot of them don't recognise themselves.'

'Yeah. I read a bit about fascism at college, sir; did an A-level in Politics. They're all about championing the social order, aren't they, maintaining law and order—that sort of thing—

but really, it's all just an excuse for the worst louts out there to run amok.'

'You might have something there,' said Walker. 'There's no hint of any racism or bigotry here, though, but it's not much different in the end; just a load of idiots making excuses for violence and disorder.'

'Does anyone have anything concrete on this guy yet?' asked DC Briggs.

Walker's thoughts once again went back to the big chap seen in the pub the night Anthony Singelmann died. Alex also said the man threatening him was large. It could have been one and the same, but large males were not exactly in short supply around Blackpool.

'Tom from The Blackpool Tower Dungeon, the guy in the Grim Reaper costume at the pub, said he may have seen the big fella at the pub at his show,' said Walker. 'So, I actioned a list of customers from that day, checking the bank card records of people who paid. I was hoping Tom might identify the guy he saw from those, but we got nothing. Now it makes sense, if he had all that cash—he wouldn't have paid by card. I also thought it might be good to find out if they also have any photos of customers—CCTV, tour photos that punters can buy, that kind of thing. But again, no leads. It was a longshot though; I'd expect any offender to be avoiding such things, of course. I also actioned a wider scale, more in-depth analysis of CCTV footage in the area from Blackpool's new CCTV Control Centre. It's state of the art, you know, had a two million quid upgrade recently. I'm hoping to get something from that, but we've yet to get the results back. It takes time, apparently. We need to chase that up, ASAP.'

'I'll get on that,' said DC Ainscough.

CHAPTER TWENTY

'Good man,' said Walker. 'Right, let's get this show on the road.'

DC Briggs looked unsure, with them not really being able to prepare properly for a press conference that would likely be shown all around the world—or at least a part of it. She was nervous, and rightly so. This was one of the biggest press conferences of Walker's career, and it was certainly the biggest of DC Briggs's relatively short stint with the Criminal Investigation Department. Plus, they'd already seen some of the grilling that Superintendent Stone had got, and her superior, so he didn't expect they'd go any easier on them. Stone would be there again, on hand, like last time, should any questions arise that didn't concern Walker, but this part of the conference was for him, she'd said, for questions that fell more in his purview, as Chief Investigator of the first two killings. Despite this explanation, though, he couldn't escape the feeling she wanted him out there to take some of the flak. 'But shouldn't we—'

Walker waved a hand, dismissively. 'There's never going to be enough time to prepare for this properly. Better just to wing it, not to get too hung up on the presentation. We'll just explain the facts as we know them, try to stick to talking about the first two killings—it's come from the top, we mustn't talk about anything else in any detail. The rest is just a bandwagon effect, copycats running amok, maybe an organised attack, but we just don't know yet. It's up to Superintendent Stone to step in if any questions deviate from our remit. But, if we can get more people staying at home for a few days, then at least we can keep more people safe. And if we can get some eyes and ears out there from people who can't stay at home, looking out for a large guy acting suspiciously, wearing a mask, then all the better. Who knows, we might even get a tip off.'

DC Briggs still looked unsure but nodded anyway. 'Okay then, Chief,' she said. 'You're the boss.'

Walker looked at DC Hardman, his muscles almost bulging out of his suit, jaw clenched, brow furrowed. 'DC Hardman. You're coming along too. We need someone to scare these journalists, keep them under control a bit. And I think you're just the man,' he said.

'Roger that,' said DC Hardman. 'No problem at all.'

CHAPTER TWENTY-ONE

'Could we have some quiet out here, please?' shouted DC Hardman. There were so many of the mass media turned up this time that they were having to hold the press conference and issue the statement outside of Blackpool Police HQ, just as Superintendent Stone and her superior had before them, despite it now spitting with rain. Some of the HQ staff had placed a book plinth there for them to stand at, put a few notes on, look more professional. Not that the notes would be of much help, given the circumstances, but they did give him some sense of comfort, just in case he got lost and forget what he needed to say. Sometimes, these days, his head got foggy, his thoughts slow, even when he wasn't sleep deprived. He hoped this wouldn't be one of those times.

The crowd piped down a bit after DC Hardman's bark, started to settle—which is exactly why he was there—until Walker felt that was as quiet as it was going to get, so he made a start. Superintendent Stone stood in the background, ready to step in if needed, alongside DC Briggs, who was there more for moral support again, and to possibly answer any lower-level questions pertaining to the investigation.

'Thank you everyone for coming,' he said, at a volume sufficient enough for people to hear him. He didn't have a microphone on this occasion as the Blackpool station PA was playing up. 'As you know, we've had quite the night. There has, sadly, been an unprecedented amount of violence, property damage, and vandalism on the streets of Blackpool during the November fifth celebrations, along with several fatalities—as Superintendent Stone has already outlined.' Cameras clicked, journalists scribbled, held microphones and mobile phones in the air, hanging off his every word. This was a *big* story, and somehow, in his twilight years, after only just coming back from illness and all, Walker found himself at the very centre of it. He started to get those heart palpitations again, really needed to pop a pill. It wasn't the kind of stress he needed at the moment—social anxieties. But it would have to wait. He couldn't take pills in front of the press. It wouldn't be a good look. They'd dig into his medical history, perhaps his personal history too, rummage around into things he didn't want touched. And there was quite a bit. No, it would have to wait. He'd just have to suck it up, soldier on. At least the doctor had said the palpitations weren't caused by anything physical, so that was something. He went on...

'At present, in addition to the two murders we're currently investigating—those involving Anthony Singelmann and Michael Tracy—which occurred prior to the November fifth riots, we now, as you know, have several more fatalities in Blackpool as a result of these riots. We do not currently have any evidence that any of these killings were conducted by the same murderer—but we are looking into any possible connection, and doing everything we can to catch this dangerous individual. We believe he may have contributed to

CHAPTER TWENTY-ONE

an online group chat that is being looked at in connection with the November fifth riots, but the use of...' Walker looked down at his notes. *'Virtual Private Networks,'* he said, 'or VPNs, has made locating the source of these comments difficult. We also have reason to believe that this public group has been siphoning off users to a private group somewhere, which again our killer could well be involved in. So, we have our very best in computer forensics on the job, and we are confident it will just be a matter of time before the killer of Anthony Singelmann and Michael Tracy is located, and anyone frequenting these forums with information relevant to these killings would be well advised to come forward while they still have the chance.'

Walker looked down, took a breath—but slowly, so those watching wouldn't notice. He flipped over the notes in front of him, not to read anything, but simply to take a moment, get his thoughts together. He felt DC Brigg's gaze, close beside him, probably getting nervous, wondering what he was doing. But her presence gave him strength. He was glad she was there, even in a silent capacity. She was a rock; someone he could increasingly rely on.

'For the time being, we will continue to approach the murders of Anthony Singelmann and Michael Tracy as separate incidents from the November fifth riots. Myself, DC Briggs, and our team will be heading this investigation, while Superintendent Stone will be approaching the riots, I believe, as an unequivocal terrorist incident.' He looked at Superintendent Stone, inviting her to speak. She stepped forward, took the invitation, took his place at the book plinth.

'As you know, I've already provided an extensive statement on our approach to the November fifth riots, but I would add that it seems this action has been taken by the Kindness Matters Movement, if indeed it is an organised movement, to intimidate the public for the purpose of advancing an ideological cause, ostensibly that of forcing people to be kinder to each other—but under the threat of vandalism, violence, or even death,' she said. 'This lies at the very heart of the government's definition of what "Terrorism" is. It seems that the bulk of people jumping on this bandwagon are being manipulated by the "Be Kind" framing into supporting actions that are wholly antithetical to that principle. It is not a legal requirement for people to be kind to each other, but even if it were, it is not the place of the general public to enforce such laws—that is our job. This is a gross violation of people's individual liberties and freedoms. No matter how vicious and cruel people are, we have a justice system to deal with that. Our justice system might not be perfect, but we strive to make it better, and a lynch mob is not the answer to any problems and issues. This is the basest, cruellest expression of human savagery, and those extremists out to bring so-called order by such rampant brutality are misguided at best, naïve malcontents led astray by more malicious individuals. At worst, they're just thugs looking for an excuse to be thugs.'

That was good. It seemed she'd had time to prepare for this, even if he hadn't, Walker thought. She went on.

'We will therefore be employing our counterterrorism policy in this matter, namely that of CONTEST, which will involve strategies used to prevent further acts such as this, pursuing those guilty, protecting the public, and preparing for any further attacks so as to minimise such an impact, should such attacks unfold,' said Superintendent Stone.

Cameras began to click some more, and Walker got the

feeling the journalists in front of them were more than starting to itch to ask some questions. Superintendent Stone must have also felt this, as she didn't pause, and hurried along her speech.

'As noted, I will personally be heading the investigation into the suspected terrorist acts carried out on November fifth, while DCI Walker and his team continue the separate investigation into the murders of Anthony Singelmann and Michael Tracy,' she said. 'Rest assured that DCI Walker and his team are working tirelessly on the case, with my full confidence that this dangerous killer will be brought to justice. If indeed our killer has been in contact with any of these other offenders, or if he knows any of them personally, then this may well turn up some leads on the crimes committed on November fifth as well. Either way, the general public should be aware that anyone involved in the Kindness Matters Movement will be extensively investigated over the coming weeks and months by the Lancashire Constabulary, with no stone being left unturned—no pun intended.' She closed her eyes for a second, probably wishing she'd not said that. It was a bad choice of word given her surname, and it sullied an otherwise well-rehearsed sounding speech. She pressed on, raising her voice slightly, 'So, I'd urge people to refrain from interacting with this group in any way, either online, or in person—as you will be treated as a terrorist suspect if you do. As noted, it's only a matter of time before we're able to digitally track the sources of these communications and collect physical evidence from the crime scenes themselves. It goes without saying that we're taking this matter very seriously, and we'll do our very best to find out who is responsible for this and punish them accordingly. You may now ask any questions you may have.'

Cameras exploded and arms shot in the air in unison.

'DCI Walker?'

'Inspector?"

A few more shouts came in his direction. They wanted him—wanted *his* head on a platter for all of this.

'Er, that's enough, everyone,' shouted DC Hardman, reinstating order once more before they lost it completely. 'Wait for Detective Walker to choose one of you, please.'

Walker stepped forward and chose someone from the front row by pointing at them, someone who looked harmless enough—for a member of the press, anyhow. It was a youngish woman, brunette, well-groomed and polite looking; pale, possibly an Oxbridge graduate by the look of her, her back straight, her posture exemplary. Perhaps she was in the wrong job, Walker thought. Journalism was a cut-throat business; he knew that only too well.

'Laura Cooper, The Guardian Newspaper,' she said. Damn. She was a national journalist. They were all here. 'DCI Walker, this is clearly a large-scale incident, and one that, as Superintendent Stone says, you're obviously taking very seriously. We understand you'll be working with intelligence partners on this—the CTPNW, Counter Terrorism Policing North West will be involved?'

Walker gazed at Superintendent Stone, looking for guidance. They probably wanted to talk to him because he was more likely to say something dumb, trip himself up— Superintendent Stone was more educated, eloquent, hence him being her inferior.

She huffed. 'DCI Walker is heading the investigation into the murders of Anthony Singelmann and Michael Tracy. Our time is very valuable. If you have nothing else—'

'Could you expand on the nature of the organisation in question, and its ideological underpinnings?' said the journalist.

Walker knew what she was getting at. Whenever there was a stated terrorist incident of any type, the press and everyone else assumed it was some kind of radical religious group, probably Islamic—which was often not the case. He knew Superintendent Stone would want to quash any such narrative there and then.

'We are certainly not aware of any religious ideological underpinnings at this time, or indeed any other ideologies, just what the messages left have called for—people being kinder to each other. However, this is now being used as a vehicle for violence, a form of extremism that could involve radicalisation to the far-right. Whatever their reasons are, it will be of no consolation to the families of the people who've died, and the hypocrisy of it is clear for all to see: they want people to be kinder or they'll start hurting or killing them. How is that an advocation for kindness? Next question?' said Superintendent Stone, pointing to a man at the back, someone Walker recognised from the last press conference, someone from a local rag, if memory served.

'Phillip Taylor, Blackpool Gazette.' That was the chap, the one who suggested the police weren't adequately protecting the people of Blackpool. Maybe she should have chosen someone else. She'd have to be careful, make sure none of her words could be twisted—but Walker was confident she was smart enough, and experienced enough, to handle him. 'We're all devasted at the events of last night, as I'm sure everyone involved was. Could you comment on the large amount of cash that was apparently thrown off of Blackpool Tower this morning, and how you think this ties in with the violence and unrest?'

'Mr Taylor, thanks for your question. We're certainly looking into that possibility, that the money released onto the streets of Blackpool was in fact connected to the violence and unrest of the previous night. We have no firm evidence to substantiate this as of yet, but we are working hard, and we will let you know when we have made further progress. That will be all for now. Thank you.'

Some of the press moved forwards, a few of them starting to ask further questions, but DC Hardman stepped in, and most of them retreated, knowing they weren't going to get anywhere past the burly-looking detective. He managed to safely shepherd Superintendent Stone, Walker, and DC Briggs back inside Blackpool Police HQ, which was nice and quiet by comparison, the large glass panels of the outer shell of the building doing their job and insulating the noise.

Superintendent Stone nodded and got on her way, just like last time, quickly disappearing upstairs, perhaps needing a moment to herself, while Walker approached the woman manning the front desk. It was Reception Officer Kate Maloney again, the same woman who'd been there when they first arrived.

'Officer Maloney,' said Walker.

'Kate. Remember?' she said, smiling, speaking with the same friendly tone that she had earlier. 'How'd it go?'

'Kate. What do we have waiting for us up there?' asked Walker.

She looked down at some documents in front of her. 'Quite a bit, actually,' she said. 'We have seven arrests connected with

CHAPTER TWENTY-ONE

the events of last night, and...'

'And what?' asked Walker.

'And... you're not going to believe this: one of them just came in here claiming to be the killer of Anthony Singelmann and Michael Tracy, and the founder of the Kindness Matters Movement,' she said. 'That one turned up here of his own accord, literally just now, while you were talking to the press. He wasn't brought in by one of our lot. We're holding him for you, in one of the cells.'

'I see,' said Walker, his first thought being that this man might be an imposter, but then some hope flooded in, chasing that thought: the idea that this thing might be all over, that they might have their man. 'Have any of the others been interviewed yet?'

'I believe so,' said Kate. 'The Counterterrorism Unit have been in here, and the Police Support Commander who was in charge the night of the riots. It's all coming and going today. Everyone's getting involved. But I've been notified by the CTU that you and DC Briggs, or anyone else from your investigative team, are only authorised to interview this man who claims to have killed Anthony Singelmann and Michael Tracy.

'Roger that. What's the name of this man then?' asked Walker.

Kate looked down at some documents on her desk, found the relevant one.

'The name he gave us is Jonny Scawthorn,' she said. 'ID checks out.'

Walker turned slightly, found DCs Briggs and Hardman looking over his shoulder.

'We got something, Chief?' asked DC Briggs.

'It seems so,' said Walker. 'Come on.'

CHAPTER TWENTY-TWO

'Why are you here, Mr Scawthorn?' asked Walker, DC Briggs sat beside him, cradling a steaming cup of milky PG Tips tea. The events of the previous night, and the investigation in general, were starting to take its toll on all of them.

'I already told you. I'm The Defender,' he said. 'I started the Kindness Matters Movement. I'm turning myself in.'

'And the cash that was thrown off the Blackpool Tower this morning?' asked Walker. 'Was that you too?'

'Made someone do it,' he said. 'Some Polish guy.'

Walker sat up a little straighter. He wasn't just some nut job after all—at least, not a nut job who knew absolutely nothing: he knew about Aleksander. But that didn't mean he was who he said. 'Do you know his name?' he asked, probing further.

'Aleksander, something. Jenniski?' said Jonny.

'Janowski,' corrected Walker. 'Aleksander Janowski.'

Jonny looked at Walker, right in the eyes, without hesitation. He was calm, confident, unafraid. 'Well, it seems you know better than me, so why are you asking?'

'We're just trying to get all the facts straight, Mr Scawthorn. We're going to need to put you in a line up, have Mr Janowski identify you,' said Walker. Jonny was a large bloke, but not quite as big as Walker would have expected The Defender to be. Still, he looked strong enough, and it was definitely possible that he could have pushed Anthony Singelmann over the Blackpool Tower Buildings and hauled Michael Tracy up on that rope on the Promenade. It wasn't impossible—some people's muscles were more efficient, could do more with less.

'Do whatever you have to,' said Jonny. 'I just want this all over with now. It's done.'

'Jonny. If what you're saying is true, why did you incite violence in the town, and then give money to people? Did you feel guilty afterwards?' asked Walker. 'Because people have died?' He instantly regretted this line of questioning because he was leading the interviewee—a rookie mistake—but it was too late; he'd just have to go with it.

Jonny seemed to clam up with that, wrestling with something.

DC Briggs leaned forward in her seat, put her cup of tea down. 'It's okay, Jonny. You came this far. Just tell Detective Walker what he needs to know, and then this can all be over.'

Jonny smiled. 'Let's hope so,' he said. 'I threw the money off the Blackpool Tower so people would have some motivation to stop, that's all. It went too far. People were using the movement to actually be unkind to each other, to use it as an excuse for violence, rather than to stop it. That's not what the movement is all about. It was supposed to bring peace. The money is simply meant to encourage people to be nicer, that's all, to motivate them.'

'And where did you get this money from, Jonny? That was a *lot* of cash,' said Walker.

'That's my business,' he said.

CHAPTER TWENTY-TWO

'Well, now it's our business too, I'm afraid,' said Walker. 'Where did you get it?'

Jonny shook his head. 'That I can't tell you, Mr Walker. I have to protect my source. It was an anonymous donation.'

Walker breathed a heavy sigh, knowing they now had another important entry to log in their action book.

'We're going to look into this further, Jonny—much further. We'll delve into every bit of your business. By the time we've finished, we'll know everything about you: what you eat for breakfast, when you lost your virginity, what time you have sodding bowel movements every day, the lot. Are you sure you don't want to save us some time, tell us what we need to know?' asked Walker.

'All you need to know is this is all over now, and I'm responsible,' said Jonny. 'I'm turning myself in, confessing.'

Walker leaned forward over the desk, on his elbows, staring at Jonny. 'Okay, let's get down to business. Start at the beginning, Jonny. Talk me through the first murder, every detail.'

'I've nothing much to say about it, other than he had it coming,' said Jonny.

'Well, we're going to need a little more than that,' said Walker. He looked at DC Briggs.

'We need the details, Jonny,' was all she said, but she said it better than Walker, calmer, softer, friendlier.

'Look, Anthony Singelmann—I didn't know he was called that then, but I do now—he was a real piece of work. I pushed him, off the Tower Buildings. He hurt some girl, then pissed off the bloody roof. He had it coming.'

Walker raised an eyebrow, looked at DC Briggs, before turning his attention back to Jonny. 'And the second murder?'

'I know his name now too—Michael Tracy. Real scum, that one. A violent troublemaker. Would have probably raped some poor girl too if I'd not been there. I bashed him in good and proper,' said Jonny, his lip turning up in a snarl. 'The world is better off without him.'

'And the murder weapon?' asked Walker. 'For the second murder.'

Jonny hesitated. 'Grabbed some stick off the beach, some driftwood or something. Used that. Threw it back when I was done.'

He was lying. Forensics were convinced the blunt force trauma that caused the death of Michael Tracy was done by a snooker cue, one with a very distinctive branding. But he did seem to know a lot about the case—too much to not be involved at all.

'What about clothes? What were you wearing whilst carrying out these two attacks?' asked Walker, probing further, trying to get something to tie him to the two scenes— just in case what he'd thought was driftwood was an old, weather worn snooker cue lying on the beach.

'Burned 'em,' he said. 'Put them in the rubbish on bin day.'

'Are other people involved in this?' asked Walker.

Jonny shook his head. 'I never had any contact with anyone else personally—just what you see online, on that forum. They're copycats, that's all. They're using what I did to cause trouble.'

'And your motive? Why did you really kill these two men?' asked Walker.

'I told you—because they were scum, and the world will be a better place without them,' said Jonny. 'I used to be a bin man one time, a Waste Operative they called us. I guess I still

CHAPTER TWENTY-TWO

am, in a way.'

'And do you have anything else to add?' asked Walker. 'Can you provide us with any more details about these two murders?"

'I think I told you enough already,' said Jonny, looking like he probably said more than he'd intended. 'I did it. What more do you want? I'm not saying anything else. I want a lawyer.'

Walker looked at DC Briggs, who shrugged her shoulders, confirming that they'd probably now come to a dead end on this one for the time being. They'd run some background checks on him, see what they could turn up. 'We'll talk to you again soon, Jonny. In the meantime, if you can think of anything we might need to know, please call one of the staff, and I'll be right down here,' he said.

Now Jonny leaned forward, put his arms on the table and rested his head on them, closing his eyes.

'Let's go,' said Walker. 'Take him back to the holding cell.'

DC Briggs nodded. 'Will do,' she said. 'Come on Mr Scawthorn. Let's be having you.'

CHAPTER TWENTY-THREE

With several days having now gone by, Walker and his team had been able to recharge, somewhat, as there'd been no further violence or incidents concerning the Kindness Matters Movement in the interim—not that they knew of, anyhow. Things had certainly calmed down some in Blackpool, and they'd all had time to take stock, go over everything they had—which was a lot—and start to analyse all that data. There had been some disappointments along the way—Blackpool's CCTV Control Centre had surprisingly turned up nothing of use, despite all that money invested in the facility. But, despite this setback, Walker still felt they were making some tentative progress, although there was still some way to go yet.

After Jonny Scawthorn's confession to the murders of Anthony Singelmann and Michael Tracy, they'd got permission to hold him for ninety-six hours— as these were exceptional circumstances—so they could run extensive background checks on him. And these checks had turned up even more than Walker had hoped. What they'd found was that Jonny's sister, one Samantha Taylor, had been involved in a rape case that had gone to court, and a couple of years later, she'd committed suicide. Her marital name—*Taylor*—had

CHAPTER TWENTY-THREE

jumped right out at Walker: that had been the surname of the journalist from the Blackpool Gazette, the one who kept turning up at all the press conferences. He'd been her bloody husband, Jonny's brother-in-law of all things. It seemed too much of a coincidence.

The problem was that Jonny's claims of bludgeoning Michael Tracy to death with a piece of driftwood did not add up—they knew the death blow had come from a snooker cue with the "Thurston and Co" branding on it. So, while he knew things he certainly shouldn't, which made him a very prominent person of interest, he didn't know everything, and that probably meant someone else did the killing—unless he'd mistaken an old snooker cue lying on the beach for a piece of driftwood, which seemed unlikely. It wouldn't be the first time some lunatic had claimed to be a killer when they weren't, though, and it wouldn't be the last; the world, Walker thought, was a funny old place. This seemed the more likely scenario, then, as things stood—that he *was* such an imposter. He wondered whether Jonny might be protecting someone, or whether he just wanted to claim the killings as his own, like a trophy, like a badge of honour. He wasn't sure yet—wasn't sure about anything—had only his policing instincts to go on. And these instincts were telling him to look deeper.

They were back in the Incident Room now—Walker, DCs Briggs and Hardman, and DI Hogarth—going over things together, when DC Ainscough—the only member of their team who'd not been in the room—entered. He was carrying a pile of newspapers, at least twenty or thirty of them. Walker had sent him out on a mission to get them. He had a hunch.

'You got *all* of them?' asked Walker, raising an eyebrow to make sure he'd followed his instructions to get every story from every publication.

DC Ainscough dropped the pile on Walker's desk and started to spread them out. 'I did,' he said. 'Been all over to get these. I even drove to Fleetwood for the Fleetwood Weekly News.' He rummaged through the newspapers and found the one he was talking about. 'This one,' he added, pointing to it. 'It's big news, local and national.'

Walker started to dish them out to the team, a few each, on desks that were still laid out for a U-shaped seating plan, an arrangement they'd kept, encouraging more discussion for the case.

'Start reading, folks,' he said. 'Look through these reports with an eagle eye. Try to find any information about the crimes that shouldn't be public knowledge.' His hunch was they'd all come up blank except for the ones he kept to read for himself: the Gazette articles by Phillip Taylor—the brother-in-law of Jonny Scawthorn, the man who claimed to be this Defender character and killer of Anthony Singelmann and Michael Tracy.

Walker had been mentally counting the newspapers while dishing them out. 'Thirty-two,' he said. 'We have thirty-two newspaper stories about the Kindness Matters Movement and the murders that took place. Let's get reading. See if you can spot anything, any detail that shouldn't be in the public domain. Go.'

Walker came across the article in The Guardian first—which he also had in his pile as he wanted to see what the nationals were saying—the one written by Laura Cooper, the journalist who'd asked him about the nature of the Kindness Matters Movement at the press conference. He picked it up.

CHAPTER TWENTY-THREE

The story had made the front page. The headline: "Blackpool Terror".

'Short and to the point,' he muttered.

'She certainly was,' said DC Hardman, who was sat next to him, smirking—seemingly his attempt at a joke.

'The headline in this: not exactly creative, is it?' said Walker, feeling a little disappointed in the woman, who he'd initially liked, from their brief encounter. He mentally shook it off, remembering the pickle he'd got himself in by getting involved with that other female journalist, Emma Thompson, the one from Granada Reports. He didn't want that again. Plus, he still had some hope that he might eventually make things right with his wife, get back with her. Stranger things had happened—even in the past few days. He quickly scanned the article, handed it to DC Hardman. 'Here. You read this one', he said, putting it in the younger detective's pile. He wanted to get to the ones by Phillip Taylor, see if they could get anything on him before approaching, interviewing him. If he had anything to do with all this, any involvement at all, they needed some leverage first, some kind of evidence or oversight in his reports that might get him talking.

He picked up a copy of the Blackpool Gazette, an article by Taylor on the front page. This had a notably different headline to the one in The Guardian: "Be Kind: No More Violence", with a subheader stating, "People of Blackpool Urged for Peace in Wake of Bonfire Night Riots". That was interesting. He'd avoided the tawdry sensationalist focus on terror, focussed more on the message instead, talked about the aftermath, the money being thrown off the Tower, and calls for peace.

'The nationals want to make everything terror-related, don't they?' said DC Briggs. 'It sells newspapers, unfortunately.'

Walker looked up for a second. 'That it does,' he said, before going back to the Blackpool Gazette article. He began to read it out loud. Listen to this from the Blackpool Gazette, everyone.

Violence erupted in Blackpool last night, halting November Fifth celebrations with tragic results. Five people were killed, twenty-three seriously injured, and seventy-one cases of vandalism reported. The Kindness Matters Movement is under investigation for the chaos. Authorities urge calm, stating the situation is now under control. A mysterious £100,000 was thrown from Blackpool Tower, seemingly to promote peace.

This violence follows the recent murders of Anthony Singelmann and Michael Tracy. Singelmann, 42, Head Clown at Blackpool Tower Circus, fell from the Tower Buildings, dying shortly after. His brother, Nathan, expressed sorrow but noted Anthony's long-standing unhappiness. The funeral is set for November 19th.

Michael Tracy was found hanging from the Sea Wall, beaten and with high alcohol levels. Known for causing trouble, his death adds to the community's distress. Chief Detective Inspector Jonathan Walker, recently back from health issues, leads the investigation. The outcome remains uncertain, with some questioning the decision to assign DCI Walker to the case.

'Son of a bitch!' said Walker, getting annoyed at that last part. 'How'd they find out about my health? That's private and confidential. He has no bloody—'

CHAPTER TWENTY-THREE

'Take it easy, Chief,' said DC Briggs. 'Loads of people know you've been off work with health issues. Maybe someone mentioned it to a family member. Word travels. You know how it is. A good journalist could easily dig around, find something like this.'

'Well, bastards are gonna get me kicked off the case with talk like that,' he said.

'Oh, and who's going to take over? Mr Hardman here?' said DC Briggs, jokingly, clearly trying to defuse the situation. She succeeded. Walker shrugged it off, carried on reading.

The November fifth violence, a non-religious terrorist incident, will be investigated separately by Superintendent Lucy Stone of Blackpool Police HQ. While possibly linked to these two recent murders, different attackers are suspected as several November fifth deaths occurred simultaneously. Investigations are ongoing.

'Wait a sodding minute,' said Walker, pulling the newspaper article a bit closer to his face, scanning it, rereading a section that he'd just read, but this time just in his head. *Michael Tracy was found hanging from the Sea Wall, beaten and with high alcohol levels.* 'Did we release the bit about Tracy hanging from the Sea Wall and being drunk at the time of his death?' he asked. 'Didn't we cut him down before anybody saw?'

'I... believe that's right, Chief,' said DC Briggs, her eyes getting a little wider, telling him that he might have something. 'So, either someone's been saying something they shouldn't, or...'

'Or this guy— Phillip Taylor—the journalist, knows something that *he* shouldn't,' said Walker. 'And he's forgot that he shouldn't know, got careless.' It was the confirmation

Walker wanted. He was involved somehow, as was Jonny. Jonny Scawthorn wasn't just some online shit-stirrer who'd latched onto this vigilante and his cause without any real involvement in the actual killings. He knew too much. He'd most likely been helping somehow, assisting the killer. As for Taylor, he could be the group's pet journalist, someone sympathetic to their cause because of what happened to his wife, someone who might also have something to gain by having a big story to build his name on. The man would have to be psychopathically mercenary to only be out for personal gain though, so… maybe he was a true believer too? Someone they'd radicalised, perhaps, got deep into the head of. Walker would have to inform the counter-terrorist task force about this, let them do their job—see if these guys had any involvement with the riots too—while he went off to interview Taylor himself, see if he could link him to the two murders he was investigating.

'You're damned right he knows something he shouldn't!' said DC Briggs. 'Or maybe he wants us to know. House call?'

Walker looked at his watch. It was 10:47am on a Tuesday morning. 'Well, he's most likely at work now, so let's head down to the Blackpool Gazette, catch him there, see what he has to say for himself.'

DC Briggs smiled. 'You're gonna give him hell for doubting your credentials, aren't you, sir?' she said.

'I'm gonna give him hell if he has anything to do with all of this shit,' said Walker. 'End of.'

CHAPTER TWENTY-FOUR

Arriving at Avroe House, an immaculate new build and the home of the Blackpool Gazette, Walker and DC Briggs entered to be greeted by a secretary manning the front desk. A plump lady with rosy cheeks and glasses, she looked like she could handle herself.

'Can I help you?' she squealed. Her voice was high-pitched, a bit annoying, but somehow friendly.

'Yes. I'm DCI Walker of the Lancashire Constabulary, here with my colleague DC Briggs. We're looking to speak to a Phillip Taylor, one of your journalists here? It's a matter of some importance.'

'Phillip? Yes, of course. He's in the office now, going over his latest copy. Shall I ask him to come down?' asked the woman, who Walker could now see was called Phillis from her name badge.

'No. That's quite alright,' said Walker. 'Just point us in the right direction, if you wouldn't mind, Phillis.'

Phillis smiled. 'Phillip and Phillis. Go on. Make a joke. Everyone else does. People keep saying we're brother and sister.'

'And are you?' asked Walker.

'No. Course not,' she said, laughing, her voice going even

higher. 'He does have a brother-in-law, though. He's been here a couple of times, Jonny... something. Nice lad.'

'Would that be Jonny *Scawthorn* by any chance?' he asked.

'Scawthorn. Yes. I think that's it. He signed in here whenever he went up,' she said, taking an open journal from the front desk and flicking back a few pages. 'There. *Jonny Scawthorn*. Phillip Taylor's brother-in-law. Routine visit. Do you know him?'

'You might say that,' said Walker, looking at DC Briggs. 'You stay here, guard the entrance, just in case. I'll go up, talk to Phillip.'

'He's not in any trouble, is he?' asked Phillis. 'I do hope not. Phillip is such a nice man.'

'Are there any other exits in this building, Phillis?' asked Walker.

'Not really,' she said. 'Except for the fire doors. But I'd get a buzzer going off if anyone opened any of those, and a light would flash on my dashboard.' Walker furrowed his forehead, questioning the system they had, which sounded a little unusual. 'We are very fire safety conscious here,' she said. 'We have a lot of valuable documents to protect.'

'Phillis. Listen to me very carefully. If you can see that one of those fire doors has opened, you must tell DC Briggs immediately. Do you understand?' asked Walker.

'Yes,' said Phillis, suddenly seeming less confident, maybe a little afraid.

'Now, where is he?' asked Walker.

'On the second floor,' said Phillis. 'Go up the stairs, over there, turn left at the top, and then go right to the end. The furthest door at the end, labelled "Writer's Room", is where you should find him.'

CHAPTER TWENTY-FOUR

Walker nodded and started heading towards the stairs, but before he could reach them, Phillis said, 'Er, Detective Walker, I think we might have a problem.'

'What is it?' asked Walker, already guessing at what the problem might be.

Phillis grimaced. 'Just got a little buzz, and one of the lights on my dashboard has come on. It's one of the fire doors. Someone just opened it.'

CHAPTER TWENTY-FIVE

'God damn it!' said Walker. 'Let's go. You head around the left side of the building,' he said to DC Briggs. 'I'll go the other way. See if you can see him. Go!'

'Got it,' she said.

They exited the building and Walker headed one way, DC Briggs the other—just like he said. If Phillip Taylor got away now, things were going to get even more complicated. A manhunt was always tricky and could take time and significant resources. Sometimes, they never found who they were looking for, as Walker knew only too well. His last case in Chorley had seen the mastermind behind the crimes get away—one *Doctor Alfred Johansen*—one evil bastard, as far as Walker was concerned, who'd now skipped the country and got away, for the time being. He was damned if that was going to happen again.

They arrived at the open fire door in question roughly around the same time, with Walker and DC Briggs approaching a middle-aged man, stood there, smoking something. It wasn't him—they knew what Taylor looked like from the press conference, and this was someone else.

'Excuse me. Have you seen Phillip Taylor?' asked Walker.

The man suddenly saw them, flicked his rollie away like a

CHAPTER TWENTY-FIVE

schoolboy might to try to hide it before he was caught red handed.

'I was just...' said the man, a little sluggishly, eyeing Walker. 'Who are you again?'

Walker pointed to the ID card handing around his neck. 'DCI Walker, Lancashire Constabulary. Sir, have you seen Phillip Taylor?'

'What? It was just a rollie, for crying out—'

'Sir. We're not here about...' Walker smelled the marijuana now. So that was why the man was freaking out. 'Just tell us if you've seen Mr Taylor?'

'You mean Phil? He had nothing to do with this. I'm Graham Hopkins. We work together. I'm really—'

'Shit. He's still upstairs,' said Walker.

'Who is? Phil? No. Phil just left. Looked at his phone, said he had something urgent to do. It was him who suggested coming out here, to take a break,' he said, looking sheepish. He appeared a bit stoned, his brain probably not quite clicking into gear fast enough. Then he rolled his eyes, the realisation likely now hitting. 'Hey. Is Phil in trouble?'

'Do you know where he's parked?' asked Walker, but before Graham could answer, a car raced past—a red Ford Focus—giving him the answer, kicking up some dirt as the tyres squealed. He'd been parked out back somewhere, behind a skip full of rubbish, next to some bushes. The car hadn't been visible from their vantage point, not until it just flashed past them, that is.

Walker got up close to Graham, right in his face. 'Graham, was that Phillip Taylor's car?'

Graham reluctantly nodded, seeming a little scared. 'I'm sorry,' he said, but Walker wasn't interested in his misdemeanour. Their man was getting away. They had to get back to their car, get on his tail, and fast.

* * *

Walker pulled the pool car over outside a Subway Sandwich shop. 'Damn it. He must have gone the other way. We guessed wrong.' He had his arm on the back seat, already backing up onto the footpath, turning around. 'What's the other way? Promenade again?'

'Yeah, but. Oh no,' said DC Briggs, looking at a Google Map on her phone.

'What?' asked Walker.

'The airport. It looks like Blackpool Airport is that way too. I'm sorry, Chief. I should have… I'm not really familiar with this area.'

Walker banged on the steering wheel with his hand, not so much angry with his colleague, but because one of their main suspects was getting away, his frustration boiling over. 'Contact base and get them to call the airport. Make sure Phillip Taylor doesn't take a flight today. Make sure he doesn't go sodding anywhere.'

* * *

'Jonny. We know Phillip Taylor has something to do with all this. How's he involved?' asked Walker. He had Jonny

CHAPTER TWENTY-FIVE

Scawthorn back in an interview room, with all current available resources being dedicated toward bringing Phillip Taylor in. There wasn't much Walker could contribute to that search right now, not with regard to eyes on the ground, anyway. His time was better spent trying to find out where Taylor might be heading, and who else could be in on this thing. And for that, Jonny seemed key. After all, he had claimed to be the killer of Anthony Singelmann and Michael Tracy, and he'd known about Aleksander Janowski, the man who'd been manipulated into throwing all that cash off the Tower. He knew something. It was just a question of getting it out of him or finding the evidence they needed. He was also the brother-in-law of Phillip Taylor, the journalist who'd known some details about Michael Tracy's death, details he shouldn't have known. So, either Jonny had been giving his brother-in-law information about the two murders—information he may have got from the real killer—so Taylor could write about it, or... there was something more.

Jonny shook his head, screwing up his face. 'No.'

'*No*, what, Jonny?' asked Walker. 'We know he's a journalist. And we know you're related. Were you tipping him off, telling him what you or someone else was doing? Or was he involved in some other way? Are you covering for him?'

Walker wondered whether Taylor might have put Jonny up to forcing Janowski into throwing that money off the Tower for the sake of a big news story—to make a name for himself—and now he'd gone on the run knowing he was interfering with a murder investigation. But that was a *lot* of money, too much to throw away for the sake of a story, so he guessed there was more to it. Another possibility was that Taylor had orchestrated the money drop after panicking, not expecting the riots to be so bad, wanting to make amends for something, which would suggest he was somehow culpable or at least complicit in fomenting or instigating the riots. He could have been active on that Facebook group, agitating things to make the story bigger, then shitting himself when it really kicked off, leaving five people dead. Or perhaps Taylor could have been the initial spark for it all, the Defender himself, the serial murderer, and again he panicked when it all spiralled beyond what he'd intended. This final possibility seemed less likely, but it was still an idea that Walker had to pursue.

Jonny shook his head some more and then put his head in his hands.

'Jonny. We're going to find out what happened here eventually. We already ran some background checks, confirmed that Phillip Taylor is your brother-in-law. We'll catch up to him sooner or later. You might as well save us all some time, tell us what went on,' said Walker.

'He *was* my brother-in-law, you mean,' said Jonny, beginning to cry. 'And so what? That doesn't mean anything.'

DC Briggs was with them, as she usually was in key interviews. She leaned forward towards Jonny, offering some support. They didn't know if he was guilty of anything yet—despite his claims—and until it was proven otherwise, they had to treat him with respect.

'It's okay, Mr Scawthorn,' said DC Briggs, passing him a plastic cup full of water, and a box of tissues. He looked her in the eye for a split-second, seemed grateful for the warmth.

Walker waited until he'd calmed down some before he spoke again. 'What do you mean he *was* your brother-in-law, Jonny?'

Jonny took a deep breath. 'I mean my sister, Sammy, is…' He couldn't say it.

CHAPTER TWENTY-FIVE

'She's what?' asked Walker. He was aware his sister, Samantha, had died, committed suicide, from their background research, but he wanted to know exactly what Jonny meant—whether Phillip and Samantha might have filed for divorce prior to her death.

'She's dead,' said Jonny. 'She died.'

Now it was Walker's turn to lean forward. He felt this was a crucial part of the interview, and the investigation as a whole, but he didn't want to appear too eager, so he backed off a little, leaned back again.

'And… can you tell us a little more about that?' asked Walker.

'Why?' snapped Jonny. His sadness suddenly turning to anger. 'What has that got to do with anything?'

'Well, that's for us to decide,' said Walker. 'Several people have died, and two of those you claim have been murdered by yourself. So, we need to know exactly what drove you to this—your underlying motive. You said something about wanting to get rid of those who are rubbish, making the world a worse place. But there must be more to it than that, some underlying psychological imperative. Is it something to do with what happened to your sister?'

'And if you didn't kill those people, you need to tell us who did, Jonny,' added DC Briggs, stepping in as she saw fit. Walker trusted her enough by now to let her go with it when she felt something was worth pursuing. She had a way with people that Walker didn't, saw things he couldn't—she was sensitive, perceptive. So, with his experience, and her people skills and intuition, he thought they were starting to make a good team. 'And you have to tell us… even if that person *is* your brother-in-law. It's the right thing to do.'

'Was,' said Jonny. 'Sammy is not Phillip's wife anymore. How can she be if she's dead? So, he *was* my brother-in-law.'

This was not legally the case, of course. Sammy was still Phillip's wife, even if she was dead. But Jonny obviously felt strongly about it, so Walker left it at that.

'We get it,' said Walker. 'We understand.' He knew that any confession to the crimes could just as easily be retracted in court, claimed to have been given under duress. And without any proper evidence, the case could easily collapse. So, they needed a full picture of how exactly the crimes went down to get forensic and other corroborating evidence, make the case airtight. '

'Can you tell us how Samantha died?' asked Walker. There was no other way to ask such questions—or at least none that Walker knew. He had to be blunt, to the point, or he'd lose him.

'She… killed herself. In the bath. Took some pills, some whiskey. Phil found her there, when he got home from work, under the water.' Jonny was clearly still very grief-stricken. 'He called me and I went over, before they took her away. 'I can't get her face out of my head. It didn't even look like her. Not really.'

Walker took a quiet breath, gave Jonny some time. Some things couldn't be hurried, despite the urgency of the situation, and this seemed to be one of those times. He glanced at DC Briggs, just fleetingly, but enough to tell her to write all of this down. She got on it, immediately. This unspoken understanding they'd developed over a course of months working together was becoming invaluable to him.

'Okay, Jonny. Did the two men you claimed to have killed— Anthony Singelmann and Michael Tracy—have anything to do with your sister's death? Did they hurt her in some way, lead to her depression, anything like that?' asked Walker. He was taking a shot, trying to keep him talking, knowing he could be way off.

'Course not,' said Jonny. 'They were nobodies. Arseholes.'

'Look, we took DNA swabs and fingerprints from you, and we couldn't find anything at the crimes scenes, or on the bodies, that are a match to you,' said Walker. That wasn't completely unusual, of course. Taking a few precautions like wearing gloves and tight-fitting clothing could mitigate such evidence. They did find some DNA at the crime scenes, from various individuals, but nothing that matched Jonny or anyone in their database, and nothing that was a match to both crime scenes. That didn't mean Jonny didn't do it, but it did cast some significant doubt on what he was saying, so more probing was required. 'What exactly were you wearing when you carried out these crimes?'

'Just some old jeans, and a hoodie with a T-shirt underneath,' said Jonny. 'I told you; I got rid of 'em.'

'No gloves?' asked Walker.

'Oh... yeah. Some leather gloves. Sorry, forgot about those,' added Jonny, although it seemed to Walker he was just making it up at this point. He'd told them the murder weapon was a random piece of driftwood, but they knew it wasn't. The death blow was conclusively from a snooker cue butt end. They still had nothing tangible to link him to the crimes.

'When we find your brother-in-law, Phillip, we're going to test him too, see if he's a match for anything. If you're protecting him, you need to tell us.'

Jonny looked down. 'He said that some horrid lady was unkind to Sammy, the day before she killed herself. Some woman called her "a stupid bitch" or something, for no reason, when she was just out shopping. She already suffered with depression. Had for years. But that was the last straw. I think she couldn't take the way people are with each other anymore. She just wanted people to be kinder.'

It was all starting to stack up a little bit now, at least the motive side of things. Phillip's wife had killed herself, had told him it was because people were no longer kind enough to each other, and she couldn't live in a world like that. So, either him, or Jonny, or both, had hatched a plan to go on some kind of mission to clean things up, make Blackpool a better, safer place. They were claiming it was all about kindness and compassion, of course, but this was a lie. They hadn't been corrupted in pursuit of a worthy aim at all. No, it was about bloodthirsty rage for moral transgressions: it was about punishment. They were on a moral crusade, driven by anger and hatred—even if they didn't realise it themselves. And they'd gone too far, had started killing people. Perhaps they thought they were some kind of anti-heroes, taking out the trash. But once people start to see others as trash to be taken out, Walker thought, it's not kindness they're after, but moral purity. And this was a slippery slope to all manner of crusades and purges and pogroms, eradicating whatever the glorious leader proclaimed as "degenerate". It was just plain wrong. They were just murderers at the end of the day. It wasn't their place to judge how people acted, or to punish people for their crimes, no matter how much pain they were in.

'Jonny. The weapon you claimed to have killed Michael Tracy with does not match what we believe dealt the death blow. We need to know. Did you really kill those two men?'

CHAPTER TWENTY-FIVE

asked Walker.

Jonny smiled a pained smile and nodded his head.

'For the record, the interviewee has just nodded their head to indicate that they did murder Anthony Singelmann and Michael Tracy. Jonny, did your brother-in-law, Phillip Taylor, have anything to do with the deaths of these men, and the subsequent November fifth riots and murders?'

'Phillip is completely innocent. He simply wrote about the murders and the riots, that's all. I gave him some anonymous tip offs, so he could be there first, ahead of all the other journalists. I gave him information that nobody else could know,' said Jonny. 'I'm sorry. I didn't want to implicate him.'

'What information?' asked Walker. 'What did you tell him.'

'Just… some details,' said Jonny. 'I don't really remember now.'

That made some sense—provided one possible explanation of how Phillip knew that Michael Tracy had been hanging from the promenade. But it didn't explain why Phillip Taylor was running. There was something more, either that Jonny wasn't telling them, or that he didn't know about himself.

'Is there anything else, Jonny?' asked Walker. 'You should know, your brother-in-law is running. There's a wide scale search in operation to bring him in. He's in potential danger if he doesn't give himself up. If you want to help him, to protect him, then you need to help us find him.'

Jonny shook his head, grimaced. 'He's running because it was him who gave me the money. Two hundred grand. Sold his house after Sam died, said he couldn't look at that bathtub anymore. He got a much smaller place, gave the rest to me, said it was Sam's half and was what she'd have wanted—to give me a new start. He gave it to me in cash, just in case I didn't want to pay tax on it or something. He probably just thinks this large cash withdrawal makes him look guilty. Or he's put two and two together and knows it's me, freaked out, didn't know what to do. Maybe he wants to talk to me first? He doesn't know I'm here yet, does he?'

'Do you know where he might have gone, Jonny?' asked Walker. 'It's important. If what you say is true, we need to verify that, get him safe.'

Jonny shook his head. 'I'm sorry. I have no idea. Except maybe my place.'

They'd already had a team of CSIs and PCs thoroughly search Jonny's home, still had a couple of PCs stationed there watching, just in case. Taylor hadn't been there. Walker felt sorry for Jonny, in a way, what happened to his sister and all, but he was still a criminal. At the very least, he'd wasted police time and could be charged with perverting the course of justice—a serious offence carrying a maximum penalty of seven years imprisonment—and at worst he was a serial killer like he claimed. The world might have chewed him up and spat him out, just like it did with so many, Walker included. But it's how you react to such adversity that's important, he thought, and this was not the way.

'Mr Scawthorn, I'm not formally charging you just yet as we still have no actual evidence that you committed these crimes, other than your say so—no murder weapon and no forensic evidence. Nothing. However, if we find firm evidence that you *didn't* commit these crimes, you will be charged with wasting police time and perverting the course of justice, which potentially carries with it a significant prison sentence. Is that clear?' asked Walker.

Jonny nodded.

CHAPTER TWENTY-FIVE

'Do you have anything else to add?' said Walker. Jonny shook his head. They'd now take this to the CPS, try to get the relevant paperwork to search Phillip Taylor's residence as well. They were now on an evidence-finding mission to verify if what Jonny had claimed was true or not.

'Mr Scawthorn, are you sure you have nothing else to say?' asked Walker again, probing one last time.

'People should be kinder to each other,' said Jonny, stubbornly.

'Well that I probably agree with,' said Walker. 'But this has not been the way to convince them. Not the way at all. One way or another, Mr Scawthorn, whether you're telling the truth or not, you're going to prison for a very long time.'

Jonny smiled, like he was trying to hide it, but couldn't. Walker didn't quite know what to make of that, but it didn't change anything, not a jot. He was going down. They'd find what they needed, in time. Walker was sure of it.

CHAPTER TWENTY-SIX

Taylor stood at the glass-fronted enclosure of the orangutan section at Blackpool Zoo. One of the orangutans had come right up to the glass and was kissing a little boy, who was sat in a wheelchair. It kissed him right on the lips—only the glass separating them. The boy was delighted, and the onlookers clapped. It was a lovely moment. These beasts could be so gentle, so loving, he thought, but also so vicious and destructive too. In this sense, they were so much like their human counterparts.

Sam had loved coming here, watching the animals. She'd said they were well looked after, had good lives at the zoo, and she'd known something about it too—she once worked over at Knowsley Safari Park, in Prescot near Liverpool, when she'd been younger, had a degree in Zoology and everything. But she hadn't done anything like that in years, hadn't been able to hold down a proper job because of her depression. Ironically, not working in such environments had probably only served to make her mental health worse. Being around animals seemed to calm her, helped her find peace, took her outside herself somehow. It had worked for her, to a point—at least for a short time. So, he'd brought her here sometimes, to try to help, until she did what she did, that was… that day.

CHAPTER TWENTY-SIX

He still hadn't completely forgiven her for it. He missed her terribly, every hour of every day. But he knew she must have been in a lot of pain to do what she did. And he knew why, God damn it, and it was up to him to do something about it. It made his blood boil and his heart weep, all at the same time. His emotions were all stretched and pulled in different directions, like a squishy ball being fought over by some sugar-fuelled children. He hoped he might finally find some small peace when this was all over, when he did what he was planning, and if he didn't... well, he figured he could always join her, do something similar—end it.

When the orangutan he'd been watching was finished with kissing the little boy, its eyes all big and soft, it went further back in, grabbed some kind of bottle, perhaps a container with some food inside, just before another of the orangutans got to it—a younger looking male, by the looks of it. A brief fight broke out between the two of them; they struck each other with a warning blow, before the younger male backed off, taking the worst of it. The blow would probably have been enough to seriously injure a human, possibly kill them, even. But the beast appeared strong enough to take it, and simply ambled off, disgruntled, and started climbing on some of the installations the zookeepers had made for them. The previously kissy victor just chewed on the bottle thing, sticking its tongue inside, while eyeing its challenger some more.

Taylor had seen enough, came back outside, found a bench to sit on, choosing one tucked away so he could get some distance from the crowds. At least it had stopped spitting with rain. He took his Apple MacBook Pro laptop out from his brown leather satchel, put it on his lap, and opened it up. He connected the laptop to his iPhone service using the Bluetooth function, as he always did when he was out and about so he had an Internet connection on the computer as well. Then he opened up a Microsoft Word document. Other journalists preferred more contemporary writing software like Evernote or Scrivener, but Phil was old school. He'd always used Word.

The document he opened up was named "For Detective Walker.doc", and the headline: "Blackpool DCI Halts Kindness Matters Movement: Should He Stay?". It was an article he'd prepared as an insurance policy, should the detective become a problem—as he currently was. He'd rooted into Walker's past, gone deep. Following digital trails was one of his specialities, as was coding and hacking. He knew how to enter virtual places he shouldn't be in—something he'd learned as a teen. He had a way with computers, for sure. And now he was prepared to break the law to find what he wanted.

The detective had obviously hidden what he'd found well, had not wanted any of it to get out in the open. But it would— *be out in the open*—if he carried on. He went through the article one more time, proofreading for any grammatical or spelling errors, using Grammarly, a virtual typing assistant he found useful, to double-check. It read:

As the search continues for the killers of Anthony Singelmann and Michael Tracy, it has come to light that DCI Jonathan Walker, aged 53, currently leading the case, has recently endured two lengthy hospital stays for a rare recurrent form of meningitis and associated encephalitis, which could relapse at any time, causing headaches, auditory and visual hallucinations, fatigue,

CHAPTER TWENTY-SIX

and emotional problems. When asked to comment on this, one prominent member of Blackpool Council, who wishes to remain anonymous, questioned whether DCI Walker is the most suitable person for this job moving forward, due to these on-going health issues, along with further question marks surrounding the longstanding DCI.

The well-known detective, who has undergone a number of disciplinary hearings during his three-decade long career, also has a chequered past. As a teenager, he was cautioned for breaking and entering, and was known to drink heavily and take recreational drugs during this time—perhaps a result of the little-known death of his younger sister just a few years earlier, an Amanda Morris, who was brutally raped and murdered in Standish in 1987. The then youthful Jonathan Morris later changed his surname to "Walker", after his mother remarried following his father's death—a name that he still uses, possibly to cover his former identity. Amanda Morris's killer was never found, and it can be speculated that Walker may have begun a career in policing in order to try and find her killer himself.

Recently though, there have also been some worrying issues with DCI Walker being accused of violence in the field, which raises questions about his mental stability. One person of interest in a previous case, a Darren Hawley from Rufford, stated that: "When he wrongly arrested me, he kicked the shit out of me, made me piss myself. Then later, when he was searching my place, he pinned me up against a wall, strangled me. I couldn't breathe. It was awful. One of the neighbours saw everything. The man's a maniac. I was just grieving for my son!" Hawley has since been cleared of any crime and emerged as an innocent party.

Professor Tim Chapman, who teaches Criminology at Salford University—a leading light in the campaign against police bru-

tality, and the author of "Echoes of Injustice: Police Brutality in Modern Britain"—has urged that in light of these findings, the Lancashire Constabulary should action an internal investigation in due course into the suitability of DCI Walker to maintain his current position and head the aforementioned case. While every homicide investigation is crucially important so that the offender can be caught and punished and no more people get hurt, this current case has the added importance of being intertwined with the large-scale November fifth riots and killings in Blackpool, which is a separate investigation being headed by Superintendent Lucy Stone. "In such a situation," said Professor Chapman, Superintendent Stone "should really be assessing the suitability of the DCI involved in the case"—a case and outcome that is fast becoming increasingly important to the people of Blackpool. When interviewed, many residents of Blackpool also expressed wishes that, in light of recent events, regardless of the outcomes of these cases, the people of Blackpool will resolve to be kinder to each other, so that their precious seaside town can be a better place to live once more.

Article by Phillip Taylor, The Blackpool Gazette.
P.Taylor@BlackpoolGazette.com

Taylor had tried to get in Walker's head a bit, fill in the blanks where need be. But he thought he had him. This was a man who was clearly haunted by his sister's death, who more than likely joined the force to pursue her killer, and who'd do anything to carry on doing that. He was a livewire who cut a few corners now and again, got a bit rough. It wasn't exactly Taylor's best work, and there might be some issues with possible defamation to address if the Editor-In-Chief caught sight of it—it might need some considerable editing if it went to publication—but that didn't matter. The point was to send a message to this DCI, that his life would be turned upside down if he pursued this any longer. He needed him off the case—or, at least, he needed him distracted while he did what he needed to do. It would be beautiful: all that vile hatred, all the scum of society, all destroyed at once. But he needed time to put his plan into action, and the way things were going, he wouldn't have that time.

He attached the document to an email, copy and pasted DCI Walker's email address into it, and then added the subject "Urgent Information Attached", before pressing send.

That should do it, he thought. *That should distract you enough to buy me some time, do what I need to do. Good luck, Detective.*

CHAPTER TWENTY-SEVEN

Freddie Ward settled in for the night, turned his light off. He was lucky enough to be housed in a one-man unit and was even more fortunate to be serving his sentence at HMP Kirkham, an open prison just south and east of Blackpool—a prison holding a tad over six-hundred men in twenty-four residential buildings. He'd served more than four of his seven-year sentence for the supply of a Class-A drug—namely his drug of choice, heroin, but also some cocaine too. He'd confessed to dealing a significant amount, and it wasn't his first offence. So, he'd been handed the maximum possible penalty. But that wasn't his biggest regret. His biggest regret was dragging his boyfriend, Jonny, and his family into all this.

As a result of his good behaviour while inside, though, he'd be out on probation soon—he'd got a release date and everything. Over the past few years, he'd missed Jonny something rotten, more than he'd expected, even after all this time. *Johnny Rotten* he'd used to call him. That was the nickname of John Lydon, the former singer of punk rock band the Sex Pistols. It was a joke they'd often made together, with Freddie calling Jonny 'rotten', and Jonny then asking if he wanted him to get his sex pistol out. It was crude, sure—not for everyone—but it was a private joke, and one they'd

CHAPTER TWENTY-SEVEN

enjoyed immensely. But they wouldn't be joking anymore. Not after what happened. It was all so terribly messed up. It was unfixable.

His single dad had never accepted he was gay, tortured him about it. He was old-fashioned, small-minded. So, when he'd finally been brave enough to introduce him to Jonny, in a stupid, deluded attempt to win him over, his dad had predictably gone mad—kicked Jonny out, called him all sorts, then proceeded to knock Freddie around, said he was beating some sense into him, trying to help him; said he was just confused, that his hormones were playing up, or some shite. He was in his twenties, for God's sake. It didn't even make any goddamned sense. He told his old man to go screw himself, of course, gave him the finger and everything, spat his own blood back at him in defiance. He didn't dare hit him back though: his dad was much bigger and stronger. It was after that when Freddie really started hitting the drugs hard. Heroin took all those bad feelings away, all that pain and anger. Everything spiralled out of control so quickly. Before he knew it, he was working as a courier for this shady, dangerous-looking lot in exchange for smack, agreed to store a brick for one of 'em. He'd stashed it in the room Jonny was sleeping in at Sam's house; but one night, Freddie had been off his head, went looking for Jonny at Sam's place, and this scary guy everyone called Razor turned up. He'd led him right there. The guy forced his way inside, kicked the door in—where there was only Sam, home alone, before they'd turned up—found the gear, then accused Freddie of nicking it. He then proceeded to beat Freddie up even worse than his dad had, broke his sodding nose, said he was a just a stupid junky poof and he was gonna show him and his boyfriend's poncy family what was what; before making him watch, knife at the ready, while he beat and raped Sammy right in front of him. If only his mum hadn't died when he'd been in his early teens, none of it might have happened. He'd gone down the wrong path, somehow, was a complete mess, got in above his head. While it was all happening, it was like he was outside himself—and not just because of the drugs—he just watched, psychologically detached, unable to do anything to stop it. He was so sorry to her afterwards—Sammy—but apologies didn't help one jot. It had been all his fault, after all.

When it was all over and Razor left, she'd told the police everything. She had to. Freddie had become dangerous to be around. So, he'd stayed there at the house and confessed to everything; all except who the drugs had been off, and the name of the guy who'd come. They'd kill him if he said anything—probably Sam and Jonny too, so he just had to take it on the chin, man up. He actually wanted to be punished too, to be locked up somewhere, to get off the drugs. Jonny hadn't spoken to him since though—at least not face-to-face—and why should he? There was no other way of putting it: Freddie had hidden drugs in his sister's home—a *lot* of drugs—and got her goddamned raped. There was no getting away from that. It was unforgivable, even if he had been smacked off his head.

The only light at the end of the tunnel—apart from hearing on the grapevine that Razor had been killed shortly after in a gang attack—was that the judge had sent him to an open prison due to 'mitigating circumstances', as they'd called it, what with him being an addict and doing what he did to get high. Seven years was still a long time, but he couldn't argue he didn't deserve it. Especially in light of what happened

CHAPTER TWENTY-SEVEN

afterwards. That was even worse: Sammy was *dead*. She'd killed herself two years later. He'd got a hateful letter from Jonny shortly afterwards, telling him in no uncertain terms that he was to blame, that he should kill himself too. He almost had as well. Or tried to, at least. But he'd changed his mind at the last minute, realised he was a victim too, that they were all suffering. He'd found God while in prison, you see, was a changed man. He was seeing things much more clearly now he wasn't on the drugs, perhaps for the first time in his life, knew that God loved him—loved all of them—no matter what. He'd just made some mistakes, that's all. He was lost, but God was showing him the way now, lighting the path. It was all much clearer. He was being tested.

He'd eventually managed to forgive himself for what he'd done, which was massive. And, in the end, nobody really knew why Sammy had killed herself. It's not like she'd done it right after that awful incident. Maybe she'd been depressed all along, he thought. Or maybe it was something else. No-one really knew, nobody except for God, that is.

Freddie lay down on his single bed, took a deep breath, and closed his eyes. This time next week, he'd be out—not completely free, perhaps, but he'd be back out there, amongst free people. And if he behaved himself, got on the straight and narrow, and stayed there, he'd serve out the rest of his sentence on probation, and then he could move away, start fresh somewhere. He could become a whole other person, do better, redeem himself somehow. Who knows, he thought, it might even be all okay one day.

CHAPTER TWENTY-EIGHT

Walker and DC Briggs headed to the home of Jonny Scawthorn to see if they might spot anything their team could have missed. They hadn't been able to get a warrant to search Phillip Taylor's residence yet, despite his connection to Jonny and Sam, and him showing himself privy to information about the killings he shouldn't be. The CPS had initially said it was too circumstantial to get a search warrant, that he might just have been tipped off. Then DI Hogarth had confirmed the sale of Phillip Taylor's house, which was easy enough to verify, apparently, money from which Jonny claimed was used to throw off the Tower. But his superiors had been wary of the optics of raiding a journalist's house, even with Phillip seemingly taking flight to avoid questioning, and wanted them to back off until they got a bit more, made it watertight.

DC Briggs was in the driving seat this time, with them taking turns these days so one of them could always take a little break or work on whatever needed working on remotely.

Walker's phone *pinged* and he checked it. 'Never should have let you set this thing up for email alerts,' he said. 'It's getting bloody annoying. Most of it is junk.'

DC Briggs glanced at him, before putting her eyes back on

the road. 'But not all of it, eh?'

She was right. It wasn't junk this time. He was in his inbox now in the Outlook app. The message was from Phillip Taylor.

'Pull over,' he said. DC Briggs did as asked and he read through the message without saying a word.

'Well, what is it?' asked DC Briggs after patiently waiting for thirty seconds or so.

The bastard had tried to do a hatchet job on him, but Walker's initial thought was it might actually be a good thing. The guy had got desperate, incriminated himself of being seriously invested in Walker backing off with this. He'd been digging around for some dirt on him to use as leverage. He knew everything, about Walker's sister, about how he'd got a little rough with some of the suspects from past cases. And although not explicitly stated, it was clear that if he didn't back off on the current investigation, Taylor was going to publish the article, try to discredit everything about him, make his personal tragedies a morbid public spectacle. But it wouldn't work. This would hang the guy out to dry on the stand. If he was just some random journalist, what he had *might* be enough to create a public shitstorm that would put pressure on Walker's superiors to take him off the case. But he was a suspect with direct ties to the confessed killer, a suspect who was himself on the run. This warning shot just made him look guilty as hell. In his opinion, it was an ill-advised attempt that smacked of desperation. But he needed his colleague to confirm his thoughts. He felt he could trust DC Briggs now, felt he could talk to her, about almost anything, and he increasingly valued her opinion.

'It's from Phillip Taylor,' he said.

'Okay,' said DC Briggs, opening her hands for a second, taking them off the steering wheel, urging him to go on.

Walker plucked a couple of eyebrow hairs out with his fingers—a habit he sometimes had whenever he was getting highly strung. He leaned across to her, speaking softly. 'There's a little problem, but I think it might not be a problem at all. I think it might help us, with the case, I mean.'

'Go on,' she said, now looking a bit worried.

Walker licked his lips. Taylor had still got to him a little, finding what he had. His mouth was exceptionally dry. 'He knows things about me. He's done his research, found things that no journalist ever has.'

'Okay,' she said. 'Like what? It must be something important if we're sat here instead of searching Jonny's Scawthorn's house.'

Walker went on. 'Look, remember what I told you about my sister?' He'd not told her everything about what happened to his kid sister, Mandy, or how he'd chased every single tiny lead he had over the years. He'd certainly not told her how he was completely obsessed with finding her murderer, how that was why he'd gone into policing in the first place, or how he'd separated from his wife because she'd had enough of his obsession and his family's neglect, this single-minded focus. But he had explained his sister had been killed when he was a teenager, and that her murderer had never been found.

'Of course I remember what happened to your sister,' she said. 'It was heart-breaking. What about it?'

'He knows all about it. God knows how he found out. There aren't many people who know—just my wife, you, Ron, a few others, like yourself,' he said.

'Ron?'

CHAPTER TWENTY-EIGHT

'Superintendent Hughes,' said Walker. 'He knows as well.'

'Oh. So... what of it, Chief? I know you don't want more people knowing, but what if they do? Everyone will understand,' said DC Briggs, but she didn't know the half of it yet. He was just getting started.

'He knows about my illness too. Makes it sound like I'm not fit for duty,' said Walker.

'But we all know you *are* fit for duty,' said DC Briggs. 'We all get ill from time to time. You've recovered. He has nothing. The court won't have any issue if we follow protocol. Hey, you have recovered, haven't you?'

Walker still got bad headaches, dizziness, brain fog, and some fatigue, but he played it down, didn't tell anyone about it.

'Course,' he said, lying. He hadn't even told the doctors. They were just long-term side effects, nothing he couldn't handle. Nobody needed to know. 'So, what do you think?'

'I think this email makes him look guilty as hell,' said DC Briggs. 'And I think we can use it. He's desperate. He's made a big mistake.'

'That's what I thought too,' said Walker, glad to have his idea confirmed.

'He might have helped kill those people. Or he might just be trying to protect his brother-in-law. Or there could even be something else. But whatever it is, he's involved somehow, he's interfering with a criminal investigation, and we need to bring him in,' she said. 'We need to search his place.'

'Well, they should give us that damn search warrant now, at least, after this,' said Walker. 'It's a clear attempt at blackmail in my view, trying to force us to back off. I'll run it by Superintendent Stone, get it back with the CPS. He's guilty as sin. If we don't have enough to connect him to the murders, we can certainly bring him in for blackmail and extortion now, and for interfering with a criminal investigation, like you said.'

'Is there anything else I should know?' asked DC Briggs. Walker reluctantly nodded his head, and she took a deep breath. 'What is it?'

'Remember the suspect on the Rufford case, the drunk—Darren Hawley?' asked Walker.

'How could I forget?' said DC Briggs.

'Well, I may have got a little rough with him at one point. We were desperate to find that girl, Emily, remember? I had to push him, to get information,' said Walker.

'So, you just *pushed* him?' asked DC Briggs. 'That's it?'

Walker screwed his nose up. 'Maybe a bit more than that. Quite a bit, actually. But he has been exaggerating, and we did have a girl's life to save.'

'I see. And is there any possibility that anyone else saw this, to corroborate his story?' asked DC Briggs.

'There was a neighbour knocking around. They might have seen something,' said Walker. 'Maybe. But there was no problem until Taylor started looking for dirt on me.'

'Then there shouldn't be a problem now, should there?' said DC Briggs, but giving him a look that seemed like a warning shot.

'Okay, so… we need to get this guy in custody. If he's sentenced for any part he played, anything he publishes after that will have no credibility anyway.'

'And we could also talk to the Blackpool Gazette, tell them he's under investigation for two murders, that he's made an attempt to blackmail a senior officer, and that they shouldn't publish any more of his articles for the time being,' said DC Briggs. 'It wouldn't exactly be a big ask in the circumstances.'

'Sure. But we still can't absolutely guarantee the information in Taylor's article won't make it into the public domain. The man knows what he knows; he's found out, digging around, and that means other people can find it too. Plus, he might just publish it on some blog somewhere, or on some online discussion forum.'

'With the greatest of respect, sir, *so what?*' said DC Briggs. 'It would just be a profile of a police officer devoted to the pursuit of justice due to a terrible personal tragedy, one who's heroically overcome a recent personal illness. Yes, there's an accusation of police brutality in there from a former murder suspect, but it was never investigated, and there's probably more than a few folks crying "police brutality!" over the slightest touch from one of us. Don't worry about it. The suspect never filed a formal complaint, did he?'

'No,' he said. She might not be so blasé if it was about her and her personal life, he thought, but she was basically right. The guy had nothing. He was just desperate—but *why*, Walker didn't yet know. He took a deep breath, took a moment to get his head down in the heat of battle, quietly assessed the situation. 'Okay. You're right. He has nothing on us. Let's go get this guy.'

'He has nothing on *you*,' she corrected. 'He never mentioned me!'

'Fine. What I mean is we must get this guy, find out what his involvement is,' said Walker, 'regardless of these silly threats'. In the unlikely event he did lose his position because of these accusations, one of the other detectives would figure things out. And Walker wouldn't ever stop looking for his sister's killer, whether he was a police detective or not. So, that made little difference. What would happen would happen.

DC Briggs nodded, looking impressed at the way he was taking it all. She probably expected him to be angrier at being blackmailed, but the way he saw it, it was only going to help their case, help them get that warrant to search Phillip Taylor's home.

'Let's go then,' said Walker. 'I'll make a few calls on the way, see if we can get that warrant for Phillip Taylor's house expedited, ASAP.'

CHAPTER TWENTY-NINE

Taylor didn't even know how they could call it a "prison". HMP Kirkham was an open prison that hundreds of prisoners had absconded from since opening. He'd read that from 1998 to 2003, some 911 inmates had got out, and things hadn't got much better. In the past few years alone, over a hundred more prisoners had escaped. It was awful. There was no other word for it. Rapists and murderers who'd been downgraded to Category D just because they'd behaved themselves for a while and were coming to the end of their sentences could simply hop over one of the low-lying fences and be on their way. It was like the authorities weren't even trying. Some schools had more secure boundaries, in his opinion. It was hardly helping to keep the public safe. So, when he'd found out that Freddie Ward—the bloody bastard who'd been responsible for Sammy getting beaten and raped because of his drug dealing—was serving out his sentence there, Taylor had been furious, wanted to kill him. From what he'd seen, it was more like a holiday camp than a prison. And then the real gut-punch; six months ago, he'd discovered Freddie would be out on probation soon, that he'd be free again to do what he did: deal drugs, get people hurt, destroy lives. Well, not on his watch. He wouldn't be hurting anybody ever again if he had anything to do with it. Even if it was the last thing he did, it would be worth it, he thought. He had nothing much to live for now, anyway, not with Sammy gone. She was everything to him. He just wanted justice for her—*real* justice, not this—and maybe a little redemption too, for his own sins and indiscretions. He'd not been perfect either. He needed to be forgiven for what he'd done. He knew he'd made mistakes, that it was time to make amends.

Sat in the car, in the darkness, lights off, next to the boundary to Kirkham Prison, Taylor contemplated what he was about to do, steeling himself. He ate a Nature Valley peanut and chocolate protein bar to get some energy for the task ahead, washed it down with a bottle of orange-flavoured Lucozade Sport. He was treating it like a sporting performance, doing his very best to prime himself, prepare. He was taking every aspect of it very seriously—nothing left to chance. He couldn't fail; he wouldn't. He'd tooled up, as they say, dressed all in black, even, like a goddamned ninja. He certainly looked the part—or at least he thought he did. Not that any of that mattered. All that really mattered was that Freddie Ward would be no more if he succeeded in what he was about to do. And he *had* to succeed, no matter what the cost. That good-for-nothing druggie had to pay: *really* pay—she'd killed herself because of what he did, after all. An eye for an eye was what it said in the Bible. Or at least he thought it did. He'd never actually read it. Not all the way through, anyway. If God existed then he'd screwed Taylor over, good and proper, and Taylor didn't want any part of it.

He had a tool belt, with various weapons attached; a couple of knives—real sharp ones—a metal wrench, a pepper spray,

CHAPTER TWENTY-NINE

a cannister of spray paint, a nail gun, and more. He was ready. He got out of the car and put the belt on, making sure it was properly secured. He'd had it all prepared, in the boot, ready. He'd planned this meticulously. This was to be the *coup de grâce* of the Movement, to really show this scum of society that they weren't standing for it anymore. He'd read that somewhere—liked how it sounded.

The fence aligning the open prison really was an absolute joke. Anyone could climb over there with ease. But at least that made his job a little easier: if prisoners could get out, then he certainly could get in too.

He hopped over the fence and got inside the prison grounds proper. He was wearing all black—clothes he'd also prepared in the car boot—including a hood and his black face mask, just in case he was able to make it back out of there unscathed, and in case the prison guards had any pepper spray of their own. He knew where Freddie was—which building, which unit, everything. Phil had interviewed a prison guard using his Blackpool Gazette ID, an article, he'd said, that was to be about staffing levels at the prison, and a lack of funding and resources. The guard had been only too happy to carry out the interview, providing it all remained confidential and he stayed anonymous, as he believed it might lead to some benefits for them, or something, if the government sat up and listened. They'd talked about Freddie's case, about how drug dealers like him, even rapists and murderers, were absconding because of inadequate staffing levels and trade unions, and Phil had been able to steer the conversation towards where Freddie was, exactly, and how different types of prisoners were segregated. The guard had verbally mapped it out for him, how the units were organised, everything.

Right now, Taylor was also carrying something else too, in his hand—a tranquilizer dart blowpipe that he'd purchased easily enough on the web, pre-loaded with a dart filled with Propofol, a general anaesthetic that would knock most people out. While he'd considered getting some chloroform at first, his research had quickly informed him that it didn't quite work how it did in the Hollywood movies, or on TV, didn't knock people out as quickly as popular culture would have us think. The feathers on the darts he'd got were bright pink—not exactly appropriate but at least he'd easily be able to see where they hit, which is perhaps why they were designed that way, he guessed. He had nine more darts sitting inside a sheath on the back of his tool belt as well. They all had caps on, to stop him pricking or scratching himself. But thankfully, such a prick wouldn't be enough to inject the sedative anyway, as it was the force of the impact, he'd learned, that triggered the injection mechanism. He'd use the darts on the prison guards, get them out of the equation. He figured they'd all have to be pretty big, working in a prison, so he'd loaded a generous amount into the darts; but not too much—didn't want to kill them. He thought he might use some on the prisoners too, if he had any left, then do some of the bastards in, give 'em a proper sentence for their crimes. But the main target was Ward. He wouldn't render him unconscious, not if he didn't have too. He wanted to look him right in the eyes while he took his life, watched it drain out of him, wanted him to know exactly what was happening.

This was it. Taylor looked up at the sky, said a silent prayer to Sammy, and headed towards the compound at HMP Kirkham.

CHAPTER THIRTY

'No laptop,' said DC Brigg. They were at the home of Phillip Taylor, having gained entry forcefully because of the warrant they'd managed to expedite. The search was finally deemed urgent enough given Taylor was potentially involved in a serial murder and was on the run, coupled with his recent blackmail attempt on Walker. 'Probably got it with him and sent the email to you from that.'

'As expected,' said Walker. 'You get anything else?'

They'd just completed their individual searches, having divvied up the house to get the task done quicker, and were now getting together to discuss their findings.

'Not a whole lot,' said DC Briggs. 'He's pretty careful, clean, if he did anything. But I did find something in the kitchen bin, right at the bottom, amongst the rubbish. This…' She had a small item in her hand, what looked like the pink feathers of a dart. 'Googled it. It's not of the sporting variety. More like that you'd find on a tranquilizer dart.'

'Shit,' said Walker. 'Bloody idiot. He's going to get more people killed.'

'What do you mean?' asked DC Briggs.

'Well, this isn't like in some spy film, is it. A flaming fool amateur like him injecting a powerful anaesthetic by guesswork is a recipe for disaster. There's good reason why the police don't use such methods as non-lethal options.'

DC Briggs nodded her understanding. 'This is bad, isn't it?'

'Well, none of the current victims had been sedated. Not according to the toxicology reports. He's planning something else. He *is* involved. I can feel it. He didn't just supply the money.'

'It seems that is a distinct possibility, sir,' said DC Briggs. 'If he isn't involved in any animal care in some way, or anything like that, which there is no evidence of. But what's it for?'

Walker thought about it. 'It doesn't make sense. Throwing the money off the tower like that, it seemed contrite, regretful about what happened. Seemed like whoever was behind it realised they'd made a mistake. There's been nothing else since. I thought it might be done now we have Scawthorn. I even half-expected Taylor might turn himself in at some point too, admit any part he played, or confess that he was just trying to protect his brother-in-law or something.'

'Perhaps he will,' said DC Briggs. 'Maybe he just has one more thing to do, for Jonny, or for—'

'Oh, hell,' said Walker, an idea popping into his head. He got on his mobile phone, called the station. 'It's DCI Walker. Could you pull the file on Samantha Taylor, please, remind me of the details? Yes. Beaten and raped two years before her suicide by one Richard Peterson, A.K.A. 'The Razor', now deceased, killed by a rival gang member. I remember that much. What else?' Walker listened. 'Got it. Thank you.' He hung up and looked at DC Briggs. 'Samantha Taylor's attacker had come to her house looking for a 1.5kg bag of heroin, hidden there by one Freddie Ward, now in prison. And get this… He mentions in his statement, Ward was the

CHAPTER THIRTY

boyfriend of one Jonny Scawthorn, the victim's brother.'

'Shit. You think Taylor is going after this Freddie Ward character?' asked DC Briggs.

'Ward is currently serving seven years at HMP Kirkham, about to be released on probation. So, I think it's a distinct possibility Taylor *is* going after Freddie—maybe before Jonny gets incarcerated, in case he gets assigned to the same place, goes after him himself. Call the staff there, let them know they may be about to have an intruder.'

CHAPTER THIRTY-ONE

'There's no answer,' said DC Briggs.

'You sure you got the right number?' asked Walker, now driving, heading towards HMP Kirkham as fast as he safely could, nose to the steering wheel, rain battering off the windscreen with wipers on full speed, visibility limited.

'Got two numbers,' she said. 'Both getting no response. It is night time, I suppose. They might be short staffed.'

'Or they could be up to their necks in it,' said Walker. 'Call the station. Get some backup.'

DC Briggs frantically tapped on her phone and Walker could just about hear it ring above the elements. 'DC Briggs again. Yes. Let Supt Stone know we think Anthony Singelmann and Michael Tracy's killer might be on his way to HMP Kirkham. No, not Jonny Scawthorn. Yes, he *is* in custody. It's his brother-in-law, Phillip Taylor. Just... Just tell Supt Stone, would you? Oh, and tell her he's likely armed and dangerous. This is an emergency. People's lives may be in danger.'

'And tell them to look out for a red Ford Focus parked somewhere on the perimeter of the prison—Phillip Taylor's car,' said Walker. 'That could be his entry point and getaway.'

'And...' said DC Briggs. 'Oh, you heard that. Great. Will

CHAPTER THIRTY-ONE

do.' She looked at Walker and hung up. 'They got it. They'll run a check on the plates too if they find any cars parked up suspiciously, ID the owner.'

'Look, if he has got in there—and from what I know of HMP Kirkham, there's a distinct possibility he has—then he's probably armed. Perhaps even better than the officers there. They'll only have the usual batons and PAVA sprays. This maniac could have anything,' said Walker. 'He could do a lot of damage. We need to be ready.'

'But *we* only have batons and irritant sprays,' said DC Briggs, looking concerned. 'Do you think he might have a gun?'

'Anything is possible,' said Walker, as he lost the car for a second going around a bend a bit too quickly, before wrestling it back under control. 'But I'd say that's unlikely. Guns are not that easy to get hold of here. It's not the bloody Wild West, is it?'

'You could have fooled me. Then what are we going to do, Chief? What's the plan?' asked DC Briggs. 'The man could be extremely dangerous. You saw what the killer did to that second victim. He caved his darned face in. Maybe Jonny was lying. Maybe it was Taylor that did it after all, and he *was* protecting him for some reason—perhaps to give him time to do this?'

'Look, we don't know anything for sure, not yet. But, if Taylor's here, we're first gonna try to talk him down,' said Walker. 'The man's probably doing this because he's hurting, because he lost his wife—not because he's some psycho maniac. She was raped, got depressed, killed herself. Imagine how he feels. He probably just wants justice for her.'

'And do you think serving a few years in a prison like this, and then being released, *is* justice for some druggie who brought violence into an innocent woman's home?' asked DC Briggs. 'Do you think it's enough?'

The rain was easing off now, making driving easier, and quicker. Walker glanced at her. 'That's not for me or you to decide,' he said. 'That was the judge's job. If he was an addict, that might be deemed to be mitigating circumstances. There might be other things off the record too. You know a lot of offenders have all kinds of problems. Most of them are ill and just need help. The system fails them somehow. I don't know. But what I do know is that you can't just go around killing people if they aren't being polite enough. And it's my job to bring people in who break the law. It's not a perfect system, DC Briggs—everyone knows that—but it's the best we currently have.'

His colleague, nodded, in agreement, checked the equipment she had on her belt, making sure everything was secure and fastened properly. They were getting close now.

'Okay, Chief. Let's go get this guy,' she said. 'Make sure nobody else gets hurt.'

* * *

Taylor had managed to get behind Building C without much trouble. There'd been a prison officer knocking around, surveilling the area, but he'd been able to navigate around him easily enough under a combination of the cover of darkness and the pouring rain. Plus, they were looking for people getting out, not someone getting in, so that made his task that bit easier. There were various garden-type sheds on the

CHAPTER THIRTY-ONE

grounds, so he'd been able to move from one to the next, hiding behind them each time while the guard had their back turned, until he'd got close enough to the barracks. But this next part wouldn't be so easy—gaining entry to the building itself.

The door would be locked at this time, so he'd have to wait until the guard came over to enter, knock him out, grab his key. He had two options with this: he could jump him, pepper spray his face to stun him a bit, and then knock him out with the wrench. That was one way. But he didn't want to hurt him too badly, and he wasn't a hundred per cent sure they'd *just* get a concussion. He could bloody accidentally kill them if he whacked 'em too hard, and he didn't want that. So, he waited around the corner, peering around it, blowpipe in hand, hoping for a good shot with the tranquilizer dart. If he could get it to penetrate their skin, the Propofol would hopefully do its job, anesthetise them, put 'em out cold within a minute or so—if his research was correct. And if it didn't, they'd likely be disoriented at the very least, perhaps partially incapacitated, and then he could move in with the pepper spray and wrench—go to plan-B. But it was a risk. An unsuccessful dart could alert them to the situation, and even with a successful shot they'd no doubt try to quickly shout or call for backup before they passed out. However, the rain was providing a symphony of noise—white noise—to muffle any cries for help, and he was close enough to get to the man within mere seconds before he realised what was happening and could react properly. He decided to go with the dart first. He deemed it an acceptable risk. He didn't want any innocent blood on his hands if he could help it. That was the last thing he wanted; the guy could have a wife, and kids, someone just like Samantha, perhaps, someone that special. But he knew that no approach was without risk. He could have put too much Propofol in the darts—it was tricky to get the right dose without knowing the person's weight—it could go wrong in any number of ways; but at least he was trying. If it went wrong, it would just be… collateral damage.

The officer was approaching now, he'd just had a smoke and was taking the last drag and flicking the filter on the floor. He was a big chap, middle aged, overweight but strong looking. He hoped he'd loaded a suitable amount of Propofol onto the darts. The guy was a rhino. It was good that he was distracted with his ciggie though, just long enough for Phillip to get out into the open, aim the blowpipe and fire. The man was wearing the white cotton shirt and tie that all prison officers wore but with the black jumper and jacket over the top, which Taylor thought might not be thin enough for the dart to penetrate. So, he decided, on the fly, to fire near the top of the man's legs, looking for a fleshy thigh.

The shot hit, stuck in one of his legs, and he looked down, grabbed the dart, looked at it, seeming confused for a second. Taylor was already running at him at full pelt when the officer threw the dart down and reached for his radio. But before he could call for help, Taylor tackled him on impact, knocking him to the ground, quickly wrapping himself around the guy's arms, barely just managing to stop him from getting loose, struggling in the dirt. It took a minute or two for him to be out completely—seemed like an age to Taylor as he held him, but he finally went limp. When he was, Taylor took a few breaths, got himself together, and then grabbed the keys hanging from the man's belt. Before going in the building though, with some considerable effort, he just about managed

CHAPTER THIRTY-ONE

to drag the prison guard by both ankles, taking him around the corner, out of sight. It was some weight, but he was big and strong enough to manage it. Then, he undressed him, turning him this way and that, got into his uniform. It took some time, but it was worth the effort. They were about the same size in height—which was lucky, and any excess shirt he just tucked into the pants. It was slightly baggy, but passable: some people didn't like the tight fit. The uniform, he thought, would distract both staff and prisoners for long enough so he could incapacitate them too.

He went back to the door, now looking like a prison guard himself. There were several keys, but some were obviously not for this door, too big or the wrong shape, but he found the right one easily enough and got inside. There was a long corridor. He started checking the individual sleeping units, one by one, opening the doors. Most of the prisoners were already asleep, some looking startled as he turned the lights on and off, checking to see if Freddie Ward was there. He knew exactly what he looked like. He'd met him a couple of times when the guy was Jonny's boyfriend, also had a picture of him at home from a newspaper article—the one documenting Samantha's assault. Some of the prisoners seemed confused to see him, as they should be, as they wouldn't recognise him, but would just as quickly assume he was a new guard with him wearing the standard uniform. None of them said anything.

One of the other prison guards came out in the long corridor now, frowned at seeing him. 'Hey. We weren't expecting any—'

'Staffing levels deemed too low,' said Taylor. 'Was sent by the Governor for the night shift. He's been trying to ring. He's not going to be so happy with you boys in the morning.'

'Oh,' said the guard, getting closer. 'I'm Officer Bright. Where'd they get you from?'

'HMP Garth,' said Taylor. 'I'm Officer Terry. Nice to meet you. I just met the other chap outside. Do you have a Freddie Ward here?'

'Freddie? Yeah. He's in 12C, just down the hall. Why?' asked Officer Bright.

Taylor now had the PAVA spray and baton that all prison guards have, but he also had a few more weapons tucked in his belt underneath the jumper and jacket he had on.

'Oh. My cousin knows him,' said Taylor. 'Asked me to check on him, see if he's doing alright.'

'Well, he'll probably be asleep now. Why don't you—'

Taylor took the opportunity to remove the PAVA spray from his belt, stick it in Officer's Bright's face, and hit the button. A jet of liquid came out and got him in the face. He yelped like he had wet fire in his eyes, sucking in oxygen in ragged breaths, holding his face and going down. This gave Taylor enough time to remove one of the Propofol-loaded darts from the tool belt sheath tucked under the jumper and jacket and stick it in the man's arm. He'd be out cold in a couple of minutes, just like his colleague. Taylor straddled him, muffled his cries for help the best he could by removing one of the man's leather shoes and forcefully shoving it in his mouth. It seemed to take forever, again—probably a bit quicker than last time though, maybe less than a minute—but he eventually stopped wriggling and lost consciousness. That was one more down, and he hoped the last of them in this building.

He opened another of the cell doors, but this time didn't turn the light on. The prisoner inside was still sleeping—

CHAPTER THIRTY-ONE

snoring. It was a single person unit. It was perfect. He jabbed the prisoner in the arm with another of the darts, made sure he wouldn't be waking up anytime soon. He barely stirred, just rubbed and smacked the little prick the dart had made like he'd just been bitten by a mosquito, before going into an even deeper sleep. Then Taylor dragged the unconscious Officer Bright into the cell with him, exited, and closed the door.

He walked a little further down the hallway, made it to unit 12C—the cell Officer Bright had said Freddie Ward was in. This time, Taylor took out the wrench in one hand, and a knife in the other. He wouldn't be using the PAVA spray or the anaesthetic darts. He wanted the bastard to see everything, to be lucid, to feel every blow, every cut, before he turned his lights out for good. He didn't even care if he made it out of there alive at this point. He just wanted the man dead, gone from the world, so he could rest in peace. *There are consequences to your actions,* Taylor thought. *There has to be. Otherwise, people can just do anything, hurt each other as much as they want.* It was time for change. Time for some accountability. To change the world step by baby step. Freddie might not have been directly unkind to Sammy, but there were all kinds of unkindness in the world. The bastard who'd raped her was already dead—or he'd be going after him first, really hurting him too—but Freddie had caused the whole thing, had hidden a large supply of stolen drugs in their goddamned home! That was a type of unkindness too, in his book, putting innocent people in danger, lying to them, disrespecting them, insulting them. She was dead because of him. Actions had consequences and now this junky scum had to be punished—*properly* punished, not this liberal, namby-pamby bullshit. Society had become way too decadent. Things had to change. He had to make an example of him. And perhaps his actions now would act as a catalyst, like that guy who'd set himself on fire in Tunisia, Mohamed Bouazizi or whatever he was called, the man who'd started the Arab Spring—those anti-government protests in the Middle East. Maybe his actions wouldn't be so far reaching, but if they helped make a few people's lives that bit better, that was good enough for him. Maybe there'd be another guy somewhere— a guy just like him—whose special person, the love of *his* life, would this time recover, live a happy life together. If Freddie hadn't done what he did, Sam would be alive now, with him. He knew it in his bones.

This was it. He was ready. He opened the latch on the door to cell 12C, kicked the door open, and went inside.

CHAPTER THIRTY-TWO

Now parked up at HMP Kirkham, Walker and DC Briggs exited the car to find a half-naked fella staggering towards them—a big guy wearing only underpants.

'There's... there's someone...' said the man, seeming disoriented.

'Sir. Calm down. Tell me who you are?' asked Walker.

'I'm Officer Collymore, one of the prison guards. I was just having a smoke, putting it out. I don't know what the hell happened. Who are you?' asked the man.

'I'm DCI Walker,' he said, showing the man his ID card. 'And my colleague DC Briggs.' He was just giving the man a few seconds to get himself together. Despite the urgency of the situation, he knew any information he could get might be vital. It could even save lives.

'Where are my clothes?' said Officer Collymore, shivering a little, his lips going blue.

'I'm afraid we have a situation here—an intruder. We think he wants to harm one of the prisoners,' said Walker. 'Maybe even kill them. What's your staff number and full name, Officer Collymore?'

'David George Collymore, staff number... 9524100,' he said.

'Check it,' said Walker, so DC Briggs got on the phone, tapped on it, dialled a number.

'It's DC Briggs. We have an urgent situation. I need the staff number of one David, George Collymore, please.' She waited. 'You got it: *9-5-2-4-1-0-0*. Thank you.'

'Okay, George,' said Walker. He held out the key fob to his car. 'Take this and get in our car. You're in no state to help right now. Get the heating on. Get warm. Wait for us there. We'll come check on you when we're done.'

Officer Collymore hesitated, but then took the key fob and pressed it. Walker's Audi pool car flashed, telling him which car it was for. 'Okay, fine,' said the man. 'I do feel a little groggy.'

'How do we get in?' asked Walker.

'He took my keys. Took everything. All the billets have the same key. Use the intercom, tell them who you are, and one of the guards will come out. If there's no answer, try one of the other billets,' said Officer Collymore. 'Get another key.'

'Is Freddie Ward in this one?' asked Walker.

'Yeah. How did you know?' Officer Collymore frowned. 'Is he the one in danger?'

Walker got moving. 'We think so,' he said, turning back. 'Which room?'

'Er... 12C, I think,' said the Officer. 'He'd already turned in for the night. Had a shower.'

Walker nodded and got to the entrance of the nearest billet, pressed on the intercom. It buzzed. No answer. DC Briggs was right behind him.

'I'll go try another unit,' she said. 'You keep trying?'

Walker nodded. 'Quickly now,' he said, as he pressed again, but he got the distinct impression they were already too late.

CHAPTER THIRTY-TWO

* * *

'Oh, my God,' said DC Briggs. They were looking at the mangled body of Freddie Ward in Room 12C—or, at least, they assumed it was him. It was hard to tell, even with the digital mugshot that DI Hogarth had sent over for comparison. 'He didn't deserve this, not for what he got sent down for.'

Walker got on his two-way radio. 'We have one prisoner fatality, and one prison officer down here, and there may be more yet. We need immediate medical assistance and a search party out looking for the intruder and probable offender, one *Phillip Taylor*. Suspect is likely armed and very dangerous, over.'

'We're on that,' came the reply. 'We'll have someone with you shortly, and all available PCs out looking for the offender. Over.'

Room 12C was now an active crime scene. The deceased Freddie Ward had been left next to a wooden desk and chair, a broken kettle lying next to him, having obviously been used as a weapon to bash him with, maybe even scald him by the look of his blistering, red-raw skin. He'd also suffered numerous lacerations, possibly done with a knife, most of them superficial—like the killer had wanted him to suffer first—and finally his head had been bashed in by what looked like a solid, heavy object, like some kind of crowbar or tool perhaps, rather than the kettle, which was too lightweight to cause such extensive damage. It wasn't a neat job, far from it. This had clearly been done in a hurry. But there did appear to be some method to the madness, if one looked at the details.

'I've never seen anything like it,' said Walker. 'A civilian breaking into a prison to kill an inmate. I've heard of many an inside job, but not this.'

There was the signature writing of The Defender on the wall of the room too, this time with black paint on the white wall. It said, simply: "Be Kind."

'This is messed up,' said DC Briggs.

Walker shook his head. If anyone ever hurt *his* wife—even if they were currently separated—he didn't know what he'd do. And if he ever came face to face with his sister's murderer, he had a pretty good idea what he would do. He'd had dark fantasies about it for decades. But this was just an idiot who hid some drugs in someone else's place. He hadn't raped Samantha Taylor. He deserved something, but not *this*.

'That it is,' he said. 'Wait…' He noticed the writing on the wall seemed to go behind the bed, which meant he'd have to have moved the bed to do it, otherwise some of the paint would have got on the sheets. 'Help me move the bed.'

DC Briggs did as asked and they slid the single bed over easily enough. At the bottom of the wall, where the bed had been covering, it said: "One More To Go…"

'Shit. We need to find this guy, and quick. God only knows what he'll do next, or who he'll try to kill. It's like he doesn't care anymore—doesn't care what happens to him—and that makes him a very dangerous animal. Get forensics over here, but I think we're well past that now. We know exactly who we're after. It's just a case of catching up to him before he does any more harm.'

'Gotcha,' said DC Briggs.

'Oh, and check some of the other units on the way out, make sure the other prisoners are okay—and I'll do the same,' said Walker, suddenly wondering if it might not only be Freddie

CHAPTER THIRTY-TWO

Ward that Taylor was targeting here.

'Will do,' said DC Briggs, but Walker suddenly had an ominous feeling about the whole thing; after all, this was a building full of people who'd likely been unkind at some point, in one way or another—and if he knew one thing, it was that this guy didn't like people who were unkind.

CHAPTER THIRTY-THREE

A voice came on Walker's two-way radio just as they were leaving the billet that Freddie Ward, and several other prisoners, had been killed in. They were mentally and physically exhausted. It had been an absolute bloodbath: twenty-two *dead* on the last count—most of them shot with tranquilizer darts before having their throats cut. Taylor had gone manic on this one, completely on the rampage, taking down as many criminals as he possibly could before getting away. Most of them probably slaughtered while they slept. There was also one more prison guard who'd been anesthetised and dragged into one of the cells—the tranquiliser dart still in his arm—but this one hadn't woken up. His pulse was low, his breathing shallow; he'd probably been given too high a dose. He was in trouble, might not make it, Walker thought. The other guard, the one who had woken up, was now being treated by paramedics.

'Sir? DCI Walker? We got his car—matches the reg supplied—but it's been deserted. He must have got away on foot. Maybe he saw us. Over.'

That potentially made things a whole lot harder. If he was driving his car, with them knowing his registration, at least they could have squad cars on the lookout for him, check

CHAPTER THIRTY-THREE

all available CCTV, that kind of thing. But with him on foot, he could go anywhere, off-road, over farmer's fields, down dirt tracks, in woodlands. He could easily hide. Walker knew that over ninety per cent of land in England was of non-developed use, meaning it was either agricultural, recreational, or relatively untouched. He'd been involved in many a manhunt like this—and he was happy to call it that without fear of being reprimanded by his young subordinate, DC Briggs, for use of sexist language. A *manhunt* was what it was, pure and simple. And they were almost always men. If they could get police helicopters here quickly enough, the Police Dog Unit should be able to track him and point them in the right direction. But it was still just much easier to find someone travelling by car than it was to find someone on foot, who was prepared to go off the beaten track. If he slipped through the net, they'd have to rely more on a member of the general public calling it in, reporting something suspicious. And that could take weeks, months even, to get a lead, if at all.

'Sir?' came the voice again.

'Roger that,' said Walker. 'Keep looking. If we don't find him soon, he's gonna slip away. And approach with extreme caution. This man is extremely dangerous. There are more dead than we can count here. Over.' He looked over at DC Briggs and put his radio back on his belt. 'He's gone. But fortunately, he did leave us one clue as to where he might be heading.'

'*One More To Go?*' asked DC Briggs.

'One more to go,' said Walker.

'And you don't think he just meant the next prisoner in that building do you, and then he got carried away, couldn't stop, did more than he planned?' said DC Briggs.

'No. It doesn't feel like that at all,' said Walker. 'I think HMP Kirkham was one to him, and then there's going to be something else, one last thing on his list.'

'But what?' said DC Briggs.

'Well, we find out what or who that is, and we might just be able to bring this guy in after all.'

* * *

Walker stood at the head of the Incident Room, in front of an Evidence Board that now contained an increasing number of interconnected photographs and names. The latest photograph was that of the deceased Freddie Ward, the picture of his bloodied corpse inside Room 12C at HMP Kirkham had been printed from the Internet. Taylor had freaking posted the picture himself on the Tower Forum, signed 'The Defender', before the police had instructed Facebook moderators to take it down—the photograph, the message board, the whole sodding lot. On the Evidence Board, Walker also had a photograph of HMP Kirkham with the number '21' written on it with a red marker pen, meant to represent the bodies of the other twenty-one prisoners who'd been killed there. It had been a mass execution that even Walker, in all his years of experience, had never witnessed— not to this extent and number, anyway, or the nature of the killings. It had just been so clinical, so efficient, brutal. This guy was no journalist. He was a killing machine.

'I think he's going to murder again,' said Walker. In front of him sat DCs Briggs, Ainscough, Hardman, and DI Hogarth.

CHAPTER THIRTY-THREE

The atmosphere was solemn, to say the least. A lot of people had died on this case—the body count was staggering: twenty-nine dead in total now. It was unprecedented. There was a feeling that they could and should have done more, although Walker wasn't quite sure what that was. It was a feeling he always got whenever innocents died on their watch. Not that all of the deceased were completely law-abiding and guiltless this time—some of them might even have had it coming. But that didn't matter, really. There was no excuse for this, no justification. 'At least, that's what we can deduce based upon his message: *One More To Go.* It seems that's exactly what he intends—to kill someone else. But who that might be, we do not know. And since he's still currently at large, someone out there could be in danger as we speak, so we need to figure this out as a matter of urgency, redeem ourselves just a tad here. Someone else's life is at stake, and it's up to us to save them. Nobody else can do it. Right, let's focus. What do we have? Detective Hogarth? Can we get anything from the digital photograph he posted online?'

DI Hogarth gave it some thought. 'You're right. I considered that myself. But the Exif data is removed by sites like Facebook before publishing.'

'The *what?*' asked Walker. 'Please speak in a language we can all understand, Detective. Time is of the essence here.'

'Sorry. Exif—*Exchangeable Image File Format.* Every digital photo that people take contains a whole host of information that most are not aware of. Things like time of the photo, location, the type of device used to take it, and more. I might be able to get Facebook to provide this information, which they automatically remove from such photos, but they're not easy to deal with, and it can take time. I'm not sure it would be worth it, as we already know the location the photo was taken in, and the time.'

'But we don't know the make and model of the device used,' said Walker. 'Chase it up. Find out. You never know. It might come in useful.'

'Will do,' said DI Hogarth.

'Anybody else?' asked Walker. 'We need something. Ideas, please? What are we paying you for here, people?'

DC Ainscough cleared his throat to get the room's attention. 'I looked into Phillip Taylor's bank account activities, got a warrant to search his bank statements. It seems he got a significant sum of money from a conveyancing solicitor—just over £200,000. I Googled his old address, found the sold price on Rightmove. It fits the amount and date. And the most important thing: it was withdrawn in cash from this account just a couple of days before that money was thrown off the Blackpool Tower.'

'Well, we can be pretty sure that's the same money then,' said Walker. 'Look, we already know this guy's guilty. We even have him on CCTV at the prison, pulling his mask down for a few seconds to get some air.' He stabbed at a photo of this on the wall with his finger to highlight exactly what they had. 'It's a clear match for Phillip Taylor. We have him: hook, line, and sinker. We even have his DNA confirmed at the crime scene of Michael Tracy as well, now.' They did too, and Walker had been ecstatic when that report had come in, made his job a whole lot easier. When they'd first taken DNA samples from the crime scenes, Phillip Taylor hadn't been in their database. But they'd done their jobs—got his DNA off the sodding toothbrush at his home, got a match. 'All we have to do now is bring him in.'

CHAPTER THIRTY-THREE

'Dude's obsessed with kindness,' said DC Hardman, blurting it out a bit like he was just thinking out loud, maybe a little surprised himself that he'd actually said it.

'*Dude,*' said Walker, glaring at him. 'What is this, Wayne's World?'

'Wayne's what? Sorry. I just meant… I don't know what I meant. That this one more person he's planning to kill is someone who he sees as being the unkindest, I guess,' said DC Hardman. 'The climax to his plan? The real devil as he sees it?'

'Okay. Let's make a list of possible victims, based on who he might deem to be the unkindest person in this town,' said Walker. 'Interview all his work colleagues, family members, anyone he might have spoken too. Make sure you speak to Graham…' Walker looked through his notepad, flicking it several times before he found the right page. 'Graham Hopkins. They worked together, may have been close. Find out if Phillip had a chip on his shoulder about anyone else, if he was complaining about anything. Press this Graham character with threats about prosecuting for drug use—he was smoking some weed when we met him, and he was freaking out about it. He'll talk, I'm sure of it. Then make a general list of the most hated people in Blackpool at the moment. It could be someone famous, or in the public arena—a politician. He could be going after anyone. Maybe he wants to make one last big statement, make front page headlines. Hell, he might even be writing the piece himself.'

'Oh, there's one more thing,' said DC Ainscough. 'Anthony Singelmann's missing tooth; it was finally found on the first floor of the Blackpool Tower Ballroom. Seems it came out on his way up to the roof. So, either he fell over drunk and knocked it out himself, or he had an altercation with someone, got hit.'

'That's good information,' said Walker. 'But it doesn't help us much right now. I assume you checked for any CCTV footage in the ballroom and beyond?'

'Of course, sir,' said DC Ainscough. 'Nothing available.'

Even if they had someone nearby at the right time, it would be circumstantial evidence, at best. They couldn't prove who knocked that tooth out, and even if they could, it wouldn't prove that they killed him as well.

'Chief,' said DC Briggs. 'It's just a thought, but what if that *One More To Go* statement was referring to himself? What if he intends to kill himself?'

'Then I suppose our job will be made a little easier,' said Walker, perhaps a bit too coldly. 'But let's try to find him before he does that too, eh? We need some closure on this, for all those people, for ourselves, for the community. We don't just need to get him, we need to understand exactly why he did what he did, why he went to these lengths, once and for all.'

'That we do,' said DC Briggs, seemingly in complete agreement. 'What are we going to do, Chief?'

Walker gave it some thought. 'Remember when we thought Anthony Singelmann's brother might have killed him over that woman? And then Phillip Taylor's wife was raped because of her brother's boyfriend's stupidity. It makes me think about family connections. Let's see what other family this guy has, see if there's anyone else hiding away in his closet—a brother, a sister, some dark family secret, perhaps. People don't just start killing masses of people because their wife committed suicide. People have emotions, sure. But they don't do this.

CHAPTER THIRTY-THREE

They just don't. There's something more here. There has to be—some childhood trauma, or a long forgotten mental health condition that's resurfaced. It all starts in the home, as they say, doesn't it. Let's dig a little deeper, see what we find. Maybe there's a lead there, or someone he might stay with if he needs some respite, time to recharge—somewhere he thinks we wouldn't know about, or someone he really trusts. He must need a little rest after all that. But we have to hurry, or it'll already be too late.'

CHAPTER THIRTY-FOUR

'I've got something, sir,' said DC Ainscough. The young detective was doing his part, getting through some of the donkey work. Every case needed someone like him—someone willing to look through seemingly endless documents and paperwork and cross tabulate all the findings. 'Managed to get a hold of birth certificates for Phillip Roger Taylor and one Thomas Ryan Taylor. They have the same parents listed. And get this...'

'What?' asked Walker, who was just about to head out with DC Briggs, talk to some of Phillip Taylor's work colleagues, see if they could offer any further information about him.

'They were born... *on the same day*,' said DC Ainscough. He let it settle for a few seconds. 'Twins, obviously.'

'Well, that is interesting,' said Walker. 'We need to find out if Phillip has contacted his brother. If they're twins, they might be close. And if they are he'd be on his list of people to contact if he needed to go into hiding. You got an address?'

'I do,' said DC Ainscough. 'But it's not local. Shrewsbury of all places. I got a landline for him, but no answer.'

'Right. Get the local police down in Shrewsbury to pay this brother a visit,' said Walker. 'Explain the situation. Find out if these brothers have been in touch, or whether there's any

CHAPTER THIRTY-FOUR

reason to believe Phillip might be there.'

'Do you think he might be in danger, Chief?' asked DC Briggs. 'Could he be the *One More To Go?*'

It was a stretch, and Walker knew it might also be nothing. He'd had more dead ends in his career than he cared to remember. He always found it funny how the successes typically get remembered by everyone, but the ideas that come to nothing were typically conveniently forgotten, brushed under the carpet. He wondered if there might be some kind of clever, scientific name for that phenomenon. But there was no time for such musings now. They had to follow up on every idea, and fast—and that meant checking on this brother.

'Anything is possible at this point,' said Walker. 'We've already seen on this case the complications that arise between siblings. DC Ainscough, you also talk to Jonny Scawthorn again, try to find out if there was any bad blood between these twins, if they were in touch at all. '

'Will do,' said DC Ainscough.

Walker wondered whether Jonny might also be in Phillip's sights now given that it was him who'd brought Freddie into Sam's life. If Phillip felt he'd served his purpose now, he could be the "One More To Go."

'We'll talk to Phillip's work colleagues, see if they've ever seen or heard of this Thomas character, try to find out what kind of relationship they had from them,' said Walker. 'Contact me immediately if you find anything.'

'Got it,' said DC Ainscough. 'Hey, what if they're identical? What if Thomas is passing himself off as Phillip? We wouldn't be able to tell whose DNA is whose, would we?'

Walker rolled his eyes. 'Come on. This isn't a Netflix drama. It's Phillip who has the motive, the money, and Jonny as his accomplice. And unless Thomas is a journalist too, it's highly unlikely he'd be able to pass himself off as his brother for... however long.'

'Sorry, sir,' said DC Ainscough. 'Just a thought.'

'Noted,' said Walker. 'And, DI Hogarth, you do what you do and work some magic, try track this guy down. DC Hardman, you're coming with us.'

'Delighted,' said DC Hardman. 'Fieldwork is my forte, as always.'

Walker felt they had to do something, anything, act now. Momentum was key, forward movement. 'Right. Let's—'

Before they could leave, though, Superintendent Lucy Stone entered, without knocking, blocking his path. She glared. 'DCI Walker. My office,' she said. *'Now!'*

* * *

'What the *bloody* hell are you doing, Detective?' asked Superintendent Stone. She was furious, and rightly so. Her town had become a war zone, its institutions a joke. 'I've never seen anything like it. None of us have. It's a shitting disaster. Couldn't you have tipped us off a little sooner? By the time we got our team over to HMP Kirkham, all hell had broken loose, as you well know.' She wasn't as polite and well-groomed as the last time he'd seen her, that was for sure, or as well spoken. It looked like she hadn't slept or groomed herself in ages.

Walker shook his head. 'There really wasn't much more we could have—'

CHAPTER THIRTY-FOUR

'*Don't* you say we couldn't' have done more. We can always do more. The security at that prison was a sodding joke. Anyone could have got in and out,' she said.

'But that's not our—'

'And don't interrupt me when I'm speaking, Detective,' she said. 'As soon as you found out Freddie Ward was in that prison, and that it was his actions that led to Phillip Taylor's wife being raped, you should have informed me so that the prison guards could have been on high alert, no matter how improbable a break-in might have been. It was my call to make.'

'Well, I tried to inform the guards, but—'

She put her hand in the air, motioning for Walker to stop talking, and sat down at her desk, leaving Walker standing, twiddling his thumbs like a little schoolboy in trouble with his headteacher.

'And you should have warned us about what this guy might be capable of. The reports say you found the feathers of a tranquilizer dart at his house? What if he'd been training his followers to do the same? It could have been ten times worse,' she said, shaking her head. 'That should have been on my desk ASAP as well.'

'I believe the correct procedure was followed,' said Walker, stubbornly. She was being unreasonable. All these things took time, and he couldn't just call her every time they found something.

'We got something else too. My team brought in a kid after some other kid was caught in the act of graffitiing a motorway overpass and gave him up, said he'd been boasting about his involvement in the Anthony Singelmann murder and the KMM. The kid's identified Phillip Taylor from some photos. Said he paid him to write the "Be Kind" message next to Singelmann's body. This is something you should have followed up better on the case. Why am I doing *your* job?' asked Superintendent Stone.

'But... that's not fair. This could have been brought to my team first,' said Walker.

'That's it. I'm taking you off the case,' she said.

'You're *what?* We're just—'

'I said do not interrupt me!'

Walker sat down, deflated. He'd never been taken off a case before. Not ever. Not in the middle of it, anyway. The case was just reaching its climax. They didn't have any time to lose. If they handed over the investigations to someone else now, all could be lost. Phillip Taylor could get away, disappear somewhere, kill again, even.

'Well? Don't you have anything to say?' asked Superintendent Stone.

Walker hesitated, having already been cut off several times. 'I...' He gave it a little thought, knowing this might be his one chance to change her mind, stay on the case.

'Look, we've just discovered that our prime suspect, Phillip Taylor, has a brother—a twin brother. We think he might know something, might even be Phillip's intended final victim. He tipped us off that there was "One More To Go". Wrote it on the prison cell wall. If you take me off the case now, there'll be a lack of continuity in the investigation. It's at a really vital moment in proceedings,' said Walker, hoping that would do the trick to dissuade her.

'Don't you think I don't already know that?' asked Superintendent Stone. 'The press is all over this. They're looking for a scapegoat. You know someone's neck is on the line, there

CHAPTER THIRTY-FOUR

always is.'

'Look, with the greatest of respect, Thomas Taylor's life, or whoever is next, is more important than any one of our jobs,' said Walker. He meant it too. He didn't mind losing his job if no one else were to die. 'I'll happily resign once it's all over if you still feel the same. Just let me finish the case.' He wasn't sure if he meant that part though, about resigning. He guessed he'd deal with it when the time came. He just had to keep working.

Superintendent Stone sighed. 'Don't mess up anymore,' she said. 'How's your health?'

'Oh, I'm right as rain,' said Walker. 'I just need a bit of rest when this is all over, that's all.'

'Well… Keep me informed of any further developments. Our Intelligence Team has been successful in the arrests of eleven men and one woman in conjunction with the November fifth riots and violence. We just need to get the man responsible for all this, the one who inspired it, maybe even organised some of it too,' she said. 'We just need Phillip Taylor. Can I trust you to bring him in? I can provide more resources now, if you need it.'

'Yes. That would be very helpful,' said Walker. 'I need to know everything possible about Phillip and Thomas Taylor. Can you get your intelligence team on that?'

'I can,' said Superintendent Stone. 'But find him, and fast, Detective. Or we might all lose our damned jobs.'

CHAPTER THIRTY-FIVE

'You alright, Chief?' asked DC Briggs. Walker had just come out of Superintendent Stone's office, probably looked a bit pale, or shell-shocked, or both. But at least he was still on the case—for now.

'Never mind me. Have I missed anything?' asked Walker, hoping something might have come in during the short time he'd been away from the Incident Room.

'Negative, sir,' said DC Briggs. 'I think. DC Ainscough is on a call, though. I'm not sure if—'

DC Ainscough suddenly held the phone in the air, away from his face, his words stuck in his throat.

'Well, what is it, detective?' asked Walker. 'Spit it out, man.'

'It's... that was... *Thomas Taylor*, sir. I just talked to the twin. Shrewsbury got his mobile number from a neighbour on a neighbourhood WhatsApp group with him, said he hadn't been seen for days. Kept going to voicemail, but I left a message and finally he got back to me,' he gulped. Something was wrong. 'He said his brother has him, that he had to be quick because he was coming, that he was going to hurt him—he was whispering, sounded terrified—gave us an address, and then there was a loud noise, like someone had just thumped him or something, and the line went dead.

CHAPTER THIRTY-FIVE

'What was the address?' asked Walker.

'5 Blundell Street, Blackpool,' said DC Ainscough.

Walker clicked his fingers. 'DI Hogarth, do a search, tell us what you can about that property.'

'Already on it,' said DI Hogarth. He tapped away on his keyboard for several seconds, until he stopped again, staring at the screen. 'Got it. 5 Blundell Street, Blackpool.' He typed on his keyboard a little more, increasing in speed, if anything. He looked up at Walker. 'It's an Airbnb.'

'Short-term housing rental?' asked Walker, thinking he knew what that was, but being not entirely sure, needing confirmation.

'That's right,' said DI Hogarth. 'He's rented somewhere nice and private.'

'Well let's get over there,' said Walker, already moving. 'Before he sodding kills him.'

* * *

'Phillip Taylor. This is the police. Come out with your hands up.' The trained Hostage Negotiator, a stocky middle-aged bald fella called Harry Keen, was using a loudspeaker, stood outside of Number 5 Blundell Street. They were all wearing body armour—some in stab vests, who were shielded behind police cars for extra protection, while others had bullet proof vests on in case Phillip Taylor had somehow managed to get hold of a gun, stood further up front. Walker was wearing one made of steel—not the highest level of protection available, but close. It was the best they had. *'Phillip. We need to talk to*

you.'

The front door opened, slowly, being pushed just a few inches by whoever was inside; and there were several Authorised Firearms Officers from the Firearms Unit with weapons pointing right at that door, just in case a rapid and fatal intervention was required. Their Commanding Officer was stood close by, barking orders for them to take up key positions, motioning for some of them to move closer in case they needed to breach.

'We need you to come out and lie down on the floor, face down,' said Officer Keen, glancing across to the Incident Commander, a skinny chap who looked almost at retirement age, who would have been assigned by the Force Incident Manager. He too wore a bullet proof vest. They were heavy and uncomfortable. Walker was sweating in his, but it was still better than taking a bullet. The Incident Commander nodded, urging Negotiator Keen to press on. *'Mr Taylor.'*

The door opened some more, and a man came out, covered in blood. He was holding something—maybe a knife; it was hard to tell. But that made everyone a bit jumpier, and some of the AFOs moved in a couple more steps, getting closer, fingers on triggers. The Hostage Negotiator held his free hand out, motioning for them to step it down a touch, and he lowered the loudspeaker, getting ready to speak without it.

Walker initially recognised the man as Phillip Taylor, but unlike the last time he'd seen him, this man appeared gaunt, unhealthy, looked like he hadn't eaten or slept in days. This made Walker think that maybe this was his twin brother, Thomas. He was wearing the prison guard uniform from HMP Kirkham, which was also covered in what looked like dry, older blood—probably from the carnage at the

CHAPTER THIRTY-FIVE

prison. Walker thought perhaps Phillip had dressed him in the uniform to confuse matters, try to frame him.

'Mr Taylor, I need you to put the weapon down. Now,' said Walker, calmly but firmly, just like he'd been trained all those years ago.

Taylor looked at the knife in his hand with an emotion Walker couldn't quite pin down, like he was surprised, or like he'd only just realised it was there. Walker wondered whether Phillip might have slapped it into his hand just before shoving his poor traumatised brother out the front door to take the fall for him. The man let go of the knife like it was a hot iron—but it lingered there for a microsecond, the stickiness of the blood keeping it momentarily attached to his finger—before it fell to the floor, gravity doing its thing.

'I didn't...'

The man looked a bit insane, like he'd had a breakdown, like it was all too much for him—not the driven, mad, obsessed person that Walker had Phillip Taylor pinned as. It was surely the terrified Thomas who DC Ainscough had spoken to on the phone, but there was a nagging doubt—perhaps that's what Phillip Taylor wanted them to think. If it was Phillip though, he was a hell of an actor: this looked like a person who was broken, who'd gone to hell and back, several times.

'I need you to get down on the floor, put your hands on your head,' said Walker. 'Before this lot get nervous. Do it now.'

Taylor slowly got to his knees, first putting his hands on his head then removing them, perhaps thinking better of it, not quite knowing what he was supposed to be doing.

'Just lie down on your belly, and then put your hands on your head,' said Walker, realising he needed some more specific instruction. 'You are Phillip Taylor, aren't you?' If it was Thomas, he'd deny being Phillip, and if it was Phillip trying to pull a fast one, pretending to be Thomas, he'd also deny being Phillip. But much to Walker's surprise, the man nodded, eyes wide.

'I...' He was still on his knees, staring at Walker, almost begging. 'My brother. He brought me here, and then he...'

Walker glanced across at DC Briggs again. Something didn't feel right; she furrowed her brow, confirming his feelings. He clicked his fingers, got a couple of PCs to move in, cuff the guy, before pushing him to the floor, one of their hands firmly on his head, keeping him there. Some of the others went inside, the armed AFOs going first, cautiously.

'Clear,' one of them shouted. A few seconds went by that seemed like hours or days before a PC came back out.

'*Paramedics!* In here. Quickly. We have one male, seriously injured, possibly deceased—we're not sure—looks very similar to the man on the floor; same face, build, even the same haircut, identical,' said the PC. The paramedics responded immediately, mobilised, got inside with some equipment. 'The ID in his wallet says "Thomas Taylor"'. Looks like his throat has been slit. There's blood everywhere. Two of the PCs are putting pressure on it as we speak, just in case he's alive.'

Walker bent down next to the man on the floor. 'Phillip Taylor, we're arresting you for the attempted or actual murder of your brother, Thomas Taylor, and for the murders of Anthony Singelmann and Michael Tracy. You do not have to say anything, but it may harm your defence if you do not mention when questioned something which you later rely on in court. Anything you do say may be given in evidence. Do you understand?'

'But I didn't do anything,' he said. 'He did it to himself. This was all his fault.'

CHAPTER THIRTY-SIX

'Well done, Chief!' said DC Briggs as Walker entered the Incident Room at Blackpool Police HQ for what he hoped might be the last time, at least in the near future. They were all clapping—DI Hogarth, and DCs Briggs, Hardman, and Ainscough, plus a few of the PCs who'd been involved in the operation as well. He was never a big fan of such back slapping, but they'd all worked so hard, and they deserved to have their moment of glory. 'We got him. Hopefully this is the last of it. It's all over.' More applause and literal back slapping, this time.

Walker sat down at the head of the table, gestured for everyone else to take a seat as well. The killing spree at HMP Kirkham now overshadowed the deaths on Bonfire Night, but Walker wasn't convinced this would completely stop the ball that had been set in motion in the form of the KMM. He dearly hoped the arrests they'd made on November fifth might have collared all the people responsible, and in combination with the capture of Phillip Taylor, the whole thing could now peter out. But he worried the arrests they'd made on Bonfire Night could have missed the worst agitants and perpetrators, and the noisiest could kick up a rumpus in support of their Defender in the weeks to come, leading to similar violence.

CHAPTER THIRTY-SIX

'Any word on our Mr Thomas Taylor? He make it?' asked Walker.

'Apparently he's in a critical condition at the hospital, but he's alive—for now,' said DC Briggs. 'What's Phillip Taylor saying about all this?'

'Says he wants his lawyer,' said Walker. 'Won't say another word until he's talked to them.'

'Well, I suppose that's sensible,' said DC Briggs. 'But it's not gonna help him a jot.'

'We have pretty much everything we need,' chipped in DC Hardman. 'DNA from the crime scenes, his brother as a witness—if he recovers—the cash withdrawn from his account two days before it was thrown off Blackpool Tower, and him on CCTV at the prison, pulling his mask down for a second. It was him, alright. Then we caught him in the same clothes that he put on at the prison too—the uniform. We have the lot. Even have his fingerprints on the knife that he cut his brother with, the one we saw him holding.'

It was a lot of evidence. He had to admit that. But something was gnawing at Walker. Phillip said his brother did it to himself, that it was all his fault. He wanted to know what that meant, or it would haunt him, always forever wondering. He hated loose ends, but unfortunately it was often part and parcel of the job and he'd lived with more than he could count already. It was one of the many things that kept him up at night. Now, though, he had to take things at face value— Phillip Taylor had the motive and means to do all this, and it was hard to imagine anyone could cut their own throat just to frame someone else. It was all too fanciful. He wondered what his brother's role was in all this, whether he'd angered him somehow, started the ball rolling, and whether he now blamed him for everything he'd done. Whatever it was, he wanted answers.

'What is it, Chief?' asked DC Briggs. She was getting to know him well now, instinctively knew something was wrong.

'I'm not sure. Something didn't quite feel right,' said Walker. 'Did you see how Phillip Taylor looked? He was malnourished, traumatised.'

'Yeah. We all saw it,' said DC Hardman. 'We've looked at his medical record. He had some mental health issues—had counselling, was on sertraline, an anti-depressant. He probably lost the plot, went off at the deep end. It wouldn't be surprising. He did come home to find his wife had killed herself in the bath. That kind of thing is obviously very traumatic.'

'Yeah, I know,' said Walker. 'And I suppose you're right.' He got up to leave and everyone followed suit, got back to celebrating, chatting amongst themselves as they were leaving. Only DC Briggs stayed behind, waiting for everyone to go, giving Walker the eyes to tell him she wanted to have a word.

'What is it, DC Briggs?' asked Walker.

'You're still not happy,' she said, speaking quietly as there were still some people yet to leave the room. 'There was a time when I'd have told you to go home and rest, that it was all done, that you were being paranoid. But...'

'But what?' said Walker, although he had a pretty good idea where she was going with it.

'*But...* I've come to realise you have a really good instinct for such things, and if you're not happy about something, we should follow it up,' she said. Everyone in the room had now left, so they could speak normally.

CHAPTER THIRTY-SIX

Walker couldn't shake the fanciful idea that what Phillip Taylor was claiming might be true—his brother Thomas *could* have been impersonating him, had kept him locked up, had wanted to frame him; and he'd been willing to risk his own life to achieve that aim.

'Aren't identical twins also genetically identical?' asked Walker.

'Er... monozygotic twins, they're called. Covered it a little in my psychology module on my degree. Yes, I think they might be,' said DC Briggs. 'Will have to check, but yes, that sounds about right. So, that would mean...'

'It would mean the standard DNA testing techniques that we used would not differentiate between the two brothers,' said Walker with a little more urgency in his voice. 'DC Ainscough had raised this concern and I dismissed it, thought it too fanciful. But I'm not sure now. They even had the same haircut. All we really have is a wallet and ID on one of them, which could have been planted, and some fingerprints on the knife, which could have been forced into his hand. The DNA test tells us nothing. It could be from either of them: we thought we had a match from Phillip Taylor's toothbrush, but the DNA found at the crime scenes could equally belong to his brother, Thomas. No dental records, and no fingerprints on file as no previous convictions. I mean, who has no dental records these days?'

'People who fear the dentist, I suppose. Oh, my...' said DC Briggs. 'We've got to get to that hospital.'

'Yes, we do. Come on. Let's go. You make a call on the way, tell the PCs we have stationed there to watch Thomas Taylor well, make sure he doesn't go anywhere until we get there,' said Walker.

'Okay, Chief,' said DC Briggs, appearing jaded, but trying to galvanize herself for the task ahead. 'It's probably nothing though, right?' she added.

'Probably,' said Walker. 'The odds are against it. But let's get over there anyway, try to be there when he wakes up, see what he has to say for himself.'

'*If* he wakes up,' said DC Briggs, while they were on the move, going down the stairs to the ground floor of Blackpool Police HQ.

'*If* he wakes up,' repeated Walker. 'But I have a funny feeling he might.'

On their way out, DI Hogarth caught them up, out of breath. 'We got something,' he said, bending over to catch his breath. 'The hospital just called. They've had some trouble down there. Someone posted on the Facebook group just before we arrested Phillip Taylor, said the Defender was being taken to Victoria Hospital after being beaten by police and taken into custody. An angry mob has been, stormed in, and our three PCs down there couldn't hold them back, got hurt in the chaos by the sound of it. And apparently, Thomas Taylor slipped away in the confusion.'

'Shit,' said Walker. 'Go, go, go!'

CHAPTER THIRTY-SEVEN

'He was right here before the trouble started, detective.' It was one of the nurses at Blackpool Victoria Hospital, the shift manager. 'He was being carefully watched by the police officers you had stationed here, the ones who are now being treated for injuries. Thomas Taylor's wound seemed serious; he was sleeping, had been given some strong painkillers that make you drowsy. I don't understand it.'

Walker was furious. 'And nobody saw him leave? Not one of you?'

'I'm afraid not. We were keeping an eye on him too before those people forced their way in, but things got a little crazy after that. And it's not like we don't have other emergencies to attend to. People's lives are at stake here. We can't just stand guard for one patient who isn't really in any state to stand up, never mind move around. And we can't have people bursting in here like this, causing trouble.'

'Well, it seems he was in such a state to stand up, *because he isn't here now*,' said Walker, instantly regretting his outburst. The nurse was only doing her job. It was up to them to police people, and they'd failed in that. They should have had more PCs on him from the start, just in case anything like this happened. 'I'm sorry. It wasn't your fault. So, he's been missing since those men came in here, causing a ruckus?'

'Yes. We had to prioritise treating the PCs first. They've been beaten up badly. And then we realised Thomas Taylor was gone. We didn't know what to do. We've had a couple of staff out looking for him while we were waiting for you, but they haven't found anything yet. He might have left the premises,' she said.

'Thank you. That will be all,' said Walker, just as a male doctor arrived in the room, spotting the lanyards around Walker and DC Briggs's necks.

'Do we have a problem here?' asked the Doctor. 'I'm Doctor Michaels, here to see Thomas Taylor—the knife attack. Where is he? Isn't this his bed?'

'I'm sorry. He's gone,' said the nurse.

'Gone?' said the Doctor. 'What do you mean *gone*? He died?'

'No, of course not,' said the nurse. 'I mean, he left the ward, and we can't find him. These detectives here need to speak to him. Urgently.'

'His injuries,' said Walker. 'How serious are they?'

'Well, we've just got the results in,' said Doctor Michaels. 'They're actually not nearly as serious as they first appeared. He no doubt lost a lot of blood. But the attacker somehow managed to miss the exterior, interior, and anterior jugular veins. Trachea is intact too, just some minor damage, but no evidence of any major aspiration of blood or seepage into the lungs. This is more a laceration of the neck, with some muscle and minor veins cut, causing the bleeding you witnessed, rather than a cut throat. He was very lucky. It's almost a miracle it wasn't any worse.'

'Or it wasn't,' said Walker.

CHAPTER THIRTY-SEVEN

'Excuse me?' said Doctor Michaels.

Walker was thinking maybe it wasn't just lucky the laceration had missed all these major arteries and the windpipe, which would have almost certainly killed him. He wondered whether it had been done by design to dupe them.

'Let's get a widescale search out looking for this guy,' said Walker. 'Even if he's not done anything wrong, he's still wounded and in potential danger. He may be having some kind of episode. Or he's confused due to the drugs you gave him. Maybe he isn't—'

DC Briggs was staring at someone coming into the ward, her mouth open, eyes wide, so everyone turned around, took a look. It was Thomas Taylor. He was sat up, on a bed, being wheeled in by one of the medical staff. He looked to still be in shock a little, but appeared lucid, and relatively unscathed apart from the large bandage around his neck, which was soiled with blood. He kept touching it, tentatively. It was obvious very sore.

'Mr Taylor,' said Walker.

'It's Tom,' he said. 'You can call me "Tom".'

'What the hell are you doing?' said the nurse to the man wheeling him in. 'I didn't authorise this. Where's he been?'

'Found him sat in the cafeteria, eating a muffin, drinking some coke. His neck was bleeding—wound must have opened up again—so I brought him back here,' said the man. 'Thought it best to use a gurney in case he got dizzy, fainted. He shouldn't be off the ward in his condition.'

'Well, I know *that*,' said the nurse. 'He wasn't supposed to be. Thank you—for finding him and bringing him back, I mean. Can you help me get him back on the bed as well before you go?'

The man did as asked and they guided Thomas Taylor onto the hospital bed, before tucking him in and getting him comfortable.

Walker and DC Briggs got some chairs, pulled them up near the bed.

'We're going to need to talk to him now,' said Walker. 'As a matter of urgency.'

'Understood,' said Doctor Michaels. 'Nurse. Give them a few minutes and then get that bandage changed and the wound cleaned up. See if any of the stitches have broken.'

The nurse nodded and left with the doctor, leaving them to it.

'Mr Taylor... Tom. I'm Detective Walker. Do you understand what has happened to you?' asked Walker.

'Yes. I do,' said Tom, feeling his neck again where the bandage was, here and there, inspecting it with his touch.

'Can you tell us, in your own words, what happened?' asked Walker.

Tom nodded, took a moment, swallowed, albeit with some difficulty.

'I was at my home in Shrewsbury. It was late at night. I was taking out some rubbish to the wheelie bin, felt something stab my arm—thought I'd been bitten by a bug or something at first, but I had this dart in it, with some pink feathers on. I thought it was some kids, messing about. I whipped it out, but it was too late. I passed out. When I came to, I was in some car boot, but squeezed in real tight. I'm not the smallest of chaps, am I? My legs and hands were bound with gaffer tape, and there was something shoved into my mouth, stuck tight with the same tape. I couldn't move. Could I get a sip of water?'

CHAPTER THIRTY-SEVEN

Walker gestured to DC Briggs, and she got up, went over to the sink, brought back a plastic cup full of water, gave it to Tom. He nodded his thanks and took a sip.

'And when was this?' asked Walker.

'November sixth,' said Tom. 'I remember because the air was still thick with smoke.'

'Go on,' said Walker.

'I was in there for what seemed like an eternity. I was tired, needed a piss. When the boot opened, I was in a garage, my brother's face looking down at me. It was... Phil—Phillip Taylor. We're identical twins.'

'We know. And had you had any recent contact with your brother prior to him kidnapping you like this?' asked Walker.

'We were estranged. We weren't on speaking terms,' said Tom.

'And why is that?' asked Walker.

'Well... because of the affair... I had, with Sam, his wife, after... She was down, depressed, and he wasn't there for her,' said Tom.

'I see. So you weren't on speaking terms, and he just turned up and kidnapped you. And then what happened?' asked Walker.

'He kept me there, at this place, tied up, bound, gagged. I don't know how long for—for a few days, maybe? I begged him to let me go. Said he was going to pin everything on me. He took a swab from my mouth, pulled some of my hair out with tweezers. Said I deserved it because of what I did. He was all twisted up, full of rage,' said Tom. 'Then he flipped. Said he was going to kill me instead, that I deserved no less, that I was just like the others.'

'The others?' asked Walker.

'I'm not sure what he meant by that. I had my mobile turned off, had it tucked into my sock the whole time. So, when I finally got free, I turned it back on, saw your message, and called you guys back. Did he do something bad? Did he kill someone?' asked Tom.

'Yes, Tom. We think he did something bad. Several people are dead,' said Walker.

Tom put his head in his hands. 'Oh, my God,' he said. 'It wasn't his fault. It was just all too much for him I think, what happened, to Sammy. She was raped, you see, and then... she killed herself. I think he's gone mad.'

'Tom. I'm afraid your brother is going to go away for a very long time for this,' said DC Briggs, obviously feeling the need to interject at this stage, offer some more feminine support in that soft tone she did. 'He's not going to be able to hurt you anymore.'

'It'll be either prison or a secure mental health facility,' added Walker, in a much less soothing tone, although he tried. 'He'll no doubt undergo a full psychological evaluation prior to trial.'

'I see,' said Tom, lifting his head up again. 'Can I go back to Shrewsbury now? I've never really liked it here. I want to go home.'

Walker looked at him, wrapped in bandages, his brother having almost just killed him, his world turned upside down. It would take time to get over this, to process it. He'd probably never get over it. 'As soon as you get discharged from the hospital and no longer need inpatient care, as long as we have enough evidence to support your account by then, you'll be free to do whatever you like.'

'And if you don't—have the evidence, I mean?' asked Tom.

CHAPTER THIRTY-SEVEN

'Why don't you just focus on getting better for now,' said Walker. 'And we'll see where we are when you're all recovered. Hopefully we'll have this all tied up for you by then.'

Tom nodded. 'Thank you, DCI Walker.'

'We'll need to take your fingerprints from here, assuming that the medical staff won't clear you to come to the station yet,' said Walker.

'Sure,' said Tom. 'Whatever you need.'

'And we'll also need to keep several more of our officers stationed here, for your own safety, you understand?' said Walker. 'There's been a lot of trouble lately, and we don't want to take anything for granted.' He didn't want to say it, but he also wanted to keep Tom contained until they had firm evidence of his innocence; and he'd make damned sure they had better security this time and more officers on him, just in case there was more trouble.

'I understand,' said Tom.

Walker nodded back, tapped his hands on the top of his thighs and then pushed up into a standing position. He glanced at DC Briggs and raised his eyebrows. They had what they needed for now—but they still had to verify what the man had said, get his prints from Phillip Taylor's car boot, perhaps, try to get a witness or some footage of the car in Shrewsbury. It wouldn't be easy. But it was doable, at least. It felt like the case might be nearing its end, if they could just find that evidence to corroborate his story.

'Shall we?' he said, a little wearily, ready to get out of there, having spent far too much time in hospitals himself over the past few years; in fact, he was absolutely sick to the back teeth of such places.

CHAPTER THIRTY-EIGHT

'Mr Phillip Taylor, we need to take your statement pertaining to the events at 5 Blundell Street in Blackpool, and regarding the deaths of Anthony Singelmann and Michael Tracy on Blackpool Promenade, along with any role you played in the November fifth violence and unrest in Blackpool. Do you have anything to say?' asked Walker.

The man was now sat with his lawyer—a Mr Pitt—who unlike his theatrical counterpart was an unremarkable fella with a well-presented but notably cheap suit and steady haircut, and a close shave. He wore round glasses and held a pen and leather-bound notepad. DC Briggs sat on Walker's side of the table, as per usual.

Mr Taylor looked at his lawyer, for guidance, or permission, one of the two. Mr Pitt slowly nodded, allowing him to speak.

'I'm the victim,' he said. 'My brother held me captive. He's gone mad. I thought he was gonna kill me. He cut the tape binding my hands and feet, removed the tape from my mouth, and then slit his own throat. I don't know what happened after that. I was in shock. He must have put the knife in my hand at some point. It's all a blur.'

Walker hadn't been expecting that, but nothing surprised

CHAPTER THIRTY-EIGHT

him anymore. He was far beyond that. He sighed, knowing they officially had a big, big problem. What they had was both brothers now claiming that it was the other one who held them captive, did the crimes—identical brothers with the same or almost identical DNA, no dental records, and no fingerprint records in the database. He knew there were major issues in prosecuting someone who claimed their identical twin did the crime; he'd read about such cases and the problems associated with disproving such claims. He looked at Mr Pitt, wondering whether he'd put him up to this, but the lawyer seemed to read Walker's mind and shook his head.

'Tell me the details that led to this situation?' said Walker. 'Don't leave anything out.'

'Well, Tom turned up several days ago. I wasn't pleased to see him because…' Phillip looked at the wall, seeming reluctant to say what needed to be said.

'When exactly?' asked Walker.

'I think it was… the day after Bonfire Night. Yes. I remember because there was still smoke in the air,' said Phillip.

That was what his brother had said too. Uncanny, thought Walker. 'Go on. Why weren't you pleased to see him?'

'He… had an affair with Sammy,' he said. 'My wife. Before she died, obviously. She confessed to me just days before she…' He was upset, struggling to get the words out.

His brother had said that too. Not that he was surprised about this revelation, what with what had gone on in the case so far. It seemed this kind of thing happened more often than people realised. 'I see,' he said. 'And had you had any recent contact with your brother prior to him turning up like this?'

'No. I hated him. Hadn't seen him since Sam died—at the funeral. He tried to contact me a few times after that, but I just blocked him. I didn't want to see him ever again. He was my brother, my twin brother, and he slept with my freakin' wife! It's so messed up, isn't it?' He was vigorously rubbing his forehead now, sweating, clearly in some distress—either that or he was doing some very convincing acting.

'Okay,' said Walker. 'I get why you might be angry with him, I really do, why you would want to hurt your brother. But you're saying the opposite—that he tied you up. What you're saying actually serves to support his statement, I'm afraid: that you hurt *him*.'

'Mr Taylor—' said his lawyer, obviously having some concerns, not sure if Phillip should go on.

'I want to tell them what happened,' said Phillip, so Mr Pitt simply shrugged his shoulders and allowed him to do so. Phillip's lawyer wasn't the most assertive. Like many people, he'd probably fallen into the wrong job.

'Okay. But you're refuting that you hurt him, and what you're saying is that he made you *his* captive and then eventually hurt himself. Why would he do that?' asked Walker.

'I don't know. He said I wasn't kind to Sammy, that I blamed her for what happened—the rape—that she was lonely. Said I should be punished. But then maybe he felt guilty, for the part he played? I have no idea,' said Phillip.

Walker gave it some thought. The man wasn't completely making sense. 'So... you're suggesting he hurt himself because he felt guilty about the affair, and also perhaps how this affair impacted on Sam's mental health. And that he also blamed you because of what happened to her. But—'

CHAPTER THIRTY-EIGHT

'Please don't lead my client,' said Mr Pitt, before clearing his throat, suddenly seeming unsure about himself, losing confidence. 'Please let him say what he wants to say. He can make his own statement.'

Walker was annoyed but couldn't deny he was in danger of leading the suspect in his line of questioning. He needed to back off, let the man speak, shackle his own emotions about it. 'Please provide your statement now,' he said.

'Well, that's it, really,' said Phillip. 'There's not much more to tell, except the details. That's about all I know. I'd been locked up for days. I wasn't sure what he intended to do. He took swabs of my mouth at one point and pulled some of my hair out with some tweezers—said it was my fault Sammy was dead, that I should be tried for murder. All I know is he took me captive, locked me up for God knows how long with very little food or water, and then he forced me into that bloodied uniform you found me in, set me free, and cut himself. I think he must have gone mad, had some kind of mental breakdown. He needs help. The next thing I know, you're all there, telling me to get down on the floor. And now I'm here.' He began to sob, like it had all been too much for him.

'Someone claiming to be Phillip Taylor attended a press conference we held just after the Bonfire Night violence,' said Walker. 'Was that you?'

Phillip shook his head. 'No,' he said.

'And you had nothing to do with the murders of Anthony Singelmann and Michael Tracy?' asked Walker.

'Absolutely not,' said Phillip. 'But I had been running stories on them for the Blackpool Gazette.'

'Are you saying that your brother Tom has been masquerading as you since November sixth, the night after Bonfire

Night? That he managed to take over your job, interact with your boss and colleagues, without being rumbled?' asked Walker.

'I don't know. I guess if you think you saw me at a press conference on November sixth, then that must have been him, because it wasn't me. Like I said, he took me captive,' said Phillip, the tears now subsiding a bit.

'Do you have anything else to add?' asked Walker.

'I don't know...' said Phillip. 'He took my phone. I used Face ID on it, so he was able to easily open it, access my online banking. Said he was going to make a large withdrawal.'

'Do you play snooker, Mr Taylor?' asked Walker.

'No. But my brother used to. He liked that, what's his name... Ronnie O'Sullivan: *The Rocket*, they call him, because he's quick.'

'Anything else?' asked Walker. Phillip shook his head. 'We're keeping you here for at least twenty-four hours, Mr Taylor, while we figure all this mess out,' said Walker, not sure if they'd be able to untangle what they'd been told in that time, which was a big problem. 'DC Briggs, take him to the holding cell and meet me in the Incident Room promptly. We've got work to do.'

CHAPTER THIRTY-NINE

'Get as many officers on Tom as possible, at the hospital. Just in case there's more trouble down there. I don't want him getting away,' said Walker.

'We've already got quite a few down there,' said DC Hardman.

'Well get more,' snapped Walker.

'Okay. I'll do that,' said DC Hardman, picking up a phone and getting on it.

'This is an absolute shit-show,' said Walker. 'Has been from day one. The CPS are never going to allow this. Not unless we can conclusively prove which one of them is responsible for all this.'

'If it was *one* of them,' said DC Briggs. 'They might both have been in on it.'

He'd already considered that, of course, but hadn't wanted to say anything, hadn't wanted to bring the idea into the universe in case it made it true, somehow. That would really complicate things, even more than they already were. But it still seemed unlikely, given that Thomas would have had to masquerade as a journalist to accomplish this. 'Well, that might be possible too, I suppose,' he admitted, 'but for now, we'll assume that one of them is telling the truth,' said Walker.

'DI Hogarth, where are we on forensics?'

'It seems that standard forensic DNA testing cannot differentiate between monozygotic, identical twins—as you probably already realise. Fingerprints and dental records can, but as you know we have neither on record, as it seems the twins had no convictions and were not partial to a dentist either. However, there are more advanced techniques for differentiating DNA these days, which could shed some further light. This would involve some ultra-deep next generation sequencing aimed at identifying rare mutations. But it's far from guaranteed, of course, especially with the resources available to us,' said DI Hogarth. 'But there's a chance.'

'Well, if that's not guaranteed, and the DNA evidence we found at the crime scenes cannot be pinned to one or the other with the initial tests, then we need something else—a backup—some hard evidence. DC Briggs, at the hospital back there, Tom called me "DCI Walker". Did you notice that?'

'Er, I suppose so,' said DC Briggs, cocking her head to one side, inquisitively. 'What of it?'

'Well, I've been thinking about it—it's been bothering me—and I'm pretty sure I introduced myself as Detective Walker. Didn't I?'

'I'm not sure, sir,' she said. 'Maybe.'

'Well, if I did, how does he know my bloody rank if I didn't tell him?' said Walker.

'I suppose he probably saw it on your card,' said DC Briggs, referring to the ID card he always had hanging around his neck on a lanyard.

'It was cold, wasn't it? Had my jacket on. The ID card was tucked underneath. I had to get it out for the nurse, and then

CHAPTER THIRTY-NINE

I shoved it back in, out of the way—I remember that much,' said Walker.

'Oh,' said DC Briggs. 'Then maybe he's seen you on the telly, or he's read about what's been going on in one of the newspapers.'

'Possible, but unlikely,' said Walker. 'Especially since he's supposed to have been held captive since November sixth, and this whole thing only really became national news after that.'

Superintendent Lucy Stone entered, abruptly, without knocking. 'Detective Walker. My office. Now.'

It was a drill Walker was now getting used to. Last time, of course, she'd almost thrown him off the case. He wondered whether his luck had run out, but he wasn't even sure he could do anything much more to move the case forward anyway. It seemed to have reached a standstill.

Walker followed and sat down in Superintendent Stone's office, with her closing the door and sitting opposite him. She seemed less flustered this time, more *on it*, focussed.

'Tell me where we are with this case?' she asked. 'You got him, right? Are we well positioned to take this to the CPS now, prosecute?'

'Er, there's been a little problem,' said Walker.

'A *little problem?* Go on,' she said.

'He's an identical twin, and both twins are claiming the other one framed them,' said Walker, pausing, letting it settle, waiting for the inevitable explosion.

'You're kidding? What is this? Some Sky documentary True Crime bollocks? This is freaking ridiculous,' she said, at her wits end with the case, seeming just about ready to pack it all in. 'You must have *something*.'

'Well, we have DNA evidence from the first two crime scenes, but that could have been planted,' said Walker. 'So even if advanced forensic techniques can distinguish between the twins' DNA, which is not guaranteed, it might not help much if they both claim the other one planted their DNA at the crime scene—which it seems they are. They both referred to their mouths being swabbed, and hair being pulled out by tweezers while they were held captive; they're both saying they were held captive by the other. We're persevering to find prints at the crime scenes, or anywhere that would support their claims, as these would be unique, even for identical twins. But as yet we have nothing. They also both have matching haircuts—short back and sides, about the same length—no tattoos, piercings, notable birthmarks, scars, or blemishes, nothing really to differentiate the two, so eyewitness testimonies aren't going to help us much in that regard too.

'Oh, my God. Could this be any worse?'

'Both of them have motive to frame the other. Thomas Taylor apparently had an affair with Phillip Taylor's wife, Sammy. While Phillip Taylor said he's been accused by his brother of being very unkind to his wife since she'd been raped by Freddie Ward, suggested he blamed her for it. That's why Sammy might have got close to Thomas, because she needed more support and understanding; and *he* could blame Phillip for her suicide for this lack of kindness. I'd say Phillip's motive is the stronger of the two, though,' said Walker. 'Just a touch. If Thomas did have an affair with Phillip's wife, his own brother, then that provides really strong and clear motive, I'd say. Then again, if Thomas was in love with Sammy, and he blames his brother for her death for some reason, then

CHAPTER THIRTY-NINE

that is equally possible. We've started by questioning the friends and colleagues of both men, trying to establish who was doing what and where throughout the weeks and months leading up to this, while the Defender was building up to the first murder. Unfortunately, it seems Thomas was a bit of a recluse—no friends, unemployed, so no colleagues either. His neighbours knew little about him too, other than having his number on a local neighbourhood WhatsApp group, couldn't say whether he'd been there or not. One said they might have seen some lights going on and off recently but couldn't be sure. His kitchen was stocked with ready meals and snacks, so he could have survived like that for weeks or longer without needing any deliveries or going out. There was some post on the floor when we went in, with dates going back several weeks, but he may just have not bothered opening it if he was depressed—which his behaviour suggests he may have been. It's a real head scratcher, hard to definitively prove one way or the other at the moment with what we currently have, if they're both claiming the same.'

'Then get scratching then, Detective Walker!' said Superintendent Stone. She was losing it again. Frustrated with the whole case, as were Walker and his team. They'd come so far, only to be blocked at the final hurdle. 'We cannot have a situation here where both these men go free.'

'Well, one of them must have disappeared several days ago. We just need to find some evidence of that, somehow,' said Walker.

'The press, the public, my bosses, everyone are looking for some kind of a result, and it's up to us to give them that,' said Superintendent Stone.

'What, even if we get the wrong person?' asked Walker.

'They can't both walk,' said Superintendent Stone. 'They just *can't.* So, make sure you do get the right one, somehow.'

Walker gave it some thought. 'With no dental records and the same DNA, the one thing we have at the moment to distinguish between these two brothers is that they'll have different fingerprints—even identical twins have variances in their prints. I have no doubt that whoever committed these crimes was careful, but mistakes can always be made. Let me do a little more snooping around, see what we can come up with. There's still a lot of evidence to go through yet, lots to analyse. Who knows, we might get lucky.'

'Just get me a result, Detective,' she said. 'If this one goes unsolved, we're finished. You hear me? All of us: *finished.*'

CHAPTER FORTY

'Where are we going, Chief?' asked DC Briggs.

Walker was grabbing his jacket, mobile phone, and car key fob from his desk, ready to move, but then stopped in his tracks, an idea forming. 'Wait,' he said, suddenly rooting through a mountain of paperwork on his and other officer's desks. There were tons of it from the case—they hadn't had a chance to go through all of it yet. 'The three-quarter length snooker cue I took from Q's Sports, as evidence—I had it actioned to be dusted for prints, and the place in general. No match came back, but that was before we had Phillip and Tom Taylor. We can't prove that whoever touched that cue used the murder weapon, but it could point us in the right direction, and it would add to the weight of evidence.'

'Here, got it,' said DC Ainscough, who'd been helping with the search.

'Give it to me,' said DI Hogarth. 'I'll scan the prints and check now. But we only have Phillip Taylor's fingerprints as yet, so we need to get Tom's as well. Just running it now… No. Nothing. It's not from Phillip.'

'Supt says we need to close the case with a positive result or we're all gonna be in deep shit,' said Walker.

'And what does that mean, exactly?' asked DC Briggs.

'I think she means we'll all be fired if we don't bring home the bacon,' said Walker.

DC Ainscough squinted behind his glasses. 'Well, I'm vegetarian, so—'

'Don't get smart, Detective,' snapped Walker.

'I wasn't… I didn't mean…' stuttered DC Ainscough. He actually wasn't the type to be a smart-arse, was probably just trying to lighten the mood; but his timing was off—way off.

'Never mind,' said Walker. 'I think we need to focus on the fingerprints. This is the only bit of evidence that's going to actually distinguish between these two.

'Unless the genome sequencing is successful,' added DI Hogarth.

'Yeah. Unless that. But that's a real longshot by the sounds of it, plus it may have been planted if one of them was holding the other captive. For now, we have to assume that won't be successful, or won't hold up in court, and go out and find something else,' said Walker. 'It's not looking like we're going to find the murder weapon from the killing of Michael Tracy—the snooker cue butt end—he could have got rid of it anywhere: in the rubbish, in the sea even. We got no prints back from the tranquilizer darts, but the prints we have from the abandoned car do match those of the man we have in custody who claims to be Phillip Taylor. Let's go through the CCTV footage again from the prison, see if he takes his gloves off at any point, touches anything. If we can find prints from one of them at the prison, then we have them, for those murders at least. That would be good enough to put them away for a very long time—probably for good.'

'Sounds like a plan, Chief,' said DC Briggs, but not sounding

CHAPTER FORTY

entirely convinced. She was right, it was a longshot, but then again, most cases were solved by taking a punt like this, seeing what turned up. It was a matter of staying in the game, taking enough shots, and eventually one would inevitably go in, land, get them a result—if they were lucky. It was how he worked.

'DI Hogarth, can you hook us up to a big screen in one of the conference rooms so we can all look at the footage together?' asked Walker. 'The more eyes on this the better. It's all in the details.'

'Can do,' said DI Hogarth. 'Why not.'

'Great idea,' said DC Hardman. 'Sometimes some of the small details can be missed on one of these little laptop screens.'

'I agree. Come on then,' said Walker. 'Let's go take another look.'

* * *

'There,' said Walker. 'Go back a few frames.'

They were looking at CCTV footage taken from HMP Kirkham, the night Freddie Ward was murdered. They'd seen it before, but not on a projector screen in a darkened room, one that was about five feet by seven feet. It provided a whole new perspective.

DI Hogarth did as asked, went back on the footage a few seconds, and started it again.

'Look, 'said Walker, standing up now, pointing at the projector screen with his pen, then lightly tapping on it, making the screen move around a little, then thinking better of it, backing off a few centimetres. 'He backs into this door a tad, touches it with his hand—the one he just removed a glove from to put the strap of his mask back over his ear. He's distracted by a guard coming. He probably doesn't even remember. It all happens so quickly—so quickly that we almost missed it ourselves.'

'Wow. I think we've got him, Chief,' said DC Briggs. 'We've really got him.'

'Not yet. Get forensics back over there, immediately, and make sure all prison staff have been told not to clean anything until they get there. I don't want anyone messing this up. It's too important,' said Walker.

'I'm betting it's Tom,' said DC Hardman. 'Slit his own throat, pinned it on his brother—sick bastard.' Everyone looked at him, not seeming too impressed with his little outburst. 'I'm sorry, but... that's what I reckon.'

'Well, we do get a quick glimpse of their face when they pulled the mask down to take a breather, and it's definitely one of the Taylor brothers,' said Walker. 'The only question is: *which one?* Let's mobilise, people. DC Ainscough, you make sure we have Tom Taylor's prints, and get some extra security on him while he's still at the hospital. It's important. Get him arrested and cuffed to the bed if you have to. And as soon as he's discharged, get him in here. DC Hardman, see if you can get any more from Phillip's work colleagues. Ask them if he'd been acting any differently recently—any change in body language, mannerisms, way of speaking, that kind of thing. If Tom has been impersonating him, someone may have noticed something. And DI Hogarth, you can check the phone records of the two brothers, highlight any calls between them that might help call their statements into question. They both

CHAPTER FORTY

claimed there hadn't been any recent contact with the other. DC Briggs, you come with me. We're going back to HMP Kirkham. I want to be on site for this one, make sure all goes smoothly, see if there's anything else we can spot over there we might have missed before. This is going to be key.'

'Okay, Chief,' she said. 'And if we can't get any prints there?'

'Then we'll try to find some of Tom's fingerprints at the Blackpool Gazette offices, see if he's been masquerading as Phillip,' said Walker. 'But failing that, we'll very much be back to square one, Constable,' said Walker. 'And we might all be working the checkouts at Asda next week.'

CHAPTER FORTY-ONE

'This is it,' said Walker. This is the section of the door that he touched—right... *here*.' He was pointing with his pen again, the same one he'd recently used to touch the projector screen with, when he'd pointed at the very same part of the door on the CCTV footage.

He was talking to a Crime Scene Investigator, a Fingerprint Expert from the forensic team—a middle aged fella without a single hair on his head; something Walker thought might be beneficial for someone in his line of work. 'If there's anything there, we'll get it,' said the CSI. 'Don't you worry about that.' He had a Scottish lilt to his accent, maybe Edinburgh. 'I just need a few minutes.'

Walker and DC Briggs stood back, let the man do his job. 'Let's take another look at Freddie Ward's unit.'

The quarters Freddie Ward had been sleeping in, and killed in, like many of the other units, was still an active crime scene, and was therefore currently unused. There was still some police tape on the door, reminding staff and anyone else not to go in there. One of the prison staff unlocked the door for them, let them inside.

'Smells a bit,' said DC Briggs, cracking open the window. They were already wearing nitrile gloves and plastic shoe

CHAPTER FORTY-ONE

covers, as per procedure, so as to not contaminate the crime scene.

'Well, there's still some congealed blood on the floor, isn't there,' said Walker. 'We asked them not to clean it up yet, remember? Careful not to step in it.'

The bed was still moved out from the wall as they left it, revealing the writing spray-painted onto the wall behind it. 'Be Kind. One More To Go…'

Walker crouched down, looked at it. Nobody else had actually died since the carnage here, which made Walker wonder whether there might still be one more to go—one more person to be murdered. On the face of it, it appeared that the last victim was supposed to be either Phillip or Thomas Taylor, whichever one wasn't doing the killing. But it all had the feeling of a master plan about it. He'd come across killers with big plans before, who'd put all the pieces of their jigsaw puzzle in place, before hammering in the final piece.

'It takes a hell of a lot to cut your own throat, Chief,' said DC Briggs. 'Who can do that? The killer must be Phillip, mustn't it?'

Walker looked at her. 'You'd think so, wouldn't you?'

'We just need his prints on that door,' she said. 'Then we have him. And if it turns out to be Tom's prints, then… well, it's pretty unbelievable what he's done, brutal.'

'It sounds like you're almost in admiration, Detective Briggs,' said Walker, frowning. He'd seen Police Detectives be impressed by crimes before, and he didn't like it, not one bit.

'No, not at all,' said DC Briggs. 'I just mean it's probably the most unlikely scenario here.'

Walker stood back up, straightening his clothing. 'But it often is the less likely scenario that emerges as the truth,' he said. 'That's why we let the evidence lead us. I don't think there's anything else here.' He looked at the Bible on Freddie Ward's bedside table, picked it up, looked through it.

'Looks like the guy found God. It's often the way when a terrible crime or transgression has been committed, isn't it?—they want to find forgiveness. Do you know anything about the story of Cain and Abel?'

'Yes, of course,' said DC Briggs. 'Cain killed Abel, right, because he was jealous or something—or was it the other way around?'

'No. I think that was it. He was jealous because God accepted Abel's sacrifice, but not his own. So, according to the scriptures, Cain became the world's very first murderer,' said Walker. 'He was then condemned to a life of wandering.'

'Brothers,' said DC Briggs.

'Brothers,' said Walker. 'Either they're thick as thieves, or they hate each other.'

'You know, for someone who isn't religious, you certainly know a lot about the Bible,' said DC Briggs.

Walker was still flicking through Freddie's copy of the Bible, but then stopped, finding a piece of paper tucked away in there. He took it out, unfolded it: on it, it said "I forgive you – S."

'What is it, Chief?'

'I'm not sure. Maybe something from Samantha Taylor. It says she forgives him,' said Walker. 'If it's her.'

'But somebody didn't forgive him,' said DC Briggs. 'Or he wouldn't have ended up like this.'

'Let's see if the CSI is done yet,' said Walker, pulling his gloves off and exiting the room, DC Briggs following.

When they got back out, the bald CSI from before was just

tidying his things away, looking like he was done.

'You get anything?' asked Walker.

'I did,' said the man. 'But it could really be from anyone in here, so don't get your hopes up just yet.'

'Oh, I never do,' said Walker. 'Don't you worry about that. I never do.'

CHAPTER FORTY-TWO

Walker entered the Incident Room they had at Blackpool Police HQ, the door slamming the wall as he did. He walked in with purpose, perhaps a little too aggressively, and everyone—DI Hogarth, DCs Ainscough and Hardman, and a couple of PCs—looked at him, one of the PC's mouths dropping open.

'Right, what do we have, people?' he asked, his voice raised, still pumped up, feeling the case reaching its climax. 'Hardman?'

'Talked to Phillip Taylor's co-workers. Some of 'em said he's been acting a bit funny recently—hasn't really been himself. When I pushed them for more, they said he was unusually scatty and distracted, forgetting where things were and what he was supposed to be doing—that kind of thing,' said DC Hardman. 'I also asked if he was forgetting anyone's name, but they said not. When I looked on the Blackpool Gazette website though, all the staff are listed there with photos, so he could have easily memorised the names of anyone he hadn't met before—if he was the twin, I mean. That's all I could get, I'm afraid. It's hard to say whether this strangeness is that of an imposter, or that of someone going off the rails, I'd say. Did you get anything? From the prison? Those prints?'

CHAPTER FORTY-TWO

'DC Ainscough? Did you see Thomas Taylor?' asked Walker, ignoring the Detective's question. He needed to get information first, not give it out. Everything was on a *need-to-know* basis, and that he didn't need to know right at this moment.

'I did,' said DC Ainscough. 'He's in a bad way—his condition seems to be declining. Got his prints though. Logged them in the system.'

'Good,' said Walker. 'We're just waiting on the prints we got from the prison off that door. Forensics will send it over any minute now. DI Hogarth, you looked at phone records. Anything there?'

'No. But… Just got an email come in from Forensics. They sent a report with a copy of the fingerprints they got. You're not going to believe this,' he said.

'What?' said Walker.

'It's Tom, isn't it. The prints from the prison are Thomas Taylor's, right?' said DC Hardman, getting excited.

'I did say no bets, right?' said Walker, gruffly, annoyed at the interruption. 'Go on.'

DI Hogarth smiled. 'He's right. The prints taken from the door at HMP Kirkham are from one Thomas Taylor.'

Walker banged on the table with his fist in delight, and everyone *whooped* or shouted.

'Yes!' said DC Ainscough, getting uncharacteristically carried away.

'We did it,' said DC Briggs, who'd been stood just behind Walker the whole time.

'We did', said Walker. Everyone looked relieved, DI Hogarth still with a broad smile on his chubby face too. There were few good moments in CID, but occasionally, like this, when they finally got a result, it all seemed worth it.

'Cut his own God damned throat,' said DC Hardman. 'That takes some doing.'

'It certainly does,' said Walker. 'But that's where we are. It was Thomas Taylor who'd been wearing that prison uniform, the one we found Phillip Taylor in. Phillip explicitly said his brother forced him into it when we took his statement, obviously to try and frame him. It almost worked too.'

'Jesus. Poor chap,' said DC Briggs. 'He was telling the truth all along. His brother had tied him up, done all those terrible things, and was planning to pin it all on him, walk free. It's unbelievable.'

'Well… we've got him now. Let's get down to the hospital, arrest him officially, make sure he's properly secure and in custody,' said Walker.

'Oh, he's already secure,' said DC Ainscough. 'Got several bobbies still stationed outside the ward, and Thomas is cuffed to the bed now. He wouldn't get far anyway. Looks like there were some complications with his injury or something.'

'Well, we'll get down there and make sure anyway. I want to see for myself, make sure everything is watertight down there,' said Walker.

DC Hardman got up, slapped Walker on the back. 'Congratulations, Chief.'

DC Briggs also touched his arm. 'We did it,' she said. 'Looks like we're all gonna keep our jobs after all.'

Walker nodded but wasn't entirely sure whether that was even a good thing. He felt jaded, tired of it all—the murders, the chasing, the tragedies, loss. But at least Tom's print found at the prison corroborated his brother's story of being forced into the guard's uniform. 'It seems so,' he said. 'Come on then,

CHAPTER FORTY-TWO

let's tie this one off, get it done and dusted. DC Ainscough, please tell Phillip Taylor he'll be released very soon, that he won't face any charges. I'll talk to him myself when I get back and do the necessary.'

'Will do,' said DC Ainscough.

'It's been a pleasure working with you all,' said Walker, wondering whether they ever might all work on a case together again in the future—but, as always, assuming not, as teams tended to change from case to case, depending upon what skillsets were required. 'Thank you for your efforts, everyone. You did good.'

CHAPTER FORTY-THREE

'Nurse. What's going on here?' asked Walker. There was a flurry of activity in the ward that Thomas Taylor had been assigned to, doctors and medical staff crowded around Thomas's bed, frantically going about their work.

'Out of the way, Detective,' said the nurse. 'Let us work, please.'

Walker stepped out of the way, along with DC Briggs, mirroring him, giving the staff more space to come and go.

'It looks like his organs are shutting down,' said one of the doctors. 'Get another IV in him, quick. That one's empty. Who's been on him?' The doctor was annoyed. Someone hadn't been doing their job properly. 'He needs more fluids and antibiotics. He's in septic shock.'

'On it,' said one of the male nurses.

'We need to get prepped for surgery. Get him in theatre, now!' said the Doctor, and then they wheeled him out of there, still cuffed to the bed.

DC Briggs looked at Walker, eyes wide, eyebrows raised. 'He's not going to make it, is he, sir?' she said.

Walker shook his head. 'I have no idea, but that didn't look good,' he said. 'Not good at all.'

CHAPTER FORTY-THREE

'After all this—us finally getting the evidence we need for a conviction—he's not going to go to prison after all', she said. 'Incredible.'

'I'm afraid that is now a distinct possibility,' said Walker. 'Let's follow, take a seat outside the theatre, see what happens. We'll have to inform his brother if he dies, of course.'

'Yeah. And despite everything, it's still his brother—and his *twin* brother at that. There'll be a lot of mixed emotions there,' she said. 'That's going to be difficult. Poor man, after all he's been through already.'

'Well, let's not get ahead of ourselves. Let's wait and see what happens, first,' said Walker, but he held little hope that Thomas Taylor would survive. It irked him that the man wouldn't be incarcerated for his crimes, but at least they had an explanation for what had gone on now—a conclusion. Samantha's suicide had been caused by cruelty, and the man who loved her wanted vengeance on the specific people he saw as responsible and harboured a loathing for what he saw as wrong in human nature, until he eventually went off the rails. The message that scumbags need their skulls cracking struck a chord with folk and it snowballed online into the Bonfire Night riots as their own thing, while Tom carried on with his mission. The only thing he didn't know was whether Tom had participated in those riots and killings himself—Supt Stone's team had not been able to rule him out of all of those—and it was now possible that the truth of this might die with him. He hoped not; and there was still hope. The investigation was still ongoing, and Tom wasn't dead yet. 'Maybe he'll live. The one thing I've learned about this job is you just never, ever know.'

***

The same doctor from earlier came out of the operating theatre, wiping his hands on some paper towels and popping them in a nearby bin. He breathed a heavy sigh, wiped his face, before seeing Walker and DC Briggs sat there, looking up at him.

'You the detectives?' he asked.

Walker and DC Briggs got up, addressed him, just as a couple of nurses also came out and went on their way.

'That's correct. I'm DCI Walker, and my colleague DC Briggs. What do we have?' asked Walker.

'I'm afraid the surgery was unsuccessful,' said the Doctor. 'Several of his organs failed due to septic shock, a result of an infection—methicillin-resistant Staphylococcus aureus, more commonly known as MRSA.'

'Oh, my,' said DC Briggs. 'That's just so common in hospitals around here, isn't it? I know several people who got such infections while in hospital, and one or two that died too. It's just awful.'

'Well, it is what it is,' said the Doctor. 'We do our best to keep things sterile.'

'No, I'm sure that you do,' said DC Briggs, stuttering. 'I didn't mean…'

'What she means,' said Walker, looking at her, 'is that you do incredible work under the circumstances. We've been chasing this guy for a long time. We're just a little disappointed that we couldn't complete our job and get a conviction, that's all.'

The doctor nodded. 'I understand,' he said. 'But the disappointment should be that another human being has died,

CHAPTER FORTY-THREE

regardless of what he's done.'

Walker wondered if he might still be saying that if he knew what Thomas Taylor had done—probably not. He may even have treated some of his victims, before they'd died, the ones from the carnage of Bonfire Night, if Tom had been involved in that too.

'Well, thank you for your time,' said Walker, and the doctor started to walk away. 'Oh, just one more thing.'

The doctor turned back around. 'Yes?'

'Did Thomas Taylor say anything, before he died. Was he conscious at all?' ask Walker.

'Before we put him under with a general anaesthetic, he did mutter something, over and over. Something about people being kinder?' Does that make any sense?' said the Doctor.

'Oh, it does. It makes perfect sense,' said Walker. 'You don't watch the news much, do you?'

The Doctor shook his head. 'Don't have the time. And I see the news every day, right here. This is where it all happens.'

And with that, it seemed the case against Thomas Taylor was abruptly closed.

CHAPTER FORTY-FOUR

'Phillip Taylor. I'm afraid we have some bad news,' said Walker. He had him in one of the interview rooms at Blackpool Police HQ, DC Briggs beside him. They were tying off the case, processing the final paperwork, and informing Phillip of the death of his brother before letting him go.

'It's Tom, isn't it?' he said. 'He's dead. He killed himself.'

Walker nodded, as solemnly as he could. 'I'm afraid your brother didn't make it, Mr Taylor.'

Phillip broke down, head in hands, crying. He started shaking his head. '*Stupid bastard,*' he said, muttering. '*Why'd you do that? You didn't have to do that.*'

'I'm sorry. It's all over, Mr Taylor. You may go home, now. Resume your life. I'm sure the good folks at the Blackpool Gazette will be happy to offer you some bereavement leave. You can rest up at home, build yourself back up. You must have lost a lot of weight while you were being held like that.'

He looked at his arm. 'I suppose so,' he said. 'So, I'm free to go?'

Walker nodded. 'We found the evidence we needed. We know it wasn't you that went to HMP Kirkham, killed those people. We know it was your brother, that what you said was

CHAPTER FORTY-FOUR

true, that he made you change into that prison uniform he took, made it look like it was you that was there.'

'I see,' said Phillip. 'This is going to make a hell of a story. Sorry... once a journalist, always a journalist.'

'There's no need for apologies, Tom,' said Walker. 'After what you've been through.'

'Phillip,' said Phillip. 'I'm Phillip, not Tom.'

'Sorry,' said Walker, scrutinising him. He was just checking, trying to trip him up. One last check, just in case. 'You may go now, Mr Taylor.'

Phillip Taylor got up, took a last look at Walker and DC Briggs. 'I'm sorry about all this,' he said. 'He was my brother, I should have... I'm sorry.'

And then he left.

* * *

Now back in the Incident Room, everyone was busy packing up, getting everything in boxes—all the documents and bits and bobs. DC Hardman was just coming through with one heavy-looking box of folders when Walker and DC Briggs entered.

'Another one for storage,' he said. 'Man, this was a big case.'

'Man?' said Walker, reminding him of his rank.

'Sorry. DCI Walker. There's just so much stuff!' he said, seeming happy the case had finally reached a conclusion.

DC Ainscough was also packing a box full of his personal belongings—his laptop, various stationery, glasses case, and some candies, but DI Hogarth was still sat there with his computer open, ever the workaholic.

'Er… Wait a minute. You're all gonna want to see this,' he said, his voice bordering on urgency. Walker had heard that tone before. It meant he had something. 'Maybe you should put those boxes back down for now.'

'What is it, Inspector?' asked Walker, wondering what kind of curveball his work life was going to throw at him now, having already had more than a few.

'I'm not sure yet. Wait. It might be nothing.' He tapped on his laptop keyboard for a few seconds. 'Okay. Here it is. Oh… *shit*,' said DI Hogarth. He didn't swear much, so Walker knew it was something serious. 'Have you let Phillip Taylor go yet?'

'Yes, he's just gone, a few minutes ago,' said DC Briggs, her eyes getting wider.

'Then get him back in here, *now!*' said DI Hogarth, and DCs Briggs and Hardman scrambled, got out of there.

'What is it?' asked Walker, before also heading for the exit.

'It's the results from the genome sequencing, from the two twins—they found a discrepancy; they've been able to definitively determine which twin the DNA sample from the Michael Tracy case came from…' He looked at Walker, for once not milking what he'd found, but seeming genuinely in shock. 'It was from Phillip Taylor.'

* * *

'He's gone, Chief.' It was DC Briggs, out in the street nearby Blackpool Police HQ. She was out of breath, having been

CHAPTER FORTY-FOUR

running around, looking for Phillip Taylor. 'Could have got a bus, or a taxi—anything, really. He had his phone. The desk staff gave him all his belongings, as instructed.'

Walker paced up and down, head down, before stamping on the floor in frustration. 'Damn it,' he said.

'DC Hardman is still looking. He ran off—he's fitter than me—said he'd ring if he found anything,' said DC Briggs.

'God, I hate it when they run,' said Walker, having been in a similar situation with their previous big case, over in Chorley; one that ended in tragedy when that young boy had killed himself. He didn't want anyone else dying. He had to catch up to Phillip Taylor and bring him in before he hurt anyone else. 'Let's get the car, survey the area, and get all available resources on this as a matter of urgency.'

'Agreed,' said DC Briggs. 'Chief, did they do this together?'

'I'm not sure of anything right now, but it's starting to look that way,' he said. 'Unless Phillip claims the DNA was planted by Tom, which is also possible—although that doesn't fit with the timeline of his story. Or maybe Phillip planted Tom's fingerprint at the prison somehow, to frame him.'

'But if they did do it together, why on Earth would they do that?' she asked, on the move, as they headed over to the car park.

'Well, *that*, is the million-dollar question now, isn't it?' he said. 'We could press Jonny some more. Maybe he knows something, but I doubt he'll talk. Right now, though, first, we just need to find this guy.'

CHAPTER FORTY-FIVE

'Chief, we've got him.' It was DC Hardman this time, speaking to Walker on his mobile.

'You've *got* him? You mean he's cuffed, actually in custody?' asked Walker, wanting confirmation.

'No. We've not actually *got him*, got him, but he can't go anywhere, I mean. He's up the Tower,' said DC Hardman. 'Blackpool Tower. Went up there of his own accord, by all accounts. Weird. He has a knife, apparently, and a big bag, but he's not hurt anyone—yet. Made everyone get out of there, sent them down in the lift. He's up there right now, alone. God knows what he's doing. He's no way of getting down because the lift operator took the key. Had to, to get everyone out of there. So, either he didn't think it through, or he wanted it that way.'

'Shit,' said Walker. 'He's planning something. Wants to go out with a bang, probably. These nutjobs always do. He has no intention of leaving. Get that place watertight. In fact, get the surrounding area evacuated as much as humanly possible, just in case.'

'In case what?' asked DC Hardman.

'I don't know yet. Just do it. We're on our way. Be there soon,' said Walker, before hanging up.

CHAPTER FORTY-FIVE

'Oh, good God, whatever next,' said DC Briggs, probably not quite believing what was going on, despite her now racking up some considerable experience of this kind of thing in a relatively short space of time. 'What do you think he's going to do this time?'

'I really have no idea,' said Walker. 'But it can't be anything good—not with his track record. Let's just hope we can get to him before he does anything else. Come on.'

* * *

Walker was now back in the lift he'd gone up the Blackpool Tower in just a few days ago with DC Briggs—the brick-red coloured metal girders whizzing past them once more as they went up, and up. He was with his partner again, but this time DC Hardman had joined them too, just in case they needed some extra muscle. The tour guide had shown them how to use the lift, and they were operating it themselves with the dedicated security key—the one that Phillip Taylor had given up control of for some reason. Walker decided to take the key and leave its operator behind, so no one else was put in danger.

'Almost there,' said DC Hardman, who was voluntarily manning the lift controls. He was the proactive type, all right, ready to take control, do what needed to be done. Walker liked that, though—it allowed him to focus his thoughts, get mentally prepared.

Walker got his baton out in one hand and his taser in the other, and DC Briggs followed his lead. DC Hardman looked at them and nodded.

'I'll use these,' he said, showing them his meaty hands. It was better if one of them had some hands free, in case Phillip needed to be manhandled, or if some other tasks needed doing, so Walker said nothing.

'Just expect the unexpected,' he said, before the lift came to a standstill. Unlike the last time they were in this lift, though, DC Briggs didn't look relieved when it stopped moving, like previously, her unease about the situation possibly overriding her obvious discomfort with heights.

They got out of the lift, cautiously, took a little look around. The place looked deserted—there was no one, at least not near the lift.

'Right. We stick together,' said Walker. 'Clear each area and level as we go.'

The lift couldn't be operated without the key they'd been given, and DC Hardman had that, stuffed in his trouser pocket. Phillip Taylor wasn't going back down the way he'd come up, not unless he was in their custody, or if he took them all out, nabbed the key. He was there for the taking, but he'd put himself there voluntarily, and that bothered Walker. It felt like a trap. He was definitely up to something—the question was, *what?*

'Smells a bit funny in here, Chief,' said DC Briggs. 'Different to last time. Clean, somehow. Almost sterile.'

Walker took a deep inhale through his nose. She was right. 'Maybe they just cleaned?'

DC Briggs smelled the air again. 'Oh, that's not a cleaning product, sir.'

Walker bent down. There were patches of moisture formed on the floor and walls. He wondered whether it might always be like that as a result of the damp sea air. He wiped his finger on some, tentatively tasted it. He knew that taste, knew it well from periods in his life when he'd been struggling, when he'd needed something to get through the day.

'It's vodka,' he said. 'Someone's been spraying vodka everywhere. He's going to start a fire. Find him, quick. We stick together. And if this thing starts to go up, we head back to the lift, immediately. Got it?'

DCs Briggs and Hardman nodded, in agreement.

They slowly moved through the level of the Tower Eye they were on—the level that featured the SkyWalk, the famous glass-bottomed viewpoint that Walker and DC Briggs had been on before, when they'd seen the graffiti on the Promenade below. It was still there, telling everyone to "Be Kind", but Walker only glanced at it this time, walking straight over the glass floor while they cleared the area, checking for any items left behind, or any other clues, being careful not to slip on any of the vodka residue or pools of it that had been left here and there.

'Right. We've been all around,' said DC Hardman, speaking softly in case Phillip was lurking somewhere, listening. 'This level is clear. Let's go up.'

Walker nodded and took the lead, creeping up the winding metal staircase that took them to the next level. They walked all the way around the platform, which had again been doused in the same flammable liquid, but again there was nothing, and they went up one more level—one more winding metal staircase, going ever higher.

'This is the last level open to the public,' said DC Briggs. 'Right?'

'That's correct. You were paying attention during the tour

after all,' said Walker. 'Last is the Crow's Nest, right? For maintenance only.'

DC Briggs nodded, confirming what Walker remembered. 'What's he doing up here?' she asked, more to herself than anything as they continued with their search. 'He's planning to torch the place, kill himself in the process? Send one last message? This is nuts.'

'Or jump off with a parachute,' offered DC Hardman, but Walker didn't take that comment too seriously. This wasn't a Tom Cruise film; it was real life.

'Well, if we don't stop him, we'll never find out why he's doing what he's doing. Keep moving,' said Walker.

They finished surveying the level, which didn't take as long as the previous level, as it was smaller—each level of the Tower Top becoming tighter as it graduated upwards and inwards, moving towards a final nexus point, just like the case. They got to the final staircase, the one leading up to the Crow's Nest. There was a metal gate closed over, preventing the public from going up there, but there was no padlock on it, as one might expect, to keep people safe.

'This thing should be locked. Did anyone mention him getting a maintenance key?' asked Walker.

'It's chaos down there,' said DC Hardman. 'Haven't had a chance to talk to everyone yet. It's possible. Or he just nicked some keys.'

'Well, unless he slipped by us when we were moving around, he must be up there,' said Walker, pointing with his eyes towards the Crow's Nest. 'And if he did slip by us, he'll have nowhere to go, so let's check up there first. I'll go. You two stay here. It'll be too tight up there anyway. We'll just get in each other's way. I'll call if I need you.'

CHAPTER FORTY-FIVE

'Chief?' said DC Briggs, with a look of concern. 'Is that wise?'

'It's okay. I have these.' He held up his baton, which he held in his dominant right hand, and the taser, in his left. 'I'll call you,' he said, firmly, and with some finality.

'Okay. But be careful,' said DC Briggs.

'Go get the bastard,' offered DC Hardman. 'I'm here if you need me.' He looked pumped, ready for action—would probably be disappointed if he didn't get any at this point.

Walker looked up, opened the maintenance gate, and started to very slowly climb the stairs.

* * *

'You took your time, didn't you?' It was Phillip Taylor. He was leaning against some of the outer railings of the Crow's Nest, looking at Walker, who only had his upper body up into the final level of the Blackpool Tower yet, having not made it off the stairs.

'Mr Taylor. *Phillip* Taylor. We made a big mistake letting you go.' Walker took a few more steps up, one by one, and got onto the platform itself. 'We now have the evidence we need to charge you for the murders of Anthony Singelmann and Michael Tracy. You need to come with us. You do not have to say anything, but it may harm your defence if you do not mention—'

'I told you: Tom took some samples,' he said. 'Hair and spit, that kind of thing. Probably planted it at the crime scenes.'

'But you said he only came the day after Bonfire Night,' said

Walker. 'Your story doesn't add up.'

'Then... I don't know. Maybe he broke into my place before that, got some more samples from there,' said Phillip.

'Then why the hell are you here?' asked Walker.

'Why are you?' asked Phillip.

Walker thought the man didn't seem in his right mind, was a bit confused, unfocussed, scatty. He had dark bags under dead-looking eyes. There were some other items to one side of the Crow's Nest, what looked like a scuba-diver's oxygen tank of all things, and a rucksack.

'Phillip, we believe you have a knife, have been threatening people with it, coercing them. I need you to put the knife on the floor,' said Walker, raising the taser up, pointing it at him.

Phillip took out a knife from his pocket, still in its sheath. But instead of dropping it on the floor, he removed the sheath and placed the blade of the knife on his own neck.

'Put the gun down or I'll cut myself,' he said. 'Just like Tom did.'

'Easy, Mr Taylor.' Walker did as asked and carefully placed the taser back in its holster.

'And the baton,' Phillip added. 'On the floor.'

'Mr Taylor, you really—'

'Do it!' he said.

'I'll place it in its holster, but that's it,' said Walker, doing so. 'There. Empty handed. Now what?'

Phillip smiled. 'Now we reward the people for being kinder to each other,' he said.

He walked over to the rucksack, Walker never taking his eyes off the man, putting his hand back on the taser, ready to release it should it be required. Phillip unzipped the bag, took out some money, while also carefully watching Walker

CHAPTER FORTY-FIVE

for any sudden moves too.

'Another hundred grand,' he said, throwing a wad to Walker, who caught it.

On the top note had been written "Be Kind" in a black marker pen, and on each of the subsequent notes as Walker flicked through.

'You can have that,' he said. 'For helping to stop some of this scum. We've been pretty much doing the same job, after all.'

Walker threw it back to him. 'No thanks. I already get paid.'

Phillip failed to catch the wad, unlike Walker, but it dropped nearby. He picked it up, put it back in the bag. Then, he started to cut the safety netting surrounding the Crow's Nest, making a hole just big enough to throw the money out, but probably not big enough to throw himself out after it. A gust of wind blew through, making them both wobble a touch. 'It's my last wish—to give back to the people. May I?'

Walker nodded, not seeing the harm in it. 'If you'll come quietly once you've released the cash, you may.'

Phillip smiled again and proceeded to throw the cash out of the hole he'd made, taking each individual wrapper off every wad by ripping them with the knife he had, watching the notes fly and spread out as they fell, the wind catching them, making the money travel far and wide. It took some time, but Walker left him to his task, watching his every move until there was no money left.

'There,' he said. 'All done.'

'Good,' said Walker. 'I need you to come with us now. I'm going to have to cuff you, Phillip. I need you to turn around and put your hands behind your back.'

'Do you know what the Olympic flame symbolises?' asked

Phillip.

Here we go, thought Walker. They always wanted to talk when it was too late, when they'd accepted the game was up—whatever that game was. Everyone wanted to explain their side of the story, their perspective, even psychopaths. Everyone just wanted to be listened to.

'Phillip.'

'Continuity between the ancient and the modern, the old and the new—the flame never going out. We could use a bit of that now, don't you think?' he asked. 'Some of the old ways were far better—politeness, respect, community.'

'Sure,' said Walker, not wanting to encourage him just yet, wanting to get him secure first. 'But I'm going to need to cuff you now.'

'Don't you want to know what happened? Why I did what I did?' asked Phillip.

So, it *was* him. He was practically admitting it. And Walker did want to know. He knew it would haunt him if he never found out what happened. So many people had died because of this man. He needed to know what made him tick. He needed to know *why*. But first he needed to get those bloody cuffs on.

'I'd rather we talked about all that down at the station,' said Walker. Phillip grabbed the oxygen tank, dragged the bag over. 'What do you have there, Phillip? What's this?'

He took something out of the bag. 'Blowtorch,' he said.

Shit. He was going to start a fire, probably try to cause an explosion with the oxygen tank. 'Where'd you get that from?' asked Walker, wanting to stall, slow him down, keep him talking while he thought what to do, his mind getting frantic, going into overdrive.

CHAPTER FORTY-FIVE

'Had it in storage, not far away,' he said. 'The cash too. That was the last of it. Quite good these little storage facilities, aren't they? God knows what else people hide in there. You should do some raids sometime.'

'So, you want to light this place up, that it?' asked Walker. He looked down the stairs. 'Briggs, Hardman, get out of here. Now.'

There was a pause. 'You said to stick together, sir. Not going anywhere without you,' shouted DC Hardman.

'Okay, Phillip. Let's talk here then,' said Walker. 'Explain to me why you did all this.' Phillip put the oxygen tank and the blowtorch back down, but close enough he could get it should Walker make a move, which he was preparing to do imminently.

'You'll probably even help me when you've heard my story,' he said.

'I doubt that, Phillip. But go on. What started all this? I heard your wife died, right? Suicide?' said Walker. 'That's tough. Tough for anyone. But what happened to her, before—that's terrible. That must have been really difficult for you, Phillip.'

'Her brother's sodding boyfriend, of all people, brought some drug dealer into our house and the bastard raped her. Can you believe that? Blamed his daddy for hitting him, or some bollocks, said he got hooked on drugs. Freddie Ward. She'd just had a miscarriage, for Christ's sake. Bet you didn't know that, did you? She was already suffering. Do you really think the world is not better off without the likes of him?'

Walker actually found it pretty hard to disagree with that, in itself, but people couldn't just go around killing others. It would be anarchy. Society would crumble.

'But we found your brother's fingerprints in the prison,' said Walker. 'Were you in on this together?'

'I already told you Tom had an affair with my wife,' said Phillip. 'After Sammy was… violated, like she was, by that animal, one of Freddie Ward's lot, we grew apart. I couldn't touch her anymore. It just made me think of *him,* that bastard, inside of her. I got all twisted up, wondered whether she might have even led him on, at one point. I was hurting too, and I had trust issues. I suppose she got lonely, started spending some time with Tom, who kept visiting. I thought nothing of it at first, was glad to get some time on my own, truth be told. But then, one day, she confessed that she'd kissed him, that they'd slept together. My trust issues turned out to be a self-fulfilling prophecy. Said she was lonely, needed support, needed more—from *me*. It was all so confusing. I was furious with Tom, hit him, told him I was never going to see him again. I tried to make it right with Sammy—didn't want to lose her, couldn't imagine my life without her—but it was already too late, I guess.'

'But why'd you start killing people?' asked Walker.

'The day before Sammy died, some woman had a go at her while she was shopping. Sam said she didn't even do anything, just got in her way a little bit. The woman exploded, called her all sorts—really hurtful things. She was already depressed with everything that had happened. I guess it was the last straw. Sammy was such a kind-hearted soul, you see. She just couldn't stand it when people were unkind to each other. The way the world's becoming, I suppose she just didn't want to be a part of it anymore,' said Phillip. 'So, she… did what she did.'

'And then what happened?' asked Walker.

CHAPTER FORTY-FIVE

'I just… couldn't get over everything that happened. I tried to throw myself into work, but nothing helped. I sold the house. It was too big for just me, and memories of her were everywhere in it, a lot of them bad ones. So, I got rid of it, made just over two hundred thousand in profits after buying a smaller place. I got this idea to start rewarding people who I saw being kind to each other. Not much, just a hundred quid here, or two hundred there, depending on how kind the act was. I wanted to use that money for good. I was hoping word might get around, that people might start to behave better if they thought someone was watching, paying attention, ready to reward them for being kind. I thought something good might come out of Sammy's death, somehow. But instead, I just started noticing more and more how people were being so rude to each other, how they were ruining each other's day because of the slightest little thing.'

'I see,' said Walker, eyeing the oxygen tank and blowtorch again, just for a second. If he put the blue flame on that tank, it could blow, and with flammable liquid sprayed everywhere too, he knew the whole tower could go up, with them in it. The lift might be compromised as well. They'd be screwed. 'So, what did you do next?'

'*Chief?*' shouted DC Briggs. '*You okay up there?*'

'*Just give me a few more minutes,*' Walker shouted back before returning his attention to Phillip. 'What did you do next, Phillip?'

'I started to punish people who were being unkind,' he said. Walker had thought as much. They'd already noted the rise in such attacks in the local area in recent weeks and months, that there'd been several previous incidents of a less lethal nature. Superintendent Stone had said there could be any number of reasons for this uptick in crime, but Walker had felt in his bones otherwise. It was too coincidental. 'Beating people up, damaging their cars or property, that kind of thing.'

'And did people start being kinder?' asked Walker, his thoughts racing out of control, wondering what the best move was. It wasn't just himself he had to think about—DCs Briggs and Hardman were just below, waiting for him, in immediate danger. He had to get them out of there, but he also had a responsibility to help this man stay alive if he could, get him in custody, get him to trial. It was a balancing act. The people needed closure—many sons or brothers or grandsons had been killed as a result of the Kindness Matters Movement, a couple of women too—and this was not the end they needed.

Phillip shook his head. 'No. It didn't work. People respond best to abject fear, not little rewards or relatively low-level punishments like that. You have to put everything on the line.'

'So, you started killing people,' said Walker.

'It wasn't planned. I mean, I had the idea, but it wasn't planned that night, with Anthony Singelmann. I was having a drink and saw this argument start up with this clown—I mean an *actual* clown, as you know. He went outside with this woman—she was small, I thought it was a little girl at first, but she was just a small adult—and he pushed her over. It looked like she really hurt herself. It was awful. There was no excuse for that. So, I followed him, not quite knowing what I was going to do. I saw him get into an altercation with some other chap, a really big fella, and then he went up to the roof of the Tower Buildings, fell asleep. I watched him for hours, wondering what I should do. Then he woke up and took a piss off the building. There could have been anyone down below. Can you imagine, a clown peeing off a roof like

CHAPTER FORTY-FIVE

that? I'd had enough. It was despicable, awful. So, I pushed him off. Paid some kid to graffiti the street below with the message.'

'Be Kind,' said Walker. 'We know. We found the kid.'

Phillip nodded, seeming almost impressed. 'Next was Michael Tracy. It was the anniversary of Sam's death, so I wasn't in a good frame of mind, looking to punish someone, hurt them, just like I was hurting. He was a real piece of work, though. Deserved it. I'd been tracking him for a while. Real scum. Getting rid of him was just good housekeeping—taking out the trash before it made everything smell. I did the world a favour there. No doubt.'

'And how does Tom fit into all this?' asked Walker. 'Why did we find his prints at HMP Kirkham. Were you trying to frame him, because of what he did—with your wife? Did you make a fake fingertip or something, somehow, make a mould with modelling clay, perhaps, create a latex copy?'

'I actually thought about something like that. Believe me. But no. Actually, I got in touch with Tom, just after Bonfire Night—told him everything, that there was a way I'd forgive him: *if* he helped me, got on board with the plan. I explained that you'd never be able to prosecute if there was any doubt about which one of us did it. He was all contrite about what he did, and angry about Sam's death too. We're very similar you see.'

'Because you have the same DNA,' said Walker.

'Because we have the same DNA,' said Phillip.

'Unfortunately, you do not have the same fingerprints,' said Walker. 'And your brother got sloppy with that. It was him who carried out those murders at HMP Kirkham, wasn't it? But he made a mistake.'

'He did,' said Phillip, looking down, clearly still in grief over his brother's death. 'And he wasn't supposed to cut himself so deep too. We wanted to pretend to blame each other, cast some considerable doubt over everything, and then neither of us could be sentenced. But we never anticipated him getting an infection like that. We studied about how he should cut himself, exactly where and how much. We even practiced on some uncooked pork. It was supposed to be brilliant, and he promised to follow through, get it done, be careful. We actually started to get a little close again, once we had a common goal. I think I forgave him.'

'So, by blaming each other, and muddying the waters, you thought you could get away with it?' asked Walker.

'We did. Tom wanted to do Freddie Ward himself. He was just as cut up about Sammy's death as me. So, I let him. I gave him that one. He didn't need much encouragement either. He's always been a bit mentally unstable, you see. He's had his problems. And then we made it look like one of us had been held captive, and made it unclear as to which one,' said Phillip, seeming somewhat proud of himself for evading capture for so long. 'I'm glad Freddie Ward is dead, and nothing you or anybody else can say is ever going to change that. He ruined my life. I didn't tell Tom to kill anyone else at that prison. He decided that all by himself. He must have had a manic episode.'

'So, why'd you throw that money off the tower just now, if people respond more to punishment, as you say?' asked Walker, still stalling. Anything was better than him grabbing that blowtorch.

'Call it compensation, he said. Some people got hurt in all this who shouldn't have—I accept that now. We went too far,' said Phillip. 'It all went too far. We got carried away, unfocussed, our emotions getting the better of us.'

'Then why don't you stop now, before anyone else gets hurt?' asked Walker.

Phillip thought about it. 'You are free to leave,' he said. 'I'm not forcing you to stay. If you get hurt, it's on you.'

'*Chief!*' shouted DC Briggs. She sounded a bit frantic now.

Phillip picked up the blowtorch, turned it on.

'Phillip. You don't have to do this,' said Walker.

'Oh, but I do,' said Phillip, as he took a few steps over towards the oxygen tank. Walker had his hand on his taser now, ready to use it. 'I had an epiphany, you see: *it's me that's the most guilty of all*. If I'd been kinder to Sammy after what happened to her, more understanding—if I'd really dug deep and dealt with my own inner demons—she might still be alive. I was awful to her, before and after that. We argued all the time. I was so stubborn, always wanting to be right, always wanting to win. What I didn't realise is that by winning, I really lost everything.'

Walker's fingers twitched now, ready to pull the taser out at any second, use it as soon as Phillip got that flame anywhere near the oxygen tank.

'So why the dramatics?' asked Walker. 'If you want to top yourself, you could just do it somewhere quiet, privately.'

Phillip smiled perhaps the saddest smile Walker had ever seen. 'The people of Blackpool need to remember this, need to cement it in their minds. Symbolism is a powerful thing, Mr Walker. We all remember the Twin Towers in New York, right? The drama of those airplanes hitting? Would we remember so well if it was just some low rise building that had been bombed? Probably not. When they see the top of this Tower on fire, like an Olympic torch, exploding, with money raining down, they'll remember all right. They'll think twice in future about being rude or insulting someone just for the sake of it. People will be nicer, and kinder. At least, that's my hope.'

Walker thought about the tarot card he'd been shown by the reader at the Pleasure Beach, the one called 'The Tower', a depiction of a burning tower struck by lightning. It seemed so prophetic now. She said it meant something bad was going to happen—a disaster, danger, crisis, or sudden change. She'd been right about that much, and the prospect of the Tower now being set on fire was eerily on the nose.

'I think they're already going to remember all of this, Phillip. You don't need to do anything more,' said Walker.

'You'd better go now,' said Phillip.

'*DCs! Get out of here!*' shouted Walker at the top of his voice.

Phillip Taylor went to point the blowtorch at the oxygen tank, but Walker pulled the taser, got him perfectly on the leg, but not before Taylor could get the flame on the tank, holding it there with willpower alone while the taser went about convulsing his body. Walker hadn't expected that. The man was right: he was stubborn.

'*Shit,*' said Walker, dropping back down the stairs, two or three steps at a time, leaving the taser behind, dropping it as he went, and just in time too: there was a *huge* explosion, flames singeing his clothing as he went, then there was a trail of fire on the floor too as the vodka started to light up, spreading everywhere. DCs Briggs and Hardman were still there too, not far away, and they all started running, trying to outrun the spread of the flames behind them, jumping down the next flight of stairs.

CHAPTER FORTY-FIVE

'What about Taylor?' asked DC Briggs, as they ran some more.

'Too late. He'll be dead already,' shouted Walker. 'Come on.'

They got to the lift and DC Hardman put the key in, got it moving, the structure starting to shake and vibrate as another explosion went off.

'Hold on,' said Walker, grabbing a railing in the lift, the others doing the same. He looked up at the ceiling, imagining the cable beyond, holding the lift, hoping it wouldn't break, leaving them to fall hundreds of feet below. 'Just… hold the bloody hell on.'

CHAPTER FORTY-SIX

A firefighting helicopter dropped its load on the Blackpool Tower at 3:42pm, putting out much of the external blaze, long before individual firefighters got up to the top of the Tower itself to attempt to secure the structure. Walker had since learned from one of the staff that there are 563 steps from the roof of the Tower Buildings to the top of the Tower, which maintenance staff use for the upkeep of the structure. So, as the lift was now deemed to be unfit for use due to being compromised by the fire, the firefighters had to use these steps to make it up there. Not a good day for them, no doubt, but some of the people of Blackpool were looking pretty happy, with their pockets, pants, and socks stuffed full of cash, smiles as broad as the Promenade.

'Long live the Defender,' said one man, as he passed by them with a big grin on his face, almost skipping along. Walker and DCs Briggs and Hardman were sat on a nearby bench, looking up at the Tower, recuperating.

Paramedics had also arrived and had similarly taken the long trip up the Tower by stairs. Some of them would not make it, Walker thought. Not all paramedics were that fit—in fact, many were overweight or had health issues of their own. They certainly weren't of the fitness standard of the

CHAPTER FORTY-SIX

average firefighter, anyway. The standard health check test of a paramedic these days was to climb a staircase carrying a medical kit. This was something else entirely. This was a test of extreme endurance. Had Walker and DCs Briggs and Hardman known about the staircase themselves, and had access to it, they'd surely have used it rather than risking the lift—especially DC Briggs, who was terrified of the thing. But they were later told that access to the staircase would have been locked anyway, and only accessible by particular members of staff. The firefighters and paramedic teams had obviously been given a key to enter this staircase to conduct their work.

'I think he's going to be disappointed, that guy,' said DC Briggs, still sat down, recovering. 'That was a *big* explosion. I don't think The Defender is going anywhere. I don't think he's going to live long at all.'

'Yeah. I'd be very surprised if he made it,' said Walker. 'He's most likely a goner.'

'They'll probably use all this in their house of horrors over there in the years to come. It'll become part of the attraction,' she said.

'How'd he blow it up then?' asked DC Hardman.

'Oxygen tank and blowtorch,' said Walker. 'Had it in storage somewhere locally, he said, brought it here.'

'Jesus,' he said. 'That would do it, alright.'

'He explain anything—why he did it?' asked DC Briggs.

'He gave *an* explanation,' said Walker. 'But I'm not sure it made a whole lot of sense, to be honest. I'll tell you later.'

'Well, he was right about one thing,' said DC Briggs. 'If kindness was the norm, the world would be a better place. I think I'm gonna make more of an effort from now on.' She looked at Walker and DC Hardman. 'This is the part where you say you will too.'

There was a pause while they all said nothing. 'I should call my wife—my ex, I mean. She'll be worried sick if she sees this on the news. I am still the father of her children, after all. I told her I'm working a case at the Tower,' said Walker. 'She'll be frantic.'

He got up and walked off to one side, along the Promenade, looked out at the sea. It was a windy day, as it often was by the Irish Sea, and the waves stirred, going here and there, much like his emotions. The phone rang, and his ex-wife, Dawn, answered.

'Hi. Yes, I'm okay,' said Walker. 'You've been trying to ring? Sorry. I had it on "Do Not Disturb" mode for a while. Sensitive situation here. I know… it always is. Yeah. I'll call by when I'm done, see the kids. They okay? Great. See you then.'

He hung up, missing his family, but knowing things would probably never be the same again. Although he'd re-established contact with his wife and children, she'd made it clear they wouldn't be getting back together, not anytime soon, anyhow. Not while he was still a detective. She never could stand it—him being away so much, being so vacant, out of touch, emotionally and physically. He thought she might have already met someone else. He was still too obsessed with finding his sister's killer to be a good husband and father, he knew it. It was what he did. It would be what he would do when he went back home today—look through the latest possible leads, trying to revive a cold case that was long since dead in the water.

Now that his call was finished, he went back over to DCs Briggs and Hardman.

CHAPTER FORTY-SIX

'Everything okay?' she asked.

'As good as it could be, in the circumstances,' he said. 'At least they're talking to me these days.' He sensed the self-pity well up in himself and tried to let go of it. He knew how dangerous such emotions could be—knew that was probably a large part of Phillip Taylor's emotional make-up, that it probably contributed to what he did in some way. He'd have felt that it wasn't fair, that people should be punished for making his and other people's lives a misery. But Taylor also knew deep down, in the end, that he was partly responsible himself, that he hadn't been kind enough to his wife. It had taken him time to get there, and a lot of people had died in the meantime, but he'd got there in the end, it seemed—found that realisation, and he'd killed himself for it. At least, that's the conclusion Walker had come to based on what the guy had said and the evidence they'd accumulated. It never ceased to amaze him how people could so easily put aside their ethics and let their basest impulses run amok. He'd seen it many times throughout his career, and it was also something he had to constantly work on himself whenever he looked into the face of evil. Phillip Taylor's motives seemed straightforward enough: it had been guilt driving him as much as anything, blame and loathing projected outward. In the end, he'd recognised his folly, had an epiphany, and wanted to make amends in some small way. That's why he'd been throwing the money off the Tower.

Walker also recognised, much like Phillip Taylor, that he was to blame for his own personal predicament, that he should have spent more time with his family, been there for them, attended to their needs. That's why he was now living alone. It was because of his obsession with his work, with finding his sister's murderer, with making sure that nobody else got hurt, or at least saving *some* people. His thinking was that if he couldn't save his sister, then at least he could save a few others, find atonement that way. He still blamed himself for what happened to his kid sister when he'd been just a teenager himself—for not keeping an eye on her properly. Unfortunately, by going down this road, he'd lost that which was now most precious to him in the whole world: his wife and kids. But he knew he couldn't just drop his work, go back to them a new man. It didn't work like that. You can't just change who you are, what your destiny is. Some things just don't work out. It's not a fairy-tale life. He knew it. It was brutal, unforgiving. But then he had something of an epiphany himself: *that's why kindness really does matter.* Because everyone has their own struggle. Everyone is fighting their own personal war. And every second is a battle to be won or lost. Unfortunately, for the people of Blackpool, Phillip Taylor had lost too many of those battles, and had done some terrible things himself, the message getting lost in his own emotional turmoil.

'Shall we get out of here, Chief?' asked DC Briggs, getting up off the bench with him. 'I'm just about done.'

'You both go if you want to,' said Walker. 'You did a great job today. I'm going to stay here until they bring out Phillip Taylor. You know how I am about tying cases up, dotting all the i's and crossing the t's.'

'I do indeed,' said DC Briggs. 'Give me a call when you've recovered a bit then. We could go for an early lunch or something, tomorrow, before work?'

'I'm sure you can find someone your own age to eat with,' said Walker, knowing that he'd be in no mood to socialise

CHAPTER FORTY-SIX

after something like this, would need time to decompress. 'Enjoy your free time.'

'I could always do lunch,' said DC Hardman, chirpily, who was a similar age to DC Briggs. He got up off the bench too now, ready to go, and she looked at him, eying him a little suspiciously.

'Actually, on second thoughts, I should probably see my sister tomorrow,' she said. 'I might have lunch with her. But thanks.'

DC Hardman smiled and looked at Walker, perhaps thinking he was trying to set them up, and appreciating the try. 'No problem,' he said.

'Alright. Be off with you then. I'll see you both tomorrow to hopefully start getting things tied up properly on this one. There might be a fair bit to get through though—it could take a few days,' said Walker.

'Okay. Bye, Chief,' said DC Briggs.

'See you tomorrow, Chief,' said DC Hardman, as they both walked away together.

Walker looked up at the smoking Blackpool Tower once more, taking it all in, sitting back down again now that they'd gone. This was another case he wouldn't be forgetting in a hurry, one that would be keeping him awake at night, going over and over it in his mind, wondering whether he could have done anything more, or better, to have prevented all those deaths. In the end, it was all on him—he'd been in charge. The weight of responsibility was extremely heavy, and it came with a good degree of guilt, and remorse, and a whole heap of other ineffable emotions he couldn't pin down.

If he'd smoked, now would have been the time he'd have sparked up, took a drag. But he didn't, so he just took in deep breaths of seaside oxygen, trying to rejuvenate himself.

He sat there, letting his thoughts drift, for he didn't know how long. He was tired, needed to lie down, get some healing deep sleep. But something wasn't letting him yet. Something was still nagging at him, on the fringes, just out of reach. It was a feeling he'd had before, and he'd learned to trust his instincts—or at least to entertain them, see where they took him.

There was some activity at the base of the Tower, so Walker stood up, starting walking over. People had begun to gather, and more and more were coming, even as Walker was getting over there. A crowd was forming, some were the people who he'd seen picking up the cash, but there were others arriving too, many more of them. By the time Walker got over there, the crowd had begun to part, not for him, but for the people coming out of the Tower Buildings. It was some of the firefighters and the medical staff. Walker managed to hustle his way to the front of the crowd, showing his police ID card to a number of people on the way in order to ease his way through. He saw the firefighters were carrying someone on an emergency stretcher: it was Phillip Taylor. He was blackened charred, and wore an oxygen mask, but it seemed, miraculously, that he was somehow still alive, otherwise he wouldn't have been given a mask at all. Walker was shocked. He didn't think anyone could survive an explosion like that. He must have got lucky somehow, the exploding cannister flying off in the opposite direction, or the debris missing him altogether, the flames going upward instead of outward. He didn't know the intricacies of such pyrogenic effects. All he knew was that Phillip Taylor had survived—at least for now.

And that was not all. Taylor was stirring. He put his

CHAPTER FORTY-SIX

arm in the air, tried to sit up, took the oxygen mask off, so the firefighters carrying him stopped walking, let the paramedics attend to him, but Taylor pushed them away. It seemed he wanted to say something to the crowd of onlookers. Everybody went quiet, their attention focussed on him.

'Be kind, everybody,' he said. That was it. His voice was croaky, but he spoke loudly enough so that most people heard, and for those who might not have, at the back, people repeated it for them, the message flowing through the crowd like a wave. Then people started to cheer, whip themselves up into a frenzy. They clearly loved him—despite everything he'd done. He was their hero, for trying to do something to clean up the town, to make it a better place. It stuck in Walker's throat a bit, his ego getting the better of him. After all, it should have been them, the police force, who were getting the accolades. It was them who were policing the place, after all, stopping things from escalating into all-out anarchy, putting their lives on the line. Then he went from anger to guilt in a second, realising that if the people were so discontented, then they couldn't have been doing a very good job. Some things needed to change, for sure, some structural changes in the Force, more funding, more resources, less red tape. They wanted to do their jobs, and do it well, but at times there were too many barriers and obstacles stopping them, too many hoops to jump through.

Walker fought his way to the front—right to the front.

'Get him in the ambulance,' he said. 'Now.'

The paramedics did as asked, and Walker followed, getting in the back of the ambulance with Phillip Taylor and one paramedic. It was just about big enough for the three of them. The crowd *booed*, some of them realising or knowing who

Walker was, knowing that Phillip Taylor, their Defender, was about to get arrested.

Once everything was organised and settled back there, Walker closed the doors to the ambulance, and they slowly got moving, navigating through the crowd, some of them banging on the side, shouting.

'Keep your head up,' said one of them.

'We await your instructions,' said another.

'Frigging hell,' muttered Walker. He knew it wasn't over. The man had started something—something potentially big—and it wasn't going to go away overnight.

'What?' said the paramedic who was with them. 'I'm Ben, by the way.'

'I need to cuff him to the stretcher,' said Walker, and he leaned across, grabbed Phillip Taylor's wrist, attached the handcuffs. 'Mr Taylor. Are you conscious?'

Phillip nodded his head, the oxygen mask now back on, but his eyes remaining closed.

'Mr Phillip Taylor, I'm arresting you for the murders of Anthony Singelmann, Michael Tracy, and for your involvement in the November fifth riots, in addition to the direct or indirect role you played in the murders at HMP Kirkham, and the death of your brother, Thomas Taylor. You do not have to say anything, but it may harm your defence if you do not mention when questioned something which you later rely on in court. Anything you do say may be given in evidence. Do you have anything to say?'

The ambulance went over a bump in the road, jolting them all upwards, the stretcher and handcuffs rattling and clinking around.

'I did it for Sammy,' he said. It was as good as a confession.

CHAPTER FORTY-SIX

'Then you'll be going to prison for her too, Mr Taylor,' said Walker. He had his man. Job done. Now he just had to help clean up the monumental mess he'd made.

CHAPTER FORTY-SEVEN

Walker and his team from the Taylor Twins case—DCs Briggs, Ainscough, and Hardman, a couple of PCs who'd been working the investigation, and Phillis, the front desk staff member at Blackpool Police HQ—sat in the Dutton Arms on the Promenade in Blackpool. They were all crowded around a small table, looking at a TV mounted on the wall, which was currently streaming Live News from the BBC.

'Violence erupted today in Glasgow after a new start-up of the Kindness Matters Movement established itself there. The movement, which was founded by the now incarcerated Phillip Taylor, who killed two men in Blackpool several months ago, separates itself from any such violence, and operates under a banner of peace. However, similar unrest to that witnessed on November fifth in Blackpool has been seen in towns and cities all over the UK in recent weeks—the worse of it being in Birmingham, where two more people died. A franchise has also been set up in the United States and Canada, with some property damage and arson occurring in New York, Dallas, and Winnipeg. We will continue to provide coverage on this as the story progresses. Now in other news…'

CHAPTER FORTY-SEVEN

Walker had the TV remote, which he'd got from the bar staff, and turned the telly off.

'Unbelievable,' he said. 'The man is a god-damned terrorist. Or a fascist. And now he's given other like-minded folk a reason to be violent. He's seduced them into it in the name of liberation.'

'Or he just really loved his wife?' offered DC Briggs. 'And didn't want others to suffer the same fate.'

'Or both,' said DC Hardman. 'It's like that Fight Club franchise, from the film, isn't it?'

'Or the book,' said DC Ainscough. 'It's one of Chuck Palahniuk's. The book is even better. It's a commentary on fascist movements, about a bunch of guys with their masculinity in crisis, feeling emasculated by what they see as a decadent state of the social order, and the protagonist conjures up this strong man alter ego who does exactly what you said, seduces them into violence in the name of liberation. Before you know it, he's bringing in uniforms and the like, unquestioning conformity. It's been a massively prescient book, really, when it comes to far-right ideological drifts like the KMM.' Walker had never heard of it and didn't much care. There was enough drama in real life for him. But what DC Ainscough said did resonate with what seemed to be happening with the KMM.

'What? Chuck who?' said DC Hardman. 'Sorry. I don't really read books.'

DC Ainscough looked confused, like it was news to him that not everyone read. 'Then what do you read?' he asked.

'Mags,' he said. 'I like a good mag, me. Always have.'

Walker threw the remote on the table in front of them. 'Sometimes life reflects art, as they say, I suppose,' he offered.

About a week after Phillip Taylor had been arrested, an automated email newsletter had gone out to hundreds of people, via a service called Mailchimp—a company that specialises in marketing automation. In the newsletter, Taylor had detailed what he'd done, had urged people around the world to continue his work, by providing a detailed list of instructions and a template for continuing the Kindness Matters Movement. He'd even got a branded logo for it and everything: "KMM". One of the instructions in this letter was to ensure the message went viral, not just in the UK, but globally. Each of those opening the email would send it to twenty other people, while YouTube videos would also be made and uploaded en masse. It spread like wildfire, going to every corner of the Internet. Pretty soon, movements would emerge in places like South America, China, the Philippines, and Australia too. There were already extensive forums from those areas discussing it, at length. Discontent was rife around the world, it seemed, and people just wanted to be happier, to live in a world where people were kinder to each other. It was a noble mission, in many ways, but like many noble missions, it had been corrupted, used for those who craved violence and chaos. It was the Arab Spring all over again, or the London riots of 2011, perhaps, but this time the people didn't want emancipation or less police brutality, they wanted *kindness*. In Walker's opinion, though, there wasn't a lot of kindness in beating a guy to death for being cruel or vicious. This was "kindness" as a rhetorical guise for respect, discipline, and good behaviour as defined by authoritarianism. It was a violation of people's individual liberties and freedoms. It was the root of fascism.

It's soft times that creates soft people, Walker had heard

CHAPTER FORTY-SEVEN

somewhere, and this inevitably leads to hard times, and the requirement for harder people to get through it. It's a historical cycle that just keeps running. Of course, Walker agreed the world would be a better place if people were more polite to each other, more courteous—like they were back in his day—if community spirit was fostered again, if the old bobby-on-the-beat got back out and about, maybe. But movements like this were going too far. People's ideals and wishes were not above the law. It was them who were breaking the law, hurting people, causing damage. He knew he was on the right side, despite that side not being perfect. This approach was just going to create more hardship.

Even the man who'd started the movement—Phillip Taylor—had been corrupted by it, his own message, his own ideology of kindness; he'd used it to connect to his dark side, his rage, his violence, to purge himself and his feeling, to use people as his emotional bin. Consequently, he'd killed at least two people and had been given a life sentence for his crimes. His brother-in-law, Jonny Scawthorn, and his friend, Danny Bagley, had also been handed hefty custodial sentences for their role in developing the Kindness Matters Movement, and for inciting violence in Blackpool on November fifth. It turned out Jonny had made a promise to his sister, Sam, before her death, to look out for her Phil, no matter what—a promise he'd no doubt not fully understood at the time. So, he'd shadowed his brother-in-law after her death, discovered what he'd been doing, and kept watching, ready to help and support if need be. He'd confessed to everything once Phil had been given a life sentence, though, said he wholeheartedly supported the cause, had only wanted to help and protect him. He'd been given twenty years. Danny Bagley had also, in an unsuccessful attempt to get his sentence reduced, confessed to the part he played, had stated Jonny confided in him at some point, told him everything, and got him on-board with the Movement and what Phil was doing, which Danny had willingly done as a result of the awful things that had happened to *his* sister. Danny had lied about seeing Phil in the pub that night when he'd been working—to similarly protect him and keep Phil away from any police enquiries—and had helped to stoke emotions on the Tower Forum and organise the riots. The judge had come down on him hard for this, more than Walker expected, given him fourteen years as well, ten of which were to be served in prison. In court, Jonny had also said he was glad his ex-boyfriend, Freddie Ward, was dead, and that he'd have done the same thing if he'd been put in HMP Kirkham—which had perhaps been in his thinking when turning himself in and claiming to be The Defender, that and protecting his brother-in-law. But it was all done now, all put to bed, in Blackpool at least. The problem was that the Movement was now spreading, globally, and this left Walker feeling guilty, somehow, that they should have stopped it, somehow.

'Look, I don't think we could have done any more, Chief,' said DC Briggs, somehow sensing Walker's feelings. 'We did everything we could, under the circumstances, I think.'

'Yes, but the circumstances shouldn't be what they are,' he said. 'We should have more staff, more resources, more intelligence.'

'Hey, what are you trying to say?' said DC Hardman, grinning. 'I'm smart, me.'

'A smart arse, maybe,' offered one of the PCs, a jovial fella who was a bit chubby around the chops. He laughed heartily,

CHAPTER FORTY-SEVEN

and it gave them all a lift to hear it, Walker included. It was good to hear there was still some humour left in the world, some light.

'Well, it's not in our hands, anymore,' said Walker. 'There are other police forces, other cities, in other countries who will deal with this now, along with national crime agencies and anti-terrorist organisations if need be. It's likely that members of the KMM will eventually be pipelined into existing far-right groups anyway, and the KMM will just be used as a recruitment tool. We were at ground zero on this, that's all, unfortunately. And now it's going to evolve however it's going to evolve. But you did a great job, everyone. I really mean that.' He did too. They wouldn't have got as far as they did, as quickly as they did, without good teamwork and a willingness to do what needed to be done. It often went without saying—it was part of the job—but on this occasion he *wanted* to say it. Perhaps the ethos of kindness had sunk in after all.

Everyone nodded their appreciation of his words and took a sip of their drinks, most of them non-alcoholic ones, as some of them would be back on duty soon enough, working other cases. Not Walker, though. He'd been given some time off—a two-month suspension while they reviewed the case and his leadership of it. It wasn't the first time in his career he'd been suspended, and he needed some time to recharge anyway. His health had been going downhill again during the investigation, all the stresses and strains that went with it. So, he was having a real beer, a good old-fashioned Foster's, on tap. He finished it off—there were only a couple of swigs left—and then stood up.

'Good luck to you all,' he said, standing, getting his jacket on, ready to leave. 'DC Briggs, hopefully I'll see you in the

New Year.'

'I'll see you out,' she said.

They went outside the pub together, pulling the collars of their jackets up high, protecting themselves from the wind. It was starting to rain too, the sun already going down, lowering the temperature further.

'Did you want to say something?' asked Walker.

'No. I just wanted to… You will call me, won't you, if you need some company?' she asked.

'I'll be fine, Constable. Just focus on your work. You still have a couple of other cases to tie up too, remember?'

'I do,' she said, but her face softened, her eyes too. Normally, on the job, there was a hardness to her, despite her having the ability to be empathic and always say the right thing—there was still a toughness to her. But not now. She let it all drop, seemed to reveal her true nature. 'Take care of yourself, Jon.' She never called him that. She reached across, took Walker by surprise, kissed him on the cheek.

'I thought you weren't drinking alcohol, DC Briggs,' he said, a little stunned.

She started to walk away. 'I'm not,' she said, without even looking, putting her arm in the air to wave goodbye.

And with that, Walker started to head to his car. He'd only had the one beer, after all—was well within the limit. At least she'd not pulled him up on that.

The kiss made him think about his wife though—the tenderness from a woman's touch like that, made him miss his old life. But there was no going back. Not now, anyway. He looked back at the Blackpool Tower.

Be Kind, he muttered to himself. *Be sodding kind.*

EPILOGUE

Walker sat in his flat on Silverdale Road with the curtains closed, despite it being early afternoon. He was just about to tuck into a ham sandwich on white bread, when his phone rang—the landline. It was the station, in Skelmersdale. He'd been off work for six weeks now on suspension while they reviewed the Phillip Taylor case—still two weeks to go until the final verdict. If they wouldn't let him back on the force, it wouldn't stop him working. He had a backup plan in that eventuality: to become a private detective. It wouldn't necessarily give him the criminal cases he was so used to, something to really get his teeth into, but it would help pay the bills, allow him to continue to financially contribute to his family despite being separated from them. Plus, doing such work would allow him to keep his ear to the ground, so to speak, to keep working with the police from time to time when a private case spilled over into illegality—when he'd have to inform them of any such activities. It might allow him to maintain his contacts on the Force, to look out for any leads in his sister's cold case.

'Hello?' he said. 'Jonathan Walker.'

'Jon. It's Ronald Hughes. I've been trying to reach you on your mobile. How you doing?' It was *Superintendent* Ronald

Hughes from Skelmersdale Police Station—his boss, and his friend.

'I'm...' He looked around the room. It was a real mess. He didn't do well when he wasn't working—never had—had too much time to think, to stew. 'I'm doing okay,' he lied. 'Do you have any news? About my review?'

'You'll be fine on that one, Jon. I put my ear to the ground. The review is going to clear you of any wrongdoings or neglect of any duties. It seems you all followed procedure, this time. They've just been waiting for the full two months to elapse, I guess. Probably want to make it appear that full diligence has been done on this one, the case being what it was, which I'm sure it has. Given that it's now a full-on international concern what with such movements springing up all over the world, it's understandable they'd want to do this, to tie off any loose ends, make it watertight. You know how the media are with these things. If there's something to find, they'll inevitably find it. Anyway, I'm asking them to expedite the review and get you back in a little early,' said Supt Hughes. 'Something's come up, you see.'

Walker took a bite into his sandwich anyway. He was hungry, and he was comfortable with Supt Hughes. They were old friends by now. Supt Hughes's wife sometimes asked him round for dinner, even. 'What do you have?'

'Cold case in Lytham St. Annes,' said Supt Hughes. 'A body's been found in the sand dunes there, right on the coast. Forensics reckon the corpse has been there for over ten years, female, young-ish, by all accounts. They're currently searching the area, trying to see if there are any more. They're using ground-penetrating radar in the immediate vicinity.'

'I see. Doesn't sound very urgent, though, if it's been there so long, or very close to our catchment area,' said Walker. 'Why bring me back early for this? Not that I don't want to come back early. I do. But why—'

'Remember the Sally Fielding case?' asked Supt Hughes.

Of course. Walker remembered it well. She was the first cousin of Deputy Chief Constable Harry Potts, one of the highest-ranking police officials in Britain at the time. He was now retired, but he still no doubt had a number of high-level contacts in the Force. She'd gone missing in the summer of 2011 and was never found. He remembered the year because it was the same year as the England riots, an especially cool summer as he remembered it—something he'd been thinking of more recently due to what happened in Blackpool.

'I remember,' said Walker. 'She was taking a little holiday alone in Lytham, wasn't she? Never made it, according to the reports—her car found deserted just outside Birmingham somewhere as I remember.'

'That's right,' said Supt Hughes. 'Still on file as a missing person, she is.'

'So, what? They think it might be her for some reason?' asked Walker.

'Oh, they're pretty sure it is her,' said Supt Hughes. 'They've extracted DNA from the bones, matched it to the family's DNA. Whoever that was is a relative of the Potts family.'

'Jesus,' said Walker. 'And now they want the bastard who did it, as a priority I suppose.'

'Harry Potts was one of the highest-ranking policing officials in Britain. So, yeah, he'll want to know who killed his cousin. Apparently, they were close when they were young,' said Supt Hughes. So?'

'When do I start?' asked Walker.

'I'll try to get you back ASAP, if possible,' said Supt Hughes. 'You well?'

'Fighting fit,' said Walker. 'I'll want DC Briggs on it with me if I'm to do it.'

'Yeah. I heard you're working well together these days. That's fine,' said Supt Hughes. 'Wait for my confirmation and then assemble your team. This is going to be another extensive investigation, DCI Walker. No stone will be left unturned. Call it your chance at redemption, for past indiscretions. They're going to want a positive result on this one. It might be your last chance to make things right. You haven't exactly been making those at the top happy with your results of late, no offence.'

'None taken. Understood,' said Walker.

'Oh, and there's just one more thing,' said Supt Hughes. 'I've got a message for you from Superintendent Lucy Stone, over in Blackpool.'

'What's that?' asked Walker.

'She thanks you for the work you did on the Taylor Twins Case, and wanted me to inform you that, unfortunately, Phillip Taylor killed himself in prison this morning, suicide— hung himself somehow. Was found by one of the staff.'

It wasn't what Walker wanted to hear. He never liked to learn that a criminal of this nature and magnitude had taken the easy way out, wouldn't be punished by the state. 'I see,' was all he said. There was nothing more to say. 'Thanks for letting me know.'

Supt Hughes paused, swallowed. 'I'm afraid there's more.'

'What is it, Ron?' asked Walker. They were close enough for him to be able to call him that, when he was off duty, at least.

EPILOGUE

'He wrote a suicide note. Said he was *Thomas Taylor*, not Phillip. Said they swapped identities, to confuse us, or something. Said they'd had copies of their fingerprints signed by a lawyer, just in case we convicted one of them, said it was all Phillip's idea. But in the end, he decided he didn't want to get out, that he wanted to die instead. That was the general gist of it. Superintendent Stone thought you'd want to know.'

She was right. But he wasn't happy to hear they hadn't actually solved the case, that they'd had to rely on a confession in the end. It had all been such a mess, this one, right from the get-go. It had been a real-life house of horrors, something that belonged to that Tower Dungeon at the Blackpool Tower Buildings—and it no doubt would in the years to come.

'Right. Thanks for that, Ron. 'I'll see you soon,' said Walker, before putting the phone down.

He took another bite of his ham sandwich, washed it down with some lukewarm milky tea. Then he looked for his mobile phone, couldn't find it at first but found it wedged down the side of the sofa cushion, opened it up to find several missed calls, some of them from Supt Hughes. It was time to move on. He got on Google, searched for Sally Fielding, found a photograph of her. She was young, early twenties, attractive. It was another sad waste of a young life, if it was her.

'If I get assigned to this, I'm going to find who did this to you, Sally,' he said. 'I promise you that. I'm going to find him and lock him up, so he can't do this to anybody else, even if I have to sift through every grain of sand.'

He meant it too. He threw down what was left of the sandwich on the plate, his emotions stirred. What appetite he had was now gone and his thoughts turned firmly to what had gone on in Lytham St. Annes, and what he was going to do when he got there. There was a body waiting for him, and it was up to him to find out what happened to them, and how they got there—and this time, he resolved to make sure the person who did it was *really* punished, one way or another.

A Note From the Author

"Thanks so much for reading my book, *The Tower*. I hope you enjoyed it. Please could you be so kind as to leave a **review** on Amazon? (Goodreads and Bookbub also appreciated) I read *every* review and they help new readers discover my books. In fact, they're invaluable for my career and the continued lives of DCI Walker and the gang. So... please, do it now before you forget! (and I'll keep writing)"

J.J. Richards

SIGN UP to my mailing list at **J-J-Richards.com** for news of new releases and more!

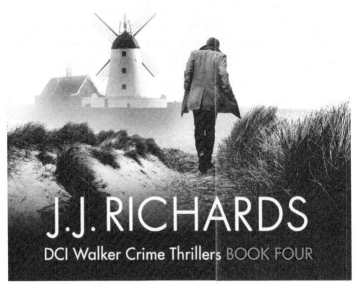

Coming soon...

Printed in Great Britain
by Amazon